SILVERWITCH

OLIVE KENNEDY, FAIRY WORLD MD, BOOK FOUR

Tamara Grantham

Silverwitch
Copyright ©2016 Tamara Grantham

ISBN:978-1-63422-233-4
Cover Design by: Marya Heiman
Typography by: Courtney Knight
Editing by: Chelsea Brimer

For more information about our content disclosure,
please utilize the QR code above with your
smart phone or visit us at

www.cleanteenpublishing.com.

"And the dreams that you dare to dream really do come true."
-From "Somewhere Over the Rainbow." Lyrics by E.Y. Harburg.

CHAPTER
One

I'M WATCHING YOU.
I know you. I'll take your magic and destroy the world.
Soon.
Everyone you know will die.
And you will die with them.
Theht's voice was becoming harder to ignore.

———— ❧ ————

"I can't help you," I said.

Zack Zimmerman's mouth gaped open. "But you said you could help anyone—never failed to cure a client."

"I said I could help anyone who's been to Fairy World. You haven't been."

"But the test showed magic had touched me. How is that possible?"

"There are several possibilities. You could have come into contact with a creature from Faythander on Earth and some of its magical residue could have touched you, thus contaminating the test. It's also possible that my own magic could have interfered."

Zack exhaled, obviously annoyed. "Has that ever happened to anyone else?"

"No."

"Then how do you know it happened to me?"

"Because there has to be a logical explanation."

"Yes, there does. I've been there. I swear to you, it's the only thing that explains my mental distress and my abnormal collection."

"Mr. Zimmerman," I said, "usually patients don't collect the articles you described."

He pulled at a chain around his neck. An egg-shaped pendant hung suspended from the bottom. The jewel was unusual, a black stone with veins of gold that shimmered in the sunlight. "I just bought this one off eBay, but I've got dozens more at home. I can't stop collecting them. It doesn't matter how expensive or how rare. Have you ever priced Fabergé eggs?"

"I can't say that I have."

He swallowed. "I got this one on sale for twenty-two grand."

Sheesh.

"Yes, that's quite a lot."

"Can't you see how this is affecting my life? My job at the news station is suffering. I can't even give a good weather forecast anymore. Not to mention my wife and kids. I need help!"

My heart sank. I wish he knew how much I wanted to help him. But wanting to do something and being able to do something were two different things.

"I wish I could help you—I truly do, Mr. Zimmerman—but I don't know how. My clients usually collect dragons and fairies, not eggs."

"But what about the sci-fi movie stuff? I've got a huge collection of every *Enterprise* seen on a TV screen. Please, doesn't that count?"

I placed my hands atop my mirror box. The test hadn't replayed a single memory from his past, although he had reacted to elven magic. However, since Theht had intruded on my mind a week earlier, my own magic had slowly been growing weaker and more erratic, and could possibly have been interfering with the test. As heartbreaking as it was, I could do nothing for him.

"Do it again," he said.

"Excuse me?"

"Do the test again."

"I don't think the results will be any different."

"I don't care. You have to try again. There has to be an explanation for what's happening to me."

Sighing, I opened my laptop. Five small figurines rested on the velvet lining. Dragon, elf, Wult, pixie, and goblin.

"Give me your hand," I instructed.

He did, and I held it over the first figurine, the dragon.

Magic flowed from the mirror and filled me with its power, though it didn't react with Mr. Zimmerman's presence. We moved to the elf, and just as last time, a faint flair of blue magic glowed around his hand.

"You see that light, too, right?" he asked.

"Yes. I see it."

"Then I've been there. Doesn't this prove it?"

"Not necessarily." I lifted the statuette and held it out. "I need you to touch the figurine, just like last time, and then place your other hand on the mirror."

He did as I instructed, and as he touched it, nothing happened. No magical flare, no images. Nothing. An empty mirror stared back at us.

"If you'd been to Faythander," I said, "we would see some form of a memory being replayed, but there's nothing there."

He stared at the glass, his eyes filled with determination, as if he were willing the memories to appear. But the glass remained empty and cold, reflecting only the harshness of his reality. Finally, with a sigh of disgust, he moved his hand away from the mirror.

"What's wrong with me?"

"I wish I knew."

He gave me a shrewd glance. "Do you?"

"Yes. I would like to be able to help you."

"You're a liar. You said you could fix anyone, and you can't."

Ouch.

"That's uncalled for."

"Is it?" He stood abruptly, marched to the door, marched back, grabbed his briefcase, and stomped back to the door. "How much do I owe you?" he asked.

"No charge."

He nodded once, grabbed the door handle, and left the apartment. Han Solo, my cat, jumped on my lap, tickling my nose with his bushy gray tail, so I patted his head.

"Well, that was a great way to start the day, don't you think?"

Han mewled, nudging my hand. He'd been in heaven ever since we'd arrived back home in our apartment, but before that, the poor thing hadn't been fond of the camper trailer I'd rented for the Ren Fest. After I'd returned from Faythander, it had taken a bit of coaxing to get him to come out of hiding.

Purring, he made himself comfortable on my lap. I had tons of things to take care of and debated on moving him away, but I'd always been a pushover, so I let him curl up.

My mind was a million miles away, back in Faythander, as I recalled the last minutes I'd spent with Kull, my newly reunited... boyfriend? Could I call him that now? We'd finally reconciled, yet with a piece of Theht inhabiting my consciousness, I felt I could never be close to him. How long until I could no longer control the goddess? What if I hurt him? Or worse, what if I killed him? I still hadn't told anyone what Theht had done to me, and I wasn't sure if I would ever be able to admit it to anyone. Not even to Kull.

Even so, I missed him more than humanly possible, and despite the goddess lurking in my head, I still wanted to be with him. He had the unique talent of calming my fears. Plus, he was a gorgeous Wult warrior, which only made the business of our being apart even worse. Not being in the same world with him put me in a dark mood.

A knock came at the door, so I pushed Han off my lap, crossed to the door, and opened it. A man with piercing golden eyes, a pressed white suit, and striking silver hair stood tall on my doorstep. He carried a wooden cane carved with a dragon's head on top. Looking regal in every sense of the word, he gave me gentle smile. It took me a moment to find my voice.

"Fan'twar?"

"Hello, Olive."

My stepfather made it a point never to cross worlds. In fact, I hadn't seen him in a human form since I was a kid, and I couldn't remember the last time he'd been to Earth.

"What are you doing here?" I asked.

A low growl rumbled in his chest, and I heard the dragon in his voice.

"I've got bad news, I'm afraid."

CHAPTER *Two*

I SAT ACROSS FROM FAN'TWAR IN THE BOOTH AT A HOLE-in-the-wall Italian restaurant. It had been a Taco Bell in another life and had been reincarnated to serve the best pizza and breadsticks on the planet. As we placed our drink orders, I found myself still in shock that he'd crossed worlds and taken a human form. As of yet, he still hadn't given me a great explanation for why he'd come to Earth.

He'd wanted to go out for lunch and sample Earth Kingdom cuisine. I'd refused at first, eventually admitting the sad state of my checking account, which had only given him reason to take me out on his dime. I couldn't argue—dragons were loaded.

So, we'd ended up here.

"Do you know why I've come?" he asked.

"No. I'm pretty puzzled, to be honest."

"Yes, I assume you must be quite confused. I had at one time made it a point never to cross to Earth at all. The memory loss is not something I wish to experience, and memory charms have never worked well with dragon magic. Furthermore, Earth magic will frequently transform dragons into crocodiles or lizards, giving them the intelligence of primitive animals and making it impossible for us to create portals to return home. Of course, one need only take a human form before crossing to avoid those side effects."

"Interesting. You know, I don't think I'll ever look at lizards in quite the same way."

The waitress arrived with our drinks and a breadbasket, which filled the air with the scent of buttered garlic. After taking our orders, the waitress exited to the back and I turned my attention to my stepfather.

"So why did you come to Earth?"

"Hmm..." he growled, sounding more dragon than human, "I am troubled over the elves—particularly the elven queen."

Chills prickled my skin. Anything having to do with her was never a good thing.

"What about the queen?"

"She has been gaining a fair amount of support from the elven nobles. While she stands strong as elven leader, I suspect she is not satisfied."

"You think she wants to rule more than just elves?"

"Indeed."

"Short of assassinating you, I don't see how she plans to do it."

"There are powers in Faythander that are stronger than me, young one."

"Maybe. But it's not just your powers that make you ruler. You respect all races, and so they respect you. She doesn't. In fact, most races hate her. And if she kills you, she'll be making more enemies than she has now."

Fan'twar sipped his soda, made an odd face, and then stared at the brown fizzy liquid. "The beverages have changed since I was here last. What is this?"

"It's basically liquid sugar with carbonation. It's called Coke. Do you like it?"

He took another sip, then swallowed, his brows knit in concentration. "It has an odd flavor. Reminds me of a mold-worm custard. What is yours?"

"It's called Dr. Pepper. Try it." I scooted the glass toward him.

He took it and sipped the soda. "Yes," he said, "I prefer this. May I?"

"Sure."

I reluctantly scooted his Coke toward me, trading drinks with him. Yet another reason why I could never live with Kull or Fan'twar in Earth Kingdom—I'd never get the luxury of finishing my own drinks between the two of them.

"Now," Fan'twar said after a long gulp, "you are correct that the queen would be foolish to try and kill me, but there are other ways of gaining rule in Faythander. Have you ever heard of the lost isle of the Tremulac Sea?"

"Of course. It's Faythander's version of King Arthur if I remember right."

"Not exactly. While Earth Kingdom's King Arthur promoted peace and equality, symbolized by the round table, the nobles of Tremulac did the opposite."

"But there are similarities," I said. "Each story spoke of a magic sword, and each told of kingdoms being united, although one story did it more peacefully than the other. Why do you bring it up?"

"Because, the power used by those who ruled Tremulac was hidden away, and most assumed it was never in danger of being resurrected again. Now, that may not be the case."

"Euralysia plans to restore Tremulac?"

He nodded.

"But, how?" I asked.

He reached inside his suit pocket and pulled out a slim leather book. As he passed it to me, I noticed the pages were brown with age and the red and gold paint on the covering had faded. I took it from him.

"What is this?"

"It is a journal I discovered many years ago, written by Dracon, one of the Madralorde brothers of Tremulac Isle. While it is incomplete, it may be of help to us."

As I carefully flipped through the brittle pages, I found a map and drawings of various weapons coupled with descriptions among the entries.

"Does it say anything useful?"

"Most of the entries are vague, although it does tell us that there were seven brothers, and each wielded a magical weapon of incredible power. They used these weapons not for peace, but for power. The journal does not say how these weapons were forged—a secret the brothers took to their graves. It is also missing several pages that I believe speak of the lost sword of the Madralorde."

I nodded. "'The only weapon more powerful than fate.' Yeah, I remember the stories, but I'm surprised she's looking for it. Quests for make-believe swords seem like a waste of time."

"You only say that because no one has found it."

"No. I say it because it doesn't exist."

"That's not entirely true. I've come across some knowledge that leads me to believe the sword is indeed real. Also, if the queen didn't believe she could find it, she wouldn't be searching for it. If she does find these weapons, then she will gain the power to not only overcome me, but to control any power she chooses, including Theht."

The waitress arrived from the kitchen with a cheese pizza, although my mind wasn't on the food. Fan'twar eyed the pizza, then took a slice and nibbled a bite.

"Do you like it?" I asked.

"It's acceptable. Not quite as good as the meat pies Charl prepares."

"She cheats. I swear she adds a little magic to those pies."

He gave me a slight grin. "Good cooking does not require magic, young one."

"You're right. It requires skill and luck. And I have neither."

Fan'twar laughed. "I suppose your lack of culinary skills is partially my own fault, as we spent more time training in magic than learning to cook, didn't we?"

"Yes, but I wouldn't have had it any other way."

I took a slice of pizza and placed it on my plate as I mulled over our conversation, still curious about the story of the seven brothers and the lost sword.

"I'm confused," I said after taking a bite. "If the seven brothers were able to harness Theht's power, and if they used it to create incredibly powerful weapons, then why aren't they ruling Faythander now?"

"That is a bit of a mystery. I have read the journals, researched the ancient tomes, and learned that historians agree—the brothers did indeed have the ability to control Theht's powers. Why they were unable to complete the ritual is a mystery."

I eyed him. *Mystery* was a word Fan'twar didn't use often.

"Don't you have any theories as to what happened?"

His eyes darkened, and—as if on cue—clouds covered the sun outside, making the room grow dimmer. "There are some who claim the castle on Tremulac Isle is cursed."

"Cursed how?"

He shook his head, his eyes seeming to wander to a different time. "Something evil happened in that castle, although I do not know any more than that."

I tapped my fingers on the table as I mulled over his words. Fan'twar wasn't easily spooked. *What had happened in that castle?*

"In order for the summoning to work," Fan'twar said as he took another slice of pizza, "the seven weapons will have to be restored, and the elves know this. One of the weapons—

the staff of Zaladin—is now hidden in the vaults in the silver-witch's castle."

Silvestra, the dragon silverwitch, was not one of my fa-vorite people. I had only met her once, but with the amount of power she wielded, once had been enough. She had tak-en Kull's sword in exchange for our passage to the top of her mountain—a deal that still bothered me.

"Do the elves know the witch has the staff?"

"I am sure they must know it by now, and they have suc-cessfully stolen from Silvestra in the past, which makes it only a matter of time before they attempt to steal from her again. We cannot let this happen. You control the magic of both Earth and Fairy World. The witch controls dragon and black magic. Technically speaking, you are equals, which means you have the ability to beat her."

"I'm sorry, but I'm very confused. You want *me* to beat her? Why can't you?"

His gaze wandered, and he shook his head. "It would not be possible."

"Is it because of a dragon code of honor or something?"

"No."

I crossed my arms. "Then why?"

He sighed. "It is best for me to keep my distance from the dragon, for there are other dealings that must be handled. Al-ready the elven queen seeks out the Madralorde sword. Of all the weapons, the sword is the most powerful. I cannot allow the elven queen to find it, and so I must make sure the sword stays protected. That is why I have come to you. I must try to find the sword, so you must remove the staff of Zaladin from the dragon's castle."

"Can it be done?"

"Yes. I have faith in your abilities."

"Well, that makes one of us." I stared out the window at the cars driving by and people walking past, wondering how it was that I always got myself into these situations.

"I'm not so sure I should. For one thing, my magic is still unstable. A man came for a spellcasting today, and while he's never been to Faythander, I can't rule out the possibility that my magic is interfering with the spell. What happens when I confront the silverwitch?"

"I never asked you to confront her."

"Then what do you want me to do?"

He took a sip of his drink, then carefully replaced his glass on the table. "I want you to steal from her."

"Steal?"

"Yes."

"You do realize I have no experience in thievery whatsoever."

"I do not expect you to do it alone. In fact, I have employed one of Faythander's most successful thieves to assist you."

"You've got to be joking."

"Indeed I am not joking. He waits for you now in the Wult outpost near Dragon Spine Mountain."

Someone please shoot me now.

"So, who is this thief?"

"His name is Maveryck, and he has been waiting in the Wult village for several days. I believe he was monitoring some riots that he thought to take advantage of. I'm not sure of the details, but he has been planning something else there at the inn. You should have no trouble finding him."

"That's *if* I choose to do this. You've never worked with thieves before. Why now?"

"Because I would much rather steal from the dragon than confront her directly. After our quest to Dragon Spine's peak, I can imagine that dealing with her again would be impossible. You must have faith in your abilities, for you are now in a position to do much good with the powers you have honed."

My powers. I still hadn't told him what Theht had done to me while she'd held me captive in the cave. She'd intruded on my mind, altered me, but I still wasn't sure of the extent of the damage. It didn't matter though. She'd shown me a vision of me destroying the world, and although I had trouble accepting it, I knew deep inside that it was true. I was the Deathbringer, and it was only a matter of time before my magic became so volatile I could no longer control it.

"Olive," Fan'twar said, "we were all surprised when you so suddenly left Faythander to return to Earth Kingdom. It seemed abrupt, to say the least, and it not only confused me but also troubled the Wult king most acutely."

I glanced at my hands, not sure how to answer.

"I do not wish to pry into what happened to you in the cave with Theht, or what other pains you may have experienced throughout your life. You were abandoned by both of your birth parents, which has resulted in some emotional trauma."

"Emotional trauma? If you're suggesting that's why I left,

then you're wrong. I left Faythander because I had things that needed attention here on Earth."

"Is that the only reason?"

I gave him a sharp look. "Yes."

He eyed me. "Are you sure?"

"Yes, I am."

I hoped he heard the warning in my voice. This was a subject I would not discuss.

"Very well. As I said, I do not wish to pry."

I took a deep breath. Being angry with Fan'twar would solve none of my problems. Besides, he was making a big deal out of nothing. I fully intended to return to Faythander, although I had wanted to take care of a few more things before I went back. Life never cooperated. If he was suggesting I had issues, then he was wrong. Absolutely wrong.

We left the restaurant and returned to my apartment. The wind picked up, making the November day turn chilly. Fan'twar made a few comments on the weather as we crossed the parking lot back to my building. Just as on Faythander, his golden eyes shone brightly in the sunlight.

"Have I offended you?" Fan'twar asked. "I've never mastered the art of human interactions, I'm afraid."

"No. I'm not offended. Disappointed, maybe. Balancing my lives on Earth and Faythander hasn't been easy. Sometimes I feel like two different people."

"Yes, the feeling is quite understandable."

A breeze blew past, whipping the dark reddish strands of my hair against my cheeks. My short-cropped hair accentuated my elven ears instead of hiding them, which drew stares at times, but I'd learned to embrace my differences. Yet, being from two worlds didn't always go as smoothly as I would have liked.

When we made it up to my door, I turned to my stepfather.

"Fan'twar," I asked, "do you believe I will destroy the world?"

He paused before answering, his golden eyes focused on me. "I am more afraid that you will sacrifice your life to save it. Do not worry over these things. Life has a way of working itself out, and all the time you spend worrying about the future would be better spent in enjoying the present."

I sighed, trying to agree with him. "I'm not sure how much I'll have to enjoy while I'm stealing from a dragon's hoard with the possibility of being eaten alive looming over my head."

"You've got a good point. I do not envy you in this quest, but it is something that must be done. I would not ask it of you if I did not have the utmost faith in your abilities. Take care, young one, and do not confront the silverwitch directly, or else I fear the consequences will be dire."

"I'll keep that in mind."

"And..." a hint of a smile crossed his face, "do try to have fun. You may find there is still sport to be had in Faythander, if one knows where to find it."

I eyed him. *Sport* was a dangerous word for a dragon to use.

"What do you mean?"

"Nothing in particular." He smiled and stepped away. "I must leave you now and return through my own portal back to Faythander. I have much to attend to."

He abruptly turned on his heel and descended the stairs, leaving me alone on the landing. I watched him exit the staircase and start across the parking lot, his shock of white hair contrasting with the asphalt. He'd never been good with good-byes—typical dragon behavior. It should have bothered me, I guess, but since I'd lived half my life with him, I'd become used to it.

However, I was curious about the sport he'd mentioned. Did he have some convoluted idea to cheer me up? Because if he did, I wanted no part of it.

I went inside my apartment and shut the door behind me. Leaning against the wall, I stared at my worn sofa with Han curled into an indistinguishable gray ball atop one of the cushions. Closing my eyes, I wished I could stay here forever and never be bothered with Faythander again. As long as I was on Earth, there was no chance I could destroy Faythander and no chance I could hurt Kull. But now, with the elves attempting to harness the power of ancient weapons of mass destruction, I had no choice. I had to return.

After hastily grabbing my backpack, I started stuffing things inside. Hairbrush, toothpaste, some clothes, and the journal Fan'twar had given me. Maybe if I had a chance to learn more about the brothers of Tremulac, I'd be more capable of stopping the elven queen.

I crossed to the kitchen and opened the bottom cabinet, intending to scoop out some cat food and leave it for Han, when I found myself sitting on my butt and staring blankly at the bag of dry kitty kibbles. I wanted to see Kull again, didn't

I? If so, then why did I have that sinking feeling in the pit of my stomach? I hugged my arms around my knees. *Because I'm afraid of the future*, I admitted to myself.

Brushing the thought aside, I filled Han's bowl, gave him a scratch on his head as he rushed to the food, and opened my mirror box. Blue magic sparkled around the laptop's casing and silver screen. I ran my fingers over the five figurines, feeling the details in the pewter. Keeping my pack close, I placed my palm against the mirror's surface.

Ready or not, Faythander, here I come.

CHAPTER *Three*

I WALKED THROUGH THE WULT VILLAGE AS I FOUGHT A growing headache. Crossing worlds had taken its toll on me, and although the portals were functioning properly again, my magic was not. It had taken a great deal of energy just to open the portal, and now I had a blooming headache and sour stomach as a result.

The village hadn't changed much since I'd been here a week ago. The Dragon Spine's mountain range loomed along the horizon, its peaks tinted purple in the rising sun. Two- and three-story houses with thatched roofs sat crowded around a town square, where a cobbled path and large water fountain took up the center of the space.

The smell of wood smoke filled the air as tendrils of gray and white rose from chimneys. From a distance came the sounds of laughter and shouting, though there were no people on the streets. I paced cautiously through the village. Where was everyone? And more importantly, where was the inn Fan'twar had spoken of?

My boots echoed through the empty lanes as I focused on voices coming from up ahead. I followed the sounds, passing through the town square and onto a narrow path, and finally, I found the town's only inn—a large stone building, sitting at the end of the lane. People were gathered on the wide front porch, and children dressed in bright woolen sweaters darted through the crowd.

I stopped walking to stare at the building. Fan'twar's sense of humor got me into trouble sometimes, and I had a feeling that something was going on at the inn—something his clairvoyance had led me toward. I wasn't sure I was going to like it. Whatever the case, I knew I had to go to the inn to find the thief, but I just hoped I didn't find anything else in the process. Like too much drama. Fan'twar knew how much I hated drama.

I wandered through the crowd and up the front steps, making my way through the open double doors and into a large room. The room's walls, floor, and ceiling were crafted of deep-stained wooden timbers that smelled of rich resin. Tables and chairs took up most of the floor. Bodies were packed inside, all focused on a man standing atop a table at the back of the room. He stood in front of an enormous stone fireplace. Firelight flickered off his tanned face and dark hair, and his voice carried through the room, booming with a deep resonance that commanded attention. His clothing, made of animal hides and a fur cloak, suggested a wild appearance, yet something about his stance and the intelligence in his dark eyes gave me pause.

"Now is the time to act!" he shouted. "We've no more need of a king. Ours is an age of freedom and prosperity. How are we to live as long as our taxes go to a king we've never seen—a man who lives on the other side of the continent?

"He is a man who has never taken interest in our villages or helped us in any way at all. He fights wars that happen so far away they'll never have any effect on our lives! But that is not the only reason. It is rumored that he has lost the sword of his ancestors—the very sword that is a symbol of our kingdom, of our heritage, and of our nobility. We are a fierce, proud people. This is a new age. I say it is time we elect our leaders. We should choose people from our own villages who know our struggles. The time has come to overthrow the king!"

Shouts and cheers filled the room. As I studied those gathered, I noticed that not all of them looked thrilled with the idea of overthrowing the king, yet the majority cheered.

"I've heard the king is not fit to rule!" someone shouted.

"He's gone mad!" came another shout.

"He doesn't care about us!" more voices chimed in.

"But what do we do about it, Euric? Do you have a solution?"

"Yes," the man on the table—Euric, I assumed—yelled. "Which is why we must act now." He pulled a rolled parchment from a pocket in his cloak. "This is a petition informing the king that we're no longer loyal to him. We'll not be sending another coin in taxes to him ever again. Give me your signatures, and we'll gain our freedom!"

Cheers and whistles exploded through the room, though I got the impression that Euric had worked them up so much they would have agreed to sign away their lives. I studied the man standing on the table. People with the ability to rally a crowd to their whims were dangerous.

The cheers abruptly stopped, and I had to scan the crowd to see what had quieted them.

A man wearing a blue cloak and cowl walked inside, his footfalls thumping over the wooden floorboards. His clothing looked expensive—a dark green vest with silver buckles, and tall leather boots that looked as if they belonged in an elven court. Although his face was partially hidden by the cowl, I could tell he had a strong jaw and thick, seductive lips. He wore his brunette hair in a ponytail slung over his shoulder, and he had a lean, muscle-corded frame. The cloak whipped behind him as he walked toward the table. Although he stood of average height, his presence demanded attention.

A doglike creature with silver fur trotted beside him. I wasn't sure what to call the creature, except it looked like a mix of grimwelt and wolf, although there were no wolves on Faythander—and certainly no mixed Earth-and-Faythander breeds. The animal puzzled me. It stayed at its master's heels as he crossed the room, growling if anyone got too close.

"Who is that?" someone whispered.

"I'm not sure."

The man stopped at the table's edge, and although Euric stood over him, he visibly shrank.

"Who... who are you?" Euric asked.

"My name is not important." The stranger's silken voice carried an elvish accent. "I've come to challenge you in a duel of the sword. Will you accept?"

"A duel?" The man stood straighter. "For what reason?"

"To defend the king."

"I see. In that case, you should know that you will lose. I've never lost a fight."

"Never lost a fight? That is difficult to believe. How many fights have you fought?"

That drew a snicker from the crowd.

"More than you, I assure you."

"If that is so, then you should not hesitate to duel with me."

Euric crossed his arms. "Who are you?"

The dog growled, and the stranger snapped his fingers, quieting it. "As I've said, my name is unimportant. Will you accept my challenge?"

"First, tell me, what is at stake?"

"If I win, you destroy that scroll and vow to pledge allegiance to your king. If you win, you continue forward with your plans."

"I refuse. It is not a fair trade. I will still go forward with my plans whether or not you challenge me."

"Yet you have claimed to have never lost a fight. Winning a friendly duel will only serve to aid your cause even more, won't it?"

"I fail to see how."

"You claimed to be a member of a fierce, noble people. Perhaps it is time you proved it."

"Yes, show him, Euric! Beat him!"

Euric leapt off the table, landing mere inches from the cloaked man's face. "Very well." He held up the scroll. "If I shall sign my name in blood, then so be it!"

This only goaded the crowd more as they cheered the two men into the street. I followed the crowd outside onto the sun-drenched paving stones where the two men prepared to fight.

The gathering parted to form an empty, open area where the two men circled one another. The man in the cloak unsheathed an uncommonly sturdy-looking dueling blade with a delicate, wire pommel. It was an odd weapon, full of contrast, and I wasn't sure I had ever seen one like it. As he removed his cloak, I was surprised to find that his ears were rounded, although I could have sworn the man was elven. He placed his cloak atop the porch where his dog waited patiently, guarding the garment with its life.

Euric had no weapon and found one among the crowd. I wasn't a weapons expert, yet even I could see the nameless stranger held his sword as if he were accustomed to dueling, with a straight back and balanced stance.

As the two men prepared to fight, I scanned the crowd, looking for anyone who seemed roguish or seedy, someone who would fit the description of a thief. At this point, it could have been anyone, even someone who didn't fit the stereotype, and, as I turned to watch the fight, I had a suspicion I knew who it might be.

"Is this a fight to the death?" someone in the crowd yelled.

"Nay!" Euric answered, holding his sword high. "This is a

fight to freedom."

I couldn't help but roll my eyes as the crowd cheered. Kull had struggled against his inadequacies as a leader; he certainly didn't need someone like Euric destroying the unity he had worked so hard to build. But it seemed that was exactly what Euric had in mind. If Euric won this fight and the town signed the petition, it would mean the beginning of dissension among the Wults. Kull already had his hands full negotiating with the elves. Dealing with rebellious Wults would make his job nearly impossible.

"In our village," Euric called so all could hear, "the rules of dueling are simple. First man to the ground loses. Do you agree to these terms?"

The stranger nodded, and the men clashed swords, the sound of their steel ringing through the air. Euric gained a better position than the stranger as he parried in a forward thrust, nearly knocking the newcomer off balance. Stumbling, the stranger regained his footing and blocked a blow that would have injured his shoulder.

I stood near the newcomer's dog, who sat as still as a sphinx as it watched the fight with attentive eyes. A low growl rumbled in its throat as the next several blows resulted in its master losing his balance and nearly falling.

The dog's eyes—one light and one dark—caught my attention. It kept its head up and ears pricked forward as its master finally made an offensive thrust, gaining a few precious inches.

Again, the nameless man was knocked backward. Sunlight glinted off the dueling swords. Beads of sweat rolled down Euric's face as he swung again and again, so fast he didn't take a moment to catch his breath.

The stranger merely defended the blows, standing tall and unmoving. Several tense minutes passed without a gain for either man. Finally, the stranger took a small step forward, and then another.

Euric's cheeks had grown red, and his breathing came out in labored gasps. He'd expended all his energy, and the stranger knew it. The nameless man made quick work of his opponent, slashing his sword in a wide arc and causing Euric to reposition his center of balance in order to block the move. The stranger used the moment to his advantage. He struck fast with the broad side of his blade, hitting the back of Euric's knees. Euric fell forward and hit the ground hard.

The crowd quieted.

Euric's eyes went wide as he rolled onto his back and looked at the stranger with complete surprise.

"There will be no rebellion today," the man said and turned away. He sheathed his sword, then crossed to the porch where he grabbed his cloak.

Behind him, Euric got to his knees, then stood, still holding his sword. Rage replaced the shock on his face. Without warning, he lunged for the stranger.

Before his sword tip could impale the stranger between his shoulder blades, another sword blocked it, knocking Euric backward. Euric's jaw slacked open as he stared at the man who had blocked the blow.

The man who held the sword walked out of the crowd and into the open courtyard. He stood a head taller than the rest and wore a dark brown cloak with a cowl, but when he pushed the cowl back, a gasp came from the crowd.

"The king," they whispered.

My heart sped up as I stared at the familiar, shoulder-length blond hair and piercing blue eyes of the man who held my heart. When had Kull arrived?

Again, the timing seemed uncanny, and I had visions of Kull and my stepfather sitting around and planning just such an escapade.

Euric stumbled into the courtyard, looking confused as his eyes roved the crowd. "Your... Your Majesty," he said as he stumbled into a sloppy bow. "I am sorry. I did not know... none of us knew. That is to say—"

"Euric, is it?" Kull asked, his voice commanding attention.

Euric bobbed his head. "Please, spare my life. The words I said were spoken out of ignorance. Had I known you were here—"

"Had you known I was here, your words may have changed, but your heart would have remained the same. Do you know what I do to traitors?"

He knelt, his eyes focused on the ground. "No, Your Majesty."

"In days long past, the punishment for betraying one's country resulted in a public beheading. But as you have said, now is a new age." Kull sheathed his sword and extended his hand.

Euric glanced up, confused, but then he took Kull's hand and stood.

"Your king has not forgotten you," Kull said. "You would

19

be wise not to forget your king."

Euric nodded quickly. "I understand."

"Good." Kull smiled, then turned to the crowd. "I'm thirsty. A round of king's mead for everyone!"

The villagers clapped and cheered. Most of them crowded around the king, hoping to get a glimpse or possibly a handshake from him. I wasn't sure if Kull had noticed I was among the crowd as I wandered into the building and found an empty seat near a window, giving me a good view of the crowd outside. With the throng of townsfolk surrounding the king, it took a full twenty minutes for Kull to get back inside. The mood had changed. Half an hour ago, the townsfolk had been ready to renounce their country, and now they crowded around the king as if he were their hero.

Kull finally managed to take a seat in the center of the room. After several rounds of drinks, laughter, and a few bawdy jokes, the Wult crowd seemed in their element. I found Euric standing at the edge of the room, his arms crossed and his eyes dark.

I was sure this wasn't the reaction he'd envisioned when he'd planned his speech. As morning turned to afternoon, the crowd thinned. With his back to me, Kull still hadn't noticed I was in the room. I watched him from my spot in the corner, admiring the way he handled what could have been the start of a rebellion.

A shadow loomed over me, and I looked up. The stranger stood at my table with the gray wolf waiting at his side. As I got a close-up look at the guy, I was glad my heart belonged to Kull. Otherwise, it would have been hard not to ogle him. His quicksilver eyes glittered with flecks of purple. He had high cheekbones, a square jaw, and thick, almost seductive lips that looked as if they were holding a carefully guarded secret. He wore his long brunette hair in a low ponytail that fell down his back. Muscles corded his lean frame, and although he didn't have the bulk of a Wult warrior, his toned body suggested that he must have been physically active. His tanned, smooth skin had the texture of porcelain, and as he shook my hand, his fingers were cold, reminding me of glass.

"Are you Olive?" he asked.

I nodded, and he took a seat across from me. He turned to his wolf.

"Grace, *mauir phenine.*"

The dog sat at his side, keeping its eyes on me.

20

"What sort of creature is it?"

"She."

"Excuse me?"

"You called her *it*. However, Grace is female, so the proper term is *she*."

"Okay. What sort of dog is she?"

"She is a mix of a grimwelt and *Canis lupus*—or wolf—from Earth Kingdom."

"A mixed breed from Faythander and Earth Kingdom? How is that possible?"

He shrugged. "I have no idea."

"Really? Then how do you know she is part wolf?"

"I am privileged to be the owner of several bestiaries from Earth Kingdom. After doing a bit of research, I was able to learn of her correct heritage."

"How interesting." I eyed him. "I'm sorry, but you know my name and I'm afraid I don't know yours." Although, truthfully, I'd suspected it since he'd first walked through the doors.

He gave me a small smile. "My name is Maveryck, although I prefer the title Professional Reclaimer. Most know me as 'the thief'."

Yep, suspicion confirmed.

CHAPTER *Four*

MAVERYCK SAT ACROSS FROM ME, AND THE WOLF SAT beside him. She kept her eyes focused on me as her master and I spoke.

"I have been waiting for your arrival," Maveryck said.

It was hard for me not to stare at him. His appearance confused me. With his soft, silken voice, and his high, pronounced cheekbones, he must have had elven blood. Except for his ears, he looked as if he belonged in an elven palace.

"How long have you been waiting?" I asked.

He shrugged. "Not long, although Grace was beginning to get impatient. She grows restless when she's confined to closed spaces."

"I see. Let me get this straight, while you were waiting for me, you decided on a whim to just start a few fights?"

"It was not a whim."

"Then what was it?"

"The sky king wanted me to meet with you, but I told him I could not and that I had business to attend to. He would not relent, however, and we agreed that since I had business in this village, he would send you here to meet me.

"As for my business, I was hired to confront Euric. The king may have been planning to confront the man with me as well."

"I see. And did the sky king know of this?"

"I believe he did."

"You were all three in on this together?"

"That is correct."

Hmm, I wondered if I'd discovered the sport Fan'twar had mentioned. Was this his attempt at lightening my mood?

In a convoluted, dragon sort of way, I supposed I could see how the duel possessed a cheap sort of entertainment quality. But dueling? Really?

Dragons these days.

"To be fair," Maveryck said, "the sky king knew you enjoyed a good duel, so he told us to wait until you arrived to confront Euric."

I looked to the ceiling and quietly cursed my stepfather. It was now confirmed that dragons had the lousiest senses of humor on the planet. I turned back to Maveryck, trying to remind myself why I'd crossed to Faythander in the first place.

"When do we leave for the silverwitch's castle?" I asked.

"As soon as the others arrive, I assume."

"Others?"

"The Wult assemblage. Did your stepfather not tell you?"

"He didn't mention it."

Without warning, a pair of strong arms grabbed me from behind and lifted me off my chair. Kull squeezed me so hard I felt like my lungs would pop. Served me right for dating a Wult warlord.

"Olive," he breathed into my ear, "have you been hiding from me this whole time?"

"Kull," I gasped, "please put me down."

He shot me a broad grin, gave me a kiss on my cheek, and then placed my feet on the floor once again. I couldn't help but smile back at him. What was it about this man that made me completely lose my head?

He helped me back to my seat, then sat next to me. "You've met Maveryck?" he asked.

"Yes."

"Good. As soon as we're all here, we'll leave for that cursed mountain. We're all sick to death of negotiating with the elves. For now, the elves are satisfied with the territory they've gained in the goblins lands. When your stepfather mentioned a chance at a duel to defend my kingship and then a mission to find a lost weapon of the Madralorde, I couldn't pass on the opportunity. Plus," he leaned forward, his eyes intense, "that witch still has my sword."

A young serving girl, perhaps fifteen, stopped by our table. "Anything to drink?" she asked.

"Ale," Kull said.

"Wine for me," Maveryck said.

"Water," I answered. I'd made the mistake once of con-

23

suming Wult ale and would never do it again—I would drink gasoline first, and I would probably enjoy it more.

The girl gave a brief nod before she hustled back into the kitchen.

Grace gave a low growl, and Maveryck patted her head as two figures wearing cloaks wandered toward our table. They stopped behind Kull, acting casual with their arms folded, though neither man took a seat.

"Don't mind them," Kull said. "They're my *bodyguards*." He spoke the name with distaste. "Ever since Father passed, my dear queen mother has been increasingly worried over my wellbeing, and when she found out about my brush with the bloodthorn in Earth Kingdom, she insisted I keep those two around."

The serving girl returned with three drinks and placed them on the table. "Anything else for you?" she asked, keeping her eyes focused on the floor.

"No, that's all," Maveryck said.

She made no reply before bustling back to the kitchen.

Maveryck took a small sip of his wine, keeping his eyes focused on the two men behind Kull. "Your Highness," Maveryck said, "may I inquire as to when you believe the Wult party will arrive?"

"Soon," Kull answered. "If all goes well, they should arrive before evening." He took a long gulp of ale. "And please call me Kull. *Your Highness* was my father."

"As you wish," Maveryck nodded.

After finishing his drink, Kull took my hand. "Will you accompany me outside? We need to speak."

"Of course."

I stood with him, and we gave Maveryck a brief good-bye before heading for the exit. Euric still sulked by the doorway. His eyes widened as he spotted me holding hands with the king. His gaze lingered on my ears, but I ignored him as we exited the inn. With the current tension between the elves and the Wults, I knew my ancestry would cause unease among Kull's people. But for now, we had bigger problems to worry about.

As Kull and I walked outside, I welcomed the sunshine and crisp fall air. Kull's two bodyguards followed like shadows as we left the confines of the town and hiked toward the mountains. Red wildflowers grew in every direction, and an afternoon breeze rushed past, stirring the flowers into rolling, crimson waves.

Kull led me to a rusted wrought-iron gate in a crumbling stone wall. Hinges squealed as he pushed the gate open and led me inside, where we found several benches arranged around a tree. The guards stayed just outside the gate.

"What is this place?" I asked, staring at the stone seats and crumbling wall.

"My best guess is that it was once part of a castle of some sort. You can see the outlines of the walls there." He pointed across the flat expanse of land where crumbling walls lay like exposed bone.

I watched as he stared out over the crumbling castle, past the hills and toward the mountains. The strong set of his jaw, his eyes the crystal blue of glacier ice, his lips curved in that familiar hint of a smile—all of it reminded me why I'd chosen him. We'd had a bumpy past for sure, but now none of that seemed to matter. Wind tousled his hair, and I reached up and pushed it away from his eyes. He caught my fingers and gave me a playful grin.

"Why did you bring me out here?" I asked.

His smile faded. "To be honest, I was worried about you."

"Worried?"

He led me to a bench where I sat beside him. The two guards moved to within eyesight of us. I tried my best to not notice.

"After what happened in the cave, and then after you left so abruptly, I became concerned about you. I wanted to make sure you were well."

"I'm fine."

He gave me a suspicious glance. I dodged his gaze.

"You and Fan'twar both," I said. "One would think you two had planned this."

"We worry about you. You can't blame us."

"I wish you wouldn't."

"But do you wish to discuss what happened in the cave?"

"No, I don't."

He took my hand. "Believe me when I say I understand. It's still hard for me to speak of my father's death. I only wish for you to know that should you ever need to talk, you have but to ask."

I nodded. The calmness of his voice comforted me, and the warmth of his hands seemed to melt my chills. He held my fingers gently, though his presence gave me strength. Perhaps when I was ready, I would tell him what had happened, but now was too soon.

"Was there anything else you wanted to talk about?" I asked.

He surprised me by growing quiet, his face drawn and detached as he stared out over the witch's mountain, toward her lair. "Yes," he said. "How much do you know about this thief?"

"Nothing. I only just met him. Fan'twar must trust him somewhat, or else he wouldn't have hired him."

Kull nodded. "I can't decide if I trust him or not."

"Why not?"

He shrugged. "I don't have a good reason. It's more of a premonition, I suppose. But I feel he's hiding something, though I don't know what."

I'd learned not to doubt his insight when it came to judging people, as he had an uncanny ability to read others.

"Do you think we should try to steal the staff without him?"

"No. If we're to break inside the dragon's lair and survive, it would be wise to have someone experienced along with us. Plus, he did agree to defend me earlier. I think for now, we have no choice but to trust him. Still, I will be wary of him."

A breeze gusted past, carrying with it the woodsy scent of his hair. He squeezed my fingers gently as he gave me a playful grin.

"I missed you," he said.

"I'm pretty sure I missed you more."

He leaned forward and kissed me gently. My heart fluttered with excitement at the feel of his lips on mine, and heat rushed to my cheeks as the kiss deepened. His hands wandered to my back, and he drew me closer to him. I threaded my fingers through his hair, my chest tight as I let him draw me closer to him.

But I couldn't get the image of Theht out of my head, of her powers manipulating me as I destroyed the world—and as I killed him. The image of Kull lying dead at my feet stirred such a powerful reaction inside me that I had to push him away.

He eyed me. "Are you all right?" he asked.

"Yes." I gave him my carefree smile. "I'm fine."

"You're sure?"

I only nodded, feeling as if a hole had opened up in my chest. Here he was, mine again, and yet I couldn't get close to him. I would've laughed at the absurdity of the situation if I hadn't felt on the verge of tears.

"I have to admit," he said, taking my hand, "I did question

whether or not you would return."

His words stirred a strange emotion. Was it fear? I held his hand tight, wanting to tell him what had happened to me in the cave, to tell him that soon I would kill us all. But how could anyone admit such a thing?

"You don't wish for me to kiss you?" he asked.

How could I answer? "No—I mean, yes, I do. It's just that..."

A loud cough came from nearby, and Kull released my hand. One of his guards stood behind us. The guard, a wiry guy with shaggy hair and a large Adam's apple, bounced on his toes as he spoke. I hoped he was good with a sword. Otherwise, I saw no reason why he'd been assigned to protect the Wult king.

"Yes?" Kull demanded.

"I thought you would like to know, your sister has arrived."

"And you felt you needed to tell me this now?"

"Well, yes. She's been injured."

Kull's eyes widened. "Injured?"

He nodded.

"Where is she?"

"At the inn. She just arrived."

Kull stood abruptly. "Why didn't you tell me this sooner?"

He cleared his throat. "Well, you..." he darted a glance at me, "you were occupied."

Kull growled, making the guard shrink away. He grabbed my hand, and together we made it outside the gate and back onto the path toward the inn. Afternoon turned to evening, and as the wind died down, the field of red wildflowers grew still. The fading light turned their petals a deeper shade—the color of blood. Soon their bright hue would be gone completely, replaced by darkness.

Shouting came from up ahead. We followed the sounds until we made it back to the inn. A group of Wults stood outside, but we pushed our way through the crowd and into the building.

Kull's sister Heidel sat near the fireplace with a bandage on her arm. A spot of dark blood was visible under the gauze. She wore her long, dark hair in a braid slung over her shoulder. Although Heidel had done a good job of moving forward from a troubled past, in her eyes, I saw pain that only survivors of abuse carried with them. When I looked at her, I was reminded of all my clients who shared that same haunted look.

We made it to the table, and she glanced up at her brother.

"Where were you?" she asked.

"Waiting for you. What happened?" He nodded at the gauze wrapping her arm.

"We were ambushed. As soon as our light coach entered the valley, a group of masked men stopped our carriage as if they meant to board. Instead, they killed two of us with basita weapons before we had a chance to retaliate. We fought them off, and they escaped toward the mountains."

"Who attacked you?"

Heidel took a long gulp of her drink. "Elves. They wore disguises, but I am sure it was them. They were trained to fight. I managed to get a good look at one of their weapons. It was imprinted with the seal of a sunburst."

"Why did they attack you?" Kull asked.

"I bet they're trying to steal the staff," I said.

Kull rubbed his chin. "I don't like this. To attack so boldly is an act of war."

"Yes," Heidel said, pounding her fist on the table. "We must hunt them down and slaughter them all. We can't let them get away with this treachery."

"Patience, Sister. We must think through this carefully before rushing after them."

"I don't understand," I said. "If they wanted to stop us from taking the staff, then why did they only attack Heidel? Why not attack us, too?"

"Because," Heidel answered, "I believe they thought I already had the staff, and they were trying to take it from me. Once they learned we had not already claimed it, they made their journey to the mountain instead."

The young serving girl who'd helped us earlier came to our table and placed a basket of bread on the tabletop. "Anything to eat for the three of you? Tonight we've got boarhound stew."

"We'll take four bowls," Kull said.

"Four?" Heidel asked.

He nodded toward the stairs, where a shadowy form emerged and made his way toward the table. The wolf stayed at his side. When Maveryck reached our table, he stopped, then pushed the cowl away from his face.

"Four," Kull said.

The serving girl gave a quick nod and then hurried back to the kitchen.

"Maveryck," Kull said, "please meet my sister, Heidel. She will be joining us on our quest to reclaim the staff."

"You're the thief?" she asked.

He nodded, then took a seat at the table. With a snap of his fingers, the dog sat beside him. Threading his fingers together, he scanned each of us, his gaze stopping on Heidel.

"What happened?" he asked, nodding at the bandage.

"My light carriage was attacked by elves."

He raised an eyebrow. "Elves? You are sure of this?"

She nodded.

"This does not bode well," he said. "Elves have successfully stolen from the witch in the past. We must make our journey sooner than I expected in order to apprehend them."

"How soon?" Kull asked.

"That depends on how quickly the elves will arrive at the witch's castle." He looked at Heidel. "How long ago did the elves attack you?"

"About three hours."

"And where did they attack you at?"

"On the outskirts of the village in the forest, near the foothills."

Maveryck worked his jaw back and forth as he pondered her words. "They are ahead of us. This is unexpected. The elves will likely arrive before us and steal the staff."

"Is there any way we can get there first?" I asked.

"Not likely, but possible. I have the benefit of knowing a route that will take us into the witch's vaults without detection. But we will have to leave tonight if we wish to get there before the elves."

"Very well," Kull said, "we'll leave tonight. But once we're inside, how are we to remove the staff?"

"Leave that to me," he said.

Heidel crossed her arms. "I hope you've skills in fighting as well as thievery, or you'll not last long on this quest."

He gave her a condescending smile. "I assure you, I can hold my own."

The serving girl arrived with four steaming bowls, and the rich scent of broth filled the air. I took a bite of the stew and found it a flavorful combination of fresh vegetables and tender meat.

"How do you know of this passage to the witch's castle?" Kull asked.

Maveryck paused in taking a bite. "That is something I'd rather keep to myself until we arrive."

"Why?" I asked.

He looked at me. "If I were to reveal my secrets, then anyone listening in on our conversation would also know, wouldn't they?"

"Have you entered her castle before?" Heidel asked.

"Of course. The dragon king would not have hired me unless he knew I could get the job done."

"Then why didn't he hire you before," I asked, "when we were tracking down the bloodthorn?"

"Because I only have the ability to enter her vaults and nowhere else. I would not dare try to break through the wards surrounding her mountain. I will remind you that while I am good at what I do, my skills are limited. We will enter her vaults and nowhere else, and then we will escape."

Heidel scrutinized him. "It's unlikely our quest will go as smoothly as you think. In the past, you most likely stole from the witch when she was unaware. But this time, we've got a squadron of elves to deal with, who we'll most likely have to fight at some point. Have you been trained in combat?"

He narrowed his eyes. "Do you often question people you've just met in such a way?"

"Only those who I am trusting to aid me during battle."

"And you do not trust me?"

"I cannot say for sure. However, you are too thin and far too pretty to be a fighter. And I doubt that beast at your side would measure up against a horde of elves—or a dragon, for that matter." She turned to Kull. "Tell me again why we're taking him with us?"

I tried to keep from laughing, but I felt overjoyed that Heidel had found someone other than me to pick on about their combat skills.

"Sister," Kull said, "I would prefer if you did not insult our guest." He turned to Maveryck. "My apologies. Heidel tends to be critical, especially when she's injured or in a foul mood. Or when she is hungry, tired, upset, or has a headache. Or if it is morning."

"I can hear you," Heidel said.

Kull winked at me.

"I am only trying to point out the fact that this thief could very well die in this quest, and he does not have the proper conditioning or training in order to survive. Picking locks and wearing fashionable clothing will not help him to slay a dragon."

"He has more skills than just picking locks," Kull said.

"What sort of skills?" Heidel asked. "The training of mixed-breed animals?"

"That's enough," Kull said.

Heidel clenched her hands. "Fine. My apologies for trying to keep us all alive."

"May I have a word with you, Sister? In private?" Kull didn't wait for her response as he marched to the other side of the room.

She eyed him as he walked away but soon stood. "If you two will excuse me," she said and then followed her brother.

They moved to stand under an alcove leading to a hallway at the far side of the room. Although they spoke quietly, I decided it wouldn't hurt to eavesdrop. Having the benefit of elven hearing came in handy sometimes.

"You must stop insulting our guest," Kull said.

"Why?"

"Because he defended me earlier when you were away. He can handle a sword."

"You saw him?" Heidel asked.

"Yes."

"Why didn't you tell me this sooner?" Heidel asked. "You could have told me at any point."

"Because you were too busy berating him," Kull answered. "I don't understand what has put you into such a foul mood."

"You don't? Several of my companions are dead, and you've no idea why I am upset?"

"I'm sorry you had to witness such brutality, but that is no reason to insult our guest. He had nothing to do with your attack."

I heard her sniff as their conversation went silent. Maveryck cleared his throat, and I'd nearly forgotten he was sitting at the same table with me.

"Elven hearing?" he asked me.

"Umm, yeah." I self-consciously pushed a clump of hair behind my ears.

"I've heard of you," Maveryck said. "Daughter of an elf and human, Sky King's ward. Faythander is an immense continent, yet word travels."

"I suppose it does."

He took a bite of his stew. "They were talking about me, I assume."

I nodded.

"Anything I should know?"

"Not really."

He shrugged. "Let me guess—they don't trust me. It's nothing new. Trust is something I fail to earn owing to the business I'm in." He broke off a piece of bread and tossed it to his dog. "I can't blame them. I wouldn't trust me, either."

"Should they trust you?"

"That depends," he answered.

"Depends on what?"

"On whether or not they want the staff of Zaladin." He eyed me, trying to act casual, though I saw the shrewd look in his granite eyes. "How much do you know of the staff?"

"Not much. It belonged to one of the Madralorde brothers. If we want to stop the elves from defeating my stepfather and ruling the world, then we need to find it before they do."

"Do you know of the staff's dangers?"

I raised an eyebrow. "Other than its ability to work with the other weapons to control Theht? Isn't that dangerous enough?"

Kull and Heidel returned to our table, cutting our conversation short. Kull sat on the bench beside me, and Heidel sat across from Maveryck. She forced a smile.

"My apologies," she said. "I didn't mean to offend you. I was only trying to protect you, as I know our mission is one of grave danger. But now that I know you have skills in swordplay, I shall question you no more."

Maveryck gave her a courteous bow of his head. "Apology accepted, although not needed. I was not offended."

Great. Did this mean she would go back to picking on me?

"We should gather our things and leave as soon as possible," Maveryck said as he stood. "I shall meet you all at the foot of the old church's bell tower on the outskirts of this village."

"Why not just meet us here?" I asked.

"I've business to attend to. If you will excuse me." He turned and headed for the staircase, his expensive buckles jangling and silver hound trailing behind him.

"Business," Heidel said after he'd disappeared upstairs. "He failed to mention what sort of business, didn't he?"

"He's a successful thief," Kull said. "I'm sure he's got more than one job at a time, or else he wouldn't be successful."

Heidel crossed her arms, making her metallic armbands gleam in the firelight cast off from the hearth. "I don't like him."

"You've no need to like him," Kull said, "you only have to tolerate him until the mission is over."

"Then for his sake, it had better end quickly."

CHAPTER
Five

KULL, HEIDEL, AND I HIKED THROUGH THE FLOWER field to the old church that sat on the outskirts of the village. Although the sun had set, leaving the world in darkness, the glow of our torches illuminated our path. We walked without Kull's guards following us. It had taken quite a bit of negotiating on his part, but as he was king, he was finally able to win out. Besides, I doubted any of the guards wanted to confront the silverwitch.

Up ahead, the hulking bones of the church came into view, a crumbling stone structure with a bell tower that reached into the night sky, hiding the stars. Someone must live in the place as there were several lit candles glowing from the remaining windows. We approached the building and found Maveryck and his wolf standing outside under a tall tree. He smiled as we walked toward him and stopped under the tree.

"I'm glad you have arrived so promptly," Maveryck said. "We shall cross through the field here until we reach the foot of the mountain. The entrance to the vault is through a spellcasted cave. If you'll follow me."

He turned away from us and walked toward the open field. As we followed, tall grass brushed against our legs. The chirp of night insects stirred the air, while the soft white glow of nobbinflies appeared now and again.

Ahead of us, the mountain range was almost indistinguishable from the sky, but I could just make out the ridge where the rocky cliffs stood in a jagged line against the stars. Somewhere up there stood the silverwitch's fortress. Recalling the power she'd wielded made a chill run down my spine.

There was a reason Fan'twar had sent us with an experienced thief to her castle. Confronting her directly could very easily end in our deaths. Although Fan'twar had faith in my abilities, I doubted I stood a chance against her in a head-to-head battle.

The flat field began to slope upwards, and small stones and pebbles replaced the grass. Boulders appeared as we drew closer to Dragon Spine Mountain. The balmy night air made my clothes stick to my skin. As we trudged upward, our torches sputtered and grew dimmer as they burned through the kerosene-soaked rags.

Maveryck stopped us as we neared a rock wall. Firelight reflected off the broad, flat surface.

"Wait here," Maveryck said quietly as he neared the rock face and moved along the wall. His boots quietly crunched stray pebbles as he lightly ran his fingers along the surface, his ever-present wolf pacing at his side.

"What is he doing?" Heidel asked.

"Maybe looking for the opening?" I suggested.

"In the dark?" Heidel asked. "He doesn't even have a torch with him. How can he expect to see anything?"

Maveryck stopped a distance away from us, almost indistinguishable from the mountain. "Come," he called to us.

We did as he said and crossed the distance, then stopped behind him. As the firelight illuminated the sheer wall of rock, I noticed symbols etched into the stone.

"Runes," Kull said, "written in the old language."

"Do you know what they say?" Heidel asked.

Kull studied the three characters. "*Protect*," he said, pointing to the rune on the left. "*Power* is the rune in the center, and *enter* is the symbol on the right."

"Yes," Maveryck answered. "Your Viking ancestors knew this was a place of power but had no idea how to control it. They placed these runes here in an attempt to protect the powers that lie within the stone."

"Do you know how to control it?" I asked.

He nodded.

"How? Do you possess magic?"

"Yes, I had an elven maternal grandmother. I've got just enough elven blood flowing through my veins to control a limited amount of magic."

He turned to the wall and rested his hand on the runes. As his thumb, middle finger, and pinkie finger connected with each of the three symbols, magic gathered around him. Electric blue light swirled around his hands, then coursed under his skin and through his veins, highlighting the bones and tendons in his fingers. The light pulsed outward and ignited the runes one by one. First, the rune at his thumb, then his pinkie, and finally the middle rune glowed bright blue, flowing with an almost-liquid magic that pulsed with its own heartbeat.

I stared in awe at the three glowing runes. I'd never felt magic like his—almost as if it were a living thing—but before I could question him, the ground began to shake. Small pebbles dislodged and crumbled, and then a seam opened up in the rock face.

"Everyone step back," Maveryck instructed.

We moved away from the wall as the fissure grew into a long, narrow hallway. Sapphire-blue light sparkled from the rough-hewn walls. When the shaking stopped, we walked toward the entrance as it cast bluish light on our faces and hands. Kull got to the opening first, and he unsheathed a sword that I'd never seen him use. Its wide blade and heavy, Wult-style pommel seemed sturdy enough, yet it didn't fit him in the same way as Bloodbane.

"This will take us to the witch's castle?" Heidel asked.

"It will take us into her vaults, which are underground and separate from her castle. You won't need the torches."

Kull and Heidel doused the flames, then left the smoking torches alongside the rock face. We entered the tunnel with magic lighting our path. Bursts of azure radiated around the walls and rock-strewn ground. The ocean of light made me feel as if we were walking underwater.

The path sloped downward, the only sound coming from our booted feet as our footsteps echoed in the widening tunnel. Small crystals grew like flowers along the floor and in recesses in the walls. Most glowed blue, but occasionally we came across clusters of green or black-tinted crystals. Magic pulsed from the surrounding cave walls and through my hands, making my fingertips tingle.

As we walked, I felt the presence of Theht deep inside my consciousness, a presence I did my best to ignore. It was like a thorn under my skin, constantly throbbing, reminding me it was there.

The tunnel grew brighter as the sound of rushing water came from up ahead and the smell of damp earth filled the air. Soon our path broadened, and we stood on the bank of an underground river. Black water churned past, its rushing roar filling our ears. Droplets of moisture dampened my hands and face as we followed the path along the river.

Maveryck paused when we reached a spot where the water calmed and a path of stones broke up the surface, leading from one shore to the other.

"We'll have to cross the stones to make it to the other shore. It's not deep, but these stones are slick, so we must tread carefully."

Kull and Heidel both sheathed their weapons as we prepared to cross. Maveryck went first, stepping lightly from one rock to the next until he crossed the distance and leapt to the far shore. His wolf, Grace, followed close behind him on light feet that didn't make a sound as she bounded from one stone to the next, finally making it to her master's side.

"Who's next?" Maveryck called.

"I'll go," I said. "I'd like to get this over with."

I shouldered my pack and stepped onto the first stone. My boots slipped and I almost tipped into the water, but I managed to catch myself just in time and made it to the next stone, and then the next. When I reached the halfway point, I felt the air change and realized I must have crossed the barrier into the witch's territory.

An uncontrollable chill made me pause as Theht's presence reacted to the magic. Flexing my fists, I pushed my fear aside and concentrated instead on leaping from one stone to another, keeping my eyes on the path ahead. The sound of rushing water drowned out the pounding of my heartbeat.

Soon, I leapt from the last stone to the shore where Maveryck and Grace waited. Kull and Heidel made it across without incident, and without speaking, we followed Maveryck along the shore until we reached another tunnel. The path led us steadily upward until all sounds of the river disappeared once again.

Farther along, an elaborate carving made to look like a door blocked our path. A faint trace of bluish magic hummed through the written spells carved over the arching gateway. I felt its power as it vibrated through the wards, warming me. It was an odd sensation—one that I was unfamiliar with.

"What is this?" I asked.

"An elodise," Maveryck answered. "An ancient elven gateway."

"Elven gateway?" I asked, confused. "Are you sure? I've been around elves, but I've never seen anything like this."

"I don't suppose you would have. They aren't commonplace." He turned to face the gateway. "Once I conjure the spell, the door will only remain open for a few seconds. We will need to pass through it quickly; otherwise, we'll become a permanent part of the mountain. Are you all prepared to enter?"

We each nodded, then Maveryck reached toward the door. Just as before, his magic gathered around him and spiraled in swirls of glimmering blue light. As he released his magic into the door, I felt the hairs on my arms stand on end. The door disappeared, replaced by a dark opening. On the other side was a faint golden gleam, but I could see nothing past that.

The door was an enigma to me. I'd studied magic my entire life, so I should have heard of a door such as this at least once. But for now, I had other matters to worry over. I turned back to the open gateway.

Kull and Heidel walked through first. I followed, then Maveryck and his wolf came behind me. We stepped into an enormous cavern. Behind us, the door sealed shut with a quiet whoosh.

Around us stood immense stacks of gold, though I spotted a few items made of precious stones, bronze, or silver. The labyrinth of jewels and weapons made my head spin. Light came from somewhere—up ahead, maybe?

"Where is the staff?" I whispered quietly to Maveryck.

"I'm not sure, but the witch keeps her most guarded treasures in the next chamber on the top level. Follow me."

We crossed into an open area, and the entire vault came into view. The cavern was built like a honeycomb, with spiraling staircases and narrow bridges connecting one level to the next. Wooden and stone pillars, balconies, and bridges were embellished with images of skulls and winged demons, an ornate masterpiece that sent shivers down my spine.

"Up there," Maveryck whispered, pointing to the topmost level, "is where she puts the most dangerous objects. If we're to find the staff, I believe it would be there. Stay close."

We followed Maveryck as we hiked toward one of the staircases, our footsteps echoing through the immense chamber. As we walked, we passed a set of towering double doors.

"That is the only other entrance into the vaults," Maveryck said, "and it looks as if we've beaten the elves here."

"I don't like this," Heidel whispered. "It reminds me too much of the catacombs in the goblin lands. It was a nightmare

37

trying to fight my way out of that place."

"We will have no need of fighting our way out as long as we do not attract attention," Maveryck said. He gave Grace a gentle pat on the head, and we continued onward.

I'd never been to the goblin underworld, so I had no way of disputing Heidel's statement. But I knew she'd spent time in the goblin catacombs, and I was sure it must have been an unpleasant memory, to say the least.

We made it to a narrow, spiraling staircase situated under the dome's apex and began climbing to the top. In several places, a bridge connected the staircase with the surrounding balconies. With each stair we climbed, the height grew more dizzying.

When we reached the top of the staircase, we crossed a bridge that led us to the balconies surrounding the honeycomb. With no handrails, I focused on putting one foot in front of the other until I stepped onto the far landing. The others gathered around me after crossing the bridge. We found ourselves on a narrow balcony that circled the upper edge of the catacomb. Niches had been hewn into the rock, and inside the crevices sat assortments of objects—mirrors, crowns, daggers, and some more unusual objects like a skull, a large spider, and a lock of hair. Greenish magic glowed around each of the objects, making my skin tingle from their spells.

"There's dragon magic here," I said.

"Yes," Maveryck said. "Each of the talismans has been spellcasted. Be cautious. Do not touch anything."

We circled the outer rim of the catacomb. I detected other sorts of magic radiating from many of the items we passed, and I tried not to gawk as we neared several objects of enormous power, their magic calling to me in quiet, seductive whispers.

As we rounded a corner, Kull stopped at one of the niches. Inside the glow of the dragon's spell sat an all-too-familiar object—Kull's sword.

Bloodbane.

Kull stared at the sword with wide eyes, and his mouth slacked open.

"Was this your sword?" Maveryck asked.

"Yes," Kull said after finding his voice. "Is there any way for me to reclaim it?"

Maveryck shook his head. "No. As soon as the spell is triggered, we will only have a matter of minutes to escape from the chamber before the dragon's guards catch up to us. The sword will have to remain here."

"Is there a way to get past the spell?" Kull ran his fingers over the embellished stone surrounding the niche. "Couldn't we get around it somehow? Break through the stone, perhaps?"

"Not possible. Not unless you've brought a chisel."

"I could do it," Kull said, "if I had my sword."

"But it's surrounded by a spell," Heidel said. "Come, Brother. We do not have time to waste. We are here to retrieve the staff and nothing more."

"Then go," Kull said, "and I shall meet you at the elven door."

"You want us to leave you?" Maveryck asked.

"Yes."

"Kull," I said, "do you think that's wise?"

He turned to me, and I saw the desperation in his eyes. "What would you do if you were in my situation? We're so close. I can't leave it now that I've found it."

I stared at the sword, at the familiar broad blade and simple, unadorned pommel. That sword was more than just an object to him—it was a piece of his identity.

"Fine," I said, relenting. "I'll stay with you. I'm sure I can come up with some sort of spell to remove it."

"I don't like this," Maveryck said. "Removing that sword, if it's even possible, will take time, which is a luxury we don't have. You cannot expect me to wait for you."

"This sword is causing you to lose your judgment," Heidel said.

"I assure you, my judgment is fine. I am justified in reclaiming my sword. Go ahead without me if you wish. Olive and I will meet you at the elven door. I give you my word."

Maveryck worked his jaw back and forth as he debated Kull's request. Grace stood straight, her ears pricked forward as if listening to something, then raised her hackles and gave a low growl.

"We are wasting our time arguing," Maveryck said. "Meet us at the door if you must, but if you do not return, we will have no choice but to leave without you."

Kull nodded. "Very well."

Heidel, Maveryck, and Grace turned away and continued walking down the path until they disappeared from sight. I turned to Kull, who stood staring at the sword.

"Do you know how to get past this spell?" Kull asked.

I reached out, feeling the enchantment glowing with a

steady intensity. The characteristics of a protection spell encircled the sword, but I also felt something shielding the sword—another spell, almost imperceptible.

"That's odd," I said. "There are two spells. I can get past the protection spell, but I'm not sure about the other one." I glanced up at him. "Are you sure you want me to do this?"

"Yes. I'll never get another chance to reclaim it."

"I agree, but I can't promise I won't trigger the spells."

He smiled. "I've seen your powers. If anyone can free my sword, it's you."

I turned back to Bloodbane, its metal gleaming with a greenish tint under the light of magic. "I'll see what I can do."

Reaching out, I tried to come up with some way to remove the second spell. It would've helped if I'd known more about it. Dragon magic was fairly simple to understand, but this was different from any dragon spell I'd been taught.

As I scanned the foreign enchantment, I focused on finding the simplest information first. Splaying my fingers outward, I let my hand hover close to the spell, feeling as if the power were made of individual threads in a web. As I concentrated, I could almost see the spell, like a net covering the opening.

"The spell was created to function like a trap," I said. "If anyone were to reach for the sword and grab it, the spell would be broken and most likely alert the witch." I moved my hand just above the spell, up and down, left and right, looking for any sort of opening. "And if I were to send a spell through this one to remove the protection spell, I suspect it would also alert the witch."

"Can you get past it?" Kull asked.

"I'm looking."

After several minutes of searching and my hand tingling from the effects of the dragon's magic, I gave up.

"There's got to be a way," I said.

Kneeling beside me, Kull scanned the stone surrounding the opening. Carved into the rock on either side of the niche stood two winged skeletons. Their empty eye sockets seemed to follow Kull's movements as he scanned the encased sword. I wasn't sure what he was searching for, but if it could help him free his sword, I wouldn't argue.

After a moment of examining the stonework, he turned to me.

"Have you found something?" I asked.

"Maybe. Do you feel this?"

He took my fingers in his and placed them below the sword, in a small crack marring the stone casing.

"Is it an opening?" I asked.

"I'm not sure." He pulled out a dagger and stuck the blade inside the gap. He looked up at me. "Some of the stone has crumbled away. I think I can punch a hole through the mortar. Give me a second."

Kull worked the knife back and forth, slowly shaving away bits of dust and small pebbles, filling the chamber with the echoing sound of crumbling rocks as the broken stone fell to the floor. After creating a narrow space through the stone, he moved back.

With only a little light to illuminate the space, I couldn't see if the fractured stone opened into the sword's chamber. "Does the opening go all the way inside?" I asked.

He sheathed his knife. "I believe so, but there's no way to be sure."

"I can try to send a spell through the crack and see what happens," I said, "but if this doesn't work..."

"If it doesn't work, we run. Fast."

"I agree."

Controlling my magic would be a problem. Since we'd restored the fairies' stone, my magic had been less erratic, but it was still a pain to control both the Earth and Faythander powers. The two magics were in a constant struggle for supremacy, and I wasn't sure if I could ever balance the two. Plus, having Theht's presence in my head seemed to dampen my powers—I'd felt them weakening ever since our encounter.

Steadying my breathing, I prepared to bypass the web spell and conjure a spell to undo the protection enchantment instead. When I felt ready, I reached for the crack in the stone. "Here goes nothing," I whispered before allowing the spell to rise to the surface and then releasing the magic into the fracture.

Blue wisps of magic glowed over the stone's surface as I concentrated on sending the spell through the gap and toward the sword.

The azure wisps fed into the stone while I held my breath, praying the spell found a way through the stone and around the web spell. A tiny tendril of magic threaded through the crack in the stone, and more followed, wrapping around the sword. I exhaled my pent-up breath as the magic stripped away the protection spell surrounding the sword.

41

"It worked," I said. "I can't believe it worked."

"I knew you could do it," Kull said.

"Yes, but now we have another problem. How do we get the sword out of there without tripping the web spell?"

"Could you remove the web?" Kull asked.

"No. I can't touch it with magic or it will trip the spell."

"What if you were to make the sword invisible and move it through?"

"No. It would still be covered in magic, which would also trip the spell."

Kull removed his blade and flipped it from end to end as he stared at his sword. We were too close to fail now. There had to be a way.

"What if I were to widen the gap in the stone?" Kull asked.

"It might work. How big can you make the gap?"

"With this?" Kull held up his knife. "Not very big. I'll only be able to remove the stones that are already loose."

"Do what you can," I said.

As Kull chipped at the stones, I studied the sword. I reached out, focusing on the narrow path of non-enchanted air leading inside the sword's chamber.

"I've almost got this opened up," Kull said. A small stone fell to the ground, leaving a tunnel in the stone leading into the bottom portion of the sword's chamber.

Kull stuck his hand into the opening, but as he reached inside, his elbow got stuck in the hole. He heaved a frustrated sigh as he reached for his sword, his hand within a foot of its pommel, but failed to touch it. Pulling away, he turned to me.

"Can you reach it?"

"I doubt my arms are long enough, but I'll try."

The cold stone chilled my arms as I reached inside the hole and tried to grab the sword. I pressed my body against the stone encasement, using every bit of leverage I could muster, stretching my arm as far as humanly possible, but I failed to reach it.

It was impossible for either of us to reach it, but maybe a spell would do the trick. It wasn't my first choice, and it would be risky, but at this point, I had no other choice.

"I'll try a spell," I said, hoping I could control the magic without interfering with the web enchantment as I steadied my breathing. "Levitate," I whispered.

Magic flowed from my fingers and through the gap, then the shimmers of blue and amber light wrapped around the sword, lifting it up and moving it toward us. I controlled it downward until I was able to grab the pommel, the metal cool in my hands, and then I pulled it free through the narrow gap.

I stood, holding the sword as the pommel warmed in my hands. Maybe I only imagined it, but the faint impression of Kull's hands seemed worn into the metal.

"Here," I said, handing it to him. "Pretty sure this belongs to you."

He took it from me cautiously, as if he couldn't believe it was really his. Standing straight, he held the sword with reverence.

"It looks good on you," I said.

He smiled. "Remind me never to bargain it away again." He ran his fingers along the blade. "I've missed you," he said quietly.

I tried not to get teary eyed at the heartfelt reunion. Honestly, Kull and that sword.

"Should we get back to the doorway?" I asked.

"Yes," he said. "Lead the way."

I started down the path that wound toward the staircase, expecting to find Maveryck and Heidel at some point, but as we navigated down the steep steps to the bottom floor, I saw no sign of them. After quietly passing by the enormous double doors, we crossed back toward the stacks of treasures where we had first entered.

"Where are the others?" I asked.

"Perhaps they made it to the door already?"

"Yes. Maybe."

We made our way through stacks of jewels and coins, but my thoughts were elsewhere. Oddly, I thought of the elven door.

"Kull, have you ever heard of a door like the one we passed through to get in here?"

"No, but you know I've got little experience with magic."

"I know. I just find it odd that I've never heard of such a door. Wouldn't it have been mentioned at least once in all the books I've studied?"

"You've never encountered it once?"

"No. Not once."

Kull clenched his jaw. "That is strange."

We had just rounded a corner when a crash came from behind us. Spinning around, we found smoke filling the chamber, followed by the enraged roar of a dragon.

CHAPTER
Six

FIRE ERUPTED THROUGH THE VAULT AS THE HEAD AND shoulders of the silver dragon came into view. Screams came from up ahead, though Kull and I were far enough away that the dragon didn't see us. I followed Kull as we raced through the stacks, fearing the worst. We hadn't seen Heidel and Maveryck since we'd parted ways. Adrenaline fueled my movements as we ran toward the dragon. My heart dropped as the sound of another scream pierced the air.

We rounded the corner, and the room came into full view. Silver scales gleamed as the dragon loomed over a squadron of elves armed with basita weapons. Green magic flared as bolts from the elven weapons struck her hide. The dragon lashed out with her massive tail and struck three men. They landed several feet away, their bodies hitting the stone floor with distinct thuds, their weapons scattering across the ground.

With another roar, the dragon exhaled a fireball that struck the remaining elves. The sounds of their screams punctured the air. Some of the elves managed to take cover, but others weren't so lucky.

The body of one of the tail-struck men landed not far from where Kull and I were hiding. Blood oozed from his ears and spread in a dark pool over the ground. I debated on helping the man, but to crawl from my hiding spot meant death if the dragon spotted me.

A blast from a basita went wide and struck a stack of rolled parchments near Kull and me, and the paper ignited. Blue and orange flames licked the air as they consumed the parchments and then spread to a set of wooden pillars.

Dragon fire mingled with the blaze started by the bolt. Heat roiled from the flames, casting flickers of light through the chamber. Footsteps echoed behind us, and we turned around. Kull held his sword at the ready but lowered it as Maveryck and Heidel appeared through the smoke. Maveryck held a staff made of dark wood and carved in intricate detail. At its apex sat a blue jewel that glowed with a faint light. Cloudlike swirls moved within the ball, and ancient magic emanated from the entire staff—a power that tugged at my senses, calling to me. An old power with unknown potential.

"You found the staff?" Kull asked quietly.

"Yes," Heidel answered.

"How were you able to remove it?"

Heidel glanced at Maveryck. "Ask him," she said.

Maveryck gripped the staff tighter. "I'm a professional reclaimer," he said. "It's my job."

A roar split the air behind us. The dragon thrashed as several elves shot a net from a spear-like weapon, wrapping the dragon's head and neck in thick cording. As the dragon thrashed, the elves launched spears at her sides, tearing through her scales to impale her flesh. A fireball burst from the dragon's mouth, igniting the net.

"We must go while she's distracted," Maveryck said.

"I agree," I said.

We turned and followed Maveryck away from the stacks and toward the elven door. Pain-filled shouts came from behind us, making my hair stand on end as the sounds of ripping flesh accompanied the screams.

The elves had royally pissed off the dragon. Perfect. Just what we needed.

We sped toward the cavern's back wall, though I felt as if I couldn't go fast enough. Smoke fogged the room, its acrid scent making my eyes water. The stacks of jewels and coins blurred in my vision as we raced from the dragon.

Not soon enough, we made it to the far back wall, though I saw no sign of the doorway. Maveryck stopped at a blank space along the wall and pressed his hand to the stone. Blue light glowed around his fingers, then spread out around the stone until the outline of a door formed.

Something grabbed my ankle, and I fell, hitting my knees and elbows on the rough stone floor. Looking behind me, I saw one of the elves, his face half-burned, holding my leg.

"The staff," his voice rasped. "Give it to me!"

I tried kicking him, but he held my leg in a vicelike grip.

Behind him, the entire cavern had erupted in flame. The flames spiraled toward the ceiling as they engulfed the cavern, almost hot enough to singe my skin.

"The staff," the elf shouted as he focused on Maveryck.

He let go of my leg and leapt for Maveryck, but Kull apprehended the man, knocking him backward before he could reach the thief.

The elven door opened.

Heidel looked back frantically as Maveryck stood beside the door.

"Hurry!" she yelled.

Leaping to my feet, I raced with Kull toward the door, but the dragon's roar resounded, closer than it had been before.

Kull rounded. His eyes widened as he stood his ground, not moving, holding his sword between us and the dragon.

"Kull, what are you doing?" I shouted.

"Go!"

The dragon drew closer, her breathing loud and raspy in her chest. "Thieves," her voice hissed.

"Go *now*!" Kull yelled at Heidel and Maveryck, who still stood at the door.

I stood shocked, unable to move or process the situation clearly, but the panic only lasted a moment before Theht's presence reacted.

You've awoken me, it said.

Spirals of blinding light crackled from my fingers and engulfed the entire room. Pain spread from my fingertips to my elbows and shoulders, a burning heat that seared my nerve endings. I tried controlling Theht, tried burying her in the place where she'd been before, but she'd taken hold of my magic and I was powerless to stop her.

Sounds of human screams mingled with the dragon's roar. I saw Kull stagger as the light engulfed him, and he lost his grip on the sword. It fell to the ground, but I didn't hear the sound of its clatter. The pain of the sudden release of my magic spread to my head. My knees hit the ground as blackness engulfed me.

And then came silence.

My mind went to a strange place—a dreamlike state that made no sense. Sounds came from somewhere, drums of some sort and running water. But the most persistent sound came from Theht. I heard her whispers in my head, though it wasn't one voice, but many. With my magic already released, she had no power left to control me, so I focused on sending her presence back to the dark realms of my mind where she would be locked away. For now, at least. After that, I knew that I had to wake up.

Had Kull been hurt? Had Heidel and Maveryck escaped?

Light filtered through my eyelids.

Where am I?

I pried my eyes open, and a room came into view. A single torch burned in a sconce near me, making the rest of the room hard to see, but I was able to make out a domed ceiling soaring overhead. The same winged-skeleton motif we'd seen in the vaults had been carved on the beams and pillars supporting the walls, yet the room was smaller, and I knew I must have been inside the witch's castle.

Something moved in the corner. As my eyes adjusted, I noticed several creatures slinking through the shadows, but I couldn't make out their forms, other than that they looked fairly humanoid. The room had several doorways, and although the light was dim, my gaze snagged on the woman standing under an arched opening on the opposite side of the room.

"Silvestra," I whispered, my throat dry.

The woman walked toward me, her heels clicking over the stone floor. She was a woman I had trouble describing. Her beauty was apparent in her flawless, pitch-colored skin, her dazzling white teeth, and her light, aquamarine eyes, but silver scales covered her arms and hands. They also covered her head, forming a dramatic widow's peak. She clasped her hands together, and I noted that her fingers ended in claws with curved black nails. Silvestra had also discovered the magic word for beauty, a spell that made it impossible for me to find any physical flaws in her appearance.

I sat up, realizing that I lay not on a bed, but on a solid block of stone. My wrists and ankles were bound with manacles attached to chains, making it difficult for me to move.

As the witch moved closer, she pulled a knife from her robes. Blood was smeared and drying on the blade. My stomach twisted in knots as she stood over me, holding the knife for me to see.

"Fan'twar's ward," she said, "you dared to enter my chambers unbidden. Why?"

I tried to answer, but with my parched throat, I only managed a whisper. "The staff."

She raised an eyebrow.

"The staff of Zaladin," I clarified. "We needed it. Where are my companions?"

Her eyes darkened. "Two escaped from my castle with the staff. One did not."

I swallowed my panic. "Kull?"

She nodded.

"Is he alive?"

She held the knife closer. "Yes. He is alive. But he took the sword that I had rightfully claimed. That is a misstep he should not have made, for now he is in my power."

The tone of her voice sent a cold chill down my spine.

"He's in your power?"

"Yes. He will become one of mine."

The creatures lurking in the room's shadows came into partial view. An intense fear washed over me, coupled with the need to run as soon as I saw them. They looked as if a person had taken a human, meshed it together with a crocodile, and made it into a zombie. Their bodies were deformed and hunched over, with a large spinal column protruding from their backs, a skeletal, humanoid face with crocodilian teeth, and humanlike arms and legs that ended in claws. Rotting flesh composed of scales and flaking skin covered their emaciated frames.

My stomach soured, giving me the immediate urge to vomit.

"What..." I gasped, "what are they?"

"They are called morrigun wraiths. My servants," the queen answered. Leaning closer, she added, "They live an eternal life in this castle as my slaves. This is what becomes of those who break their bargains with me. This is what your friend will soon become."

I clenched my clammy hands into tight fists. This was not happening. This was a bad dream. I must have hit my head in the dragon's vault and was now hallucinating.

"No," I managed. "Please, no."

"Yes. This is the way it must be."

"Why?"

"Because it is the only way I can deal with those who wish to bargain with me. Law must exist. And for law to exist, punishment must be exacted. This is the way of things."

"Then take out your punishment on me," I said. "Please. Don't do this to him."

"No," she answered. "He is mine. That is something you

cannot change."

"Then why am I still alive now? Why didn't you kill me along with the elves?"

"Surely you must know."

She brushed a strand of hair away from my forehead, her scaled skin cold against mine.

"You are a unique person, Deathbringer. The one spoken of in prophecy. I will not be the one to destroy you. That task is meant for someone else.

"Your magic is a rare thing—both Earth and Faythander competing against one another. I could teach you to balance it."

"No."

"Think before you answer, child. I am offering you a great gift, one that could change prophecy if you accept my help."

Change prophecy? She had to be lying. There wasn't a way to change prophecy. But even if there were the smallest chance, shouldn't I take it?

My mind wasn't right. I couldn't possibly be considering this. Her temptation wouldn't sway me—right now, I couldn't afford to be distracted. As long as she kept me alive, I would do everything in my power to save Kull. Nothing else mattered.

"No. I don't want your help," I said, turning away from her.

She grabbed my face between her hands, her nails cutting into my flesh. "Then you will suffer along with him. I will take your magic for my own, and there will be nothing left of you but an empty shell. Is that what you wish?"

Panic made my heart beat wildly, but as I stared into her cold eyes, I knew she was deceiving me. I'd been raised by dragons, and although I was certain she was certifiably off her rocker, I prayed she had a little sanity left. If so, I would call her bluff.

"You have no claim on me," I said. "I haven't made any bargains with you. Fan'twar would tear this castle to pieces if you harmed me."

She held my face for a moment longer, but then she released me.

"If you refuse my offer, then I have no further use for you. I shall banish you from my mountain, and you shall never return again."

Two of the creatures approached me as she backed away. Rough, bony hands encircled my arms. I couldn't let them take me away—once she banished me from her castle, it would be nearly impossible to get back inside.

"Wait!" I called as she walked toward the door.

She stopped and turned around.

"Can't we reach some sort of arrangement? If I allow you to train me, will you release him?"

"No," she said, her back still turned to me. "But perhaps we can work out another sort of agreement."

She turned around and walked back toward me, her quiet footsteps reminding me of a panther stalking its prey. Her eyes narrowed as she stared me down.

"It has been a long time since I had a human in my fortress. Perhaps we will do this the proper way, as civilized creatures. My servants will help you get cleaned up, and I will provide you with a change of clothes. Then, you shall meet me in my chambers. We shall discuss what to do with you and your companion."

Her eyes grew dark, and I sensed the dragon lurking beneath her human skin.

"Do not try to deceive me, Earthlander. I have placed you under no spells for the time being, but know this—if you try to escape this castle, I will kill him."

CHAPTER *Seven*

M Y FULL SKIRT RUSTLED AS THE MORRIGUN WRAITHS guided me down a dark hallway. It had taken me twenty full minutes just to change into the dress the witch had given me, and I still wasn't sure I'd figured out how to properly lace up the corset. The heavy petticoat beneath the midnight blue skirt was overly warm, and the bodice made it difficult to breathe.

I didn't know why the witch was making me wear it now, except I supposed it had been some time since she'd had guests, and I was sure she didn't want to share her morning tea with someone wearing dirty questing gear.

The wraiths led me down yet another hallway. Without their guidance, I was sure to have gotten lost. The castle was a maze of stairs and hallways, lit with torches placed in sconces that were spaced too infrequently to give much light.

Our footsteps, coupled with the wraiths' deep, rattling breaths, were the only sounds to break up the silence. Now, with the creatures so close, I was able to see them more clearly. Greenish scales appeared in patches over dead, flaking skin. I couldn't look at them for too long—there was something so unnatural about them it repulsed me—as if they were created to mock humanity.

"Can you understand me?" I asked.

One of the creatures grunted. If they had been human once, I doubted they remembered their past. It was a sobering, disheartening thought. If the witch were capable of doing this to people, I didn't want to know what else she could do.

I wasn't sure what to expect once we reached the witch's

chambers, although I had trouble understanding her motivations. Why did she want to train me? Did she really think she could stop a prophecy from happening? As far as I knew, there wasn't a way to do it. She must have known something I didn't.

We turned down yet another hallway, and I gave up trying to remember the path we'd taken. Tall, dramatic windows framed the narrow corridor, and on either side were breathtaking views of the Dragon Spine mountain range. It was morning, and the first rays of pink and golden sunlight streaked across the sky, highlighting the clouds that spread out beneath us.

We approached a set of tall double doors carved with images of dragons in flight. One of the wraiths pushed a door open, and it gave way slowly with the squeal of ungreased hinges. I wondered how long it had been since Silvestra had spruced up the place. I supposed her time was better spent in taking away people's free will, making underhanded bargains, and generally being everyone's worst nightmare. Sounded exhausting.

We entered a domed room made of glass and stone. The wraiths closed the doors behind us, and we crossed toward the center of the space. Overhead, the glass dome glinted in the morning sunlight. I squinted as my eyes adjusted to the brightness. At the room's center sat a round table with a marble top. An assortment of fruits and breads were arranged on its surface. Silvestra sat in one of the chairs at the table, her eyes narrowed as she scrutinized me. I wanted to shrink under her calculating gaze, but I stood tall instead. The last thing I needed was her thinking she intimidated me. She did, of course—she scared the living daylights out of me—but she didn't need to know that.

"You've got a nice place here," I said, "but you should fire the decorator. It's putting off a sort of creepy vibe, if you know what I mean."

She didn't crack a smile.

"Guards, wait outside," she said to her wraiths.

The two creatures turned around and shuffled out of the room, closing the door with a loud thud behind them.

"How do you like the gown?" the witch asked.

I shifted uncomfortably, feeling awkward as I fidgeted with the ribbons lacing up the bodice. If I'd had any say in the matter, I'd have chosen something less formal, something less nineteenth-century. But as I was her "guest," I didn't have a choice.

"Where is Kull?" I asked.

"Sit," she said, "and then we shall discuss the matter."

Flexing my fists, I felt my magic gaining strength as it slowly returned. I debated on using my powers to battle the dragon, but in my weakened state I'd most likely end up dead, and then Kull would end up dead or transformed into a wraith, so I had no choice but to play along.

I crossed the room, pulled out a chair, and sat.

"Eat," she said, motioning to the sweet breads and assortment of fruits piled atop the table.

Silvestra placed a bunch of grapes and a slice of sweet bread on her plate. She ate slowly, with a meticulous grace that seemed practiced, and then took a small sip from her goblet.

I debated on refusing the food but relented as my stomach growled, and I snatched a handful of berries from a silver platter. As I put a few of the berries in my mouth, I chewed slowly, feeling the witch's eyes on me as she watched me eat.

"Why don't you tell me where you've put Kull?" I asked.

"Tonight," she said. "You will see him."

See him? This was good news. He was still alive, at least. "Is he okay? Why can't I see him now?"

Her pale turquoise eyes seemed to bore a hole through me. "He is mine, child. Whatever I do with him is my concern. You would be wise to remember this." She rested her chin in her hands, her long, claw-like nails gleaming in the sunlight. "You need to understand that I rarely get visitors in my castle. Those who dare come here either die or become one of my servants as they are trying to steal from me. Your friends with the staff are being hunted even as we speak, and it will not be long before I have them.

"As it is, I have realized that I miss having conversations with others who have magical gifts. There was a time when I was like you—unsure of my powers, afraid of what I might become. You are not the only one spoken of in prophecy."

I paused in taking a bite of bread.

"There was a prophecy spoken long ago by Lucretian—Faythander's first true druid—that I would betray my own kind, that I would become a scourge and plague. 'From the mountaintops she shall bring about the death of the innocent. Beauty taken by force shall be her prison. Her curse will be her name. She will be alone and loathed by all.' The prophecy frightened me so badly that I ran from it, only to find that by doing so, I fulfilled it."

Her words struck a chord with me. She had described exactly how I felt.

"I didn't know," I said quietly.

She shrugged. "It is of little consequence now. As soon as I knew I had the gift for black magic, I fought it. I refused to use it. But it became impossible to suppress it, and I had no other choice but to embrace the magic inside me." She opened her hand, palm up, and a black flame ignited. Even though I was sitting across from her, the heat from the flame warmed me. I could feel the magic in her flame—dark magic, though not like I'd felt in Geth, the Regaymor, or the bloodthorn. There was no taint like I'd felt in theirs. It was power, but not evil.

The flame reflected in her eyes, sparks dancing in her irises, and then she extinguished it.

"You taught yourself to use black magic?" I asked. "How?"

"Years of practice. It was not easy."

I studied her face. Most who used black magic in Faythander went insane. Perhaps she already had. If she'd been transforming people into wraiths, she certainly wasn't considered normal. But was she insane? Was there a way to control black magic without losing one's sanity?

"Tonight," Silvestra said, "I have planned a ball in the grand chamber. You will attend."

"A ball?" I asked. Had no one informed her that you needed guests in order to classify something as a ball? "Who are you inviting?"

She smirked. "You will see. Perhaps you'll understand how I pass my time here."

I eyed her. All this conversation made me feel as if she were avoiding the reason I'd come to speak to her. "What have you done with Kull? Have you transformed him?"

"You shall see him at the ball."

"You didn't answer my question. Is he transformed?"

"You shall see him soon," she said, a tone of warning in her voice. "For now, you will learn of my ways here. There is much you have yet to learn. Fan'twar has been protecting you from the truth for too long."

She whispered a word of magic, making a cloud of black mist form on the table. The food disappeared, yet as the mist dissipated, a box appeared.

"Pick it up," she said.

Wary of a trap or spell, I hesitated before reaching for it. But if her intention was to hurt me, then I was fairly certain she would have done it already.

I picked up the box, and it weighed heavy in my hands as if made of solid stone. It had a glassy, onyx texture. The box felt perfectly smooth and formed a geometrically perfect cube.

"Open it," she said.

I inspected the cube. There were no hinges or a lid of any kind. "I can't."

"Why not?"

"It's just a block of stone."

"Is it?"

Inspecting it more closely, I tried to determine what exactly the thing was. I ran my hands over the smooth black stone. It chilled my fingers as my reflection stared back from the mirrorlike surfaces. A gentle hum of magic formed inside as I stared at it.

"There's magic in it," I said.

Silvestra nodded. "What else?"

I rested my hand atop the box, trying to decide what type of magic I felt. Oddly, I couldn't detect a single color. It felt as if I were watching a black-and-white film, like all the color had been absorbed into differing shades of gray.

"I've never seen magic like this before," I said. "It's colorless, gray, but not like goblin magic... something else. Why can't I tell the type?"

"Look harder."

I cupped the box in my hands, trying to see past the facets and inside the box. When I did, I found several intricate spells blocking me from seeing inside.

"There are spells inside. They're blocking me."

"Can you see past them?"

"No."

She held out her hand. "Give me the box."

I did as she said.

She took the box from me and held it on her palm. "This is called a lotus cube. It contains a magic of sorts and was once used in training practitioners. But I will say no more, for its secrets are not ones I wish to divulge. They are for you to discover."

The box disappeared in a cloud of black fog.

"Another time," she said, then rose. "Come, I shall escort you around my palace."

I stood but didn't follow her out of the room. I still had a mission to accomplish—and following the witch around her castle wasn't helping me achieve that goal.

"What if I refuse?" I asked.

"And do what? Try to escape?"

I hesitated. Would I try to escape without Kull? It wasn't a question I wished to ponder. "I..." I couldn't answer. Not yet.

"Come," she said. "There is much I wish to show you."

Her silver dress swished behind her as she walked toward the doors. I wore no chains, she'd placed me under no spells, yet still I felt compelled to follow. As long as she held Kull, she held me. Besides, wandering the castle may give me clues as to where she was keeping Kull. I would be sure to keep a watchful eye out for his prison.

I followed the witch out of the room and into the hallway. Two of the wraiths followed us out. Despite my thick petticoat, the air felt chilly, especially as we crossed through a hallway with no windows and little light.

"You are cold?" Silvestra asked.

"Yes."

"We shall go to my garden. The sun will warm us there."

I didn't want to go to her garden. I didn't want to go anywhere except wherever it was she was keeping Kull, and then I promptly wanted to leave. Flexing my fists, I felt my power recuperating from my last spell. If it came to it, I would fight her, although I knew what the outcome would be. Still, I could always try.

Crossing through a domed foyer, our footsteps echoed through the empty room. Small tiles of varying turquoise and purple hues made up the floor to form a seascape mosaic. The coils of a sea serpent dipped and rose through churning waves. The image was so detailed I felt as if the cold spray splashed my face, as if I could hear the shrill wail of the wind and feel the floor buckling beneath my feet. Magic flowed through the room, making me realize the sensations weren't imagined, but enchanted.

After crossing through the foyer, we stopped at a door set under a deep alcove. The witch pushed the door open to reveal a garden.

As we entered the garden, the two wraiths stayed behind, watching us with their cold, detached gazes. I followed Silvestra through a labyrinth of waist-high rosebushes. The gravel path wound through the garden of fragrant red flowers, and then we entered a maze of tall hedges. Some of the paths didn't seem to have any purpose and were arranged oddly, stopping abruptly and leading nowhere. Was there some meaning to their arrangement? Some of them were large circles connected to nothing. I got the feeling that if I were standing far above the ground, their patterns would make more sense.

We stopped at a pair of stone benches placed in the garden's center. The air smelled of rain, and with the dark clouds looming in the distance, it seemed the storm wasn't far away. Birdsong filled the air as I took a seat across from the witch.

Her strange, almost colorless eyes looked to the sky, reflecting the sunlight in a way that reminded me of Fan'twar.

The castle's towers rose beyond the garden, an impressive, massive structure that seemed to stretch from one end of the horizon to the other. Most of the parapets were covered in moss, making them blend in with the surrounding countryside. Beyond the towers were the snow-capped peaks of the Dragon Spine mountain range.

Kull was in that castle somewhere. I would find him. No matter how long it took, I would find him.

"You said I'll see Kull tonight," I said. "Will he be hurt?"

"He is physically well."

"Physically? You've hurt him in other ways?"

"You've nothing to fear yet. I have a bargain to propose."

"What sort of bargain?"

"Tonight you will see. Tonight everything will be explained."

I crossed my arms, wondering if she were only making up excuses for when I would see Kull again.

"How do you like my garden?" she asked.

I sighed. She was changing the subject again. This was getting annoying. Tired of playing her games, I stayed silent and didn't answer.

"Everything has a purpose," she said as she brushed her fingers over the petals of a rose. "You might see a mere flower, but I have found other uses for living plants. Magic has a way of working with nature."

A snake appeared in the bushes. I drew back as it slithered from branch to branch, its black scales almost indistinguishable from the shadows. As it approached, the witch outstretched her hand, and the serpent slinked forward, its tongue flicking, and then wrapped around the witch's wrist. It held perfectly still, as if waiting for her command.

I kept my distance. Whether here or on Earth, snakes gave me the creeps.

Shouting came from the castle doors, and we turned to see what the commotion was about. Two wraiths held an elven man between them. As the wraiths dragged him closer toward us, his eyes widened at the sight of the witch. The elf struggled as the witch's servants brought him closer to us, but he failed to break free. The wraiths stopped in front of us.

The elven man's clothes were blackened in some areas, and blood smeared his cheek and part of his chin. He must have been one of the elves who'd attempted to steal the staff.

"What do you want with me?" the elf said.

Silvestra rose. "A demonstration."

"What?"

The witch nodded at me. "The sky king's ward is confused about what I plan to do with the Wult king, and so I thought the best way to show her was through a demonstration. You broke into my vaults, killed three of my wraiths, and not only attempted to steal from me, but tried to kill me as well. Now, Olive, you will see what the punishment is for such actions."

She circled him slowly. "Taking one's free will is a process that took me many years to learn—one that cost me personally—but it was well worth it, for now I have the magical name, a word that will strip you of your essence and make you my servant."

"Impossible," the elf said. "There is no such word."

"But you are wrong. There are many words I have learned that others have not."

The witch circled the elf. On her outstretched arm, the snake remained perfectly balanced and unmoving. The elven man shied back at the sight of the snake.

"Don't touch me," he said.

"You do not wish to be my servant?"

"I will never serve you. I will die before bowing before you."

"Brave words for an elf, don't you think, Olive?"

Her eyes darted to mine, expecting an answer, though I wasn't sure what to say. No matter what this man had done, he didn't deserve to have his essence stripped away. I couldn't sit by and watch.

"Silvestra," I said quietly, "please don't do this. You've no need to harm him."

Her eyes flared. "No? He entered my vaults and attempted to steal my possessions. He tried to kill me! Would you rather I let him go free, so that more may come and try to kill me?"

"I didn't say that."

"Then what would you have me do?"

I wasn't sure how to answer. As she turned away from me, the sky darkened. The wind picked up, carrying leaves from the garden, making the tree limbs creak. Glancing overhead, I felt power in the clouds and wind, making my arms prickle with goose bumps.

Silvestra's footfalls echoed the wind as she circled the elf. Tendrils of black magic gathered around her, and then sparks of green ignited with the black. Although the witch terrified me, I sat in awe as I studied her magic. My magical powers had grown stronger since I'd first learned to control them, and I felt fairly proficient at a few spells, but to be in the witch's presence humbled and overwhelmed me.

She stood behind the elf when the snake struck, impaled its fangs into the man's neck, and then retreated. It happened quickly. The man cried out, struggling against the wraiths holding him, but it didn't matter. The poison would soon enter the elf's bloodstream.

The witch stood over him but focused on me as a word of magic escaped her lips. The magic coalesced and wrapped around the elf's body, spiraling, compressing. His screaming pierced the air with the desperate sound of pain and fear. I had trouble listening and wished I could use my magic to stop the witch. But if I did anything, I feared what she might do to me, or worse, to Kull.

The witch grabbed the man's shoulder, her clawed fingers digging into his skin as the snake slithered off her hand and coiled around the elf's neck. The black loops constricted until he gasped for air.

He struggled as the wraiths held him between them.

Unable to watch, I looked away. "Please," I said. "Stop."

"Stop? And let him escape? No. He attempted to steal from my vault and take my life—two crimes that cannot go unpunished. He must suffer so that others will know never to follow in his footsteps."

I was reminded that this wasn't the first time the elves had stolen from her. What had they taken in the past? Whatever it had been had clearly upset her, something even now she couldn't get over.

His gasping became more infrequent as the blood drained from his face. The witch lifted her hands, and a mist of black and green magic formed—a deep, heavy magic that weighed on my senses. A blade appeared in her hand. I'd seen that blade before. It was the same one I'd seen when she'd first brought me to her castle, and it had been stained with blood. With horror, I realized now that it must have been Kull's blood I'd seen earlier.

In a swift motion, the witch grabbed the snake and severed its head from its body. The elf inhaled, gasping, as the snake's coils released. But as soon they did, the scales morphed, turning gray until they became stone.

"You will wear this collar," Silvestra said, "until your soul becomes mine."

The elf made no reply. Red welts formed on his neck, mingling with the blood and poison. His eyes became unfocused as the two wraiths dragged him away.

The witch walked toward me, still holding the knife. I stood, facing her, letting my magic gather around me.

"Do not try to harm me," she said quietly, "or you will suffer the same as him."

"Is that what you did to Kull? Is that why you won't let me see him?" I could barely contain the rage in my voice.

"You will see him tonight at the ball, so long as you cooperate and do not try anything rash. I would hate to harm him now, when you are so very close to finding him."

The hardened tone of her voice made me shudder. I wanted to lash out with my magic, but to do so meant I would lose the chance to see him at all. Reluctantly, I pulled my magic back inside and waited for nightfall.

CHAPTER *Eight*

THE TWO WRAITHS LED ME INSIDE THE BALLROOM, though that was a poor term for the room. It was a palace unto itself. My jaw dropped as I stood under the enormous pillared ceiling partially open to the air. On top of the mountain, with only a few wispy clouds in the sky, the stars burned in vivid hues of gold and indigo. Below the stars, the tops of snowy peaks glowed in the moonlight.

Fairies and nobbinflies flitted under the pillared arches, their lights mingling with the starlight. Green vines grew around the archways, and clusters of flowers bloomed in purples and periwinkle blues, filling the air with a sweet fragrance.

Several staircases spiraled to balconies that encircled the room. People dressed in elaborate clothing and wearing masks were milling about on the balconies. I felt as if I'd been transported into another realm altogether, a place so filled with magic that anything was possible.

As I waited in the room, I noticed the stars spinning overhead. Confused, I studied the sky, wondering what enchantment the witch had used to make the stars move. Although Silvestra frightened me, I had to admit that her powers were something awe-inspiring. Not only had she created the ballroom, but she'd also created my own gown. I stood under the enchanted sky and ran my hands over the silk covering my arms. The dark plum, almost-black silk shimmered in the starlight around jewels that had been woven into the fabric, and the elaborately beaded bodice gave way to a full skirt that flowed to the ground.

Nerves pinched my stomach as I waited alone in the ball-

61

room. What would Kull think when he saw me? Would his mind still be his own?

I walked toward the middle of the room and crossed over a mosaic of tiles arranged to resemble the universe. A small golden sun glinted from the center of the floor, and woven around it were planets in differing jewel tones—amethyst and garnet, sapphire and olivine. Magic emanated from the floor as I walked across it, making it seem as if I floated above the universe.

When I reached the room's center, I stared at the people crowding the balconies above me, wondering why they'd all stayed up there. Alone, I stood awkwardly, fidgeting with the lace on my sleeves until a pair of heavily carved doors standing across from me swung open.

Silvestra entered.

She wore another silver gown, though more formal than the last, with a dramatic, plunging neckline and a full skirt whose train swept the ground. Her eyes, silvery aquamarine, glinted as she crossed the room to stand in front of me.

I shied in her presence as she stood over me. Her gaze was so intense I felt the dragon hiding inside her, dangerously close to the surface.

"We welcome you to our gathering," she said.

Behind her, a large group of people entered the room, dressed as I'd seen them on the balcony in ruffled collars, masks with jewels and feathers, and gowns so exquisite some looked as if they'd been spun of gold and silver. Were these the wraiths?

A woman neared me, and I noticed her skin was mottled with sloughing scales. So this was what her wraiths did when they weren't busy being tortured. The sheer number of wraiths was overwhelming. How many people had she transformed? Hundreds?

Silvestra clapped her hands, and music starting playing. It was a haunting, slow melody played on instruments similar to cellos and pianos. Those gathered began dancing, and Silvestra turned away to sit on her throne on the opposite end of the chamber, leaving me alone once again.

I scanned the crowd, my heart pounding as I searched for Kull. What if he wasn't here at all? She'd promised he'd be here, but how could I be sure she'd keep her promise? Or worse, what if she'd transformed him already? If so, I swore I would use every ounce of my power to bring this castle down on her. I didn't care if I died. She would suffer for taking him away from me. He was the only person in the world who kept me sane, who made me feel whole and loved, and I would die if he were gone because there would be nothing left of me.

I wandered up the staircase, my heeled shoes clicking against the marble. Several people passed me, and I scanned each one, focusing on their eyes, but found only the yellow, filmy eyes of the wraiths hiding behind jeweled masks.

The room seemed even more immense as I wandered the balcony, pausing occasionally to stare down from above. The carved stone railing felt cold under my fingers as I paced the landing, glancing from one face to another, looking for Kull. I wandered all the way up to the top tier, but I still couldn't find him. I wore no mask, so he would have been able to find me if he were... himself.

Silvestra had told me he would be here, so perhaps it was time I had a chat with her. Magic gathered in my fisted hands as I made my way back to the dance floor and toward the witch's throne. People gathered around the witch, but I pushed past them to face her.

"Where is he?" I demanded.

"Calm, child. He is here."

"Where?"

She studied me for a moment before answering, as if sizing me up, wanting to understand my actions.

"He waits for you in the garden," she finally said and pointed to a small alcove with an opening leading outside.

I shoved past the wraiths and headed toward the alcove. The music faded as I wandered into the immense garden outside. The damp air smelled of rain. Water trickled through small streams, weaving through the rose bushes. I followed one of the streams down a shallow slope, walking on a stone footpath, which was difficult to do in the heels.

The dress rustled quietly as I moved down the path. Fairies flitted through the tree branches, whispering and laughing, their lights bobbing in and out of the branches. None of them noticed me, although not long ago, I'd helped to restore their starstone. Other than the fairies, the garden was empty.

I stopped walking to focus on the fairies. As I stood still, one of them flew to me and hovered, her tiny face scrunched with curiosity, her blonde hair wild and studded with periwinkle flowers.

"I know you," she said. "Are you the one who saved my

kind?" she asked in a small voice.

"Yes," I answered. "How do you know me?"

Another fairy, a male, hovered closer. "All of our kind knows you. You are the one who saved our starstone."

"I suppose word travels fast with fairies," I said.

"Yes. We owe a debt to you," the male said. "How can we assist you?"

My heart leapt. Perhaps this was my chance to escape. "Can you find Kull and get us out of here?"

They eyed each other and then looked at me. "Our magic is limited in this place. The witch only allows us here because we keep her flowers alive, but when we enter her grounds, our magic is weakened."

As usual, nothing worked out for me. "I see."

"But we will be here if you shall need us. You have but to ask."

"Thank you," I said.

They only nodded before flitting away, their lights diminishing as they flew toward the sky. My heart sank as I watched them go. Trouble always followed me. It seemed a constant in my life.

I put the fairies out of my mind and continued wandering through the garden. After reaching the hill's base, I took in my new surroundings, standing on the edge of a cliff that dropped hundreds of feet below. Walking along the cliff's edge, the sound of trickling water turned to a roar as the smaller streams combined to form a river.

Up ahead, under the silver moonlight, mist fogged the air where the river turned to a thundering waterfall. In the mist, I found a man standing on a rock wall. He faced away from me with his hands clasped behind his back as he stared over the edge.

Although he wore the same refined clothing as the rest of the gathering—a dark green tunic with jeweled collar and cuffs, dark pants, and tall boots—I knew him immediately.

"Kull," I called, rushing toward him.

He rounded, his eyes wide with surprise as I neared the distance between us. As I approached, I almost didn't recognize him. His eyes weren't his. I stopped and drew back. He looked at me as if he didn't know me.

My heart dropped.

"Kull?"

He blinked as if coming out of a trance, and the look disappeared. "Olive?"

Stepping off the ledge, he approached me, walking guardedly, and then stopped. We only stood a few feet apart, but to me, it felt like miles.

"Are you okay?" I asked him.

He forced a smile.

My insides squirmed. This was him, wasn't it? It felt as if the shadow, that constant companion that had haunted him since his father's death, that had only recently been lifted, was returning once again.

I went to him and hugged him gently, resting my head on his chest. His heart beat in steady, slow thumps. It was still him, and I refused to lose him again.

"Kull, what did she do to you?"

He took my shoulders and moved me away from him, then pulled down his tunic collar to reveal a band of stone around his neck.

"She's trying to make me one of hers."

A clammy sweat broke out over my skin. "We'll stop her. I won't let that happen to you. We can escape."

He turned to stare at the waterfall. "There is a way," he whispered, and then pointed. "Down there."

I studied the water as it barreled over the edge. There was no way to tell what lay at the bottom, but the drop didn't look survivable. "Is that the only way?"

He stepped closer to me, took my arm, and leaned toward my ear. The roaring water almost drowned out his voice.

"Listen carefully. You must meet me here after the ball. There is a hidden staircase that runs the length of the falls. We'll escape together before she changes me."

"Kull, I can't."

"Why not?"

"She said she'll kill you if I try to escape."

"Then we must go together. We'll return to the ball for a time, and we must pretend to not know about the staircase. The queen is smart, but she's overconfident. No one has escaped from this place, and so she thinks it's not possible. But that's only because she's taken these people's free will, so they have no reason to escape. She's grown lax. That's how I was able to find the staircase so easily."

Glancing past him, I tried to see the hidden staircase but could only see the mist reflected in the moonlight. What if the collar were messing with Kull's mind and making him see things that weren't there?

"You're sure there's a staircase down there?" I asked.

"Yes, I discovered it earlier when she was away."

"Are you sure we can use it to escape? What if it just leads to another part of the castle?"

"I don't know, but I'm willing to try whatever it takes to escape this place." Desperation shone in his eyes.

I wasn't sure if I should follow him or not. It didn't seem as if he were using sound judgment, but I couldn't blame him—he was about to become the queen's prisoner for the rest of eternity. Squeezing his hand, I knew I would follow him through hell and back if it meant we were together.

"All right," I said. "After the ball, I'll return here."

Kull kissed my forehead, and I took in the familiar scent of his skin and hair, the wild essence of dark forests and sandalwood. We would survive this somehow. We always did.

He returned with me to the ballroom where a new melody played, a sound that conjured sadness and heartache, two emotions that were all-too familiar. I squeezed his hand, and we crossed onto the enchanted dance floor. As we did, the other dancing couples backed away, and there was a pause before a new song started. When the music began, I found the witch still sitting on her throne, her odd, aquamarine eyes following our movements.

Something nagged at me, a feeling that I was being toyed with, but I didn't know that I had any control over it. As long as the witch controlled Kull, she controlled me. Silvestra turned away to speak to those gathered around her, but even so, I felt her presence as she kept watch over us. More than anything I wanted to escape from her, but I knew that now wasn't the time.

The floor seemed to move with the music, making the sun, planets, and stars spin along with us. Kull held me close, and as we danced, the spell enveloped us. I no longer felt hunger or fatigue or worry—the enchantment masked all feelings and emotions, and the floor became reality. We no longer danced on a solid floor, but among the stars, with their heat brushing our cheeks.

Excitement tingled through me as Kull spun me away from him and then back again. His hands held me steady as the other dancers whirled past us in colors of deep plum and turquoise. Jewels glittered, mingling with the twinkling stars, and I was certain I was no longer on Faythander, but in a completely new reality. I lost all comprehension of time as I danced through the cosmos, certain I'd never seen anything so stunning in all my life. Twinkling lights surrounded us, and I wasn't sure if it was my imagination, but I thought I heard them singing—a melody that conjured images of wind chimes.

Kull pulled me closer, and as I looked into his eyes, my heart pounded. I would never find anyone else like him. He made me happy in ways I didn't comprehend. I gripped his hand tighter, wanting this moment to last forever. In another place, maybe I would have worried at the prospect of Kull's bleak future, maybe I would have been nervous about escaping the castle, but for now, I enjoyed the dance.

When the music faded, I wasn't ready. I held Kull's hand as he led me off the dance floor, and we stopped underneath a quiet balcony.

"Did I tell you that you look beautiful?" he said.

"You didn't mention it."

He cupped my face, then ran his thumb over my cheek, making heat rush through my body. My chest tightened as he leaned toward my face.

"Then let me remedy my blunder. You look breathtaking."

"Breathtaking? That might be a stretch, don't you think?"

"It's the absolute truth."

"You know I hate wearing stuff like this."

"But you should wear it more often."

"Why? It's impractical," I picked at the lace on the sleeves, "and really uncomfortable."

"Olive," he said, taking my fidgeting hand. "Why do you not believe me when I tell you that you're beautiful?"

I looked away. "I don't know."

He placed his finger under my chin and moved my face to meet his gaze. "Do you believe me when I tell you that I love you?"

"Yes, of course I do."

"Then why did you leave?"

Because of Theht. Because I'm destined to kill you. I'm destined to kill everyone.

I wanted to tell him but didn't know how. My throat constricted. How could I be with him when I knew I would kill him?

"I'm here now," he said. "You can tell me."

"I can't," I whispered.

The hurt shone in his eyes, but he didn't press the issue.

Instead, he turned away to stare at the dancers as the music began to play.

"Do you know if the witch found my sister?"

"I think she's still searching, which is a good thing. Heidel is hopefully on the other side of the continent by now. I pray we'll be as lucky."

"I agree. We'll escape right before the last dance. We'll do it quickly. There will be enough commotion to distract her for a few minutes at least."

"Are you sure it will work?"

In my opinion, he sounded too confident. Or desperate. Either way, I didn't share his optimism.

"I'm sure," he answered, "because if I'm wrong, then it means I'll become her slave, and I would rather die than become one of them." He nodded toward the gathered dancers.

They moved without intention, as if they were marionettes in an elaborate theater, guided by others with no thought of their own. They belonged to the witch, every thought and every action, an existence worse than death.

Kull was right—we had to escape. We had no other choice.

Kull took my hand in his and led me up the staircase to the top balcony. This close to the sky, I felt as though I could reach up and touch the stars. The music sounded distant as it drifted from the bottom floor. I leaned against the stone railing. Vines grew up the marble pillars, and large, cabbage-sized roses bloomed in shades of black and red.

Kull and I stood near a set of large, open windows. I tasted the night air, chill and crisp, as a breeze brushed against my cheeks. As we stared out over the mountaintops, the moon rose higher in the sky, casting its silver light over the snow and making it sparkle.

I had to grudgingly admit that it was beautiful here. Kull wrapped his arm around my waist as we stared at the scene in front of us. Somewhere out there was the entrance to the undiscovered land and the cave where I had found Theht. The memory made me shudder, and I closed my eyes, trying to get the images out of my head.

Standing in the desert. Theht's voice in my mind as I reached up toward the sky, out into the darkness where I felt the asteroid flying through space. Using my magic to change its course. Watching as everyone died... Seeing Kull's corpse at my feet and knowing I was responsible.

"Olive," Kull said, "are you okay?"

"I... yes. Of course."

"Will you ever tell me what's going on? Ever since you went to that cave, you haven't been the same."

"I know."

"Then will you tell me what happened?"

I studied his face. "I've got to find a way to undo the prophecy."

"The prophecy about the Deathbringer?"

I nodded.

"The last time I checked, you didn't believe it was true."

"Yeah. Things changed."

"Something happened in the cave that made you believe it was real?"

"Yes."

"What happened?"

My throat squeezed shut as I contemplated telling him. I couldn't do it—not matter how hard I tried, I couldn't tell him what Theht had done to my mind. The memory was too raw and painful.

Exhaling, I rested my head against his chest. "I can't," I whispered.

He stroked my hair, making my fear retreat a tiny bit. His warmth calmed my racing heart, and I took a moment to enjoy his nearness. It seemed we never had a minute to ourselves, and when we did, we were plagued by threats of death and imprisonment. When would I ever get a moment free of fear to be with him?

A group of nobbinflies flitted past the open window, their wings shimmering with magic as they floated on graceful wings. Beyond them, the moonbeams highlighted the jagged peaks.

"When we escape, I should like to take you back to Danegeld to meet my mother."

"Really? Your mom?" The woman had a reputation of being more stubborn than her late husband. "Why would you do that?"

"So she may meet you, of course. I should like to do things properly. I know I haven't always had a desire to keep with my people's traditions, but since my father's passing, I've realized traditions are the one thing holding us together."

"Kull," I stared up at him, smiling, "you're turning into a philosopher."

He grunted. "I wouldn't go that far."

"Well, you are. And I respect Wult culture, but I'm clueless when it comes to Wult traditions. You know that, right?"

He smiled. "Not to worry. I shall teach you everything I know. I will make a Wult out of you yet."

"Do I have to wear the horned helmet?" I asked.

"Of course not. Horned helmets are merely an Earth Kingdom portrayal. Hardly accurate."

I rested my cheek on Kull's chest, thinking of my life as a Wult. A sense of peace came over me as I contemplated it, as if I'd finally found where I was supposed to be—the place I belonged. It was a strange emotion, mainly because it was the first time I'd ever truly felt it. I'd convinced myself I would never belong anywhere because in all my life, I'd never really felt like I'd known where my home was. The dragons had taken me in, and while I'd felt comfortable and loved, mingling with scaled, ten-ton giants made it hard to feel as if I fit in. Later, I'd tried to make a home on Earth, but that had felt less like home than the dragon caves.

Glancing up at Kull, feeling that sensation of butterflies fluttering in my stomach and the hopeful feeling in my heart, I felt I'd finally found where I belonged.

With him.

"Tell me about your mom," I said. "Do you think she'll like me?"

He cleared his throat, pausing before answering. "I am confident she will not find too much wrong with you."

"*Too* much wrong with me? Does she have a habit of finding flaws in your significant others?"

"Yes, actually. She still refuses to acknowledge Ket at our social gatherings."

Wonderful. Not only did she find flaws, but she held grudges, too.

"Don't think too harshly of my mother. I believe she will love you as one of her own children. She has been through many trials in her life but shows strength even through the hardest times, including my father's passing. She kept the kingdom together when I was not myself. Plus, she does much more than she's given credit for. You see? You've already got something in common."

"I'll keep that in mind."

The music below faded as the ball drew to a close.

"The ball is ending soon," Kull said. "Are you ready?"

"I guess so." It was the best answer I could muster.

We made our way off the balcony and down the stairs, watching as the crowd of people mingled, preparing for the last dance.

When we reached the bottom floor, my heart raced. I only hoped the witch was too preoccupied to notice as we slipped outside. She still sat on her throne, though she seemed absorbed in the dance.

As we moved toward the doors leading outside, a masked wraith blocked us. Tree limbs moved outside behind the man, and I could only stare past him and look at the world beyond the door.

"Where are you going?" he growled, his voice coarse and animalistic.

I'd never heard one of the creatures speak, and to hear it now made me shudder.

"We need some fresh air. Move aside," Kull answered.

Another wraith stood beside the first. Their jeweled masks gleamed in the starlight, and their eyes locked on me, making my spine tingle with fear.

"No one leaves the castle for the last dance."

"Is that so?" Kull asked.

"It is. Her Majesty does not allow it."

Kull flexed his hands. I recognized the action. He wanted Bloodbane, but without his weapon, he must have felt defenseless. Did the witch know of our plan to escape? With the guards at the door, it seemed possible.

"Very well," Kull said finally and took my arm as we turned away and walked back onto the dance floor. My stomach knotted with apprehension. Somehow we had to get outside, but to do it now would cause too much suspicion.

Kull steered me onto the floor where we avoided the other dancing couples and found a quiet spot of our own. The music pulled at my heart, weighing heavily, reminding me of the ten months of loneliness I'd endured so recently. I held Kull close, feeling his warmth. His eyes scanned the room as we danced, roving over every wall and doorway with the look of a caged animal.

"We may be able to escape through the dungeons," he said. "There is a blocked passageway that I believe leads to the stairs near the waterfall. It is not my first choice as I can't be certain where the passageway goes, but I know of no other way. Come to me tonight while she is sleeping."

I liked this plan even less than escaping through the garden. "Kull, if we're caught, she'll kill you."

His eyes searched mine. "Do you know of another way?"

"Could we try to go through the vaults again?"

"No. She doubled the guards after my sister and Maveryck escaped. It would be impossible to get inside."

"Then I don't know of another way," I answered, wishing I could say the opposite. Was there something I hadn't considered?

The music grew louder, the deep sound of the viola combining with other stringed instruments to create a tune that stirred the soul. Kull held me tight to his chest and leaned toward my ear.

"Tonight," he said, "we escape."

CHAPTER *Nine*

TWO WRAITHS GRIPPED MY ARMS TIGHT AS THEY LED me back to my chamber. I didn't fight them. Instead, I paid attention to where they led me and started to see a pattern in the castle's construction. Halls were connected with arched alcoves, and we passed three large staircases, though only one led down to the floors below. I memorized the path back to the staircase.

When we arrived at my chamber, the wraiths locked me inside the room. I changed into a pair of pants and a loose-fitting shirt that I'd found in the room's armoire. The clothing smelled musty, and based on the creases in the leather and the shirt's frayed edges, I realized I must have been wearing someone's castoffs, most likely someone who'd made a bad deal with the witch and now lived as a wraith in her castle.

I lay wide-awake in my bed, watching the moon rise over the mountains. Time passed slowly, and I felt I would go insane if I waited a minute longer. When the moon rose over the castle and out of view, I climbed out of bed, pulled on a pair of leather sandals that I'd also found in the armoire, and went to the door.

The wraiths had sealed it with a common lock, and I also felt an enchantment in the wood. I whispered a word of magic and stripped away the spell, but the lock was still a problem. I attempted to shove the door open, but it wouldn't budge.

Inspecting the door latch more closely, I knew of only one way to open it. It wasn't my first choice, and destroying the door would only make the guards realize I'd escaped sooner than I would like, but at this point, I was desperate.

"*Ignite*," I whispered.

The latch warmed and then turned bright white before it melted completely. I snuffed out the flames as the liquid metal spilled over the wood. When I pushed the door open, the flames were gone, yet the harsh scent of burned metal filled the air.

As I stepped into the hallway lit only by moonlight that shone through the floor-to-ceiling windows, I felt grateful that the wraiths were nowhere in sight. I crept down the halls on quiet feet, keeping my back pressed to the cold stone walls as I passed an open room and then wandered through another hallway.

An eerie stillness clung to the castle. Moonlight transformed the stones in the walls and floors from a harsh gray to a soft blue. The sound of my footsteps echoed quietly. Keeping my hands fisted, I made sure my magic would be ready at a moment's notice if I needed it. I tried to ignore the panicky feeling making my heart beat too fast.

It bothered me that the witch hadn't restrained me more than she had. In fact, the only chains she'd bound me with were words. Her threat to kill Kull if I helped him escape played through my head.

After I found the staircase leading below, I took the steps down. In a few places, lit torches burned in sconces, but they weren't bright enough to light the way entirely. Around each sconce I could make out carvings of winged, skeletal demons decorating the walls.

When I reached the bottom, I found a narrow hallway with a door at the end. As I unlatched the door and entered the dungeon, the temperature dropped, making goose bumps form on my skin. The smell of human waste pervaded the air.

I made my way past empty cells, some with hay covering the floor. As I neared one of the cells, I paused. My stomach heaved as I stared at the decomposing corpse of a male pixie. Backing away, I tore my eyes off the corpse and walked quickly down the hall, trying to erase the image from my vision.

Another door barred my path, and I opened the latch and entered a small room. I'd hoped to find Kull inside but found only more rows of empty cells. Where was he?

Just as I was ready to turn around and leave the dungeons for good, I noticed a door I hadn't seen earlier. My heart quickened as I opened it and entered a large cavern.

Kull's sword, along with several elven weapons, were

arranged on the wall, reminding me of trophies on display. I went to Bloodbane and touched it gently, feeling the cold chill of its metal against my fingers. The room was dimly lit, but I was able to make out a table sitting against the back wall.

Someone was on the table, and as I walked closer, my heart plunged. Kull lay strapped to the metal surface. Slashes crisscrossed his bare torso, and blood dripped from the table and pooled on the floor. I went to him and grabbed his hands. His fingers felt freezing cold, and his skin was ghostly white. His eyes fluttered open and he gasped as he tried to speak, but his whispers weren't audible. Soon, his eyes closed again.

Behind me, I heard a rustling sound and spun around as Silvestra appeared from the shadows. My mouth grew dry. She'd expected this. She'd been waiting for me.

"I thought you would come for him despite my warnings," she said. "It looks like I was right."

I balled my fists, no longer caring what she did to me for using my magic against her. Swirls of amber and blue surrounded my clenched fists until power exploded from my hands, tugging at my chest as it ripped from my body. All the fear I'd felt for Kull went into the magic. I couldn't hold the pain inside any longer. It was time for Silvestra to feel my wrath, so I used a binding spell that would burn like fire as the magic coiled around her. My hope was that the spell could hold her long enough for Kull and me to escape. Killing her was out of the question. No matter how much anger I harbored, I wasn't a murderer.

I wasn't Theht.

The magic hit the witch, but instead of binding her as I'd intended, it faded and pooled in her outstretched hand, absorbed by a black mist.

Stumbling, my energy faded and my back hit the wall. I glanced at Kull, feeling as if I'd failed him.

The witch's cold, aquamarine eyes held me in her gaze as she kept her hand outstretched. The magic mist formed a cohesive shape until it became a black box—the same object she'd shown me earlier—the lotus cube.

She stepped toward me, keeping the box between us. Its magic was so strong it made my knees weak. With my energy absorbed into the box's spell, it took everything I had just to remain standing.

"Tell me," she said. "How do you open the box?"

"I don't know."

"But you will learn."

She walked to Kull and touched the collar around his neck. Dark power pulsed from her finger into the stone band, making it glow. When she turned around, she showed me an ornate key sitting in her palm.

"The magic in this key will release the collar around his neck."

She whispered a word of magic, and green energy surrounded the box until it opened. Then, she placed the key inside. With another whispered word, the box sealed shut.

The magic in her eyes shimmered when she looked at me. "If you want to set this man free and leave my castle with him, you have but to remove the key from this box and unlock the collar around his neck."

I studied the box. It had to be a trick. "I don't know how."

"Then you must learn."

I exhaled. "Fine. But if I do this, you must promise not to hurt him any longer."

She studied my face. "Very well," she said finally. "He will not be harmed as long as you are obedient to me. You only have until the sun sets tomorrow evening to open the box. Should you fail, he becomes mine. And you will belong to me as well."

She placed the box on the table beside Kull and left the room, her footsteps echoing through the cavernous hallways until the sound disappeared.

I went to Kull and found him motionless and unresponsive. My hands shook as I took his fingers in mine. Seeing him like this frightened me more than I cared to admit.

"Kull," I said, brushing the hair from his forehead. "Can you hear me?"

He gave no reply. Only the sound of his breathing assured me he was alive.

I squeezed his fingers, wishing I could do something for him, but my magic was gone. I'd used it all up when I'd fought the witch—and what a disaster that had been. My magic hadn't fazed her. She was the only being I'd ever confronted with the ability to withstand my magic the way she'd done.

I rested my head on his chest, listening to the sound of his breathing. As long as he was alive, I still had hope.

Running my fingers over the collar, I felt the smooth ridges of the stone scales. Magic burned my fingers slowly, an intense heat filled with a power beyond my comprehension— the same power I'd felt in the box.

I turned away from Kull to inspect the box sitting beside him, then I picked it up. The stone felt cold in my hands, a seamless block with no discernible lid of any kind. Only magic would open it. But as I'd noticed earlier, only colorless swirls of energy surrounded the box, as if all the magic had been sucked away.

Or as if it had been combined.

Studying the box more closely, I found patterns of light glowing faintly from each of the six facets. I tried to make sense of the patterns. One was round with several half circles inside, but the pattern moved and faded in and out, making it hard to see clearly. Inspecting the other facets, I found different shapes—a triangle, a line that branched at the top to form a Y—but what did they mean?

Accessing the magic was impossible. I didn't even understand what sort of magic it was, much less how to manipulate it. I got the feeling the witch knew perfectly well I'd never be able to beat the spell, and that Kull and I would both belong to her soon.

But magic was what I understood, so deciphering the box's powers should have been within my abilities. Studying it again, watching the colors swirl to form patterns, I was reminded of the witch's garden. It was a stretch, but could these patterns and the paths in the garden be connected?

There was only one way to find out. I placed the box in my pocket, then gave Kull a kiss on his brow, feeling my heart thudding with worry as I pulled away from him.

"I'll solve this," I told him. "I promise."

More than anything, I wanted him to answer me, to give me some cocky remark and make me smile, to tell me to quit worrying so much, but he didn't move or make a sound. I backed away from him, glancing at the sword as I crossed the room, and then exited through the door.

The hallways seemed longer than usual as I left Kull behind. With my energy almost completely gone, I had an urge to go back to my room and get a few hours of sleep, but the drive to set Kull free was unrelenting.

As I made my way up the staircase and onto the castle's main level, I was surprised to see the sky lightening as sunrise approached. I had until sunset tomorrow evening to open the box, and time was already passing too quickly. But I wouldn't stop until I solved the mystery.

A feeling nagged at me—the feeling I'd gotten since I'd

come here—that the witch was tricking me and that I would never be able to open the box.

I pushed the thought aside. Silvestra had opened it, so it could be done. I just had to learn how. The hallways were empty as I made my way toward the gardens, making me wonder where all the wraiths went at night. Were they like vampires and slept in coffins somewhere? It wouldn't surprise me.

As I navigated through the hallways, I didn't feel quite as lost as I had yesterday. Remembering landmarks helped—the foyer with the ocean mosaic, the hallway with the floor-to-ceiling windows, the broad-stepped marble staircase—until I finally found the set of double doors leading to the witch's garden.

I pushed the doors open and stepped into the crisp morning air. Sunrays spread across the sky as I walked down the gravel path and into the garden. A gentle breeze tugged at the tree branches, making the flower blossoms flutter. My sandals crunched underfoot, and somewhere in the distance came the sounds of running water.

Up ahead, I found one of the oddly shaped paths and stepped onto it. As I walked, the path curved slightly to the left, and at the end, it branched into three lines. I hiked each path, but stopped at the end of the third path and removed the box from my pocket.

The sunlight made the glowing symbols almost impossible to see, and I had to step off the path and into the trees' shadows just to get a glimpse of the swirling symbols.

"There," I said to myself as I found the Y-shaped symbol.

It wasn't an exact match to the path, but was it close enough? If so, what next? My magic had recovered somewhat after using it against the witch, so I let my powers flow into the cube. Nothing. The mixture of Faythander and Earth magics surrounded the cube and dissipated, just as it had when I'd attacked the witch. It was as if I hadn't used any magic at all.

I could solve this, I really could—I just had to use some imagination.

What if I were supposed to use a certain spell? Could the symbol represent the word for a certain spell? But most spell words were never written down, as each practitioner used unique spells and no two spells were exactly alike.

I paced down the path. If I wanted to know more, I'd need something else to compare it to. When I found the next oddly shaped pathway, I stepped onto it and followed it around a large loop, with smaller, half-circle-shaped symbols inside it. I also recognized this symbol on the box, and I held the cube as I paced the trail, tracing the matching symbol on its side, willing it to give up its secrets.

I attempted a few more spells but got the same results as last time. After exploring the rest of the garden, I found four more oddly shaped paths, and each corresponded in most part with the shapes on the box. But whatever I tried, I couldn't activate the box's magic.

Drat.

I found a bench and sat on it, watching as the sun rose higher in the sky. I was hungry, tired, I had a headache, and it was morning. Not a good combination. Seriously. It seemed Heidel and I had something in common. My magic felt my irritability, too, and my ability to think was also suffering.

Stuffing the box in my pocket, I took the path back to the castle. Tall parapets rose into the sky, reflecting sunlight in some places, and covered in moss and vines in other spots. By the time I made it inside and back to my chamber, it was near noon.

A wraith waited outside my door, and I stopped short.

His emotionless gaze took me in.

"She waits for you," he said.

"The witch?"

He nodded. "I will take you to her."

Staring at my door only a few feet away, so close to the bed where I'd hoped to get a few minutes of sleep, I wasn't sure if I should follow him. But disobeying the witch would only make my situation worse. Been there. Done that. Wouldn't happen again.

"Fine," I grumbled and followed the wraith down the hallway.

This had better be life-or-death important.

When we approached her chamber, the heavenly scent of cooked food came from inside. As we entered, I found the round table filled with bowls of steaming soup, plates of fruit and cheese, loaves of freshly baked bread, pastries covered in chocolate, and golden goblets filled with frothy white liquid.

The witch waited beside one of the tall windows overlooking her garden. She turned around as I approached, and the murder I'd seen in her eyes when we'd been in the dungeons had disappeared.

She gave me a warm smile, one that almost made me think

she was normal—if normal meant a power-wielding, half-drag-
on, half-witch who changed people into mindless subservient
slaves. Or not.

"Sit," she said, "and eat."

I took the chair across from her, and we both sat. Maybe
if I hadn't been starving and ready to collapse from exhaustion,
I would've given some flippant remark on how I refused to eat
with the likes of her, but I was neither full nor well rested, so I
grabbed a handful of cheese and stuffed it in my mouth.

The sharp flavor melted on my tongue. I ate the fruit next,
and then the soup, which reminded me of a French onion soup
I'd eaten at one of Houston's fancier places back when I'd dat-
ed Brent—when he'd footed the bill so I could afford to eat at
places like that. I hadn't thought about my ex in a while. Although he'd recovered from the bloodthorn incident on Earth,
he still had a million questions for me. But those were worries
for another time.

Silvestra watched me as I ate, although she only nibbled
her food and took small sips from her goblet.

"Have you discovered a way to open the box?" she asked.

"No."

"Have you gotten close?"

"I've made some progress, but it would be helpful if you
gave me a hint."

"A hint?"

"Yes, you know, tell me what the symbols mean or what
language they're written in. At this point, anything would be
helpful."

"I see." She sipped her drink while keeping her eyes on me,
then placed her goblet on the table. "I can tell you that the answers are not found where you've been looking."

Awesome. I'd been looking in the wrong place the whole
time. What other good news did she have for me?

"I will also tell you that you must stop doubting yourself.
Opening the box is within your own capabilities."

"But it's not made of any magic I'm familiar with. How can
I open it if I don't even know what spells to use?"

She only smiled. "Keep searching."

She must have gotten some sick pleasure watching me
blunder around the castle like an idiot. I was sure it would give
her endless amounts of joy when I failed and became her prisoner. I had the urge to toss the box out the window and drag
unconscious Kull out of the castle—if only I could find a way to

get that collar off his neck. Hence the key. And the box. Which meant throwing it out the window wouldn't work. It looked like I was stuck playing her stupid game while Kull suffered. Some things were so not fair.

I finished the food and prepared to leave. When I scooted the chair away from the table, she stopped me.

"I do not wish for you to fail," she said.

"Really?" I asked. "It seems you've set me up for it."

"Why do you say that?"

"Because if I don't open the box in time, then you win. You get both Kull and me as your slaves. But if I do manage to open it, it means you lose, it means Kull and I escape and you're down two pawns. I don't see how my ability to open the box benefits you in any way, and so that is why I don't think it's possible. You've given me hope by handing me a key and a promise, but that promise is locked inside a box that can't be opened."

"It cannot be opened," she said, "because you do not believe it's possible."

"No. It can't be opened because you won't allow it."

"That is a lie."

"Prove it."

She stood. "All I will tell you is that I very much wish for you to open that box, because if you do, my assumptions of you will be proven correct."

"What assumptions?"

"Open the box," she said, "and you will find out."

She left the room without another word, leaving me alone to ponder the box. Silvestra confused me on so many levels. What were her motivations? What would I be proving by opening the box?

Frustrated, I left the room and returned to my task of wandering the castle's hallways. On the bright side, I'd wandered the halls for so long now that I finally knew my way around the place.

I didn't return to the gardens. If Silvestra were right and I'd been looking in the wrong place, then I would find somewhere else to look. Removing the box from my pocket, I examined it once again. It looked no different than it had before, although being inside gave me the advantage of seeing the symbols with more clarity. An idea struck me, so I found a dark, windowless room, stepped inside, and took a closer look at the symbols.

I focused on each symbol in turn, but as I focused on the circle symbol with the half-moons inside, I gasped as I saw what it really was—a human skull.

Varying shades of light gray formed the bones around the eye sockets and pronounced forehead, while darker shades made the teeth and jawbones.

Skulls on Faythander, just as on Earth, represented death, but why would a skull be on this box? Surveying the other symbols, I noted that they all seemed unchanged. None of them looked any different except the image of the circle.

What was I missing?

I hadn't seen the image of the skull in the rose garden, but I'd had a really bad perspective. Maybe it was time to get a new perspective.

I exited the room and took the stairs, searching for the castle's tallest tower. Half an hour later, after finding rooms filled with wraiths who sat silently doing mundane tasks such as washing or mending, and other rooms where the wraiths simply sat and stared at walls, I finally found the tallest tower with a view of the garden.

The tower was cylindrical, with a staircase spiraling up the center. When I reached the top, I found windows circling the room. As I stood at the glass looking out, the view amazed me. Against the sky I found a brief shimmering, as if the castle and its garden were encased in some sort of invisibility dome. The magic it must have taken to fuel such a spell would have been exponentially huge—and I could only assume the life forces of the witch's captured wraiths were fueling it. It also made sense as to why I'd never seen the castle before—not in the air while flying over the mountain, and not when I'd explored the cave to the undiscovered land at the top of Dragon Spine Mountain.

The garden spread in all directions but ended abruptly where the stream turned into the waterfall on the horizon— where I'd hoped to escape with Kull. What most shocked me was the arrangement of not only the oddly shaped paths, but of each individual plant. The entire garden was an elaborate map of Faythander.

The continent of Faythander was loosely shaped like the prehistoric continent of Pangaea, but in Faythander, the land was split into five massive kingdoms. Pixies inhabited the southlands, which were represented on the garden map with an L shape and two horizontal lines through the center. The elf kingdom was the largest and took up the eastern and central portions of the map, marked with a triangle shape and a circle in its center. On the western side, the kingdom of the dragons and Wults filled the space with symbols of the Y and a backward 3 shape. The northlands, which until recently had been the territory of the goblins, was left blank.

In the map's center I found the skull symbol but wasn't familiar with any kingdom the skull could represent.

I held the box and scanned its symbols, then matched each one to one of the symbols represented in the garden. Six facets of the box, represented by only five symbols—four that corresponded to the races of Faythander, and one that was a mystery.

The shape of the skull was located at the garden's bottom center, which was loosely where Dragon Spine Mountain stood. Since the witch's castle stood so close to the entrance of the undiscovered land, I could only assume that the skull was a symbol for it.

Alarmed at the implications, I studied the box and garden, hoping I'd missed something, but I found nothing new. I could only come to one conclusion, and it scared me more than I cared to admit.

The skull was a symbol for black magic.

CHAPTER *Ten*

I MADE IT BACK TO MY ROOM WHERE I FOUND THE WRAITH who had been there earlier. A shimmering blue dress was draped over his arm.

"What's that?" I asked.

"My Lady wants you to attend tonight's ball. She has requested you wear this."

I eyed the dress. "Do I have to?"

"My Lady wishes it."

Sighing, I took the dress from him. As I hefted the gown, I almost dropped it. The thing had to weigh more than a suit of armor. After entering my room, I locked the door behind me and then inspected the dress.

It was made of several layers of translucent fabric, and each layer was darker than the next. On the outermost layer, the entire bodice had been beaded with diamonds, and I had wild ideas of transporting back to Earth with the thing, selling it, and living the rest of my life as a millionaire cat lady.

Carefully, I placed the gown on the bed. Warm, slanting sunrays filtered through the window onto the floor and bed, making the jewels glow. I stepped to the window and looked outside. Evening was approaching. A whole day was nearly gone, and I didn't feel any closer to opening the box. I pulled it out of my pocket and studied the symbols again.

The magic was a gentle hum filled with subtle power. After learning the meaning of the symbols—each representing a different race on Faythander—I realized that the odd gray color could have been caused because the magic was a blend of all five.

It made sense. I'd never seen it done before, but that didn't make it impossible. The only way to know for sure was to test my theory, so I turned the box to face me with the symbol of elven magic—the C shape—on top.

I let elven magic flow from my hands into the symbol. Controlling the magic was tricky as all it seemed to do was bounce off the box, but I finally managed to focus the power directly into the symbol. As I did, the symbol glowed brighter. The magic surrounding the box changed color as it broke apart, creating a rainbow of colors—pink, green, and amber—on the walls and ceiling. The light dazzled my eyes. The swirling magic brushed my skin, an odd sensation with all the magics combined into one, until they finally faded, and all the blue elven magic disappeared.

The C symbol on the box disappeared.

Finally, I'm getting somewhere! I felt like jumping up and down on the bed.

My hands trembling with excitement, I turned to the symbol of the dragon magic, the Y. Although I didn't naturally possess dragon magic, I had Faythander magic, and since all magic on Faythander branched from one common source, learning to control other magics was possible. I'd been taught many dragon spells, but would they work? Saying the word for magic in the dragon tongue would hopefully do the trick.

"Einoxulus," I whispered and let the spell flow into the stone.

As before, it took a bit of artistry to get the magic to flow with precision into the shape, and it took a few tries, but finally, the magic united with the symbol. Green swirls of light surrounded the box, intermingling with the other colors until the green faded, and as before, the symbol disappeared.

Sitting on the bed, I felt my head spinning. They were simple spells, but they still needed power, which happened to come from my energy. Two spells down, three to go. I still felt like jumping up and down on the bed, but maybe with a little more restraint.

The Wult, pixie, and black magic spells remained. The only easy spell would be the pixie. Since the Wults didn't possess magic, I wasn't sure what to do about that one. Worse, I knew there was no way I could manipulate the spell controlling black magic. But I would worry about that one when I got to it. First, I had to take care of the pixie symbol.

My heart clenched as my thoughts turned to the pixies.

Sometimes I forgot that my closest pixie friend, Uli, had died, only to remember that she'd given her life to save Faythander. It was a painful reminder of the world I lived in, and I wasn't sure my fate would be any different from hers.

Breathing deeply, I pushed the thoughts of death aside and focused instead on the stone. As with the last two spells, I used an incantation I'd learned from the pixies and guided the magic into the stone. Energy drained from my body, making me glad I was sitting. Rose-colored magic sparkled above me and disappeared, leaving me with two symbols: Wult and black magic.

I rested on the bed, feeling as if the magic had taken every last ounce of my energy. There was nothing left. Sleeping would restore my magic, but did I have time? Glancing outside, I saw the sun had sunk low and turned a glowing orange that announced the end of the day. My eyes closed, and without another thought, I fell asleep.

I awoke to a dark room. My stomach churned and head pounded. Sitting up, I found the gown lying on the bed with me. I cursed as I snatched up the dress. What time was it? Had I missed the ball? Silvestra would strike me dead if I missed her stupid party.

I dressed quickly, brushed my hair, and then glanced in the mirror. Running my hands over the gown's light blue, velvety fabric and sweeping skirt, I didn't recognize the woman in the mirror. She was some ethereal creature with elven ears, bright green eyes, dark reddish hair, and a gown that was suited for a fairytale castle.

Turning away from the mirror, I grabbed the stone box before stumbling out of the room. When I approached the ballroom, music drifted into the hallway. My shoes echoed off the marble tiles until I stopped at the large double doors, pulled them open, and entered the ballroom.

Wraiths crowded the room in their customary attire of masks and elaborate clothing. The tide of bodies pressed in around me as I wandered across the enchanted floor. The lilting, calming surge of music broke up my worries. I found myself drifting over the floor, floating.

Instead of the stars and planets represented on the tiles, I floated on a silver sky. My feet touched the tops of clouds, and

I felt their mist and magic fill my lungs.

A strong hand grabbed mine, and I spun around. Kull stood behind me, although I almost didn't recognize him. Dark circles shadowed his eyes, and his skin was ashen. He looked more like a wraith than I cared to admit.

"Kull," I gasped.

He smiled. I found pain in his eyes, but he pulled me close and the pain seemed to disappear.

"I was worried you weren't coming," he said.

"I fell asleep. But I'm shocked to see you here. You weren't even conscious this morning. Are you okay?"

"Well enough. Whatever magic that witch uses is some wicked stuff." He touched the collar around his neck. "I don't feel like myself."

"You don't look like yourself, either."

He raised an eyebrow.

"Don't worry," I said. "I've made some progress with the box today. You'll be free before tomorrow evening. I promise."

I didn't admit that I had no clue how to remove the two remaining spells, but I didn't want to worry him. He looked like he didn't need any of that right now.

He leaned close to my ear. "Dance with me," he said.

His nearness made my skin tingle. I felt as if I were floating as he guided me to the center of the floor.

Dark clouds gathered beneath us as we danced. The floor seemed to melt away, leaving us to dance on thunderheads as lightning sparked through the towering clouds. He held my hand close to his heart as we danced.

He wore a black tunic with dark red garnets studding the collar. His blond hair was loose around his shoulders, and his blue eyes had the intensity of the enchanted lightning sparking beneath our feet. As he held me, I wondered if perhaps we were wrong. Did Wults possess magic?

"What are you thinking about?" he asked me.

"Nothing much."

"Nothing? You looked deep in thought. You must have been thinking of something."

"Well, I guess I was pondering whether or not Wults have magic."

He creased his brow. "Why would we have magic?"

I shook my head. So much didn't make sense. "I don't know."

Resting my head on his chest, I felt his warmth on my

cheek. The music played a cadence that matched our footsteps, slow and rhythmic. The low tones of the cello and piano combined to conjure feelings of sadness and loneliness—two emotions the witch must have intimately understood, and so did I.

I looked and found Silvestra sitting on her throne. Her eyes tracked our movements.

I'd finally found the one person who completed me, and she was going to take him away. The thought was almost too much to bear. I closed my eyes as Kull and I danced through the clouds together.

When the song ended, he guided me off the floor and under an alcove.

"Is something the matter?" he asked.

"No. I'm okay." I exhaled. "At least we're together for now, right?"

He kissed my knuckles. "Yes. We're together now. And because I swore I would never lose you again, we shall stay that way. You'll have the box opened soon, and then we'll be free of this place."

I smiled but couldn't answer. How would I ever open the box without black magic?

"Come with me," he said, "I'd like to show you something."

He took my hand and led me up the stairs. When we reached the top level, he guided me toward a balcony overlooking the dance floor, except the floor wasn't visible. Instead, the spell made it appear as if we stood above the tops of the clouds.

"It's breathtaking," I said, "even in a place like this."

"It gets better," he said, then squeezed my hand and led me off the balcony and onto the cloud tops.

Gasping, I found the clouds soft beneath my shoes, as if I walked on a thick carpet.

"Amazing," I whispered, breathless.

Hues of pink and blue spiraled through the clouds. I felt their power brush against my cheeks, warm and fluid. Reaching out, I touched the clouds as they billowed up around our shoulders.

The music drifted up to us, and we danced with the soft magic of the clouds against our skin. Steady, pulsing rhythms and low, flowing notes stirred excitement—the sound of a storm soon to be unleashed.

I knew Silvestra was down there somewhere, and I wondered why she wanted so badly for me to open the box. What would happen? What did she think I was capable of? I pondered her words and felt uneasy at their implications. Assuming I discovered how to open the Wult symbol, after that, the only way to open the box was by using black magic. It was a thought that nagged at me. I knew for a fact I didn't possess black magic. Even though my mother was a practitioner, my father had admitted he'd studied me as a child and was confident I didn't possess the art. Not only that, but I'd never in my life sensed black powers within my own.

Kull put his finger under my chin, bringing my gaze to his. "Did I lose you?"

"No. I was just thinking."

"About what?"

About whether I'm a witch. But could I tell him?

"Would you believe me if I told you my mom was a witch?"

"A witch? How do you know?"

"My dad told me. He found out a long time ago, when my mom first crossed into Faythander before I was born. I guess he was worried that I would have the same powers as my mom."

"But you don't."

"No, I don't."

"Is this what you've been worried about?"

"Maybe a little."

"But you've never manipulated dark powers. You have nothing to worry about."

"You're right. I guess I'm worried about my mom, also. If she ever returns to the elven capitol where my dad calls home, she'll be executed. The elves have a standing order to execute any witch who enters their lands."

"Where is she now?"

"I'm not exactly sure. The last I checked, she'd sold her house and taken off to tour the world. She and my dad were somewhere in Africa helping with relief aid."

"Relief aid? That doesn't sound typical for her sort of lifestyle."

"No. She's not the same person I knew as a teenager, that's for sure. Sometimes I feel like I never knew her."

The music stopped, leaving only silence as we drifted on silvery clouds, and then it started again. Glancing up at Kull, I found him deep in thought.

"Do your worries have something to do with that box?" he asked.

I cringed. I hadn't wanted to admit how very far away I

was from opening it. But I supposed I would have to be more forthcoming with him. He'd see through my lies anyway. He always had.

"Yes," I answered. "I managed to open the three sides displaying symbols that represented the magical races of Faythander, but the last two symbols have me stumped. They're the symbols for Wults and black magic, but as far as I know, Wults don't possess magic. And worse, I have no idea how to open the symbol representing black magic."

He remained silent as he pondered my words. "You're sure about this?"

"Pretty sure. I feel like I've been set up to fail, although the witch seems confident that I'll figure it out."

"I agree, which makes me believe there must be another way."

"Another way to open the box?"

"No. Another way out of this castle—another way to get this collar off my neck."

I shook my head. "I can't think of any other way."

"That's because she wants you to play by her rules. Maybe you shouldn't."

"I wish that were possible. As it is, she hasn't given me any options. If I don't open that box, we both belong to her."

He stroked my hair. "I have faith in you. If anyone can solve this, it's you. You understand magic like no one else."

"I hope you're right."

"Of course," he said with a grin. Despite the pallor of his skin, he still managed to look like his old self. "I am always right."

"Ha! It seems no matter what the witch does to you, you manage to still be your usual cocky self. I doubt even transforming you into a wraith will mask your personality."

"Cocky? Who says I'm cocky?"

I cupped his cheek, feeling the roughness of his skin. "I do. It's what I love about you."

His eyes lit up. Swirling colors surrounded him as he leaned in to kiss me. Below us, the music stopped, announcing the end of the ball. He looked up, and his eyes darkened.

"What's the matter?" I asked.

"The witch," he said. "She only allowed me a few hours to attend the ball, and then she demanded I go back to the dungeon so the wraiths can continue..."

"Continue what?"

He shook his head.

"Kull, continue what? Are they still hurting you? She promised not to hurt you anymore."

He closed his eyes, and I saw the old Kull no longer. His brow creased with worry, and pain etched the wrinkles around his eyes. "They're not hurting me—not physically, at least."

"Then what are they doing to you?"

When he opened his eyes, the pain was gone. "Nothing. I am well enough. But I must go soon."

"I don't want you to go."

He pushed a strand of hair away from my eyes. "I know. But I don't have much of a choice." Leaning closer, he whispered into my ear. "There is a tunnel in the dungeon where she keeps me. It leads to the waterfall. Use it to escape this place if you must."

Confused, I stared up at him. "I won't leave you here."

"You may not have a choice."

He turned away, but I grabbed his hand. I hated that he wouldn't tell me what was happening to him. It made me worry even more.

"Kull, what are they doing to you?"

"Don't worry about me."

He leaned forward and kissed my forehead, then he cupped my face. The look he gave me was so full of love I couldn't doubt how he felt for me, but that didn't make me feel any better about what the witch was doing to him. Then, with a small smile, Kull turned and walked away, leaving me alone.

CHAPTER *Eleven*

"DO YOU KNOW WHAT THE WULT KING FEARS?" SILvestra asked me.

I sat across from her at the breakfast table. After last night's ball, I'd returned to my room, but despite Kull's advice, I had worried about him the entire night. I hadn't slept well, so sitting here, chitchatting with the witch over a breakfast of soufflés and buttered bread only made me want to go crawl back in bed.

"Why should I answer?" I said as I picked at a piece of bread. "You told me you wouldn't hurt him, yet it seems you've found a way to torture him still. I'm tired of playing your games."

The witch pursed her lips. "You of all people should know the answer to my question—you should know what he fears."

"I refuse to answer."

She laughed. "Very well, then. Perhaps you don't know him as well as I thought."

"I know him well enough to understand when he's being tortured. I don't know how because he won't tell me, but I know you're doing something to him."

I placed the lotus cube on the table. Its two remaining symbols taunted me. Wult magic didn't exist, and black magic was an art I never had—and never would have.

"You've lied to me about Kull, and you're also lying to me about this box. You said I can open it, but that's not possible."

"I have lied about nothing. There is a way to open the box. You've not yet explored all the possibilities. As for the Wult, there is nothing I can do to stop his pain. Only you have that power."

Something about her words gave me pause.

"He's in pain because you tortured him. I fail to see how I can fix that."

"No. He is in pain because of you. Tell me, how well does he truly know you and your capabilities?"

"He knows everything."

"Does he?"

I swallowed my fear. I still hadn't told him what Theht had done to me in the cave.

"I can help you," Silvestra said. "I can show you how to defeat your enemies, how to alter the course of time, and how to sabotage prophecy."

She was bluffing.

"No one can do that. You couldn't even stop your own prophecy from happening, so how could you possibly stop mine?"

"Open the box, and once you do, your questions will be answered."

"Why can't you just tell me?"

"Some things are not meant to be spoken of."

I glanced at the box. Her words taunted me. I wanted to believe her, but deep inside, I knew it was a lie. Still, if I wanted to be free, I had no choice but to keep trying.

We finished our breakfast in silence. I left the room with a brief good-bye and once again found myself wandering the hallways, trying to be creative and think of something I hadn't tried yet, although I felt as if I'd already tried everything.

The hallway widened and then branched in two directions. I took the path to my right and ended up in an unfamiliar part of the castle.

I entered a library. White marble spanned the floors and surrounded the thick pillars that supported an arched ceiling. Veins of gold shot through the marble, complimented by images of golden ivy etched along the walls and around the square base of the pillars. Although it was a grand room with marble statues and a detailed painting of cherry blossom branches covering the ceiling, it wasn't the largest library I'd ever been in—and there were only a few books on the shelves. Kull's library wasn't as spectacular, but its sheer size overwhelmed this place.

The lack of books made the place feel empty and barren. Wandering through the stacks made me curious to know what sort of books the witch would keep on her shelves. I found a beautiful blue book with raised images of a fairy forest gracing its cover. Inside, the pages were made of a thick paper that creaked as I turned from one page to the next. It was a journal that belonged to someone named Elisabeth, from Earth Kingdom, and it chronicled her short visit to Fairy World. Magic hummed from the pages, and I felt the witch's spell bound to the journal. Focusing on the spell, an image came to me of a wraith woman I'd seen at the ball. Was the magic connected to her? It made sense. Perhaps this was her diary and the witch was using it to keep Elisabeth prisoner. I replaced the book on the shelf, feeling sick inside at its implications.

One more slave that the witch controlled. One more life taken away.

Scanning several more tomes, I realized they weren't all journals. Some were history texts written by elves, some were encyclopedias of ancient languages. I also found a few religious texts written by Wults. Some of the lines caught my attention. *A socitie built on an ancient religion, evolved over time through the magic and grace of our wourld Faythander, infusing itself until the old is transformed and becomes something new.*

Had magic changed more than just their religion? Had it changed them as well? I kept that thought with me as I scanned more books. Magic was bound to these tomes the same as I'd felt in the journal. Each book represented a person in the castle, someone who had crossed the witch or made a bargain they'd lost, and now they belonged to her.

Kull's sword served the same purpose as these books. He'd given it willingly and without hesitation. I knew when he'd done it that it had been a risky move, although we'd had no other choice. But I'd felt magic when he'd struck the bargain with the witch. I'd known something bad would happen but had had no power to stop it. And now he would soon become hers.

Frustrated, I walked away from the shelves and stood near a wall of windows overlooking the mountaintops. I kept the box in my hand and gripped it tightly, feeling its sharp edges cutting into my skin, wishing I could toss it out the window and be done with it.

Magic wrapped the box in colors of amber and purple. The stone grew so hot I dropped it, and the box landed with an echoing thud on the floor. As I studied the box, the wisps of purple faded, leaving only the amber. Coppery gold streamers danced around the smooth surfaces. After the swirling light disappeared, I carefully picked up the box. What was happening to it?

Purple was the color of fairy magic, and though its light had disappeared, I still felt the fairy powers within my box. Had the fairies found a way to help me? If so, then what were they hinting at? It must have had something to do with the amber magic—the Earth magic.

It was starting to make sense.

There was no such thing as Wult magic, but thousands of years ago, Vikings had crossed from Earth Kingdom, and although most humans weren't aware of it, Earth magic existed.

I grabbed the box and turned the Wult symbol to face me. The backward three shape burned gold against the black backdrop. Focusing, I let my Earth magic flow into the symbol. Since I'd done this several times now, aligning the magic with the symbol was getting easier.

Warm, fluid magic encircled my hands as it moved into the stone. The light grew brighter as energy drained from my body. After the spell entered the stone, the symbol disappeared.

Relief washed over me. I looked up, not seeing any fairies present but wondering if they could hear me. "Thank you," I said aloud. I didn't get an answer, but I felt they heard me.

I turned back to the box. Four symbols down, one to go— the one I dreaded most. I turned the box so the skull symbol faced me. No matter how far I'd come, none of it mattered if I didn't get past the black magic symbol. But how? I'd never used black magic before. Most people hadn't. I had seen others use it—the Regaymor, Geth, the bloodthorn. I'd also seen the witch use it, although her magic seemed less tainted, but I wasn't exactly sure why. My hands shook as I held the stone box. I'd come too far just to fail.

Pacing the library, I tried to find some clue about how to conjure black magic, but the more I pondered it, the more manipulated I felt. Surely the witch knew I didn't possess the art. She'd given me an impossible task... unless she'd intended for me to harness Theht's powers. But was she even aware Theht existed within me? It seemed unlikely, as I'd never told anyone.

I left the library feeling more frustrated than hopeful. Afternoon gave way to evening as I found the staircase leading down to the dungeon. The sound of dripping water echoed through the dank chambers as I wandered from one room to the next. With only a few hours left to break the box's spell, panic welled up inside me. I felt desperate to open it, and no matter how hard I tried, I couldn't come up with any way to do it.

My thoughts distracted me from paying attention to where I was going, and as I wandered through the dungeons, it took me longer than I would have liked to find Kull's chamber. When I finally located the room and entered, I found him sleeping on a straw mattress on the floor, covered with a rough gray blanket. Dark circles shadowed his sunken eyes, twitching behind closed eyelids. I hoped to never see him like this again, but it seemed Kull, like me, would never be free of the demons haunting him.

Kull stirred as I sat beside him, but he didn't open his eyes. The stone collar glowed faintly around his neck. It was only a matter of time before he transformed completely and became one of the wraiths.

I gently took his hand and held his fingers in mine. I'd hoped to talk to him about the box, but now I didn't want to disturb him, so I removed the lotus cube from my pocket and placed it in front of me. I'd found the secret for removing the Wult spell, so maybe learning how to overcome black magic would be possible, too.

As I sat on the cold stone floor, I whispered one spell after another, but none of them had any effect on the box. Time passed, and I knew it was near midnight when I finally stood up and paced the room. My hands grew clammy as I held the box. With only a few minutes before the spell transformed Kull, I knew I'd run out of options.

As I paced the room, I noticed Kull's sword hanging on the wall like a trophy. Silvestra was controlling Kull with the sword just like the journals and elven talismans in the library. Glancing from the box to the sword, I realized playing her game was no longer an option. Silvestra had sworn opening the box was possible—and maybe it was—if she'd given me a few months to figure it out. But truthfully, I still wasn't sure breaking the spell was something I could do.

The box grew warm as I held it. I studied the skull symbol one last time, feeling as if it mocked me. I was so done with that stupid box. Tossing it across the room, I listened as it landed with a loud clatter on the paving stones. Turning, I grabbed Bloodbane's worn handle, feeling its heaviness and perfectly balanced weight in my hands. In the dim candlelight, each nick and dent was made apparent. Each time Kull had battled was etched into the sword's surface. Every drop of blood, of sweat, of tears... well, possibly not tears—I wouldn't go that far. But every war he'd fought had been won with this sword.

Glancing at Kull's sleeping form, I prayed he would forgive me for what I was about to do. I only hoped my unholy act bought his freedom.

Placing Bloodbane on the floor, I took several steps back. This was going to be dangerous. I'd created fire hot enough to liquefy metal before, but this fire had to be hot enough to disintegrate it. Now I would find out if I had enough power within me to destroy the one talisman Kull held sacred above any other.

Good thing he loved me.

Collecting the power within me, I focused on the sword, letting my anger fuel my magic. Bands of blue and amber wrapped around my wrists and traveled in hot waves up my arms. My hands fisted, and the magic released into the sword. The fire burned from ocher to white as it consumed the blade. Heat singed my eyebrows and forced me to back away, but I kept my focus on the sword, allowing all my energy to flow into fueling the magic.

Bursts of light blinded me as the sword melted. Flames licked the fragments that fell away, casting embers that flitted into the air. In a matter of minutes, nothing remained of the sword but a black stain on the floor. Sweating and breathing heavily, I stumbled back, then rushed to Kull, so dizzy I almost fell as I moved to his side.

"Kull," I said, shaking his shoulder.

As he opened his eyes, the collar encircling his neck glowed bright. In that brief moment when his eyes met mine, he didn't know me. A wild, unsettling fear replaced his look of centered calmness, and he clamped my wrist.

"Where am I?" He breathed as if he'd come back from the brink of drowning.

"It's all right. I'm here," I said.

"Olive?"

"Yes, it's me. I'm right here."

I grabbed his hand in mine. The collar glowed brighter and then began to disappear. It faded slowly, disintegrating the same way the sword had done. His eyes opened wide as he touched his neck.

"What's happening?" he asked.

"It's okay. I destroyed the collar. You're free."

"What? How?"

"I... umm, it's a bit of a long story. I'd better tell you when we're out of this castle. Do you think you can walk?"

His heavy breathing echoed through the empty room. Finally, he sat up. I didn't know what kind of pain he was suffering, and I didn't know if the witch were responsible or not, but I did know that mental pain was worse than physical. Those deep scars no one could see healed slowly, if they ever healed at all.

I smoothed the hair away from his brow. If she'd injured him, I would not rest until she paid for it.

"Kull, what's wrong? Did the witch hurt you?"

"I..." He gasped. His eyes scanned the room as if he were a caged animal. "Olive?"

"I'm here."

Closing his eyes, he steadied his breathing. I glanced back at the door. We needed to escape now before the witch or one of the wraiths discovered that I'd destroyed the sword and the collar.

"Do you know the way to the waterfall?" I asked.

"Yes." He sat up. "It's not far."

"Can you walk?"

He nodded but was slow to stand up, so I put my arm around him.

"Where's the exit?"

"There's a doorway in the back. It's locked, but Bloodbane will make short work of the lock." He turned to the wall where his sword had hung. "Where's my sword?"

He walked to the wall, keeping his eyes on the black spot on the floor. I couldn't follow. I wasn't sure if he'd ever forgive me for this. He'd left me for ten months after his father's death. What would he do after I'd destroyed his sword?

"Kull," I said, "I need to tell you something."

He scuffed his boot on the blackened spot.

"I'm sorry, but destroying the sword was the only way to get that collar off your neck."

He was silent for a moment. What was he thinking? He'd told me once that the sword was an heirloom. How old was it? Hundreds of years? Sighing, my heart felt heavy. Kneeling in the ash, he rubbed it with his fingertips, as if paying homage to an honored friend, as if a piece of himself had died with the sword.

When he stood, he gave me a small smile, but I saw the sadness in his eyes. I almost felt I could hear his heart breaking as he walked toward me.

"We need to go," he said.

"Are you angry with me?"

"Of course not. I'd rather have my life than my sword." He sighed. "But I will not lie, Bloodbane will be missed. I hardly felt like myself without my sword, and now I suppose I'll never feel like myself again."

I rested my hand on his shoulder. "Will you be all right?"

"Yes, as soon as we're free of this place. Come, I'll show you the passage I found."

I followed him through the cavernous room and to the back wall where a small metal door sat in a stone alcove. A lock was attached to the door's handle.

"I'll try to pry the mechanism apart," Kull said.

It took him a moment, but he crushed the metal in his hands until it split apart, and then he grunted as he finally pulled the broken lock away from the door.

"Easy," he said, smiling. "I don't think anyone uses this passage much, or else we would've had a harder time of it."

"That, or you've got incredible grip strength," I said.

"Yes." His smile broadened. "I like that explanation better."

Kull found a torch and some oiled cloth and lit it as we walked through the doorway and down a winding path. The firelight flickered off the rough stone walls. Cobwebs blocked our way in several places. Up ahead came the sound of rushing water, and soon we emerged under the moonlit sky onto a ledge that jutted out from a cliffside. The rushing waterfall created a dazzling white curtain that blocked our path. Kull extinguished the torch and led me to a set of steps that had been hewn into the rock face.

"It's slippery, so you'll have to be careful."

I followed him to the ledge's edge, where the mountain's face and ledge converged, and then we climbed down the steps. My heart echoed the thundering water, and my clammy hands didn't help with the climb. But I found that some of the steps were covered in moss, which gave me a little more traction. As we descended, I couldn't help but glance up at the castle. Sometime soon, the witch would find out we'd escaped. I prayed we were on a light carriage headed for the farthest reaches of Faythander when that happened.

The descent was strangely serene as we made it closer to the forest floor. We sank past the treetops, then down toward their trunks. In several places, the thick branches reached out and touched the rocks. I felt magic in their limbs and humming through the veins of each individual leaf. Moonlight glowed a bright silver on the moss-covered steps. As we neared the ground, the sound of the rushing waterfall grew distant.

"Almost there," Kull called up to me as he stepped onto the ground.

Soon, I, too, stood on the forest floor. High above us, the towering parapets of the castle disappeared. Instead, in the moonlight, I saw the faint outline of a shimmering dome.

CHAPTER *Twelve*

"**B**ROTHER, I THOUGHT YOU WERE DEAD."
Heidel and Maveryck, with Grace still at his side, had found Kull and me as we descended the mountain. Maveryck was still carrying the staff of Zaladin. I was starting to hate that staff. It had already caused more trouble than it was worth.

"Why did you think such a thing?" Kull asked. "You know I've escaped tougher foes than the dragon."

"True. You should have been dead long ago."

"And I didn't need your aid to rescue me this time. I must be improving."

Heidel laughed. "Luck is the reason you escaped."

We walked away from the mountain and toward the light-rails. Earlier in the morning, we'd made it halfway down the mountain before Maveryck's wolf had spotted the dragon circling overhead. We'd hidden for more than an hour, watching as the wraiths searched for us. After the wraiths moved to another area of the mountain, we made our escape.

"Once we're out of her territory, she'll have a hard time tracking us," Maveryck had said.

We stayed under the cover of the tree canopy as much as we could, trading snow-covered ground for damp leaves that masked the sound of our footsteps, until we crossed the border between her land and ours.

By the time we made it to the light-rails, it was mid-afternoon. We hadn't stopped once to eat or rest, but I knew we couldn't afford to slow down. I breathed a sigh of relief when we finally climbed into a carriage.

The coach was everything one would expect from elven technology and luxury. Overstuffed, cream-colored cushions, soft, ambient lighting, and the gentle hum of the magical-mechanical engine were enough to lull me to sleep, yet I couldn't rest. I could hardly believe I'd finally made it out of the witch's castle. At any moment, I expected to wake up and find myself back in the palace, wandering through the maze of hallways, trying to find a way to open that cursed box.

Kull sat beside me, his face pensive as he stared out the coach's windows. I took his hand, and he gave me a small smile, then traced his fingers over the scars encircling my wrists. Not long ago, I'd been held prisoner by the bloodthorn, and the scars were an ever-present reminder of my enslavement. Kull bore no physical scars from his time in the witch's castle, but as he glanced at me, his eyes clouded with fear. What had she done to him?

"Kull, are you okay?" I asked quietly.

He smiled but didn't answer, then he kissed my knuckles and turned away from me to stare out the window once again. His silence disturbed me, but I wasn't sure what to do about it.

"You're both lucky to be alive," Maveryck said, breaking the tense silence. "Most who enter the witch's castle never escape."

"How *did* you escape?" Heidel asked.

"It wasn't easy," I answered. "The witch tried to make me open a box that would set Kull and me free, but it wasn't possible for me to open it, so I got creative."

"How so?"

"She destroyed Bloodbane," Kull answered.

"She did *what*?" Heidel's eyes widened. "And you're still speaking to her?"

"I'd rather have my life than my sword," he answered. "Which begs another question. Sister, where were you while I was imprisoned?"

Heidel cast a sidelong glance at Maveryck. "We were attacked by the wraiths. They'd nearly overpowered us when something strange happened with that staff. I don't know how to describe it."

Maveryck spoke up. "Its magic reacted with its reflection in the ice on the frozen pond where we were fighting, and it created a portal."

"A portal to where?" I asked.

"Earth Kingdom, as far as we could tell. When we returned,

the last remaining wraith was dead and we had the staff. After that, we returned for you."

"So you must have killed the wraith and taken the staff while you were on Earth?" I asked.

"It appears so. But now that we have it, we must be careful. If it can create portals on its own, then it is more dangerous than we imagined," Maveryck said.

"I've never heard of an object creating portals on its own," I said.

"Nor have I. There are many mysteries surrounding the talismans of the Madralorde brothers and many secrets that have been kept hidden for centuries. Now that we have it, we would be wise to keep it safe. Your stepfather will know what to do with the staff."

"Are we traveling to his mountain now?"

It occurred to me then that I had no clue where we were headed. As soon as we'd escaped the witch, I didn't care where we went as long as we headed as far away from the castle as possible.

"No, we won't travel to his mountain. Your stepfather is in the Wult lands for the wedding."

"Wedding?"

"Rolf is getting married," Heidel explained. "It all happened suddenly while you were in Earth Kingdom. The invitations had to be sent magically or else everyone would have missed the marriage."

"Are you sure my stepfather is there?" I asked. "The last I spoke with him, he was on a quest to find the lost sword of the Madralorde."

"I am certain he will be there," Kull answered. "His duties as sky king dictate that he attend the marriage of our nobles."

Outside, the carriage sped past mountains and onto open plains. Usually, I enjoyed seeing the mountains, but this time I couldn't wait to get away from them.

Were we really free from the witch? Was Kull free from her? I wasn't sure how much power she had away from her castle, and I also didn't want to find out.

"So Rolf is getting married," I said, trying to get my mind off darker matters. "When did this happen? And who is he marrying?"

Kull shrugged. "No idea."

"He's marrying a girl from the eastern clan," Heidel said. "He met her a month ago."

"A month? That was fast."

"It's not unusual for Wults to marry so quickly," Kull said. "To be honest, after my father's passing, it will be good to have a wedding in the family to lighten our spirits."

Outside the carriage windows, the sky darkened. If we were headed to the Wult lands, we'd most likely spend all night traveling.

My mind wandered as we drew closer to our destination. I'd slept for only a few hours at a time during the journey—I'd had too many mishaps on these carriages to feel completely comfortable. When the sky finally lightened, I glanced through the window to find low-lying gray clouds spanning fields of dry wheat husks. We sped so fast through the fields that the stalks blurred together.

"Still a few hours to go," Maveryck said quietly.

I turned to him. "I didn't realize you were awake."

"I don't sleep well on these carriages."

"Neither do I."

Grace shifted at his feet and let out a short whine, so he scratched her head.

"Not much longer," he said to her.

She rested her chin on her paws, and Maveryck shifted the staff out of her way. As he did, I noticed the runes etched onto its surface.

"How much do you know about that staff?" I asked.

"Not much. I do know that it was named after Zaladin, who was one of the Madralorde brothers. The legends don't all agree about the Madralorde talismans, and as of yet, no one knows for sure where the brothers found the magic to fuel the objects they created."

I studied the staff and found a bluish haze emanating from the worn wood, but the magic felt old and I feared to probe it further. The sensation was akin to touching brittle paper that would disintegrate if handled too much.

"It's been enchanted with elven magic, but I can't tell much more than that. Do you know how old it is?" I asked.

He shook his head. "There's a great deal of speculation on that topic as well. Some say the objects can't be more than three hundred years old, while others claim the Madralorde brothers lived before the Vikings arrived, more than fourteen hundred years ago."

"That's a large gap in time. Can't anyone narrow it down more than that?"

"No. When the Madralorde brothers died, they took all their knowledge with them. They hid their weapons; they destroyed their scrolls. No one even knows where their keep was located, or even if it actually existed. Not much remains of their knowledge, making it impossible to understand anything at all about them. The few surviving journals don't tell us much."

"When do you think they lived?" I asked.

"No idea, though seeing the staff now, I would say it's older than we suspected. These runes are written in an ancient elven language that hasn't been in use for more than two thousand years."

"Two thousand? That's a little older than the historians thought. But it doesn't make much sense. Wouldn't that wood be rotten after two thousand years?"

"With the proper spells in place, I believe it could last for several millennia."

I studied the staff, wishing I knew more about it.

"My stepfather said it had the power to control Theht."

"No, by itself it can't do such a thing. All seven items would have to be reunited, and even then, I'm not convinced it's possible."

"The elves think it's possible."

"True. But the elven queen is desperate, and she'll resort to extreme measures to get what she wants."

Beside me, Kull shifted and grimaced as if he were in pain. "*No*," he whispered in his sleep, but then he shifted again and the pain disappeared from his face.

"Has he always had nightmares?" Maveryck asked.

"I don't think so," I answered.

He eyed Kull. "The witch did something to him."

"Yes, she tortured him."

"No, she did something else—something to his mind."

"How do you know?"

Maveryck looked me in the face, his eyes intense as the sun's first rays streaked across the floor.

"It happened to one of my companions a long time ago. He didn't live long after his encounter with Silvestra. The nightmares were too much."

"You think the same thing is happening to Kull?"

"I believe so. There aren't many who escape the witch un-scathed."

"Can I help him?"

"No. Only he can undo what the witch has put into his mind."

My heart clenched. Theht had entered my mind, and it was already driving me insane. Had the witch done the same thing to him? I took his hand and gripped his fingers. I would not let anything happen to him. It had taken so long to get him back. Heaven help me, I would unleash every evil in the world just to bring him back to me.

Yes, you would, Theht's voice whispered.

I closed my eyes, pushing away the voice that lingered so close to my consciousness. Pondering those words would drive me insane, but the truth was hard to ignore. How far would I go to save him? Would I obey Theht? Would I become the Deathbringer?

The image of my magic connecting with the comet came to mind, and I felt as though I was there again, standing in the desert, watching my own powers bring about the destruction of the world.

"Is something the matter?" Maveryck asked.

I opened my eyes, only now realizing that my breathing had become erratic. My hands were clenched in a death grip around Kull's fingers, and I carefully pried them away, sur-prised I hadn't woken him.

"I'm worried about him," I answered.

"It's well that you are. But I would not worry too much. He's got a stronger constitution than my companion had, so he may beat it altogether. It's quite likely that the witch's influ-ence will take years before he succumbs to the madness."

"That's comforting," I said, hoping he heard my sarcasm. "Isn't there any way to help him? What if I killed the witch?"

Maveryck smiled, but I didn't like the condescending look he gave me. "That's one way to do it, I suppose. But I would advise against it."

"Why?"

"She guards the entrance to the unknown lands. If she were to die, it would unleash exponential evil into our world."

Save Kull or release evil—honestly, releasing evil didn't sound *that* bad.

Heidel stirred beside Maveryck. She gave him a small smile when she opened her eyes. Was it just me, or did her

106

cheeks look rosier than usual?

"Where are we?" she asked as she sat up.

"Nearing the Wultland border."

She cursed. "I hoped we'd be there by now."

Glancing out the windows, I found the Wult mountains looming in a hazy block of gray on the horizon. The jagged stretch of peaks extended from one end of the skyline to the other. I nuzzled into Kull's shoulder as I waited for our journey to end. His clothes still retained that familiar scent of sandalwood that calmed my nerves better than any sort of magic.

Hours later, the coach had crossed the mountains, and by mid-afternoon we'd finally arrived on the outskirts of the Wult capitol.

The keep sat away from the Wult city, secluded by forests, mountains, and a deep lake of sapphire water. We disembarked the carriage, carrying what little gear we'd managed to salvage from our quest to the witch's mountain, and made our way to the top of the hill where the Wult keep sat—an imposing structure of gray stone, soaring parapets, and red-and-gold flags that whipped back and forth in the breeze.

"The flags are new," I said as we trudged up the steep cobblestone path toward the keep's open portcullis.

"Yes," Kull answered. "They only display the flags on special occasions."

From the towers' tops came the call of trumpets. A crowd of people lined the road, some standing and others sitting on carts. Children skipped past us under the guarded eyes of their parents. A few people stopped to pay their respects to the king.

"When will the procession start?" an older, redheaded boy asked us.

"No idea," Kull answered.

We continued up the path and reached the castle gates. The guards recognized the king immediately, and an entourage of people clamored around him, crowding us and asking a million questions. Soon, I was separated from the rest of the group and ushered into a room where I was told to wait.

A servant arrived with food and a change of clothing, and I was instructed to bathe and dress. The bathwater was lukewarm, so I made quick work of cleaning up and dressing in a dark blue frock with a white mantle. As soon as I was ready, I left the room, hoping to find my stepfather. Frantic servants hurried up and down hallways, but I managed to stop one of the women as she walked past with an armful of folded linens.

"Sorry," I said, "but do you know if the sky king has arrived?"

"Aye, he's down by the lake last I heard. Are you planning to speak with him?"

"Yes, if I'm allowed."

"Ye'll have to do it quick. The ceremony starts in an hour. Oh, and I've still got these bed clothes to be put in the guest chambers." She bustled away, mumbling about the wedding preparations.

I wandered through an unfamiliar part of the castle until I found a stairway leading up to the main hallway. With all the commotion, I lost track of where I was going until I became completely lost and finally found a door leading to a courtyard outside.

On a slope behind the castle, I discovered white awnings had been erected, and beneath them were rows of tables piled with food. Wults sat and ate at the tables. Most of them drank mead and engaged in loud conversations. There were possibly more people outside than inside, and I was positive the entire Wult race had shown up for the wedding. I pushed past the bodies and finally found a trail leading down to the lake. Thankfully, there were no crowds on the trail, and I made my way down the path with the sounds of conversation fading behind me, replaced by the calming sound of waves lapping at the shoreline.

The trees' canopy shaded me from the sun, casting dappled sunlight on the leaf-strewn forest floor. Purple and green foliage fluttered in a gentle breeze, and I inhaled the scents of the forest—of fresh air that tasted of fall, with a hint of winter on the wind.

I could hardly believe I was here and not trapped in the witch's castle. Everything had happened so quickly, and escaping her had been a miracle. But were we truly free of her? Was Kull free of her?

Just as I spotted the deep blue of the lake through the trees, I heard two voices I recognized and stopped. Kull and Fan'twar.

"...several years since my father spoke of it."

"He was wise to tell you when he did. You know the implications of harboring such knowledge?"

"Yes, I'm afraid it's something that weighs on me."

The conversation stalled. What were they talking about? I remained in the forest for a moment longer, but they didn't speak any more, so I entered the clearing.

Fan'twar lay curled on the shoreline, basking in the sun with his massive head resting on his tail. It reminded me of the way my cat perched on his spot on the couch.

"Olive," Kull said, hugging me to his chest as I stood by him. "I'm glad you found us. It's madness back there. You're smart to hide here with us."

"You two are hiding?"

"For as long as we can. Until the others demand we return."

I turned to Fan'twar. "I'm surprised to find you here. Were you able to locate the sword?"

He grunted. "No, I have come to learn that it cannot be found."

"What do you mean it can't be found?"

"It took a bit of research, but after tracking the sword's history, I discovered it was taken by the druid Lucretian almost five hundred years ago. Neither he nor it have been seen since then."

Lucretian—how did I know that name?

"He was the first High Druid, correct? The one who spoke the Deathbringer prophecy?"

Fan'twar nodded.

"How did you know that?" Kull asked.

"Silvestra happened to mention it," I answered.

Kull's face darkened at the mention of the witch.

I turned back to Fan'twar. "Shouldn't this be a good thing? Doesn't it mean the elves won't be able to find the sword?"

"True, you are correct that it should be advantageous for our cause. However, I've also discovered the elves do not need the sword to bring Theht back to our world. They have already obtained five of the seven weapons, and they lack only the staff in order to summon the goddess. The sword is not necessary for the summoning—its use is for controlling Theht's powers."

"Could they control her without it?" I asked.

"It would be difficult, if not deadly, but I believe the elven queen would still attempt it."

My shoulders slumped. This wasn't the news I wanted to hear.

"I have to agree," I said, "Euralysia is determined. I wouldn't put it past her to attempt the summoning without the sword, even if it meant she couldn't control the goddess and blew up half the planet in the process."

"But we still have the staff. That counts for something,

doesn't it?" Kull asked.

"Yes. Without the staff, the elves are powerless to resurrect the goddess."

"Where is the staff now?" I asked.

"In the keep," Kull answered, "guarded at all times by thirty of my best men. There is no safer place in Faythander. The Wult stronghold has never been breached before, and it won't happen now. I refuse to let it happen under my watch."

I turned to Fan'twar. "What should we do now?" I asked. "Do you believe we should confront the elves even though they don't have the staff or the sword?"

"No. Battling the elves at this point would not be worth our time. We must focus on guarding the staff, and I still believe it would be prudent to search for the sword. If the queen did manage to somehow summon the goddess, only the sword would have the ability to stop her."

"The sword has the ability to stop Theht?" I asked, surprised.

"It has the ability to kill Theht, too," Kull said.

"How do you know that?"

Kull's gaze shifted around the clearing before he spoke. "Will you promise not to repeat what I tell you?"

"Of course," I answered. "You have my word."

What was with the cloak-and-dagger attitude? Kull wasn't usually one who kept secrets.

"I am the sword's protector," Kull said quietly.

"You?" I asked, shocked. "But... how? And if that's the case, then where is it?"

He shook his head. "Even I don't know, but my ancestors became the Madralorde sword's protector long ago. They were approached by Lucretian, who came to this very keep and asked them to protect the sword. They did so for many years, until one day, he returned for the sword and took it away. He said the Wult king would forever be the sword's keeper and told them that one day he would once again ask the king to take up the sword, and whoever wielded it would have the power to defeat Theht."

"Wow," I said, trying to wrap my mind around it. "But even you don't know where it is?"

He shook his head.

I pondered his words, recalling what I knew of the sword I'd once believed to be a myth. The only weapon more powerful than fate. The power to defeat Theht. It was almost impossible to believe, but if it were true, then it gave me more hope than I'd felt in a very long time. With Theht's presence still a constant fixture in my consciousness, would finding the sword somehow help me to remove it?

"If that's true," I said, "if Theht really can be defeated, then I think we should try to find it. What do we know of Lucretian?"

"Not much. He was a mysterious man, to be sure. He lived with the Madralorde brothers at one point and was an advisor to them until things went sour and he left."

"The Faythander version of Merlin. Yes, I remember the stories," I said with a sigh. I wasn't sure where to start looking.

"There is one who might know," Fan'twar said hesitantly.

"Who?" I asked.

"The elven queen."

"Hmm... I'm not sure she counts."

In the distance, from the castle, came the sound of trumpets.

"Well," Kull said, "the feast will be over if I don't leave soon, and I'll make the nobles mad if I don't at least make an appearance. Olive, would you like to join me?"

"Yes, I suppose. But can I have a few words with my stepfather?"

"Of course. Meet me in the clearing near the castle. I shall save you a seat." He gave me a quick kiss on the cheek and then walked away. After his footsteps disappeared, I turned to my stepfather.

"Fan'twar," I said, "Kull hasn't been the same since we escaped the witch. He won't tell me what's wrong, but I suspect the witch did something to him. Do you think she hurt him?"

He didn't answer, which worried me.

"Do you?" I repeated.

"Olive, I am very sorry you were captured by the witch. I feel I put you and your companions in grave danger, and for that, I apologize. It was never my intention for you to be captured, or for the king to endure what he did."

"Do you know what she did to him?"

"I know what she has done to others like him. It's possible she altered his mind somehow and showed him visions, but I do not know any more than that."

"What sort of visions?"

He shook his head. "I do not know."

"Can you fix him?"

"No, those are not powers I possess."

"Is there anything that can be done for him?"

"Yes, perhaps. You, Olive, may be just the person to help him. You have skills in restoring a healthy balance to those who have crossed worlds and forgotten their memories. Use your powers to help him, and you may be able to undo the witch's curse."

I nodded, wishing I shared his optimism when it came to my abilities. Would Kull ever be the same?

"If anyone can overcome the witch's curse, it is him. You have picked a noble soul to spend your time with. I can see he makes you happy. Has he mentioned his intentions to you?"

Intentions? I cleared my throat, suddenly feeling uncomfortable at our turn in conversation.

"Eh, no. He hasn't mentioned anything to me about his intentions."

Fan'twar nodded, as if he knew something I didn't.

"What?" I asked.

"I said nothing."

"No, but you gave me that look."

"What look?"

"You know—*that* look. There, see? You're doing it again."

He laughed, a deep, rumbling sound that made the pond water ripple.

"Why are you laughing?" I asked.

"No reason. You'd better go and enjoy the feast before the Wults eat it all."

I put my hands on my hips. "Did Kull say something to you about his intentions?"

"The Wults will have it all eaten soon if you do not make haste."

Eying him, I wanted to press the topic further, but knew it wouldn't do any good. He'd never tell me. I turned away and marched up the path back to the festivities.

Intentions? It made me nervous to consider what that could possibly mean. I had too much drama in my life to think of settling down, but still, if it were a possibility, I had to admit it made me happy. Then again, maybe I was overanalyzing the situation and hoping for too much. Kull had never once discussed marriage with me, and now with the witch meddling with his mind and the elves on the brink of controlling the world, I wasn't sure he ever would.

I made it back to the clearing and was relieved the crowd

had thinned, making it easy for me to spot Kull sitting with a group of Wults. Brodnik, the boisterous, opinionated Wult who'd traveled with us many times, was the only person I recognized at the table with Kull.

"Oy, Olive!" Brodnik called. "It's about time you showed up. We've nearly got all the bones picked clean."

Kull smiled as I sat beside him, and then he passed me a plate of roasted boarhound and a hunk of dark brown bread. As I took a bite of the meat, I had to admit, the Wult chefs were beyond talented at preparing a meal. The meat was so tender it melted in my mouth.

As I chewed, I noticed Brodnik had a chubby baby propped on his lap. He winced as the baby yanked his beard.

"Oy, stop that pulling," he said as he pried the baby's hand open.

"Is this your son?" I asked.

"Nay, this is my grandson Björn. He's my first grandchild."

"He's cute."

The baby cooed as his grandpa held him. He had hair as red as his grandfather's, two bottom teeth, and dimples that showed whenever he smiled.

"How old is he?" I asked.

"Nearly one year old come next week," Brodnik answered.

As I stared at Brodnik holding his grandson, it occurred to me that I'd never realized Brodnik had a family, but as I looked from one face to the other in the crowd sitting around us, with their red-gold hair and freckled noses, it hit me that not only did he have a family, but a large one.

"How many kids do you have?" I asked him.

"Nine," he answered, "including two that have passed, may Odin bless their souls."

"Nine?"

"Aye. Don't act so surprised, Miss Olive. That's an average family in our lands."

The baby started to cry, and Brodnik held him over his arm and patted the baby's back, then quietly sang a lullaby as if he'd done this millions of times before. The baby quieted.

Kull took my hand, and I glanced up at him. Did he intend to have a large family? If so, these were things I needed to know—there were many things I needed to know before he brought up the subject of his intentions. He'd told me before that there was much about Wult society I didn't understand, and I believed him.

The only way for me to learn more about Kull's world was to be here, interacting and living day-to-day with the Wults. Attending the wedding would accomplish that much, but deep down, I knew I would never really become a Wult. That thought made my heart sink. No matter where I traveled or what planet I lived on, I would never fit in.

Kull wrapped his arm around my shoulder as Brodnik continued his lullaby and the baby's eyes closed.

"Brodnik," Kull said, "you have a way with children. You should have been a nursemaid."

"Aye, I won't disagree with you on that one. I would have been perfectly happy to look after the children if I'd had my way, if there weren't always wars to fight and bellies to be fed. Olga would have preferred I stayed home and tended the babies—that is, until the babies grew into young people. Then I would give them back to her. It's the half-grown ones who cause all the trouble."

"I heard that," said a gangly girl sitting beside him. His daughter, I assumed.

From the castle's towers came the sound of the trumpets, and a group of servants hurried outside and bustled around, collecting the empty trays of food and clearing the tables. As they did, Fan'twar entered the clearing and stood with a commanding presence. He held so still he looked like a golden statue.

"Wedding's about to start," Brodnik said.

After the food was cleared away, we turned our attention to the castle doors. Two men wearing official-looking uniforms propped the doors open, and then they unrolled a long rug decorated with white tree branches and golden unicorns. They carefully maneuvered the rug across the footbridge and over the grass until they stopped under a white wooden trellis.

"Does the carpet mean something?" I asked Kull.

"It's a symbol of the path the couple will take throughout their marriage."

"Everything in the ceremony is a symbol," Brodnik added.

"It is? I guess I've got a lot to learn."

"We'll teach you." Kull winked.

The gangly young woman sitting beside Brodnik spoke up. "The branches on the rug are birch wood to symbolize the bride," she explained. Her voice had a know-it-all tone, and she reminded me of a kid who spent too much time indoors buried in books. "Birch is the symbol for motherhood and fertility," she continued, "while the unicorn represents the groom—a symbol of unselfishness and unity. The two symbols together are thought to bring good luck to a future marriage. After the ceremony, the couple will be given a similar tapestry to display in their home."

"A smaller one, I hope," I said.

"Aye," Brodnik said, "it would be mighty cumbersome to hang that on a wall, now wouldn't it?"

From the open gates, a procession of people walked down the carpeted path. They wore simple white robes, though most of them wore golden sashes or bodices with golden brocade over their clothing. The women wore their hair in elaborate braids accented with golden leaves and flowers. As the gathering reached the end of the carpet, they stood aside. A young girl came behind them, holding an odd-shaped wooden cup with two large handles on either side. The cup looked carved, though I couldn't tell more than that.

"The cup means something, I guess?" I whispered.

"Yes," Kull answered. "The cup is carved with the runic symbols for unity, and the two rams' heads are carved to form the handles, representing renewal. The bride and groom will both drink mead from the cup. They'll keep the cup in their home and drink from it again once every year on the day of their wedding anniversary."

The girl carefully placed the cup on a small table sitting under the trellis, and then she stood aside as an older woman walked down the path. A tarnished blade lay in her outstretched hands. She walked carefully, holding the sword with reverence until she reached the end of the carpet. Instead of joining the crowd with the others, she turned and faced the castle doors.

The air grew still, with only the sound of the wind as it brushed the tree branches overhead. Rolf walked out of the castle doors. He walked with a straight back, and his usual boyish grin was replaced with a solemn face and neatly trimmed beard. Instead of wearing questing gear as I'd always seen him in, he now wore a long, midnight blue robe, a silver-embroidered doublet, and polished boots. He was almost unrecognizable. I blinked to make sure it was him.

He stopped as he reached the lady with the sword, and then he also turned to face the castle doors.

The bride came last. There was no music to announce her arrival—unless one counted the sound of birdsong. As she walked down the carpeted path, several people in the crowd opened cages filled with maywelters—magical dragonfly-type creatures that lived near water. As the fae creatures flitted out, their bodies glittered in shades of aquamarine and seafoam green, reflecting in the long brown hair that spilled down the bride's back. The bride wore a golden-colored gown, and she carried a bouquet of dark purple flowers with yellow centers. I remembered Terminus calling them molfüsbane flowers.

The bride wore a contagious smile that reflected in her eyes. When she reached Rolf's side, she stopped, took his hand, and turned to the woman with the sword.

"Rolf's grandmother," Kull said. "Either she or the patron is called upon at the wedding to be the sacred sword-bearer. She will pass the sword to the wife of her grandson, who will hold it in trust for her own sons until they come of age."

I glanced up at Kull. "Is that how you received Bloodbane?"

"Yes, it was given to my mother by my grandamere, and I am—*was*—to pass it down to my sons."

"Oh." I shrank in my seat, feeling guilty for having destroyed the sword, despite knowing I hadn't had much of a choice.

The ceremony proceeded with the mead drinking, vow and ring exchange, and then laughter and clapping as the bride and groom were whisked back into the castle, where the party continued. As nightfall approached, with a growing headache and after a sleepless night, I wanted nothing more than a little solitude, so I escaped the feasting and dancing and made my way up the staircases into the less-crowded halls of the castle.

When I found Kull's library, I hefted open the solid, oaken doors, hoping to find some quiet inside. I immediately heard the sounds of shouting, so I turned away, but not fast enough.

"Olive, come in," came a woman's voice.

At first, I hesitated. What could I possibly do to get a moment's rest? I turned and entered the room. When I reached the other side of a large shelf, I came face to face with Kull, Heidel, and a woman whom I'd never met, although with her dark hair and sharp gray eyes, it was easy to tell that she and Heidel were unmistakably related.

"Olive," Kull said with a forced smile, "I'd like you to meet my mother."

CHAPTER Thirteen

KULL'S MOTHER GAVE ME A CURT NOD AS I ENTERED the library's open area at the center of the room. The cold marble tiles echoed under my booted feet, and though we were surrounded by towering bookcases, I felt isolated as I stood under the woman's gaze.

"Olive," she said, "I'm glad you've come. We were just discussing you."

"You were?"

I glanced at Kull, but he offered no explanation. Heidel also kept her mouth shut.

"Yes, we were," she answered. "My name is Halla, by the way, although I feel like we already know one another. I've heard so much about you."

"Oh. That's good, I guess."

"Yes, it is. It means we can avoid awkward small talk and get to the actual conversation." She had a musical voice, although I couldn't mistake her tone of warning. "Now," she said, "Kull has just informed me that the sword of his ancestors is lost to us forever, and that you are the one responsible."

I cringed. *This so isn't good.*

Kull spoke up. "She had a good reason."

"I don't care," Halla answered. "There is no greater act of betrayal than destroying a sacred sword. She would have known this if she were Wult."

She turned to me. "I want to hear how it happened. Maybe it will give me some sort of comfort to know how the deed was done."

My thoughts turned frantic. What should I say? I suddenly

117

lost the ability to make coherent words come out of my mouth.

"I never meant to destroy it. It was... because if I'd known, if there had been any other way... because if I'd had any other choice, I..."

She held up a hand, stopping me. "That's enough," she said quietly. "Olive, I know you are not familiar with our ways. You see merely a weapon. In truth, the ancestral swords are sacred family heirlooms. There were seventeen swords forged by Kull's great-great-great grandfather in the fires of the volcanoes of the outer isles. He gave the swords to his children and grandchildren. Before he died, he left each of his children and grandchildren with a warning. To destroy one of the swords would bring a great curse to our entire family.

"To this date, only one of our swords has been destroyed. Bloodbane."

Well, darn.

I would never in a million years dig myself out of this one. Any good impression I might have had on her was completely wasted.

"I'm sorry," I whispered. It was the only thing I could think to say.

She gave me a small smile before leaving the room and shutting the doors behind her.

My hands had grown clammy and my stomach soured. Worse, I had the insane thought that I would never marry Kull—not that he'd even asked—but if he were to ask, now it seemed he would never gain his mother's permission.

I slouched against a bookcase as the floor felt unsteady. Kull walked to me and wrapped his arm around my shoulder.

"This will blow over," he said.

"There, you see?" Heidel said as she walked toward us. "Olive, you should have saved the sword and left my brother to die."

I couldn't help but laugh. "Yeah, maybe you're right."

"We should have thought this through better," Heidel said. "You could have conjured a new sword with magic and Mother never would have known."

"She would have known," Kull answered. "She always finds out."

Heidel sighed. "Well, it was a thought at least."

"Don't let my mother worry you," Kull told me. "This wedding happened all of a sudden, and she's been doing nothing but making preparations since she found out about it. I'm pretty sure she hasn't slept for the last three days. She always says things she doesn't mean when she's like this. I can ask her for her blessing another time."

I glanced up at Kull. "Her blessing for what?"

He ran his thumb across my cheek. "Her blessing for..." he paused, "for Björn's one-year consecration."

"I see."

"All babies of noble blood are required to get the queen mother's permission before their consecration blessing. Did you think I would say something else?"

"No, Kull. I didn't. I never know what will come out of your mouth."

He gave me a lopsided grin. "You're so pretty when you're upset."

"I don't feel very pretty." Sighing, I stared at the floor. "I don't have much luck with your parents, do I?"

"Don't worry about it. As I said, give her some time and let her get some sleep. She'll come to her senses."

"Sure. She'll miraculously forgive me for destroying an irreplaceable family heirloom. Aren't you the one who told me she holds grudges?"

Heidel spoke up. "Only for a decade or two."

Kull shot her a dark look. "You're not making this any better."

"I'm only being honest."

"Stay out of this, Sister, or I may start asking you questions, like what happened between you and that thief in Earth Kingdom."

Heidel's face paled. "Nothing happened."

"No?"

"You know my memories were erased," Heidel said.

"Yes, but remembering memories and recalling emotions are two different things, aren't they?"

"Nothing happened," she ground out.

"Right. If that's true, then tell me why you two can't stop looking at one another, or why he's still hanging around the keep after returning the staff, when he should have left hours ago?"

"I'll not be spoken to in such a manner. You know I will never love any man ever again."

"Then why are you falling for him?"

"I'm not. I hate him."

"Are you sure about that?"

Heidel stormed out of the room and then slammed the doors behind her.

"You sure know how to push her buttons," I said.

Kull stared at the doors, working his jaw back and forth, the way he did when something was bothering him.

"That thief can't be trusted," he said. "He's got too many secrets, and no one seems to know anything about him. I don't even know where he comes from or who his family is, much less what he's capable of. I hope she's not losing her head over him."

"She's a grown woman. I'm sure she knows what she's doing."

"She is also still recovering from an abusive relationship that took her years to get out of. She can't afford to fall for someone who will hurt her again."

"Even so, it's her choice."

"But I'm her brother. It's my duty to protect her."

"Do you think she wants your protection?"

"She's getting my protection whether she wants it or not. I failed to protect her from Geth, and I will never let that happen again."

"Fine," I said, "but before you execute Maveryck, don't you think maybe you should find out who he is first?"

"Maybe."

"You never know—he could be completely harmless."

"A man who makes a living stealing from others is not harmless."

"True, but maybe you're worrying about nothing. She claims to hate him."

"Yes, you're right." He took my hand. "You're always right."

"I'm not *always* right."

He kissed my knuckles. "You're also very wise. It's why I love you." He sighed as he turned toward the doors. "They're dancing in the main hall and expecting me to make an appearance. Would you like to join me?"

"Not really. After attending the balls in the witch's castle, I've had enough of dancing."

"It will only take a minute, and then after that, I've been meaning to show you something. Would you like to follow me down to the river?"

"What's at the river?"

A twinkle lit his eyes. "It's a surprise. You'll see."

He led me out of the library and down the hall to a staircase that took us to the main floor where the party engulfed the entire bottom portion of the keep. I stayed close to Kull, noticing when two men appeared from the crowd and followed us. Glancing back, I recognized the man with the tall, thin frame, bad skin, and hawkish nose as one of Kull's bodyguards.

"You've still got those two trailing you?" I asked.

"Yes, unfortunately. Mother insists they follow me everywhere I go. I would argue the point, but she's impossible to reason with right now."

Sounds of lutes and harps mingled with laughter, and I found myself wishing for a Tylenol when Rolf appeared suddenly from the crowd. He clapped Kull on the shoulder and flashed his broad, still-boyish grin. Maybe the kid hadn't changed as much as I'd thought. That beard couldn't mask the naïveté in his eyes. While Rolf meant well, he'd always reminded me of a teenager with more testosterone than was good for him.

"I've found you, old man." He slapped Kull on the shoulder and barked a loud laugh, making my headache pound. "I'd almost started to think you were avoiding me."

"*Old* man? Is that what I am now?"

"Yes! As you're still a bachelor and I am not, I guess my status outranks yours, doesn't it?"

Rolf's bride walked from the crowd to stand by her husband's side. She was an attractive girl with a bright smile and long locks of dark hair, but I couldn't fathom what would drive her to marry Rolf. I only hoped she had great reserves of patience.

"Cousin Kull," Rolf said, "I'd like you to meet Brynhild, my bride."

"The pleasure is mine," Kull said as he took her hand.

She gave him a warm smile.

"Well," Rolf said, speaking with a little too much enthusiasm, "it looks like I've finally beaten you at something, eh cousin? You may have slaughtered the largest jagamoor on record, but you've yet to capture a wife as I have."

"I assure you, I am in no rush to find a wife."

"And it is well you aren't! You certainly have a kingdom to worry over, what with the elves and all. No time for courtship, I'm sure. Have you tried the boarhound?"

"Yes, it was delicious."

"Good, good—and Olive! You've come, too. I'm surprised to see you here. What brings you to the capitol?"

"I—"

Kull wrapped his arm around my shoulders. "She's with me."

Rolf raised an eyebrow. "Is she? What is she—your advisor or something?"

"A bit more than that, Rolf."

"Ah! Back together again. I'm very relieved to hear it. Let's just hope it lasts longer than last time, eh? Well, Brynhild and I are off to make more introductions. Married life can be so demanding."

Rolf laughed as he turned away from us to navigate through the crowd. I stared after him, wishing I could've given him a piece of my mind.

"Cocky little punk, isn't he?" I said.

"He's family."

"I still can't believe you gave the throne to him."

"It seemed like a good idea at the time."

The music and laughter grew louder, or maybe my headache grew worse, I wasn't sure which.

"Would it be all right if we go now?" I asked. "I think I need some fresh air."

"Yes, good idea."

He took my hand and led me through the crowd, but it took a full twenty minutes just to get outside, as every person in the kingdom felt that now was the time to stop and chitchat with the king. Kull handled it better than I could have, and I got a few polite hellos, but for the most part, I got the usual comments.

Is he with that half-breed again? I heard a few people whisper. *When do you think he'll settle down and find a real Wult woman?*

The gossip was enough to make me want to mouth off and tell everyone to mind their own damn business, but Kull thankfully led me outside into the crisp evening air, where my annoyance faded.

We walked along a path overshadowed by tall trees with branches that creaked in the wind. Brittle leaves curled from the branches, and as the wind tugged on the limbs, they were set free to spiral to the ground. The trail sloped downward, and we hiked the path with the sound of the leaves crunching beneath our feet.

The evening sun dipped toward the horizon as we traded the mountain path for a flat, rocky trail that led into an unfamiliar part of the forest. In the distance, I heard the sound of running water, and several times I spotted the river's white-capped, glacier water rushing over smooth stones.

"Where are you taking me?" I asked.

"You'll see."

Vines and green plants grew along the ground, choking the path and making it hard to see in the failing light.

"No one uses this trail anymore," Kull said, "but a hundred years ago, this was a major thoroughfare linking the castle with the village."

"Why doesn't anyone use it now?"

"You'll see."

He pointed straight ahead. I followed his line of sight and found a large structure hidden by vines.

"What is that?" I asked.

He took my hand and pulled me along with him. "I'll show you."

We walked to the building and then circled the outer wall, which was when I realized the structure was massive and seemed to stretch in all directions.

"What was this place?"

"The old abbey. It was built almost three centuries ago. No one uses it now."

He led me to a section of wall that had been cleared of vines, and we entered through an open doorway, where smells of damp earth filled the interior. His two bodyguards followed us, although I tried not to notice. Large, coral-colored flowers bloomed in some sections, while in other places, stones created floors and walls that looked almost untouched by time. In some places, the roof was still intact.

"What do you think?" Kull asked.

"It's interesting, but I'm still not sure why you brought me here."

"Because, Olive, you are standing on the site of Faythander's very first universal library."

"Library?"

"Well, soon-to-be library. I've already gotten the architects to take a look, and they say the foundation is still good. Most of the walls will have to be rebuilt, but give it a month or two, and it should be cleaned up and in good enough shape to start the construction. What do you think?"

"I... I'm a little shocked, to be honest."

"Shocked?"

"Yes. I had no idea you wanted to build a library. What prompted this?"

"I was running out of room in my own library, for one thing. Plus, I've had to keep Kitten locked up in a vault downstairs, which isn't really fair to anyone."

"Kitten—your pet T-Rex?"

"Exactly. My hope was to have the ancient dragon bones on display in a place where everyone could learn from their history, but as it is, the keep is hardly a museum. It's heavily defended and difficult for anyone but Wults to enter. My library is bursting at the seams, so I thought, what if I build a place where everyone could come? And not the way elves do it, where knowledge is kept under lock and key, but what if I made it a place open to everyone who wants to learn?" He ran his hands along one of the walls. The stones had turned a deep amber in the light from the setting sun. "And then one day, while I was out for a walk, I spotted the old abbey, and it just sort of hit me. This would be the perfect place for the library. What do you think?"

I smiled. It was good to see him happy about something.

"Yes, I have to admit, it would be a wonderful place for Faythander's library. I only hope the elves don't get involved."

"I can handle the elves. They've controlled knowledge in Faythander for far too long."

"Yes, and if they find the weapons of the Madralorde, they will be controlling it for a much longer time. Are you sure the elves will allow a place like this?"

"It doesn't matter. Elves do not rule Faythander."

"Not yet."

"No, not yet. And not ever if I have anything to do with it."

"Then we'd better find the sword before they do, or else they'll control more than just knowledge."

"Are you worried they'll find the sword?"

"I don't know. Fan'twar seems to think it's safe, but even he knows they're desperate enough to try and take Theht's power without it."

"Do you really think they would try such a thing?"

"Yes. It's only a matter of time before they find Tremulac Island and initiate the spell to call Theht back to our world. Even without the sword."

"What makes you so sure?"

"My dad's an elf. I'm part elf. I hate to admit it, but I know how elves work. They don't give up. Once the queen sets her mind to something, she'll have her way. We'd be smart to stay wary of her."

"I'm always wary of her."

In the distance, the sound of the thundering river echoed— the sound of something we couldn't see yet knew was there, just like the threat from the elves. Euralysia scared me. She'd caused the extinction of an entire race. She would stop at nothing to see her purposes fulfilled.

"Can you think of any way to stop her?" Kull asked me.

"Yes. Keep the staff safe. And I also think we should find the lost isle before she does."

"Do you know where to look?" he asked.

"No, but I do know who to ask. Maveryck knows more than he's telling us. If anyone knows where to start, it's him."

"Very well, when we return to the castle, I'll ask him." He grabbed my hand. "But before that, I've got one more thing to show you."

He led me through a weed-choked room to a tower. Half the walls had crumbled, but the stairs were still intact. We climbed up the stairs with the sounds of our booted footfalls echoing through the surrounding forest. Kull's two body-guards trailed behind.

The stairs spiraled up the tower, and I ran my hands along the warm stones to keep my balance. As the last rays of light disappeared completely, leaving only the bright glow of the moon to light our way, we finally made it to the top.

When I stepped onto the floor beneath the partially open roof, I caught my breath. The view was more than I'd expected. The towers of the Wult keep rose in the distance, surrounded by white-capped mountain peaks. Moonlight reflected off the river as it snaked down the mountain. Treetops swayed gently in a breeze heavy with the rich scent of sap. Above us, the stars twinkled red and blue, brighter than I'd ever seen them before, so close I wanted to reach out and touch them.

"This," Kull said, "will become the observatory. We'll build a telescope that will allow us to see the stars, the planets, and distant galaxies. The elves may have built a station up there somewhere on the moon, but we'll be the first to see if the rumors are true."

I stared at the moon as it glowed over the forest. Its distant light hinted at the secrets it harbored.

"Do you think it's true that the elves built a station up there?"

"No idea. But someday soon, I hope to find out."

A gust of wind brushed a few strands of hair across my face. Kull reached out and tucked them behind my ear.

"You look so beautiful in the moonlight," he said. "Almost as if..."

"As if what?"

"Nothing. Never mind."

"Nothing? Tell me."

He smiled and leaned forward, pressing his lips to my ear. "Almost as if you were made of magic."

An explosion came from the Wult keep's towers. A giant orange fireball ignited the topmost parapet, and in its glow, I saw the silhouette of a silver dragon.

Kull's face fell. All the happiness I'd seen in him disappeared, replaced once again with the haunted look—a look conjured from his nightmares.

"Silvestra has returned," he said quietly.

CHAPTER *Fourteen*

I RAN WITH KULL DOWN THE STAIRS BUT FELT THAT NO matter how fast we went, it wasn't fast enough. Time seemed to slow down as we raced up the hilltop to the castle. My only thought was of Kull's family trapped inside the burning castle.

When we neared the keep, the dragon's shrieks cut through the air. The silver dragon flew over the towers, pumping her massive wings that seemed to spread from one end of the horizon to the other. A pillar of flame burst from the dragon's mouth, igniting the keep's topmost tower.

A group of people had gathered outside the castle walls. We pushed through the crowd, though as we neared the gates, I wasn't sure what we could do to stop the dragon. She would burn the castle to the ground without a second thought.

My heart raced as we finally made it through the main gates. As we raced for the keep's entrance, the dragon screamed, and I stopped when I saw another form swoop down and block out the stars.

Fan'twar barreled into the dragon, knocking her back. The light cast from the flaming tower reflected off his gold and her silver scales. As the dragons fought, my heart clenched. Fan'twar hated violence. It had been the norm for his kind for so long, and he'd tried so hard to erase that stigma from their past, but now it looked as if he had no choice but to fight.

The silver dragon snapped her massive jaws, barely missing Fan'twar's neck. He dodged to the side, then swung his tail and hit her side, knocking her off balance. She struck at him again, but he moved away.

Overhead on the tower, the flames had been doused, leaving large clouds of smoke to replace the flames. The sharp scent of burned wood filled the air and was carried through the valley on the breeze. Bright embers flitted on air currents, drifting away from what remained of the tower.

The crowd of people grew larger as everyone fled the keep to the open courtyard. Kull's mother and Brodnik were among them. The queen's cheeks were smudged with soot, and she couldn't seem to stop coughing as they limped outside.

"Kull," she said, grabbing his arm.

"Mother, what happened?"

"I... I was in the tower when the witch appeared." Her coughing fit started again, and she motioned for Brodnik to continue.

"The witch demanded to speak to you and Olive. When we couldn't find you, she transformed and blasted a hole right through the tower."

Kull clenched his fists as he stared up at the battling dragons.

"Have you a sword, Brodnik?" he asked.

"Aye." He pulled a short sword from a scabbard at his waist and handed it to Kull. "I doubt that blade will do anything against a dragon. You don't mean to go and fight her, do you?"

"I will do what I must."

I grabbed Kull's arm. "What are you doing?"

"What does it look like?"

"Kull, no! She wants you back. It would be better to hide."

"Olive," he said calmly, though I saw the panic in his eyes, "don't you see? She'll never stop until she has me. We never escaped her at all. There is only one way to the end this."

"But it's suicide. You're no match for a dragon."

"Then you'd best stay here," he said and entered the castle.

"Brodnik," Kull's mother said, "we must go after him. We can't let him confront the dragon."

Brodnik stared up at the two battling dragons, his face pensive. "There's not a word I can say to convince him otherwise."

"Then let me speak to him." She choked as she spoke, and I knew her lungs were possibly damaged from inhaling so much smoke. "He can't do this," she said. "I've already lost his father..." Her voice wavered. "I can't lose him, too."

"Nay, it's too dangerous in there, and you need a physician."

"But someone has to stop him!"

128

I spoke up. "I'll go," I said, my eyes meeting hers. "I can stop him."

"You, Olive? But, no, I didn't mean you. It's too dangerous for you."

"It's all right. I've had a little experience dealing with dragons. And with your son—who is more stubborn than the dragons, I assure you. I'll make sure he doesn't kill himself up there."

"Are you sure?" she asked.

"Yes." I turned to Brodnik, speaking quietly. "Make sure she sees a physician soon."

He nodded, and then I backed away to enter the castle. Most of the people had cleared out, making the place eerily quiet as I took the stairs up to the topmost tower. The beating of my heart thudded loud in my ears. The acrid scent of smoke grew stronger the higher I climbed.

As I passed one floor and then another, the dragon's shrieks pierced the stillness. I reached the top of the tower and entered an enormous, circular room, where a few piles of wood still smoldered, casting their flickering lights over Kull's silhouette. He stood at the center of the room, while above him, through the room's ruined, open roof, the two dragons fought.

Against the backdrop of stars, the two massive creatures attacked one another. Sounds of ripping flesh echoed through the tower. Occasional bursts of flames blinded me as the dragons shot fireballs at one another.

Fan'twar drove his massive head into Silvestra's chest. She shrieked as she tumbled from the sky, landing with a thunderous crash on the tower's floor.

The dragon's body blurred, and soon we no longer stood over a dragon, but a woman. Silvestra lay before us, bleeding and panting for breath. Her clothing was ripped and tattered in places. Blood dripped down her face, and she wiped it away from her eyes. Sweat slicked her dark skin.

Fan'twar landed beside her. My stomach soured as I took in his injuries. Several gashes looked deep enough to puncture organs.

"Why have you come here, Silvestra?" Fan'twar demanded.

She spat at him, though her breathing was still too labored for her to speak. "This," she said and pulled something from her robes. She tossed the magic box at his feet, and it landed with a clatter on the tower's floor.

"What is this?"

"A lotus cube. It is meant to test the magical strength of a practitioner. Your ward had but to break the spell and she would have freed herself and her companion. Instead, she tricked me and stole him from my castle. I will have my vengeance, Fan'twar."

She stood slowly, and before I had a chance to blink she was at my side, her cold hand wrapping around my neck. The feel of her flesh sent shivers down my spine.

"Her blood is mine," she said.

Kull pointed the sword at her. "You will not have her."

"You cannot stop me, Wult."

"Silvestra," Fan'twar shouted, moving closer to us. He held the cube in his claws. The faint glow of the skull illuminated his face. "There is dark magic in this stone. How did you intend for my ward to break through its spell?"

"It should have been a simple task for her."

"She possesses no black magic, and she never has. I fail to see how she could have ever accomplished such a feat."

"She could have! It is within her power." Her nails cut into my skin as she wrapped my neck tighter. "How else will the Deathbringer prophecy be fulfilled if not with the black arts?"

"You are making assumptions," Fan'twar said. "The prophecy mentions nothing about black magic."

"It does. See for yourself." She flung a fireball at the floor where it exploded, a deafening sound that thundered through the room. When the fireball died down, words written in flame appeared on the floor.

Marked by death from the beginning—she will come in flame and ash, wielding the fire gifted to her of her fathers. She will cross worlds and mend the rift. She will bring death to the unbelievers, life to those marked by the ancient one. Her life will bring death, for she is the Deathbringer.

"There, that is proof. How can you deny it?"

"I fail to see how this proves your point."

"I will have my vengeance," she said. "It is well within her abilities to break the spell, and she tricked me. I cannot allow this to go unpunished. You know this, Fan'twar. It is our way. We have never allowed injustice. You of all dragons know such things. I demand retribution. She destroyed the sword gifted to me by the Wult, and then she took him from me. Never have I been so wronged. Her blood is mine."

My heart pounded in my chest. She wanted my death,

and there was nothing anyone could do to stop her. Not even Fan'twar had the ability to break his own rules. No matter how I looked at it, there was no way out of this situation.

Fan'twar's pain-filled eyes met mine. "Is it true? Did you destroy the sword?"

"Yes," I answered quietly. "It's true."

"Was there no other way?"

"No. I tried to open the box but couldn't. She would have taken him if I hadn't destroyed the sword. I'm sorry."

"She is mine," the witch said. "She has broken a sacred trust between us. She will meet her punishment."

Silvestra struck out with her magic. Icy black bands wrapped my shoulders and legs. I gasped as the magical bands cut into my flesh, piercing my skin with a pain that radiated into my nerve endings. The bands buzzed with a magical energy that absorbed my magic. I could feel my energy seeping into the bands, a slow trickle that would soon take my life.

Kull lunged at the witch with the sword, but she blasted a bolt of magical energy at him, hitting his chest. He fell unconscious to the floor as the sword clattered uselessly away.

"Kull," I called out, but as I did, the bands tightened, squeezing the air from my lungs. Tears sprang into my eyes as my vision blurred. I didn't want to die this way. The only thought that gave me comfort was knowing that with my death, the Deathbringer prophecy would never be fulfilled.

Fan'twar, I thought, *thank you for... for being my parent when no one else would be.*

I knew he couldn't hear me, but there were so many things I wanted to say and not enough time to say them. He was the only creature who'd cared for me when I was defenseless. He'd only ever shown me love and kindness. I couldn't recall a time when he'd raised his voice to me. Betraying his own kind was a regret that would follow me to the grave.

"Silvestra." Fan'twar stepped forward, his massive, spike-rimmed head blurring in my vision. "Stop this now. You must stop."

"You have no power to stop me. You know this."

The magic bands wrapped around my throat, cutting deep into my neck, burning through my skin, absorbing my magic. Energy buzzed through my ears. How long would I have to suffer before I died?

"I will not let you take her life," he said.

"But you must."

"No. There is another way. You will take me instead."

The room grew quiet. The band's buzzing stopped, although they didn't loosen and I still couldn't breathe.

"You will give yourself?"

"Yes." He didn't hesitate answering.

"You would die to save her?"

Fan'twar, no! Please, don't do this.

"I will give my life in exchange for hers. You have my word."

Gasping, I wanted to scream to make him stop. Faythander needed him. Without him, the elves would win. Theht would win. He was the only thing keeping evil from the world. If he died, everyone lost. Didn't Silvestra know this?

The blackness engulfed me, sucking away my last reserves of energy just as the bands disappeared and I fell to the ground.

"We are agreed," I heard Silvestra say before I lost consciousness.

CHAPTER
Fifteen

"SHE'S ALIVE," SOMEONE SAID.
As I opened my eyes, I found Kull standing over me. Sunlight streamed into the tower through the ruined roof, making me squint.

My first coherent thought was of the pain. Everything hurt. I glanced at my arms and found bright red welts where the witch's magical bands had burned me, and I lightly touched my neck where I felt the same sort of wounds. Inside, I felt even worse, like everything was raw and exposed, the feeling of having my magic stripped away.

My second thought was of Fan'twar.

Sitting up, I tried to speak. "My stepfather?" My voice was so hoarse I wasn't sure anyone had heard me.

Heidel stood near her brother, although I couldn't find Fan'twar. I searched the room but found only mounds of broken stone and smoking, splintered beams strewn across the floor.

"The sky king is gone," Heidel said. "The witch took him."

My already upset stomach soured even more. How had this happened? Why had he traded himself for me? I pushed the tears back as best as I could, but losing him hurt even worse than the pain of having my magic stripped away.

Kull wrapped his arm around my shoulder. "He was still alive when she took him. And she left us with a message. There may be a way to bargain for him, although we've no idea how to decipher her words. We'd hoped you would know more."

"A message?"

"Yes. Maveryck is in the library now, trying to decipher its

133

meaning."

"Maveryck? Why is he still here?"

"To help us, I suppose."

"Why does he want to help us?"

"No clue. Perhaps the thieving business took a downturn."

If I hadn't felt like dying, I would have laughed.

"Take me to him," I managed.

"Are you sure?" Kull asked. "You've been passed out for quite a while. Wouldn't you like to rest for a moment?"

"No, help me up. Please." I didn't care that I felt like death. If there was a way to bring my stepfather back, I had to know.

Kull helped me stand, and together, we made it out of the tower and down the stairs as Heidel followed us. Several people rushed past, carrying towels and medicated ointments. Shouts came from downstairs, and I found the Wults gathered and speaking in heated tones. Some of them cast wary glances at Kull as we dodged the group and entered a narrow hallway.

"They're talking about you, Brother," Heidel said.

"I don't care."

"They're blaming you for the abduction of the sky king."

"Let them. If they want to be fools and blame me for something I didn't do, then let them."

"Euric, the man from the inn, is among them. He's back to spouting treason."

Kull sighed. "I will deal with it later. For now, we've got bigger problems to worry over."

We made it through the hallways and to the library, where we found the doors propped open and several people inside. Kull's mother and Maveryck were both hunched over a table.

My head pounded by the time we made it inside. Kull found a chair and placed it by the table, then helped me sit. The room spun around me, and I had to blink several times to make the dizziness go away.

"Olive, I'm glad you're here," Maveryck said. "Maybe you can help us understand this better."

I wasn't sure what I'd expected, but seeing the magical box on the table wasn't what I had envisioned of the witch's message. How would I ever get away from that accursed thing?

"Do you know what this is?" Maveryck asked as he scooted the box toward me.

"Of course she doesn't," the queen answered for me. "Leave her to rest. She's in no position to answer questions."

"Actually," I said, "I do know what that is. It's a lotus cube, and it can only be opened with black magic."

"Are you sure?"

"Yes. Very sure."

"Then, do you know what this means?"

I reluctantly took the stone from Maveryck and studied its facets. The image of the skull I had seen earlier had changed into the shape of an oval with swirling gold patterns inside.

"It's changed from when I saw it last. It could mean anything."

Maveryck turned to the books stacked on the table. "I can't find any symbol that matches it. If we are to set the sky king free, then we need to know that symbol's meaning."

I was glad I was already sitting, or the daunting implications of my stepfather's situation would have completely overwhelmed me. I rested my chin in my hands, feeling dizzy and disoriented, my stomach ready to heave its contents, and worse, sick to death of dealing with the witch.

"When she held Kull prisoner, she wanted me to open his collar with a key she kept inside the box, but at the time, each facet had a different symbol. I was able to break through most of the spells using various forms of magic, except I couldn't break through the last symbol because I would have needed black magic to do it."

"Is there black magic in the stone now?" Maveryck asked.

I wasn't sure my own magic would function long enough to let me find out, but I knew I had to at least try. Holding the stone in my hands, I breathed deeply, then focused on the magic inside, letting its powers call to me. Inside, I found an intense swirling vortex of bright emerald magic.

"It's dragon magic," I said, "and very powerful, too."

"Dragon magic?" Kull asked.

"Yes. But that's odd, because there was only black magic before. Why did it change?"

Maveryck took the stone from me. "It's my guess that since you failed the last test, she's given you a new one. You're sure you've never seen this symbol?"

"Yes, I'm sure. When I was solving the last test, I found the clues in her garden, but I don't think we'll be able to get into her garden this time."

"Nor would I want to," Kull added.

"Me either."

"Do you think it's possible to solve?" Heidel asked.

"I don't know. When she tested me earlier, she seemed so

certain I would be able to break the spell. I think she honestly believed I could do it."

"Then it makes sense why she would be so upset," Maveryck said. "If she thought you could break the spell, then she believes you purposely tricked her."

"But I didn't. I only did what I had to do to save Kull."

Maveryck placed the stone at the table's center atop an open book. "Regardless of what happened at her castle, we now have a new mystery to solve. What is this symbol, and how do we use it to free your stepfather?" He looked at the group gathered around the table. "Any suggestions?"

Heidel crossed her arms. "I have a suggestion," she said. "Why don't you leave and let us figure this out for ourselves."

"Leave?" he smirked. "I was staying here for you, Heidel. I am deeply hurt at your suggestion."

"I hope your suffering won't last too long," she said drily.

"It won't," he said, "because I've decided to stay and help you."

"Wonderful."

"I knew you would be happy about my presence here." He winked.

Were they flirting? Honestly, I'd never pictured those two together. Could it be possible they had a thing?

Kull cleared his throat, breaking the awkward silence.

"Perhaps it's not a magical symbol at all," Kull said.

"What do you mean?" his mother asked.

"Maybe it's a symbol of something else—a landmark or something."

"You've got a point," I said. "For one thing, there really aren't many written magical symbols."

"And the ones that are written can vary between practitioners," Maveryck said.

"If that's the case, then how will we find its meaning?" Heidel asked.

"We'll have to think creatively, I suppose. I don't really have a better answer," I said.

"Brother," Heidel said, "we must gather an army and storm her castle. That is the only way to save the sky king."

"No," Maveryck said. "Violence is not the solution. If we want to bring the sky king back unharmed, then we will have to play by her rules."

"But her rules aren't fair," Heidel said, a hint of exasperation in her tone.

"They *are* fair," Maveryck said, "they just aren't logical." He picked up the box. "You know," he said, turning to one of the books. "The symbol does remind me of something I've seen before." He flipped through the pages until he stopped and pointed to a picture. Looking closely, I found the picture of a bright turquoise egg with veins of gold sparkling through its shell.

"A dragon egg?" I asked.

"Yes. It's rumored that Silvestra had an egg stolen from her, but that was a long time ago."

"A dragon's egg?" Kull said. "You might be on to something."

"Yes," I said. "I could try to open it with dragon magic."

"Do you feel well enough to use your powers?" Kull asked.

"It's a simple spell. I'll be okay."

I focused on my magic, breathing deeply, and let it flow naturally to the surface. When I felt ready, I whispered the spell to call dragon magic. It flowed in a silvery-green glow from my fingertips into the symbol on the box, but the magic disappeared as it touched the stone.

When the magic left me, dizziness clouded my vision, and I focused on taking deep breaths just to stay conscious. Kull knelt by my side and took my hand.

"Are you all right?" he asked.

"I will be. Give me minute."

"I think that's enough magic for one day," Kull said.

"I agree," the queen answered. "Obviously, we're getting nowhere. Kull, perhaps it is best to do what your sister suggested. I will sanction a small squadron of men to infiltrate the witch's castle and free the sky king. It's imperative that we get him back before the elves learn what happened. They are already trying to rule the whole of Faythander as it is, and without the sky king in their way, they'll sack every nation not willing to bend to their laws. We must get him back. We do not have time for mysteries and riddles."

"Mother," Kull said, "I do not disagree, but I'm afraid infiltrating her castle would be a huge mistake. She would find us and either kill us or make us her wraiths. Even with my best men, it is not a mission we could accomplish. If we are to free the sky king, our safest bet is to learn the true meaning of this stone's symbol."

"But how?" the queen asked. "How much longer must we try until the witch grows impatient and does something drastic? Like kill the sky king?"

"We may be closer than you realize, Your Majesty," Maveryck said. "We know the stone is powered with dragon magic, meaning the spell must have some connection to dragons. From what I can tell, the symbol most likely represents a dragon's egg. Furthermore, I've done quite a bit of research on dragon eggs as they are quite valuable in Faythander's black markets. I have a contact in the Godiaz Desert who is an expert on dragons and their eggs. If we want to know the meaning of this symbol, it is my belief we should seek him out."

The queen was silent for a moment, but then nodded. "Very well. I'm glad someone has come up with a viable solution. You must make haste to the desert. Kull, I'd like you to lead this expedition. It will give you an excuse to leave the keep."

"Why would I need an excuse to leave the keep?"

"Because there are enough rumors being spread about you as it is. If you stay here with your present company, the rumors will only grow worse. It's best if you leave."

"What's wrong with my present company?"

She sighed, glancing at me. "Must you ask?"

Heidel spoke up. "The rumors are unfounded, Mother. Those men speak of treason."

"They speak of treason because word has gotten out that he has lost the sword of his ancestors, and that the Earthlander woman destroyed it. For the time being, it would be best for him to leave the keep while we come up with some way to restore his good name. If not handled properly, this could very well lead to the unseating of the king."

The queen turned to her son. "I only ask that you be safe. The Godiaz is not a place to be taken lightly. You know I could not bear to lose you, too." She left the room without another word, her footsteps echoing until they disappeared down the hall.

Kull turned to Maveryck. "How long will it take us to journey to this contact?"

"His compound is in the heart of the desert on the eastern peninsula, so it won't take long if we use the rails. But," he glanced at me, "we'll have to proceed with caution once we arrive. Olive, you'll have to keep the truth of your identity a secret. We'll tell him you're a merchant or the like, and you're not to admit you're with Kull—and we certainly can't let him know of your connection to the sky king."

"Why?"

Maveryck threaded his fingers together. "Let's just say they've had dealings in the past. It would be best not to draw attention to your identity. Jahr'ad is suspicious of outsiders, and his compound is hidden. I'm confident I can get us inside, but he'll most likely demand you be blindfolded in order to enter."

Kull crossed his arms. "Blindfolded? I'm liking this less and less."

"Yes, but it will be worth it. Jahr'ad has more knowledge about dragon eggs and their black-market value than anyone on Faythander. He's the man we need if we're going to learn more about the symbol on the box—and ultimately return the sky king to us safely."

"But you said he hates the sky king," Heidel said. "Why would he want to help us?"

"Simple," Maveryck answered. "Because we'll pay him."

"Pay him how much?" Kull asked.

"As much as it takes, I assume."

"I don't like this," Heidel said. "We're just to follow you all the way to the Godiaz, be taken prisoner and blindfolded, and then trade all of our coin to some scoundrel because there's an off chance he'll know something about the stone? What makes you think we'll follow you on such a mission?"

Maveryck stood. "Because you have no other viable options. That's why."

"Yes, we do. We'll storm the witch's castle as I suggested earlier."

"That option doesn't count."

Heidel's cheeks reddened. "It counts more than your idea."

"Heidel, please," Kull interjected, "he's trying to help us."

"Yes, he's helping us lose all our money to some thief. I'm not so sure he won't be pocketing the money himself."

Maveryck laughed. "I assure you, I've no need of your money. Besides, I never made mention that Jahr'ad traded in money."

"Then what does he trade in? Looks? Because that's the only thing *you've* got to bargain with."

Maveryck gave Heidel a roguish grin. "You like my looks, do you?"

Heidel blushed. It was very possibly the only time I had ever seen her face turn such a heated shade of red. "I... I didn't say that," she answered, stumbling over her words.

Maveryck only smiled.

"I'm leaving," Heidel said. She turned and stormed out of the room, slamming the doors behind her.

"Well," Kull said, "two members of my family have been offended before noon, and I wasn't the one to do it. I'm moving up in the world."

CHAPTER
Sixteen

I WALKED WITH KULL DOWN THE HALL IN THE WULT KEEP, trying to ignore my growing headache, trying to stay positive about my stepfather's abduction, and failing miserably at both. We both carried our traveling packs, deciding to leave this evening to head for the desert. Maveryck and Heidel had agreed to meet us at the rails.

"At least one good thing came from our meeting with Maveryck," Kull said.

"Yeah, what's that?"

"I don't think I have to worry about my sister being interested in him."

"Really? Did you not see how red her face turned before she stormed out? She's got a crush on him for sure."

"Perhaps. But she's too proud to ever admit such a thing. She'd never allow him to get close to her now. She's got a reputation to keep up."

"I wouldn't be so sure." I rubbed my temples, hoping a little food would clear up my headache. We turned down another hall, where we found a small door at the end leading to the kitchen. A long wooden counter took up the center of the space, and Kull helped me sit on a stool by the butcher block. Smells of warm buttered bread and herbs with a hint of lemon made my stomach growl. Kull handed me a slice of bread, then ladled two bowls full of a dark, thick stew that smelled heavenly.

We sat at the makeshift table and ate. Between bites, Kull focused on me.

"Are you ever going to tell me what has you bothered?"

My spoon stopped halfway to my mouth. I wasn't ready to tell him, but then, I probably never would be. Maybe it would help if I told him the truth.

"I don't really know how to say this," I said, "but when I was trapped in the cave with the bloodthorn, Theht came to me, and she... put a piece of her consciousness inside my mind."

"A piece of her consciousness?"

"Yeah, I know it sounds odd. But I think she was trying to keep tabs on me so she could understand me better, so that when the time came..." I sighed, unable to finish the sentence. "Either way, I don't like it. My magic has been growing weaker, and I haven't felt like myself since then."

He eyed me. "And this is why you asked me to keep my distance?"

I nodded, feeling a bit of relief after finally telling him, but also wondering if he would still accept me.

He rested his hand atop mine. "You should have told me sooner."

"I guess, but it's not an easy thing to admit."

"I can understand that," he said, and I knew he was still keeping from me what had happened to him in the witch's castle.

"What about you? Have you recovered from your ordeal at the castle?"

Fear flashed through his eyes, but it only lasted a moment, and then he smiled as if to reassure me.

"Of course."

"You're lying."

"Maybe, but can you blame me? You've already got enough to worry about. I'm only trying to keep you from worrying about more."

"Still, you should tell me. I told you my secret, didn't I? It will help if you tell someone."

He rested his chin in his hands. "Millions of miles away from Earth, and still you're the psychologist."

I took his hand. "It's a habit," I said. "You'll have to get used to it."

He kissed my fingers. "I hope to have many, many years to do just such a thing."

My heart leapt at his touch. Sometimes I still had trouble accepting that he'd chosen me. But I saw pain in his eyes and knew I couldn't rest until I knew he was okay.

"Kull," I said, "you should tell me what happened at the

castle. It's better if you don't keep it in. Trust me on this one."

He shook his head. "It's not important."

"If that's the case, then tell me what happened."

"Olive, you've already got enough to worry about. You don't need to worry about my problems, too. I assure you, I'm fine."

He grabbed a few loaves of bread and wrapped them in cloth, then found his bag and packed it with the bread, some dried meat, and a few hunks of cheese. I wasn't ready for another journey, but the thought of losing my stepfather drove me forward.

We left when evening approached. My heart felt heavy as I walked away from the keep. It was one of the only places where I felt safe, but now, after the witch had taken Fan'twar, I wasn't even sure I felt safe there anymore.

Kull and I took a path leading to the light-rail. A misty rain drizzled around us, and I pulled my cloak's cowl over my head. We found Heidel and Maveryck waiting by a light carriage, although Grace was nowhere in sight. Through the dense fog, a halo of orange glowed from the coach, yet the light did nothing to settle my unease.

Before boarding the carriage, Maveryck turned to stare at each of us. Under the shadow of his cowl, his face looked ghostly, his eyes gleaming with a twinkle of silver. Moments like this made me wonder who exactly the man was.

"Perhaps I should have mentioned it sooner," he said, "but I feel I need to warn you about Jahr'ad. He's not to be trusted. In fact, I only take us there as this is the direst of circumstances and we have no other choice. It's quite possible that I will be putting your lives in danger, and for that, I deeply apologize."

Heidel crossed her arms. "And you waited until now to tell us? What if we refuse to go with you?"

"That is your choice. You may leave if you wish."

"Never. You underestimate us, Maveryck. We've dealt with cheats and thieves before. We can handle it."

"Very well. But it may be best if you follow my lead once we get there. Challenging Jahr'ad's authority will only make this worse."

"What makes you think I would challenge him?"

"Call it a hunch."

His smirk looked almost seductive as he focused on Heidel, but the moment only lasted a second, and then he turned to the carriage as the doors slid open. After climbing inside, I took a seat near the window. The coach was warm and dry, although the soft cushions and ambient light weren't enough to calm my racing heart.

As we settled in for the long journey, the coach's doors closed and, with the speed of thought, raced eastward. Outside, there was nothing to see but the swirling mist, and beyond that, darkness. Only the quiet whooshing of the carriage and sound of the pattering rain broke up the silence.

"Get as much rest as you can," Maveryck said. "I doubt we'll get the chance to rest once we arrive."

With my mind in an uproar, I wasn't sure I would get any rest at all. But soon, my mind wandered and my eyes closed, and I knew I was dreaming when Theht came to me.

In my dream, I found her sitting in my father's old office at my mom's house. Behind her, through the window, thick fog covered the garden. Only the gray silhouette of the small bird fountain was visible through the mist.

The goddess looked more human than I remembered, and I wondered if her appearance had any significance. She still wore the same red armor, and her skin was made of the same orange scales. But her eyes. Something was different. I almost felt as though I were looking in a mirror.

"Kull won't tell you what happened in the witch's castle, will he?" Theht said.

"No. I'm worried about him. But then again, I'm worried about a lot of things."

"You're right to be worried. There is a reason Silvestra was chosen to guard the gate to my lands. She wields magic more powerful than any other creature on Faythander. Not even your stepfather has the ability to stop her. He's only alive now because she wishes for an exchange, but not even that will appease her for long."

My heart weighed heavily in my chest as I thought of losing Fan'twar. He'd always been there for me. I couldn't go on without him. If I lost Fan'twar, I would lose my world. There had to be a way to get him back.

"What does she want in return for him?" I asked.

"That's for you to find out. And you'd better do it quickly."

"Why do you even care about any of this? You're planning to destroy the world as soon as you get a chance."

"Destroy the world? No. Your world will be reborn." She leaned forward and spoke quietly. "But I will not be the one to do it, Deathbringer."

A shiver ran down my spine, and the dream shifted to a different reality. Instead of sitting in my father's office, we stood in the desert—the same desert I'd seen in another vision, one I'd tried so hard to forget.

I stood alone.

"This is your curse," Theht whispered. "To be forever alone without anyone to guide or comfort you. That is the destiny of the Deathbringer. Like Ulizet, like the silverwitch, you will fulfill the prophecy, kill the ones you love, and then you shall be as them. Alone."

I clamped my hands over my ears. "I don't believe you," I called. My voice echoed through the empty expanse.

"There is no need to believe. Prophecy happens whether you believe it or not."

I sank to my hands and knees, the sand gritty as it clung to my skin. "I don't want to be here anymore."

"But you will be," Theht whispered. "You will be here sooner than you think."

I bolted awake, sweat slicking my forehead, my hands cold and clammy. My heart pounded, and the throbbing headache had grown worse. Outside, it was still dark.

"Olive," Maveryck said quietly. "Are you okay?"

His words surprised me. I hadn't realized he was awake. But then again, I wasn't sure I'd ever seen the man sleep.

"I... I don't know."

I rubbed my temples, trying to make sense of the dream. Had I really spoken to Theht? I tried to remember where I was. On the light carriage, headed for the desert. Theht was just a dream.

"Where are we?" I asked.

"We've just crossed through the outskirts near the elven capitol," Maveryck answered. "We've still got a few hours to go."

As I breathed deeply, the images from the dream faded, but I could still hear Theht's voice.

Prophecy happens whether you believe it or not.

Trying to distract myself from the dream, I turned to Maveryck. "Where is your wolf?" I asked.

"I left Grace at the keep. She hates the desert, and she hates Jahr'ad even more. I thought it best if she stayed put."

"I see." I turned to the window, trying not the notice the haunted look in my reflection. "Do you really think this man—Jahr'ad—will be able to help us?"

145

"Yes. He may be the only person in Faythander who can."

Taking deep breaths, I still couldn't shake the fear I'd felt in the dream.

"It's a shame that Silvestra appeared and took your stepfather," Maveryck said. "I had intended to help you find the lost isle of Tremulac."

"Did you know where to look?"

"Not exactly, but during one of my journeys, I came across some rare documents that held knowledge about Tremulac." He placed his pack on his lap and pulled out a slim, leather-bound tome. "I hadn't thought to look through this until now as it didn't make much sense to me before. But after recovering the staff, the allure of the lost isle piqued my curiosity, and so I took another look at it. This book was written by a historian who lived several hundred years after the Madralorde, so I can't say how accurate it is. Still, it does contain some fascinating knowledge."

"What does it say?"

"It seems the Madralorde did indeed live longer ago than most suspected. In fact, they lived at the same time Earth Kingdom's Egyptians were building the pyramids."

"Wow. No wonder it's so hard to find out anything about them."

"Precisely. I have also learned that the Madralorde brothers built their keep on the site of what had previously been an ancient temple. The locals opposed the building of the keep as they claimed the Madralorde were desecrating sacred ground. In retaliation, the Madralorde brothers sacked the temple and killed everyone in it. They... tortured them in an unusually brutal manner, and then they burned them alive. After that, they displayed the charred corpses outside the temple as a warning to anyone else who sought to stop the construction."

"My goodness, they sound like savages."

"Yes. Remember, this was before the time of Pa'horan, so they basically were savages."

"But they were also smart. They constructed weapons powerful enough to harness Theht."

"True, but they had help." He tapped the book on his lap. "This historian says that when the brothers unearthed the temple's foundation, they found a wellspring of magic, and they used the magic to forge their weapons."

"If that's the case," I said, "then wherever they built their castle must have been a place of great power. But if that's true, then finding it should be easy... but it isn't. Why?"

"Perhaps the magic no longer exists? They may have used all the magic in constructing their weapons."

Sighing, I gazed out the window. The clouds had cleared, revealing a star-flecked sky. "Until a week ago, I thought the place was a myth."

"Yes, as did almost everyone else. Everyone except the elven queen."

"Does that book say anything else useful?" I asked.

"Only that the castle was built on an island and surrounded by a large lake."

"Okay, then all we'll have to do is scour every lake in Faythander. Easy."

Maveryck's smile didn't seem to touch his eyes. "Yes, perhaps it would be easy if there weren't over a million recorded lakes in Faythander, and perhaps a million more that haven't been discovered."

"All right, maybe not so easy. Then how do you propose we find it?"

He shook his head. "We need more information, and unfortunately, the one race who has the only collection of known records from the Madralorde are the elves."

"And they won't be giving it up any time soon."

"No, and it's quite likely they'll find the island before we do."

My shoulders slumped. I wanted to argue, but I knew he was right. I glanced at Heidel and Kull, who still slept. Kull's idea of opening a library was sounding more and more appealing. It was about time someone other than the elves had all the knowledge.

"Olive," Maveryck said hesitantly, "has Heidel ever... spoken of me?"

"Uh..." I wasn't sure how to answer. "Well, I'm afraid Heidel is a guarded person. She's had a rough past, so she's not necessarily open to speaking about her personal life."

"Ah, I see. So she hasn't mentioned anything about Earth Kingdom... or about me?"

"No, but I don't expect she would. Her memories of Earth Kingdom are gone."

He nodded but bit his lip, not seeming appeased by my answers. "Do you think she would ever consider someone like me?"

I shifted in my seat, unsure of how to answer his question.

Kull would kill me if I gave Maveryck the okay to date his sister. "You know, that's probably something you should talk to Heidel about."

"Oh." His face fell. "Yes, of course. I'm sorry to have brought it up." He smiled, then turned away from me to stare out the window.

I wasn't sure what to think of Maveryck. While he was polite and seemed to want to help us, I couldn't help but feel he was hiding something.

Except for the whirring of the carriage's magically hybrid motor, the rest of the trip passed in silence. Outside, the sun rose, changing the sky from gray to cloudless pink, revealing a flat, barren landscape devoid of trees or plants of any kind. Sand stretched away from us in a seemingly endless ocean.

Heidel and Kull both woke, and we had a scanty breakfast of nuts and cheese. As I chewed my food, I glanced out the window and saw that the landscape was changing from flat, broad plains to mountains in the distance and tall sandstone pillars that rose three stories high. As we put the food away, the carriage slowed and then stopped.

"The light-rails won't bring us to the mountains," Maveryck said. "From here, we'll have to hike."

Blinding sunlight streamed inside as the doors opened with a soft, motorized whirring sound. After we climbed out, the doors sealed shut and the carriage zipped away, leaving us alone in the desert.

The tall pillars surrounded us like trees as we trudged toward the mountains. Sand billowed around us, and I tasted its gritty particles on my tongue. The dry air was swelteringly hot, and soon I was covered in sweat. When we reached one of the taller pillars, we found some shade, pulled out our canteens, and rested before going any farther.

"How long will it take us to get to this compound?" Heidel asked.

"Only a few more hours if the weather holds, but we'll have to be careful—the sandstorms here can come without warning."

After replacing our canteens in our packs, we continued hiking toward the mountains. I glanced at Kull as we walked. Without speaking, he focused straight ahead. He hadn't tried to kiss me since that evening in the Wult outpost when I'd pushed him away. The feeling of growing distant from him made a knot form in my stomach, and an idea formed that if

I kept pushing him away, I wouldn't get him back. But knowing I would destroy the world—and worse—with Theht's presence still lurking in my head, made it painful to be with him, and I didn't know what to do to make it better.

The sun beat down on our backs, hot and oppressive until I felt I was suffocating, but still we walked. The only thing that kept me going was to focus on Fan'twar. Every step I took brought me closer to freeing him.

Up ahead, strange brown cacti grew as tall as buildings. Some had magic trapped inside, and occasional bursts of blue ran through their spines and zapped the ground.

"Watch out for those," Maveryck said. "Get too close and they'll give you a nasty shock."

Dark storm clouds gathered overhead, giving us a welcome break from the glaring sun. The flat expanse of sand began to change to a rocky ground, and the gently sloping hills grew steeper as they led toward the mountains.

The rain-scented air mingled with the billowing dust clouds. Up ahead, the crumbling mountain range stood like a fortress blocking our path.

"Are you sure we're in the right place?" I asked Maveryck. "I can't imagine anyone actually living here."

Heidel spoke up. "I agree. The only people willing to make this place their home are those wishing to hide, which begs the question, why are they hiding?"

"And who are they hiding from?" Kull asked.

The wind picked up, causing the dust to obscure the air and making it difficult for us to see more than a few feet ahead. I pulled the fabric of my cloak across my face to keep the sand from entering my nose and mouth, and the others did the same. Behind me, the sound of ringing steel caused me to stop. I spun around to find Kull standing with his sword unsheathed. With the wind whipping his hair and the sandstorm as a backdrop, he looked like a true barbarian—and sometimes I had to remember, he was.

Kull motioned for us to do the same. Confused, I scanned the desert, but with the sandstorm, it was nearly impossible to see anything other than a wall of sand.

"What's the matter?" I yelled over the wind.

Kull shook his head and put a finger to his lips.

"Drop the weapon," a rough voice shouted over the howling wind. Two men wearing rags wrapped around their heads and faces appeared ahead. Both of the men carried crossbows pointed at us. "Drop it!" one of the men repeated.

"I'd rather not," Kull called back.

"Drop it, or we put a bolt through your heart."

"I'd like to see you try!"

Maveryck kept his eyes on the two bowmen as he took a step toward Kull. "Do as he says," Maveryck said calmly. "They won't hurt us as long as we follow their orders."

"I'm not in the habit of being ordered around, thief."

"Brother," Heidel said, "don't be a fool."

Kull grumbled and let his sword fall to the ground. "Happy?" he asked.

The two men with the crossbows narrowed the distance between us and grabbed our wrists, then tied them behind our backs.

Memories of being held prisoner by the bloodthorn surfaced, and I had to force myself to stay calm as the scratchy ropes tightened around my already-scarred wrists.

It won't be like that again. I won't let it be like that again.

"Maveryck?" one of the men asked as he faced the thief. "Is that you?"

"Come back from the dead?" the other man asked.

"I never came back from the dead. I merely healed from my injuries. That's all."

"Says who? That fall would've killed a normal man."

"Perhaps. But it didn't kill me. Now, do me a favor and keep those ropes off my wrists. There's no need. And untie my friends as well. They'll not harm you."

"Nay, Maveryck, we'll leave you untied, but we can't do the same for your friends. We're under orders that strangers aren't allowed inside the compound unless they're blindfolded and tied up. You know that."

"Plus," the other guy said, nodding toward Kull, "that one's hands are big enough to break our skulls."

"He'd do more than that," Heidel muttered.

"There, you see? That's the reason we take precautions." The two men stuffed burlap sacks over our heads, although I noticed they'd tied a gag in Heidel's mouth. I tried not to dry heave as the stench of sour sweat came from the abrasive fibers scratching my cheeks.

Rough hands pushed me forward. I blindly walked into the desert with the sand shifting under my feet, doing my best to breathe through the bag.

Half an hour must have passed before we finally traded

sand for a solid floor. The air cooled, and our footfalls rang out as if we'd entered a cavern. After being shoved to the ground, someone finally removed the sack from my head, and I breathed in the fresh air.

As I scanned the room, my eyes adjusted to the light coming from millions of candles burning throughout the cavernous area. Large piles of white wax dripped in puddles onto the ground. The candles were set in naturally occurring arched pillars that spanned from one floor to the next, all the way to the top of a chamber that looked several hundred feet high. My mouth gaped as I stared overhead.

High above us came the sound of dragon wings, and I spied several small sun dragons circling near the cave's ceiling. The dragons' shrieks echoed through the cavern. One of the dragons dipped lower than the rest, his wings brushing the floor, causing clouds of dust to rise from the walls and making the candles' flames sputter.

I watched the small dragon as he flew close to me. His frame was so thin I could see ribs beneath his sagging and scaled hide. Scars marred both his face and portions of his snout. He flapped his wings twice and then shot upward into the air to glide in circles with the other dragons.

I wasn't sure what breed of dragon it was. Sun dragons weren't usually so small, and these dragons had longer, narrower snouts and a larger wingspan, reminding me more of the extinct pterosaur.

Maveryck and another man I didn't recognize approached. The two men squatted near me, and the thief cut away the cords binding my hands. After he pulled the ropes away, I rubbed my wrists, feeling the uneven bumps and ridges of the scars on my skin.

"Jahr'ad, I'd like you to meet Olive," Maveryck said. "She's a traveler from Delestria."

"From Delestria?" Jahr'ad asked.

"Yes," I lied, hoping Jahr'ad bought it.

Jahr'ad gave me a careful smile. "I am pleased to make your acquaintance. I have many friends in Delestria."

He had a rough appearance, from his sand-covered, patched clothing and his worn, dragon-hide boots to his tanned, weathered skin. He wore his bleached hair in long cornrows that looked as if they hadn't been washed in years. What I found most disturbing about Jahr'ad were his eyes. They seemed too calculating, as if when he looked at me, he could see my weaknesses.

Jahr'ad shook my hand, holding it a moment longer than necessary. When he released his grip, he eyed me. "What is it you do in Delestria?"

"She is a merchant," Maveryck answered for me. "She trades in unusual items, which is what brings her here. We've much to discuss," Maveryck said.

"I see," Jahr'ad said, keeping his gaze on me. "What is she willing to trade for these unusual items?"

"We will discuss that later," Maveryck answered. "For now, we are hungry and tired, and trading anything in a generous manner is impossible to do with an empty stomach. Where are your manners, Jahr'ad? You know I have a reputation to keep, and I can't do it when I'm covered in dirt."

Jahr'ad stood. "Very well," he said with a sigh, "come inside and you'll be cleaned and fed, but after that, we negotiate. Does that suit you, *thief*?"

Maveryck rose to his full height. I felt magic emanating from his fisted hands. "You still insist on calling me that, do you?"

"I'll call you whatever names I like while you're here. My home. My rules. You get the picture?" He nodded toward me. "Same goes for you. I don't tolerate cheats or liars. When you're here, you play by my rules. Now, as you are my guests and I am your gracious host," he gave us a mocking smile, "please, if you'll follow me."

My legs cramped as I stood, but I managed to limp forward, following Maveryck and Jahr'ad through a doorway that led into a tunnel. Rust-colored rock composed the floors, walls, and ceilings. The tunnels had been roughly carved to form hallways and small rooms. We entered a room larger than the rest, with a ceiling that seemed to span all the way to the top of the mountain and a fountain that took up the room's center. Water bubbled from a stone in the pool's center, then flowed outward, lapping at the pool's edges. Steam rose from the water.

"Bathe here," Jahr'ad said, "and then meet me for the evening meal whenever you're ready."

He turned to leave, but I stopped him. "Where are my companions?"

A dark look crossed his face. "The big one wanted to give us trouble, and his sister was worse than him. We had no choice but to put them in a room upstairs."

I turned to Maveryck. "Did you know about this?"

"Yes, but not to worry. They'll be released before our evening meal. Isn't that right, Jahr'ad?"

He shrugged. "As long as I have your word, then yes, they'll be released."

Jahr'ad left without another word, his booted feet echoing down the hall until they disappeared.

I rounded on Maveryck. "What's going on?" I demanded. "Kull and Heidel are locked up?"

"They are not locked up. They're being kept in a room upstairs, and they are both perfectly fine. Would you like to bathe first?" Maveryck asked, pointing to the water.

"Bathe? When my friends are being held captive? No, thank you."

"Very well. I shall bathe first. Your friends are being held on the top level in a room at the end of the west hallway. You should have no trouble finding them."

"Fine." I turned and walked out of the room, leaving him alone. I trusted him less the more I got to know him, and I only hoped this journey ended soon with my stepfather safely returned so I wouldn't be forced to confront him.

I found the end of the hallway and took the wooden ladder leading up, then climbed onto a platform. Several people milled about as I walked through the narrow corridors, but most didn't pay me any attention. When I reached the western end of the complex, I found a room with a wooden door and let myself inside. Kull and Heidel both sat on the floor with their hands tied and gags in their mouths. Blood dripped down the side of Kull's face.

Perfectly fine? Maveryck will so be getting a piece of my mind...

I cursed under my breath and untied Heidel, removed her gag, and then moved to Kull and did the same.

"Did Jahr'ad do this to you?" I asked Kull.

He worked his jaw back and forth before speaking. "No. One of his men. I happened to mention that I thought keeping dragons in captivity was illegal, and then he struck me."

I inspected his wound, but with the blood drying on his forehead and cheek, it was hard to tell how deep it went.

"This needs to be cleaned," I said, moving his hair away from his face, "and possibly stitched. What did he hit you with?"

"A club of some sort. Made of bone. Possibly dragon bone."

Heat simmered inside my chest. "Dragon bone?"

"Yes. I think they're breeding dragons here, most likely for the purposes of illegally fighting them against one another."

"That's horrible. And highly illegal. No wonder Maveryck didn't want me telling them about my relation to my stepfather."

Heidel paced the room behind us. "What do we do now? Do we continue with this charade and continue to follow Maveryck? Or do we try to escape?"

The room was silent for a moment.

"If we escaped," Kull said, "we'd have no guide to get us back to the rails, and since they blindfolded us, I would have no idea how to get back. Even if I could, navigating through the desert with those sandstorms would be suicide."

"And we still wouldn't know how to free my stepfather," I said.

"Then I believe we should stay here," Kull said, "at least until we get what we came for."

Heidel sighed. "So we just stay here and trust Jahr'ad's men won't kill us?"

"They won't kill us," Kull said flatly.

"How do you know that?"

"Trust me. I won't let it happen."

"Overconfident, as usual," Heidel said.

"I'm not overconfident," Kull said. "I'm honest."

Heidel narrowed her eyes. "Brother, forgive me if I don't trust you to miraculously get us out of here safely. You don't understand men like Jahr'ad the way I do. He can't be trusted."

"I agree that Jahr'ad can't be trusted," Kull said, "but there is still a chance that he can be reasoned with. Not every man is as evil as Geth. You'd do well to remember that."

"He's right," I said. "While Jahr'ad may not be trustworthy, it doesn't make him like Geth."

Heidel fisted her hands. "You only say that because you share my brother's bed. You'd say anything to agree with him."

"That's uncalled for," Kull said.

"And it's technically untrue," I added.

"Why is it untrue?" she asked. "You've not shared his bed?"

"Uh, well..." I wasn't sure how to dig myself out of this one. "Technically, no."

She rounded on Kull. "Brother, is this true?"

"Whether it is true or not is none of your business, is it?"

"It *is* my business," Heidel said. "What is the matter with you? Are you damaged? How many women have you taken to bed before her? And now you will not take the woman you've pledged your heart to? How long do you think she will put up with you?"

"How I choose to spend my private life is my own business."

Heidel glanced at me. "Aren't you concerned at all?"

"Well, it wasn't really his decision completely." I could feel my cheeks heating up. I hated being put in this situation. "I wasn't really... I mean... what I mean to say is..."

"It was you who made this decision?" Heidel asked me.

"It has nothing to do with her," Kull interjected. "If you must know, after Father's death I realized I wanted to change my ways, to go back to traditional values and all that. It has nothing to do with her."

I glanced at Kull, silently thanking him for saving me from a catastrophically embarrassing situation.

"I don't believe you," she said to Kull.

"Believe what you want, but you've no reason to pry into my life, and you certainly have no right to pry into Olive's personal life."

"I have every right. It's not fair for you to judge every man who shows the slightest interest in me if I don't also have the same right to judge who you spend your time with."

"That's completely different. I've never courted a maniac bent on the destruction of the world."

Heidel laughed. "And I suppose Princess Euralysia doesn't count? The queen who is now trying to conjure Theht, which will most likely end in the destruction of Faythander? Oh, and that's right, you are now courting Olive, aren't you?" She thrust her finger at me. "The woman destined to destroy our world. I've heard the rumors, Kull—about the Deathbringer prophecies. Don't pretend you don't know what I'm talking about. Do you even know who she really is?"

My heart hit the bottom of my chest. Heidel had no idea how badly her words hurt me.

Kull rose to his full height. "That's enough," he snapped. "You are never to speak to Olive in such a way ever again. Is that clear? And just so you understand, I will never listen to your advice when it comes to relationships. You are the last person on this planet I would seek advice from. You gave your heart to a man so evil he destroyed magic, and then nearly succeeded in destroying our world. How I choose to spend my time is not your concern, and you are never to bring it up again. Is that

155

clear?"

Heidel pursed her lips. Her hands trembled as she kept them fisted. "Perfectly clear," she said quietly. "And now I see that when you told me you forgave me for my past crimes, you were lying. I don't know why I'm surprised." She choked on her words and hastily brushed away a tear running down her cheeks. "Yes, I understand completely." Turning, she stormed out of the room, not bothering to slam the door behind her.

CHAPTER
Seventeen

I SANK TO THE GROUND, FEELING AS IF MY LEGS COULD NO longer support me. It was hard for me not to hate Heidel after what she'd just said, but the hardest part was knowing that what she'd said was true.

I would destroy the world. And it was only a matter of time.

Kull knelt beside me and gently rested his hand on my shoulder. "Don't let her words hurt you."

"I won't. At least, I'll get over it." I exhaled slowly, trying to keep my emotions in check.

"She's been unusually temperamental of late," Kull said. "Not that she hasn't always had a temper, but it seems to have gotten worse over the last few days."

"It started when she returned from Earth Kingdom. She's probably dealing with feelings she doesn't understand because she's lost her memories. Being around Maveryck only makes it worse."

"Can you help her?" Kull asked.

"Me?"

"Yes. Couldn't you conjure a spell to help her remember her lost memories?"

"I guess I could try, but usually my patients come from Earth who've been to Faythander and returned. I've never really tried it in reverse. Plus, no offense, but I'm not sure I want to see her right now."

"I understand." He squeezed my hand. "She's my sister. I've dealt with her outbursts my entire life. She says things she doesn't mean when she gets angry."

"We all do, I guess." I rubbed my eyes, hoping Kull didn't see the tears trying to form.

"However, she still worries me. Do you really think she believes I didn't forgive her?"

"No, I'm sure she was only speaking out of anger."

He pursed his lips. "I hope you're right."

I squeezed his hand. Outside the door came the drifting sound of voices and an occasional roar from one of the dragons. I knew Kull and I didn't have much longer to be alone.

"Thank you for sticking up for me," I said. "You didn't have to lie for me, but I appreciate it."

He gave me a gentle smile. "It wasn't a complete lie."

"Yes, it was."

"What I said was the truth. My father's passing made me realize how important it was for me to go back to the beginning, figure out what made the old ways so important. But it wasn't until you were trapped in the cave with the bloodthorn that I really began to ponder what I believed in. I knew that if I ever got you back, I would never take you for granted. I would do things the way they ought to be done. Losing my father was hard enough, and losing you would have completely broken me. If we're to be together, I'd prefer if it happened at the right time, the right way."

When I looked into his eyes, that icy blue color of a glacier, cold, yet comforting, I knew I could never let him go. "Kull," I said, cupping his cheek. "I don't care what Heidel thinks, you're an honorable man."

Footsteps echoed in the hallway outside. We turned to find three of Jahr'ad's men, all dressed in dirty rags and with the same careworn skin as Jahr'ad, entering the room. Behind them, a woman entered. Dark red tattoos in the shapes of rune-like symbols and swirls covered her neck and arms to her wrists. She had a muscular build and a shaved head, and the hardened edge to her eyes made me wonder what sort of life she led in a place like this.

"My name is Zariah," she said. "I am Jahr'ad's consort. He wants you in the main arena. Follow me," she called to Kull and I as she turned around.

Zariah led us out of the room and down the hallway. As we made it to the ladder, I heard laughter and loud voices coming from the large inner chamber. When we stepped off the ladder and into the main chamber, we found several wooden tables arranged in the center of the room.

Jahr'ad and several dozen of his men sat at the tables. Platters of meat rested on the tables in front of them, along with bowls of broth and cups filled with dark liquid. Maveryck and Heidel stood speaking quietly under one of the room's broad arches. Heidel only gave Kull and I a brief glance as we walked by her, and then she turned away from us both.

Maveryck walked toward us. He'd washed up and now wore a simple, beige-colored cloak, dark leather pants, and a golden-stitched doublet. He wore his long, dark hair loose down his back, and his piercing, gray eyes were focused intently on us. Despite having crossed the desert and having been swept away in a sandstorm, he had cleaned up so well that he now looked ready to greet royalty.

"Olive, Kull," he said with a formal nod to us both. "I'm glad you've come."

"I'm not sure we had much of a choice," I said.

Jahr'ad walked toward us. "Our guests have arrived," he said with a leering grin as he outstretched his arms. "I am pleased you decided to join us for our evening meal. Maveryck tells me we have the pleasure of dining with Wult royalty. Please, sit and eat, and then we shall discuss why you've come."

Kull and I both sat at one of the long tables. Heidel joined us but sat a few chairs down from her brother and didn't make eye contact with him. Above us, I noticed that the dragons no longer flew overhead but were perched on the balconies surrounding us. Jahr'ad, Zariah, and Maveryck sat across from Kull and me. They made small talk for several minutes, and then Jahr'ad turned to Kull.

"Tell us," Jahr'ad said, "what news do you bring from the Wult lands? Is the kingdom still unstable without your father as ruler?"

"Who says it's unstable?" Kull asked.

"I do. The trading at Wult outposts has grown increasingly scarce. I can only assume this is because the Wult kingdom is not supporting its outlying villages the same way it did in the past."

"Our borders are safe and our people are free. Nothing has changed."

"Of course you would say that since you're the king." Jahr'ad laughed. "But what does it matter to me? I have no interest in Wults. We separated from that society long ago." His eyes met mine. "Trading is what I'm interested in."

The look of cold calculation in his eyes made a shiver run

down my spine, but I met his gaze with equal contempt.

"What is it you wish to barter?" Jahr'ad asked.

Maveryck spoke up. "Knowledge," he said, and then pulled the lotus cube from his cloak and placed it on the table. "This symbol was sent to us as a message from the dragon lady, Silvestra. Should we fail to respond, it could mean the death of someone very powerful. We need to know what this symbol means."

Jahr'ad picked up the cube and studied the facet with the golden oval. "This is a lotus cube, made of a black onyx only found in the mines near the western coast in the pixie lands. It's a rare mineral, and with the magic infused inside, it could fetch a hefty price—that is, if one is able to find a buyer willing to pay it.

"The symbol is odd. At first, the swirls look random, but I suspect there's more to it." He glanced at Maveryck. "Do I have your permission to perform a simple test?"

"For what purpose?"

"A spell to divine the meaning of these patterns. I assure you, the stone will remain intact."

"Very well, as long as you do not disturb the spell's meaning."

Jahr'ad handed the stone to Zariah. "Use a sun spell and focus it in the center-most pattern. That should do the trick."

She took the stone from him and focused on the gold pattern. Her eyes clouded with a red-tinted magic, and then she whispered a word in a low, guttural voice. Her magic repulsed me, making my skin crawl. I'd never felt magic so primitive and vulgar. The emotion it elicited was hard to describe, except the feeling was akin to experiencing violence—a sensation that set my teeth on edge.

The red magic left her lips and entered the stone. As soon the enchantment connected with the swirling patterns, the golden light coming from the pattern grew brighter and then re-formed, creating words instead of the swirls. But as I glanced at the stone, I found the words written in symbols I'd never seen before. I didn't know how much good the spell had actually done if we still couldn't read it.

She handed the stone back to Jahr'ad.

"What sort of magic is that?" I asked her.

"I'm not sure of the proper name, but I call it blood magic," she answered.

"How did you discover it?"

She cocked her head. "I came upon the power many years ago by sapping the energy from a dying magic user. I use a... *creative* process to obtain it." She leaned forward. "Would you like me to show you how it works?"

Snickering came from the men surrounding us.

"Zariah, leave her alone," Jahr'ad snapped.

"I was only jesting."

"But our merchant is in no mood for your games," he said as he turned back to the stone. "This is as I suspected. It's written in an ancient language known as rhenuroc, some also call it high dragon. Of course, it's a dead language, so no one reads it anymore, but it's not uncommon to find it written on stones such as these."

"Do you know how to interpret it?" Maveryck asked.

"Yes, I know what it says."

"Will you tell us?" I asked.

"That depends, doesn't it? What have you brought to trade?"

"Trade?" I asked.

"You are a merchant, aren't you? Haven't you brought something to trade?"

I glanced at Maveryck. "Well, I..."

"Come now," Jahr'ad said. "I look forward to seeing the latest trinkets from Delestria. Surely you've brought something of value?"

"I... I haven't brought much. That is to say..."

"You've come all the way from Delestria and brought nothing to trade? Surely you cannot expect me to believe that. You are a merchant, aren't you?" He leaned forward, his eyes narrowed. "Or are you?"

His shrewd gaze made it hard for me to make any kind of answer.

"Jahr'ad," Maveryck said, "we are not here to bargain over trinkets."

"Then why are you here?" he asked.

"We seek to challenge you in the fights. Our champion against yours."

Jahr'ad's eyes lit up. "What's the wager?"

"If we win, you tell us the meaning of the stone's symbol."

"And if you lose?"

"If we lose, then you keep the stone."

Jahr'ad frowned. "Not good enough. If you lose, then we keep the stone, plus, the *merchant* stays with us. Forever."

Kull clenched his fists. "I will never agree to that."

"Then I will never tell you what's written on that stone. Besides, you have no say. Did I fail to warn you? When you're here, you play by my rules."

"Your Majesty," Maveryck said, "perhaps you should first evaluate what challenge is being considered?"

"I don't care," Kull answered. "Whatever it is, I do not accept the terms."

"No?" Jahr'ad said. "Would you rather be tied up again? Would you accept those terms?" He laughed. "You should at least hear us out before refusing the wager. With your reputation, I am surprised you are not at least a little interested. We've all heard the rumors about you, of course. Remind me again what you're rumored to have accomplished? Wrestling a jagamoor while tied up? Perhaps we ought to tie you up again and see what happens when you challenge one of my dragons."

"Dragons?" I asked.

"Yes, love. My dragons against one of you. That's how this game works. Would you like to volunteer?"

Laughter echoed through the room.

"She won't be involved in this," Kull said.

"No? That's a shame. What's it about that woman anyway that makes you want to protect her? Is she a lover of yours? Is she a good lay?"

Kull stood abruptly, making his bench fall with a loud clatter to the ground. "Leave her out of this."

"Ah, so she does mean something to you. Even better. This just got ever so interesting. There's nothing more rewarding than taking another man's woman while he watches. What do you say, Wult? Care to be tied up and watch as I bed your woman?"

Kull lunged across the table and punched Jahr'ad in the face with a loud smack that could have split the man's skull. Jahr'ad let out a high-pitched screech as he fell back with his hands clamped over his mouth.

Jahr'ad's men surrounded Kull, while others ran to their leader and helped him sit up. When the commotion settled down, Jahr'ad got to his feet as he held a bloody handkerchief to his mouth.

"Wult bastard." He spat a mouthful of blood at Kull's feet. "I should have killed you when you first arrived. Tie him up," he shouted at his men. "If he fights, throw him to the dragons."

Overhead, the dragons beat their wings as they waited

on their perches. I glanced up to find them chained to posts. The metal loops clanked as the dragons wrestled with their restraints, looking on us with hungry gazes.

Jahr'ad rounded on Maveryck. "You should have known better than to bring this man here. What were you thinking?"

Maveryck threaded his fingers together. His calm aloofness bothered me. "If you do not wish to continue with the bargaining, we will leave."

Maveryck took the lotus cube and placed it in his pocket. He stood and turned to leave when Jahr'ad stopped him.

"Wait," Jahr'ad said. "I'm not finished with you yet, thief. Stay and fight if that's what you wish, but I have few demands."

Maveryck turned around to face Jahr'ad. "You are in no position to make demands. I am here to negotiate. That is what I do, and that is what I have always done. Do not cross me, Jahr'ad, or my trading with you will come to an end."

Jahr'ad fisted his hands. "Fine," he said after a pause. "We'll do it your way. My dragon against your man. If I win, I take the box and the girl. If you win, I get the box, and you get information."

"And," Maveryck added, "we are *all* free to leave in peace?"

"If your man wins, you shall all leave in peace. If not," Jahr'ad's lust-filled gaze flicked to me, "then one of you will not."

He had the audacity to smile at me. Gag me with a spoon. The idiot had no idea what a huge mistake he was making. Magic gathered in my chest, pulsing with a rapid heat that begged to be released. I restrained it for now, but if the man so much as touched me, he'd get what was coming to him.

"Now," Jahr'ad said, "it's time for us to choose which dragon will fight the Wult king. This is the fun part. Have you ever witnessed a dragon fight, merchant?"

"No, I can't say that I have, considering it's illegal."

"Illegal? Says who? The sky king? That beast is no ruler of ours." He spat. "In my house, we treat the dragons the way they ought to be handled—as animals. Am I right?"

He raised his arms, and cheers erupted. The dragons flapped their wings, making the candlelight sputter.

"Who's ready for a fight?" he shouted. The cheers grew louder as some of the men moved the tables to the corners of the room.

Above us, the dragons grew increasingly agitated as their shrieks mingled with the cheers. The noise grew to a fever pitch as Zariah walked to the center of the room. Dust clouds billowed around her, and the thousands of candles seemed to focus on her, like a spotlight on a stage, as she raised her arms.

Crimson magic gathered around her, spiraling and twisting. It reeked of blood and violence, repulsing me until I felt I would vomit. The dragons grew frantic, their roars turning to a frenzy.

Zariah's tattoos glowed as her magic ignited. A rhythmic pulse, like a heartbeat, came from her powers as the magic swirled upward and enveloped the dragons.

"What is she doing?" Heidel asked Jahr'ad.

"She's goading them so they'll fight. It took us some time to control the dragons. We learned that if the magic was removed from the creatures, they eventually lost their speech and their flight. Without magic, the dragons are just primitive reptiles."

"Then how are these dragons able to fly?" Heidel asked.

"Trial and error on our part. We began breeding the non-magical dragons and noticed that their species adapted at an alarming rate. Using magic to speed up the growth process also helped aid in the adaptation process. After several generations, we were left with smaller, non-magical dragons that can fly. They were also bred to be highly aggressive, which suits our purposes perfectly."

Zariah's magic surrounded the dragons, making them gnash their teeth and twist their necks as they tried to break free from their restraints. With her arms still raised, she slowly backed away and off the floor. As she stepped beside me, she lowered her arms and a red-glowing shield surrounded the inner floor to create a closed arena.

"Let them loose," Jahr'ad shouted.

Sounds of snapping echoed through the domed room as several men unfastened the dragons' chains. With a violent clash, the dragons attacked one another. I counted six animals altogether, and each one carried scars that marred their flesh. They fought with uncontrolled violence, lashing out as the magic goaded them. Wind brushed my cheeks from the dragons' beating wings. I fought the urge to vomit as the red magic pulsed around me, forcing the animals into a rage.

Backing away, I found a spot under an alcove where the magic wouldn't be so close. Sweat slicked my forehead, and I worked my hands open and closed to combat the magic tingling through my nerve endings. Closing my eyes, I tried to keep a calm mind and take deep breaths to combat the blood magic's effects.

"Is something the matter?" Heidel asked.

I opened my eyes to find her standing next to me. She was talking to me now? I decided to play along. Perhaps she was ready to be reasonable.

"I'll be all right once that magic goes away," I said. "It's not pleasant to be around."

"Hmm, sounds like my brother." She crossed her arms and leaned on the wall beside me.

The dragons fought with a wild frenzy that sickened my stomach. What Jahr'ad and his people had done to these dragons was inexcusable. Fan'twar would raze this place in a heartbeat if he knew about it, which was why Maveryck was so set on keeping me from revealing my identity.

"I wish I would have never come on this journey," Heidel said. "I knew from the start it was a bad decision."

"I'm beginning to agree with you. The only reason I did it was to save my stepfather. Let's hope we get out of here with the information we need."

"And let's hope we do it while we're still alive," Heidel said.

"Yeah, that would be nice too," I said.

"I..." she hesitated. "I apologize for what I said earlier. I know there is no excuse, but I have not felt like myself of late."

"It's okay. I certainly know what it's like to not feel like yourself." If only she realized how much I understood.

Two of the dragons clashed and fell to the ground. One made it back up and flew into the air, while the other remained on the ground. The creature struggled to get up, but even from this distance I could see deep gashes on its neck and hindquarters. Blood dripped from the gaping wounds. The glowing red magic dimmed around the injured dragon, and the beast limped out of the arena and back to its perch.

"It doesn't surprise me that my brother chooses to wait to bed you," she said casually, as if there weren't a colossal dragon fight happening right before us. "He's always been honorable to a fault, even if he doesn't show it. And now, with the weight of the kingdom resting on his shoulders, he wants to do things the right way, even if no one notices."

"If that's the case, then you should know he does forgive you. He would never go back on something as important as that."

She shrugged. "I still hate him."

"Are you sure about that?"

"Yes. He knows better than to bring up my past, especially with... other things troubling me." Her gaze focused on Maveryck, who stood nearby, studying her. As soon as their eyes met, they looked away.

"Will you help me, Olive? I have to know what happened in Earth Kingdom. I hardly feel like myself anymore."

"I can try, but I can't promise I'll be successful in restoring your memories, and it will have to wait."

Several more dragons fell until only two remained—a small, blue-gray and a larger brown, diamond-backed beast. The blue-gray had speed and agility on its side. It moved with a lithe nimbleness and used its stealth to its advantage. The brown monster looked older, with barbs lining its head and running down its neck, ending with large spikes at the end of its long, snakelike tail. Its yellow eyes looked calculating and dangerous, as if it were only waiting for the right moment to strike.

The blue-gray snapped at the larger one's neck, tearing the flesh, and the brown dragon shrieked and soared upward. Blue-gray followed. They clashed at the top of the dome, clawing and biting until they were both covered in open wounds.

Below the dragons, Jahr'ad's people cheered, their shouts mingling with the dragons' roars. In a split second, the brown dragon lashed out with a powerful burst of fire, blasting and singeing the smaller dragon, forcing it into a corner where the white-hot fire singed the blue-gray's scales. The smaller dragon fell and landed in a bloody, smoking heap on the arena floor. The smell of burning flesh pervaded the air, and I watched in disgust as several men threw ropes around the dragon's corpse and hauled it off the field.

The brown dragon watched from above like a hawk scanning its prey.

"We have a champion," Jahr'ad shouted.

Clapping and cheering deafened my ears.

Jahr'ad pointed at Kull. "It's your turn, Wult, but we can't have you fight an injured dragon. It wouldn't be fair. We'd like to see a fair match, wouldn't we?"

"Yes," the crowd cheered.

"We can't have a healthy man battling an injured dragon. It wouldn't be right, would it?"

"No!" the crowd roared back.

"Then we will even the match," Jahr'ad called. "Bring out the dragon whip. Two lashes ought to do the trick. We'd still like him a little healthy—oh, and leave him tied up. We'll see if those stories about the jagamoor are true. We're going to watch a fair fight after all!"

I cursed under my breath. Jahr'ad had gone too far this time. "What in the world are they thinking?" I muttered as I charged toward Maveryck and grabbed his tunic. Magic rippled through my veins. "You can't let them hurt him."

He glanced at my hand on his collar. "Do you think I have the ability to stop them?"

"Yes, I do. They're going to hurt him, Maveryck. You can't let it happen."

"I assure you, if I had the ability to stop this, I would do it."

Anger rose within me. "Fine. If you won't stop them, then I will."

I marched toward the crowd where Jahr'ad and Zariah gathered around a tall wooden post and prepared to tie Kull to it.

"Jahr'ad!" I shouted.

Keeping my magic trapped inside was no longer a possibility, so I let it flow from my hands and my heart, rippling in waves of amber and blue, so strong it distorted my vision.

Surprised, Jahr'ad spun around. I let my magic wrap around the man and tighten around his neck, slowly compressing his windpipe.

I am so sick of this stupid man.

Jahr'ad's men grabbed my arms, but I kept my magic wrapped around their leader.

"So," Jahr'ad gasped, "I should have known it was you. You... you're no merchant. I know who you are, Sky King's ward."

I tightened the magic around his neck, and he choked on his words.

"Release him," Zariah demanded.

"No," I shouted back. "This has gone too far. I won't let you hurt the king."

I glanced at Kull as they removed his shirt and tied him to the post. Why wasn't he fighting? Was he seriously okay with this?

Jahr'ad's face turned blue. I didn't care. Deep inside, in that place where I kept Theht's consciousness, came a surge of excitement. What would it feel like to cause another's death?

A cold sensation wrapped around my magic and snuffed it out. I stumbled and fell backward, hitting the ground, trying to make sense of what had happened to my magic. Zariah stood over me with red sparks dancing through her eyes. Her magic encased me, absorbing my own power until I had nothing left inside.

"I wouldn't try that again," she said.

Jahr'ad stood straight as he gasped for breath. "Tie her up," he said. "And keep her powers away. We'll deal with her after the fight."

Rough hands encircled my arms. Jahr'ad's men tied my ankles and wrists with thick rope that burned as it rubbed against my skin. I kept my eyes on Zariah. How had she so easily taken my powers? What sort of magic did she wield that would allow her to do such thing? I only hoped I could find a way to get my powers back.

Two of Jahr'ad's men placed me on a bench in the corner. Maveryck watched from his spot in the shadows, and after the men had left, he came and stood beside me.

"I am sorry it has turned out like this," he said. "I assure you I will do everything I can to—"

"Save your breath. You betrayed us," I said. "What were you possibly thinking when you led us to this place?"

"The information we gain will be worth the price."

"Worth the price? It will be worth watching Kull die?"

"I am confident he will not die. However, your stepfather will most assuredly die—and he will die soon—if we fail to uncover the mystery of the lotus cube."

"I still think this was a horrible idea."

"I agree these are not the best of circumstances, but you must trust me when I say it will be worth it."

Kull didn't scream as the men lashed him with the whip, but I didn't expect him to. Brown watched from overhead as Kull's blood dripped to the ground.

CHAPTER *Eighteen*

*I*SN'T ANYONE GOING TO STOP THIS? I watched helplessly from my seat in the corner as Brown leapt off his perch and circled overhead. Maveryck and Heidel both stood beside me. Heidel leaned against the wall with her arms crossed as she watched her brother struggle, tied to the post in the arena's center.

Blood dripped from Kull's back as two long slashes split his skin open. I couldn't believe Heidel was doing nothing to defend him. What was wrong with her?

"Heidel, you have to help him," I said.

"Help him? I hate him."

"No, you don't. You know he would do the same for you."

"Only if it suited his own purposes."

"That's not true. How many times has he sacrificed himself to save you?"

She mumbled something under her breath. "Fine," she said. "Perhaps you are right. But I fail to see what I can do to help him."

"Unfortunately, I have to agree," Maveryck said. "Jahr'ad's men will do the same to Heidel as they did to you, or worse."

"Then what are we supposed to do?" I asked. "Watch him die?"

The dragon let out a piercing roar. Red magic glowed from the beast's scales, from the tip of its snout to the spines on its tail. Rage fueled the dragon's movements as it circled overhead.

Kull was still tied to the post. My heart beat at a frantic pace in my chest. It couldn't end this way. There had to be something I could do to stop this.

169

"Maveryck," Heidel demanded, "you are the one who brought us here. If he dies, you will be held on charges of conspiring to murder the king."

"I have done no such thing. And you underestimate your king's abilities. You both do."

I swore. If I'd had magic right then, Maveryck would have been a pile of cinders.

"I do not underestimate him," Heidel said. "I am aware of his capabilities, and I am also *very* aware of his weaknesses."

The dragon soared lower, flapping its wings and creating a dust cloud that obscured the field. The fine sediment tasted gritty on my tongue, and I coughed as it entered my throat. I couldn't bear to watch Kull, tied up and struggling, defenseless against the monster. This wasn't a fight. This was an execution.

As the dust cleared, we found Kull standing away from the pillar on the opposite side of the room, holding the rope in his hand.

"What?" Heidel gasped. "How did he do that?"

"As I said," Maveryck answered, "you underestimate him."

The dragon soared lower and snapped at Kull, but he dodged aside. He found a discarded mace inside the arena and grabbed it off the ground. Kull swung the mace around his head, stirring the dust around him. His muscles rippled as he swung the weapon, and his face was set with grim determination. Kull was in his element, in the heat of battle, sweat beading on his naked torso and dripping down the ridges of his muscles.

The dragon dipped toward Kull once again, but this time, Kull swung the club and knocked the beast's joint where the wing met the creature's body. Smart move on Kull's part, as the dragon shrieked and crashed to the ground. The injury was enough to take away the creature's ability to fly, which gave Kull an advantage as long as he could avoid the dragon's fire.

The monster rounded, limping, with one wing dragging the ground. The beast snapped at Kull, but he jumped back, out of the dragon's reach. Brown exhaled a breath of fire that streamed toward Kull, but the warrior ducked and rolled away. Fire ignited the wooden posts and several of the wooden tables, crackling as it consumed the fuel, making smoke and embers flit through the room. The smell of burning wood pervaded the air.

Brown limped toward Kull, slowly sizing him up as he paced from one corner of the field to the other. Kull looked savage with the mace swinging in his hand, his hair damp and slicked to his forehead, sweat making the skin on his bare torso shine in the light cast from the fires.

"Come," Kull yelled, swinging the mace.

The beast continued pacing, the way a lion would size up its prey. As the creature came closer toward me, I noticed long, feather-thin spines around its face, most likely venomous.

Firelight glowed through the billowing smoke, giving the cavern an eerie, orange cast. My eyes watered as the smoke's pungent scent filled the room. I worked my hands open and closed, feeling empty without my magic. Sweat slicked my forehead, and I tasted its saltiness on my tongue.

As I watched the monster circle Kull, my heart pounded in my chest. I'd seen him take down a dozen men. I'd seen him fight goblins and slaughter dragons twice his size. I should have been confident in his abilities to take down one dragon, so why did I feel so nervous?

The beast struck out, faster than I thought it was capable of moving, and rammed its massive head into Kull's chest. Kull fell back, and the monster nearly trampled him, but Kull rolled to the side and avoided it.

"He'll be all right," Maveryck said.

"You don't know that," I said.

"You don't have confidence in him?"

"I have plenty of confidence in him, but I also realize he's mortal."

The dragon roared and let out a massive fireball. Flames exploded around us, deafening me. In the chaos, I could hardly make out where Kull had gone and feared the worst. The crowd surrounding the arena clambered away from the flames. Chunks of burning wood fell from the ceiling and crashed to the ground. Frantic screams echoed through the domed room.

"Maveryck, untie me," I called over the chaos.

"But Jahr'ad—"

"I don't care about Jahr'ad. Untie me!"

He huffed, but then knelt beside me and loosened the knots in the ropes. Heidel did the same, and then they helped me stand as flames engulfed the cavern.

A hoarse, primal scream cut through the noise, and the sounds of yelling died down until we were left with only the sounds of crackling flames.

"Jahr'ad," Kull yelled.

Through the flames, I saw Kull's silhouette standing atop

the lifeless form of the dragon. I almost didn't recognize the man, shirtless, covered in blood, his hands clenching the mace as it swung back and forth, making the chain clink. Embers drifted past him on waves of hot, shimmering air. He looked like something from a legend—something primal—a force of destruction. Was this really the same man I'd spent my time with, who'd discussed building libraries, who spent his time reading books and making friendly chitchat with elven nobles? No, this wasn't the Kull I knew.

My breathing grew shallow as I stared at the man atop the beast. Was this really the person I intended to spend the rest of my life with?

"Jahr'ad," Kull shouted. "Show yourself!"

Silence answered. As I stared around the empty balconies, the thought struck me that perhaps Jahr'ad's men had been prepared for the fire and they'd all headed into the inner chambers until the flames died out.

"Jahr'ad," Kull repeated. "Where are you?"

Jahr'ad and Zariah appeared from the flames. Streamers of crimson magic wrapped around the two as they approached Kull. Maveryck, Heidel, and I also approached the room's center. Ash flitted on invisible waves of overheated air, creating a maelstrom of flickering embers funneling around Kull as he stood atop the dragon's corpse.

Blood trickled from a small wound in his chest. The cut didn't look deep, but with the angry red streaks fanning outward around the gash, I was fairly certain he'd been infected with dragon venom.

"You killed my dragon," Jahr'ad shouted.

"So I have." Kull swung the mace and embedded the spiked ball with a low thunk deep in the dragon's hide. He leapt to the ground. His eyes smoldered as he stood straight and faced Jahr'ad.

"Now, you will tell us the secrets of the witch's spell."

"Not so fast, Wult. That dragon gave you a good dose of poison. As I see it, you'll be dead soon, so you haven't won at all. I owe you nothing."

"No, Jahr'ad," Maveryck said, "that was not the deal. He beat your dragon. Now you must uphold your end of the bargain."

Jahr'ad worked his jaw back and forth. "Fine, we'll deal in the morning."

"No," Maveryck said, blocking his path. "We'll deal now or

not at all."

"You're pushing your luck with me, thief."

Maveryck set his jaw. Grim determination shone in his eyes. "Let's hope you don't push mine."

I had to admit, Maveryck could stand his ground when he wanted.

The two men faced one another without speaking until Jahr'ad turned around and headed for the tunnels. "Fine, but this had better end quickly." He marched out of the domed area and back into the catacombs. I stayed back to keep pace with Kull.

"You're hurt," I said.

He glanced at the blood trickling down his chest. "I've had worse."

"But it's poisoned, and I don't have my magic to heal you."

"I've been poisoned before and lived through it. I'll be fine."

"You always say that," I said.

"And I'm always right."

"Brother," Heidel said as she marched toward us, "listen to Olive for once. There is a healer here in the caves. We should take you to him."

"No," Kull said. "I don't trust anyone here. If you're really worried about me, then we'll have to restore Olive's magic."

"How?" I asked.

He gave me a crazed smile. "We take it back."

"Zariah won't like it."

"She doesn't have to." Kull tromped toward the open doorway.

Heidel sighed in annoyance as she watched her brother exit the room. "You must marry him soon and take him away to Earth Kingdom. I'm done with dealing with him."

I wasn't sure how my marriage to her brother, if it ever happened, would keep her from dealing with him, but I didn't argue as I followed her down the hallway. Only a few fires still smoldered. The scent of smoke lingered in my hair. I couldn't wait to be free of this place, assuming Kull didn't die first and Jahr'ad actually cooperated and gave us the stone's message.

We entered a tunnel that ended in a single room. A wooden table took up the space at the room's center. Jahr'ad, Zariah, and two of Jahr'ad's men sat across from Kull and Maveryck. The lotus cube sat on the table's center, swirling bands of golden magic churning through the glassy surface. The object was deceptively beautiful.

Heidel and I sat on either side of Kull. Maveryck sat pensively across from Jahr'ad, his eyes narrowed in concentration.

"No person has ever beaten my venom-drake," Jahr'ad said. "The Wult must have cheated. It's the only explanation. More than a dozen men have been killed by that beast, and I've lost count of how many dragons it's bested. He's used magic—that's the only way he could have beaten it."

"However," Maveryck said calmly, "he did indeed beat the dragon. No matter how improbable it may seem, the dragon has been killed. We do not wish to keep you any longer than necessary. Tell us, what is the meaning of this stone?"

Jahr'ad huffed, looking from Maveryck to the stone. "No. I will not. I refuse."

Maveryck fisted his hands, though his voice remained calm. "Then you will no longer have the privilege of trading with me. Is that what you wish?"

Jahr'ad's cheek's burned red. "Fine," he spat, "but this had better be the last time you bring Wults to my home. It that understood?"

Maveryck nodded. "It is."

Jahr'ad took the stone in his hands and read the words. "It's a sort of riddle," he said, "which is common for one of these stones, as dragons loved dealing in riddles in ages past. This one says, '*Gold to find fortune and black to find power, but not all who seek it shall live. It is the last remaining, the end of prophecy. The talisman long sought after shall be the price paid for one who was taken.*'" Jahr'ad looked up. "It basically means that the witch will trade only one thing for whoever it is she's taken—the vachonette egg."

"What is a vachonette egg?" Heidel asked.

"A legend," he answered, "at least to some. It is a dragon egg that is rumored to have unusual properties—the ability to heal and to cure curses are a few of its supposed abilities, but more importantly, it is said that this egg is the only offspring of the witch, and the only egg to contain dark magic. Some claim its worth at more than three million gold pieces. It would fund my operations for several decades at least. In fact, my own men tried to obtain it years ago."

"How did you do that?" I asked. "Did you try to take it from the witch?"

"No, from the elves, my dear." He gave me his sly smirk. "The elves stole her egg years ago. We thought we'd be smart and take it from the elves as they weren't doing anything with it, but when we went to take it, they'd moved it. Put it in a place no mortal would ever get to it again, and that's the honest truth."

"Where'd they put it?" Heidel asked.

Jahr'ad shrugged. "Not my place to say."

"Then how are we to find it?" Kull asked.

"No idea."

"But we've come all this way," I said, "and Kull is dying because he risked his life to learn the stone's message. If you know where the elves have put the stone, then you have to tell us."

His eyes narrowed. "I don't have to tell you anything."

"Jahr'ad," Heidel spat, "I swear as Odin is my witness, I will kill you myself if you do not tell us."

"Is that a threat?"

"Of course it's a threat! How daft are you?"

Zariah's magic glistened, giving her eyes a red sheen. "You should know," she said, "that we do not respond kindly to threats."

"Then what do you respond to?" Kull asked. "We've come here for your help. We've bested your dragon, obeyed your rules, and done everything you've demanded. What more do you want from us?"

Jahr'ad's gaze flicked to mine. "I want her."

"That will never happen," Kull said.

Jahr'ad pulled a small leather pouch from his vest pocket. After opening the drawstrings, he placed the lotus cube inside, then tucked the stone back inside his pocket. "Then our bargaining is over. I've told you the meaning of the stone as you've asked. If you want more information, you know my price. If you choose not to pay it, you know the way out. I would leave quickly, if I were you. We're not accustomed to babysitting outsiders."

Jahr'ad stormed out of the room with Zariah and his men following him, leaving us alone in the room.

Feeling deflated, I slumped in my chair. "I hate him," I said.

"The feeling is mutual," Kull said.

Heidel spoke up. "But at least he told us what the cube said."

"Yes, there is that," I agreed. "What do you make of the witch's message?" I asked Maveryck.

"I believe Jahr'ad's interpretation is correct. The witch has been seeking the egg for many years, and it would make sense that she would demand its return in exchange for the release of your stepfather. However, I also believe that the witch knows how difficult is it to find the egg, making our task nearly impossible."

I rested my chin in my hands, my heart weighing heavy in my chest. It was hard not to picture Fan'twar locked in a dungeon, being tortured or beaten or starved. Even though we'd learned the stone's meaning, it seemed we'd come no closer to freeing my stepfather, and if we failed to free him, I couldn't imagine what evil the elves would unleash on Faythander. Fan'twar wouldn't be the only slave. The elves would make sure of that.

"Don't lose hope just yet," Maveryck said. "The witch's egg is mentioned in other documents, one of which is in your possession, Olive. Do you still have the journal of the Madralorde brother?"

I thought back to where I'd put it last. "Yes. It's in my pack in the room where Jahr'ad's men were keeping Kull and Heidel. But should we bother with it? Shouldn't we find a way to cure Kull first?"

"Kull will be fine," Maveryck said, "at least, for now. Venom-drake poison takes days to work through the bloodstream. I will deal with Jahr'ad and have your magic restored well before then. But before I confront him, I'd like to give him a moment to cool down. Dealing with Jahr'ad now would be impossible."

"What makes you so sure you can make him see reason?" Heidel asked.

"Because I understand his motivations, that's why. I assure you, Kull's health will be restored. While we're waiting, we might as well get back to the room and try to find out what we can about the egg."

"I agree," I said.

We left the chamber and entered the catacombs. The hallway led us through the main chamber, where I tried to ignore the gore left over from Kull's fight. We finally found the room where Kull and Heidel had been tied up, and I found my pack in the corner where I'd left it. Sitting on the floor, I rummaged through it until I found the journal. The others gathered around me as I carefully turned the pages. Outside, sounds of men's voices echoed from the hallway, though no one seemed to pay us any attention. Slanting rays of sunlight shone through the room's only window, which was nothing more than a narrow slit near the ceiling. Dust motes drifted on an unseen breeze. The window didn't help with the stifling heat. Sweat beaded on my neck as I sat and scanned the book.

Time seemed a rare commodity at the moment. We had to find a way to cure Kull's injury, I had to find a dragon's egg, and we had to do it before Jahr'ad's men kicked us out of here. No pressure.

"There," Maveryck said as I stopped on a page with a drawing of a round circle with symbols inked around the edges. "As far as I've studied, I believe these symbols represent each of the Madralorde brothers. This one is the dagger of Xacvain; this is the staff of Zaladin. I believe this bell-shaped symbol represents the shield of Yerrish. And look here—this is a list of everything needed in order to accomplish the ritual to recall Theht. In addition to the weapons, the practitioner would need several other items to accomplish the ritual."

I scanned over the list of items. "The heart of a jagamoor preserved in fae water. A fairy's wings given willingly. The first breath of fire from a black-magic dragon." I looked up. "But this still doesn't tell us where to find the egg."

"What do we know of the egg?" Kull asked as he paced the room.

"It's the only offspring of the witch, and it most likely contains black magic," I said.

"Yes," Maveryck agreed. "It's also valuable and was last known to be in possession of the elves, but where they are keeping it is a mystery."

"Jahr'ad said the elves put it in a place no mortal person could find. Where could that be?" Heidel asked.

Maveryck shook his head. "It doesn't make sense. If they put it in a place no mortal could find, then how were *they* able to put it in such a place?"

Kull rubbed his neck, and I saw the look of pain in his eyes. His wound was getting worse, and unless I got my magic back, we'd have no way to heal him. But one thing at time. First, we had to figure out where the egg was located.

"Maveryck, surely there must be someone else you know who would have more knowledge on such things?" Heidel asked.

"No. I'm afraid no one knows the dragon egg trade as well as Jahr'ad. There is a reason I risked our lives to come here."

"I still haven't forgiven you for that," Heidel said. "My brother is dying because of you."

Kull cleared his throat. "You would care if I die?"

"Care? No. Would it bother me a little? Possibly."

"Then, are you still angry with me?"

"Of course I am."

I scanned the journal as the siblings continued to argue. Something bothered me. I felt as if I'd seen the egg before but couldn't be sure until I knew what the egg looked like. My gaze snagged on a page in the back of the journal where pictures of each item had been inked onto the parchment, but the egg was only drawn in black and white, so I couldn't be sure if my theory was correct.

"Maveryck," I said. "Do you know what the egg looks like?"

"It is rumored to be very beautiful. Black with golden bands."

"Interesting," I said. "Are there any other eggs that fit that description?"

"No. The vachonette egg is one of a kind. Most eggs take on the color of their magic, making them green or bluish-green, but the vachonette took on black magic, making it the only egg of that color."

"So you're saying there are no other eggs at all that are black?"

"It's the only one. Why do you ask?"

"Because," I answered, "I think I may know someone who's seen that egg. And he's in Earth Kingdom."

Kull and Heidel stopped arguing to stare at me.

"You know where the egg is?" Heidel asked.

"No, but I think I know someone who does."

CHAPTER
Nineteen

KULL, MAVERYCK, HEIDEL, AND I SAT IN THE SMALL, one-window room in Jahr'ad's lair. The air smelled of dust and sand. I tasted its grittiness on my tongue. There were many reasons I wished to be free of this place, but getting that taste out of my mouth was pretty high on my list.

"Who do you know who has knowledge of the egg?" Heidel asked.

"His name is Zack Zimmerman," I answered. "He's a weather reporter in Earth Kingdom."

"A weather reporter?" Maveryck asked. "How would he know where the vachonette egg is located?"

"He collects rare eggs called Fabergé eggs. One in particular looked just like the egg we're looking for. I have no idea how he would have come into contact with the vachonette egg, except that he must have traveled to Faythander and seen it."

"Are you certain of this?" Maveryck asked.

"No, I'm not certain of anything. It could be a huge coincidence he collects eggs that look like the vachonette, but I don't think so. I tested him, and he has been exposed to elven magic. At the time, I thought it was a fluke, but now I believe he must have come to Faythander. He must have seen the egg we're looking for, but there's only one way to know for sure. I'll have to travel to Earth Kingdom and find out."

"We'll have to get your magic back before you can create a portal," Kull said.

"Yes, but how?" I asked.

"Leave that to me," Maveryck said as he stood tall, his robes rustling. "Jahr'ad has hopefully had a moment to cool

179

down. Plus, after his botched negotiating, Jahr'ad owes me a favor."

"You're sure you can deal with him?" Kull asked.

"I am."

"I disagree," Heidel said. "Jahr'ad won't negotiate anything unless it benefits him. It's unlikely we'll escape this place unscathed."

"I give you my word that we will leave this place without injury, but you must let me deal with him on my own terms. I shall return shortly."

He backed out of the room and left without another word. I watched him go, feeling a mixture of confusion and admiration at his brazen attitude. What made him so sure he could get my magic back and get us out of here?

"He's a fool," Heidel said, "and he's more overconfident than you, Brother. Never in a million years did I think I would say such a thing."

"I'll take that as a compliment."

"You shouldn't."

Kull leaned against the wall, his arms crossed, looking barbaric with his naked torso and blood drying on his chest. I was reminded of the time I'd spent with him in Geth's camp after he'd been attacked by a Regaymor. My heart fluttered at the memory. How was this man able to hold such power over me? Even with his injuries, he had a commanding presence, and after his fight with the venom-drake, the tales of his god-like strength would only become more exaggerated.

"Olive," Heidel said, "since we're alone for a moment, I thought perhaps... that is... I was wondering if you might... would you do the spellcasting?" she asked.

"I wish I could, but I can't do it without my magic."

"Are you sure?"

"Yes."

"Can't you at least try?"

"I suppose I could try. It might be possible to use only the mirror's magic without using my own, but I can't guarantee anything."

"That is sufficient for me," Heidel said. I went to my pack and found my mirror. After pulling it out, I sat on the floor, and Heidel sat across from me. I placed the mirror case between us.

It felt strange to do a spellcasting without my magic and here in Jahr'ad's lair, but if Heidel truly wanted her memories back, we didn't have the luxury of finding a more suitable place to perform the test.

"Brother," Heidel said, "will you kindly leave the room?"

"Me? Why?"

"Just do it," she said.

He remained in the room a moment longer, looking from the mirror to his sister, but he finally relented and stepped outside. Heidel turned to me. Sweat beaded on her forehead, and her eyes darted. I wasn't sure I'd ever seen her so nervous.

"If this works, you will not speak of what we find in the mirror, will you?" she whispered.

"I promise this will be between you and me," I said.

"Good. I have an ill feeling about what I might learn. But I must know the truth."

"I understand."

I opened the case and felt a surge of energy flow from the mirror. Its electric-blue glow warmed me. Power built within me, filling the empty spaces where my magic had once resided. I wasn't sure it was enough to fuel the spell, but it was better than nothing.

I scanned the five figurines arranged on the mirror's velvet lining, but since we were doing the spell in reverse and I was attempting this with limited magic, I left the figurines alone. Instead, I placed the mirror case on my lap and turned it to face both of us.

"Whenever you're ready, put your hand on the screen."

She hesitated, but then did as I said. As soon as she touched the screen, the magic reacted. Blue streamers of magic swirled from the screen, casting a spell that encircled us. On the screen, a city appeared. With the Eiffel Tower standing at the town's center, its identity was unmistakable.

"Where is that?" Heidel asked.

"Paris, France. In Earth Kingdom."

"I went to Paris?"

"It appears so."

"But what happened?"

"Wait, you'll see," I answered.

Soon, the scene shifted, but instead of sitting in a room looking at a mirror, we stood on the streets of Paris. Heidel spun around, her eyes wide.

"It's okay," I said. "This is just a memory. Nothing can hurt you here."

Sounds of car horns and conversations echoed through the streets. People jostled past, seeming to walk through us as if we were ghosts. We stood under a sign that read *Banque de France*.

Heidel and Maveryck stood arguing at the bank's doors until he finally went inside, leaving her alone on the street. She cursed and spun away from the bank, walking at a brisk pace down the sidewalk.

The Heidel from the memory still wore a breastplate tarnished with dark blood. Bystanders gave her odd glances as she brushed past, but she seemed oblivious as she tromped through the crowd.

"What were we arguing about?" Heidel asked me.

"I don't know. It was hard to hear your conversation over the traffic, but since he went inside the bank and you didn't, it's possible you were arguing about money. I can't be sure."

"Why is there blood on my breastplate?" she asked. "Do you think it was from the wraith we were battling?"

"It's possible. You said before you left Faythander, you were fighting off the witch's wraiths."

The scene grew darker as night approached. We hovered above a crowd of people gathered around the foot of the Eiffel Tower. Heidel stood among them. Behind her, a man with wispy white hair and wolfish yellow eyes stalked her. She spun around, but the person disappeared out of sight.

"Was that the wraith?" she asked.

"I think so. The portal crossing must have changed its looks. It must have been stalking you."

The scene shifted once again, and we hovered above an empty street near a sprawling, historic hotel. The Heidel from the memory had changed clothes, and I almost didn't recognize her.

Beside me, the real Heidel gasped. "What in Odin's name was I wearing?"

The shimmering dress hugged her chest and cascaded in a waterfall of silver fabric to the ground. Tiny crystals sewn into the silky fabric glittered in the pale lamplight. Her dark, slightly curly hair flowed around her shoulders and down her back, and I didn't mention it, but she actually looked beautiful. She walked alone down the street, and with her red cheeks and fisted hands, it looked as if something, or most likely someone, had upset her.

Her high-heeled shoes clicked over the cobbled street. A shadow darted in front of her and she stopped, then pressed her back against the wall of the building as she watched, waiting, with only the sounds of distant motors to break up the silence.

After several minutes, with no other signs of life coming from the street ahead, Heidel moved out of the shadows, only to have a form materialize behind her. The wraith moved so fast its hands blurred as it grabbed Heidel around her waist and stabbed her midsection.

The creature threw her to the ground as dark blood seeped from the wound, staining the dress.

The scene shifted once again, and we found Heidel lying on a bed in a room lit only by the pale, silvery glow of the city through sheer curtains. We must have been inside a hotel in one of the most expensive rooms I'd ever seen. The gleam of gold came from the embellished dressers, headboard, picture frames, and mirrors. Maveryck was in the room with her, wearing a suit that accentuated his lean, athletic frame. His light, purple-tinted eyes looked ghostly in the dim light.

"What's he doing?" Heidel asked.

A burst of light blinded us for a moment but then dimmed, leaving us to watch as Heidel grabbed Maveryck by his shirt collar and kissed him.

Magic jolted through me as the image faded. Once again, we were in the room in Jahr'ad's cavern.

Heidel sat across from me, her hands shaking before she tucked them in her lap and away from the mirror's magical screen, which would explain why the memory had stopped.

"That... that wasn't," she stumbled over her words, "that didn't really happen, did it? Your magic must have been compromised somehow. That couldn't have been me. I know it wasn't me. I would never..."

I didn't say anything. Those were memories she'd have to work through on her own.

"He did something to me. He must have enchanted me somehow. There was that flash of light right before I... I... You know I never would have done that willingly. I hate him."

"I know."

"Then why did I do it? Is there some sort of spell he could have used—a love spell, perhaps?"

"It's possible, but not likely. Love spells aren't what you think, and if he'd used one on you, we would know."

"How?"

"Your personality would change. You would stop eating and sleeping. Most people avoid using love spells for those reasons."

"But he must have done something to me. There really is no other explanation. I swore to myself... after Geth... I swore I would never lose my heart again."

Her breathing grew fast and shallow. She reached for her scabbard and pulled out a knife. Its pearl-inlayed pommel glinted in the sun streaming through the narrow window. She placed the dagger on her lap and studied it with guarded eyes.

"What's that?" I asked.

"An Earth Kingdom weapon. I had it after we came back, but I didn't know where it came from." She looked up at me. "He must have given this to me," she said quietly.

"Yes, that's a possibility."

"Why do you think he did it?"

"There's no way to be sure, but usually gifts are a sign of affection."

She swallowed as if to keep back the tears. "Do you think he... had feelings for me?"

"It seems possible. It's also very likely that he still does."

"I can't talk to him about this."

"You may have to."

She nodded, still staring at the dagger but not touching it. "Olive, I'm sorry, but I need some time alone."

"Of course. I understand." I closed my mirror box and replaced it in my pack, then quietly made my way out of the room.

I wasn't sure what to do for Heidel, if there was anything I could do. Her past wasn't something that would just go away. No matter how hard she tried to avoid it, her past would always be a part of her life. The best she could do was accept it and move on. I wouldn't tell her, but maybe having feelings for Maveryck wasn't such a bad thing. If he helped her move forward, then maybe accepting him would help her heal.

Walking through the empty hallways, I wasn't sure where to go next. I made my way down to the bottom floor where Zariah passed me. Her magic brushed against mine, making fear and adrenaline rush through me, but she ignored me and continued walking the other way. I hoped Maveryck would get Jahr'ad to cooperate so I could get my magic back soon. Until then, I decided I couldn't stand being covered in filth a moment longer.

I wandered into the room with the pool. Steam filled the air, making beads of sweat form in my hands and on the back of my neck. As I approached the water's edge, I found Kull resting with his eyes closed in the water.

He looked worse. The wound in his chest was streaked with red marks that spread to his collarbone. It seemed being wounded or injured was his lot in life. I supposed I would have to get used to it.

I didn't begrudge his vow to remain true until he married me. In fact, I respected him for it because it meant he intended to marry me, and that thought gave me more joy for my future than any prospects I'd had before. Not long ago, I'd resigned myself to being a cat lady and living a life of solitude with Han.

I undressed, removing my boots and socks, then took off my cloak and sand-covered pants and shirt, leaving only a bra, undershirt, and panties. As I entered the pool, Kull opened his eyes, shockingly blue as the water reflected in his irises. Sometimes I forgot what an overwhelming presence the man had. My heart fluttered, feeling light in my chest, and my stomach flipped.

The water felt almost too warm, but it wasn't hot enough to be scalding. I sat on a ledge across from Kull, the rippling water separating us. I wanted to be with him so badly the need was almost painful, and being here, with him half-undressed in the water, made the emotion nearly unbearable.

Taking a deep breath, I tried to steady my thumping heart, but it didn't help.

"Is something the matter?" he asked.

"No. Why would anything be the matter?"

He eyed me. "Nothing. Never mind."

"Never mind? Tell me."

"Very well. Your ears have gone pink."

I pressed my hands to my ears, and sure enough, the pointed tips were burning hot. Stupid elven ears. I may as well have written my emotions on my forehead. Kull slowly narrowed the distance between us. He moved so slowly the water only rippled gently around him.

My heart leapt into my throat. Would I always feel so lightheaded in his presence? The water flowed in placid waves around his broad, muscled torso, his skin turned golden bronze in the firelight. He came close enough to reach out and touch me if he'd wanted, but he held back and only looked at me with those intense eyes.

"Why are you so beautiful?" he whispered.

"I'm not. You only think I am."

185

"Have you put me under your spell?"

"Maybe I have."

He moved closer and ran his fingers up my legs, caressing my skin. My chest tightened as his hands found my waist and he pulled me to him. His lips found my ear.

"Is this what it feels like to be bewitched? Whatever you ask, I will do it without a thought. I will kill for you if you ask it of me."

"Then let's hope I never ask it."

He dipped his head lower and kissed my neck. My body melted at his touch. His hands drew me to him, pressing me against his chest. My thoughts disappeared. I only knew I wanted him and couldn't rest until I had him.

I ran my fingers over his chest, lightly grazing the small mark where the dragon had inflicted its poison, then I let my hands wander to his abdomen, where I felt the firm bumps and ridges of his stomach muscles. His gaze met mine, and I ran my fingers over his lips, caressing them, finding them surprisingly soft under my fingertips. He took my hand in his and kissed my fingers, and then he moved away. His eyes grew dark as he studied me, filling me with an entirely different emotion as lust turned to fear.

"Kull, what's the matter?"

"It's..." he sighed and looked away. "It's something the witch showed me in her castle. I've been meaning to tell you, but I wasn't sure how."

"Are you sure you're ready to tell me now?"

"Yes. Keeping it to myself is tearing me apart."

"Then what is it? What did the witch show you?"

"Olive," he said quietly, "there's more to the Deathbringer prophecy than you know. I'm in it as well."

His gaze met mine, making me shudder at the fear I found in his eyes.

"And I'm destined to kill you."

CHAPTER *Twenty*

"KILL ME?" I ASKED, CONFUSED.
I sat in the pool with Kull as the warm, steaming water splashed gently around us. He'd told me something that should have scared me, but I couldn't feel fearful yet, not until I knew more.

"That's ridiculous. You would never hurt me. Would you?"

"Of course not. You're everything to me. You're my life. Without you, I'm nothing. I know because I've been there before and it's an awful place. A dark place. If I killed you, then I would have no choice but to kill myself as well, because I could never go on without you."

His words stirred a powerful emotion within me. He'd shared his feelings with me before, but never with so much intensity.

"There is a legend my people have," Kull said, "about the end times. Some believe that our world will end in fire, and that an ancient goddess wielding flame and ash will ignite our lands and burn everything in her path. They say that only one can stop her, the one wielding the sword of Dracon. He will slay her, and our lands will be saved.

"All Wults are taught this story from a young age in our religious studies, but the legend has been around for hundreds of years, and I was never sure I actually believed the tale. Until now."

"What made you change your mind?"

"Silvestra. She showed me visions, I guess you could call them, but they weren't, really. I felt as though she'd transported me to the future. Like I was really there. I saw you, Olive. I saw Theht working through you. I saw you burn our world."

My heart stopped. I wanted to make a reply, but my mouth grew too dry to speak. I wanted to defend myself and tell him I would never willingly destroy the world, but I'd seen it happen too, and I knew as well as he that it was only a matter of time before it happened.

Theht's consciousness stirred inside my mind. I felt it there like a cancer waiting to spread.

"There's more," he said. "Silvestra's voice was in my mind. She kept repeating the prophecy over and over. She told it to me so many times that I've got it memorized. 'Only the one who wields the shadow-forged sword will have the power to stop the Deathbringer. His name will bring power. Hate shall flee from his sight, never again to return. Power to wield and power to kill. Legend will follow wherever he goes. His life will bring the death of the chosen one. His destiny shall bring peace. He shall kill the one he loves, for love shall bring her end'."

Silence filled the cavern. I couldn't speak. My stomach roiled, and I felt as if I would be sick.

"Do you think it's true?" I asked.

"Yes. Not only did I hear her words, but I saw it happen. I stabbed you through the heart, and then I held you as you passed. In my mind, it was a mercy killing."

"I don't believe it's true. It couldn't be."

"I thought the same thing. For a while."

"But now you think differently?"

"I believe prophecies happen whether you try to stop them or not."

"But it's not true. You would never kill me."

His face grew grim. "Unless the thing that inhabited your body was no longer you," he said quietly.

Lapping water filled the silence.

"But the vision I saw showed me killing you. They can't both be right."

"I got the feeling that one or the other will happen. If I fail to kill you, then Theht will use you to destroy our world."

"Then we'll stop this," I said. "If Theht takes over my body, we'll stop her. We'll do whatever is in our power to make sure it never happens, or we'll die trying. I can't give in to accepting it as truth or I'll lose hope, and if I do that, then I'll never be able to fight Theht."

Kull remained silent.

188

"Don't you agree?" I asked.

"I agree that we shouldn't lose hope. But we're wasting our time trying to fight prophecy. There has to be another way."

"Like what?"

He shook his head. "I don't know yet."

He turned and exited the water, and I did the same. We dressed quickly, though my mind wasn't on the task. I dried off as best as I could and then put on my clothes, but I couldn't stop thinking about Kull's words. There had to be a loophole in the prophecies. There had to be a way to beat them, but I knew so little about prophecies to begin with, and the one person who could tell me more was being held prisoner by the silverwitch.

The steam-filled room muffled the sounds of footsteps, but soon several people entered and gathered by the pool. Jahr'ad, Zariah, Heidel, and Maveryck stood in the room with us.

"Maveryck informs me that you wish to leave," Jahr'ad said.

"Yes," I answered, "but we'd like my magic back before we go."

"That seems awfully demanding, don't you think? If I let you go, you'll run straight to the sky king and tell him what I'm doing here. I can't let that happen."

I swallowed my panic. I knew Maveryck was too overconfident in thinking he could negotiate our release.

"What if we promise not to tell what we've seen?" Kull said.

Jahr'ad laughed. "Not on your life. Contrary to what most believe, Wults are the worst group of liars you'll find in Faythander. There's a reason I don't consider myself part of your people anymore."

Jahr'ad circled me, his boot steps ringing against the stone floor, his seedy-eyed gaze lingering too long on my body.

"But I will let you go free, and I will give your magic back under one condition."

"What's the condition?" I asked, fairly certain I wouldn't like his answer.

"One night with you."

"What?" I sputtered.

"Never," Kull shouted. "Over my dead body."

Jahr'ad threw back his head and laughed.

"Jahr'ad," Maveryck interjected, "that wasn't the bargain."

"Wasn't it? Must have slipped my mind. I thought I'd have a bit of fun before she left."

Maveryck stepped forward. "I am allowing you to pay half

price for the items I barter in exchange for letting us go freely and with Olive's magic restored. I believe that is quite enough. Jahr'ad, return Olive's magic to her, and we shall be on our way."

"Fine," Jahr'ad ground out. "Zariah, see that the *lady*," he said the word mockingly, "gets her magic back."

Zariah nodded, then let her power flow from her hands and outward toward me. As my magic returned, I felt as if I could breathe again. Going without my magic was one of the worst feelings in the world. I'd rather lose a limb than lose my magic.

Jahr'ad's gaze snagged on me. "We would have had a good time, you and I. You can't blame me for trying."

"Actually, I can," Kull said.

"Have you got a problem with me?" Jahr'ad said.

"No, I've got many problems with you."

Jahr'ad lunged at Kull, his hands balled into tight fists, aiming a punch at Kull's face, but Kull sidestepped, grabbed the man by his long rows of greasy hair, and threw him in the water. The man landed with a splash. Jahr'ad floundered in the pool, cursing and screaming. Zariah pulled a spear off her back and pointed it at Kull.

"I'll kill you for that," she ground out.

"Try it," he said.

Zariah's spear glowed with red magic as she thrust it at him. I felt her magic gathered in a whirlpool around her, ready to strike him down. I had seconds to react, so I pulled my magic inside and then flung my hand at her, letting the blue and amber swirls ignite in a blinding halo of magic. It felt wonderful to wield it again, and as my magic struck Zariah and knocked her to the ground, I was certain that felt even better.

But as the magic cleared, I wondered if I had been too late. Kull stumbled back with the spear's tip embedded in his shoulder. I rushed to him as he pulled the spear out of his flesh and tossed it to the ground.

"You deserve what you get," Zariah spat as she writhed on the floor.

Kull clamped his hand over the wound. "It's nothing," he said as I stood next to him.

"Let me see."

"It only grazed me."

"I've got to heal the venom-drake's wound, anyway. You might as well let me see."

He grumbled, but then moved his hand away. The spear

had pierced deep into his muscle tissue, and the grayish-colored fluid mingling with the blood bothered me.

"The venom-drake's poison has entered his blood," Zariah said. "You're too late to save him."

I helped Kull sit on the ground.

"I'll be fine," he said.

"Stop being brave," I told him.

He gently grabbed my fingers. "I'm not. I've been through worse. Being without you is worse."

I smoothed the hair from his forehead. "I know."

Jahr'ad climbed out of the pool, soaking wet, water streaming off him and making a puddle on the ground. "You," he said, pointing at Kull, "have gone too far." He turned his gaze on me. "Don't you dare heal him. He deserves the fate he gets. I'm warning you, if you dare use one spell on him—"

Maveryck stepped between Kull and Jahr'ad. "Need I remind you of our bargain? Killing him will ensure the end of our trading. Forever."

Jahr'ad spit at Maveryck's feet. "Then you'd better leave now before I start renegotiating. Zariah, come."

Her eyes narrowed. "Are you sure?"

"I said come!"

She lingered a moment longer before storming out of the room, following Jahr'ad. When they'd both disappeared, I turned to Kull. Healing him came easily to me, perhaps because I'd done it too many times to count. Letting the magic flow from me and into him, I felt its power run smooth and strong, an elixir that absorbed the venom and snuffed it out. As the magic worked through his blood, the color slowly returned to his cheeks. He inhaled deeply as the magic dissipated.

"We should go now," Heidel said. "I don't want to be here a moment longer than necessary."

"I agree," Kull said, standing.

"Careful," I said. "You still need to take it easy."

"Why would I do such a thing?"

"I figured you would say that."

"She's right," Heidel said. "You're not immortal, you know."

Maveryck raised an eyebrow. "Why would you use those words?"

"Which words?"

He shook his head. "Nothing. Forget I said anything. Now, if you will all kindly follow me." He headed for the door.

"Don't talk to anyone. We'll have to grab our things, and then we'll make it out."

We followed him through the narrow corridors, found our bags in the room we'd left them in, and then hurried to the exit. We got a few sidelong glances from Jahr'ad's people, but I didn't care. We were finally free, and that was all that mattered.

It took half the day to make it across the desert and back to the light-rails, but the more distance we put between ourselves and the dragon baron, the better. I half expected Jahr'ad to come after us and constantly glanced over my shoulder to make sure he wasn't following.

"Won't he come after us?" Heidel asked, echoing my thoughts.

We must have both been worried about the same thing as we crossed the hot sand with the light-rails in our sight.

"He can't," Maveryck said. "There is one thing you must understand about Jahr'ad. Greed is his only motivation. He won't risk losing his trade with me."

"But won't he worry that we'll tell the sky king of his hideout?" Heidel asked.

"Not necessarily. Jahr'ad is a nomad. He will simply pack up and find a new place. He's used to it. He's done it many times before."

"I hate that man," Kull said.

"I agree," I added.

"We all agree," Heidel said, "except Maveryck. He seems to get along with him just fine."

"I tolerate him. There is a difference." His gaze lingered on Heidel, and she quickly looked away.

Maveryck cleared his throat. "As soon as we reach the rails, I think it would be prudent that Olive journey to Earth Kingdom so she can discover more about the vachonette egg, and with luck, find out the egg's location. That is, if you feel your magic has recovered enough in order to accomplish the spell."

"Yes. I shouldn't have any problems."

I glanced at Kull, not feeling ready to go back, not ready to leave him, especially after the bomb he'd dropped on me. I wished he'd told me sooner about the prophecy, but then again, it couldn't have been easy for him to open up about it. I knew from experience. Hadn't I recently done the very same thing to him?

When we reached the rails, it wasn't long before we spotted a light carriage reflecting the sun far in the distance, zipping down the mountains. Kull squeezed my hand, and I glanced up at him, shielding my eyes as I stared into his face.

"Will you be all right?" he asked.

"I'll be fine. The question is, will you?"

He gave me a slight smile. "I shall be as well as I've ever been. You will come back soon, won't you? I fear this business with the Madralorde is more dangerous than we comprehend. Those weapons were hidden away for a reason. We can't allow the elves to have them."

"I know. That's two reasons why we need to find the egg— to free my stepfather, and to make sure the elves don't use it to summon Theht."

A breeze of hot, dry air gusted past us, bringing a cloud of sand that billowed around the open expanse of desert.

"What will you do while I'm gone?" I asked Kull.

"Start searching for the Madralorde castle, if it even exists. If the elves are intent on recalling Theht to our world, that's where they will do it."

"I agree. But how do you intend to find it?"

He shifted his gaze to Maveryck, who stood talking quietly to Heidel. "I'll start with him."

The sound of whooshing air announced the arrival of the light carriage. It sat reflecting the sun, its bauble-like exterior accented in gold, making me shield my eyes. My stomach dropped as I stared at the carriage. As soon as my companions left, I would be on my own again. I debated on making Kull come with me, but the memory loss and negative side effects were something I was sure he wished to avoid. Besides, he had a kingdom to rule and an ancient castle to find, and I knew searching for a mentally compromised weatherman was beneath him.

The carriage doors opened and Maveryck and Heidel climbed inside. Kull gave me a brief kiss good-bye and then entered the carriage. Dust billowed as the carriage sped away, leaving me alone in the endless expanse of desert.

CHAPTER
Twenty-one

I WOKE FROM THE CROSSING WITH FIFTEEN POUNDS OF cat on my face. My head spun as I pushed Han away, sat up, and tried to recall the past half hour. I remembered the others leaving on the light carriage, and then I'd opened my box and created a portal, but my memories after that were fuzzy.

Had I passed out? Usually I could withstand the side effects better, but things weren't the same as they used to be, and I wasn't the same person. Having a piece of Theht's consciousness inside my mind had changed me in more ways than I cared to admit, and not being able to tolerate the side effects from the portal crossing was proof of it.

Han rubbed against my face, his silky gray fur tickling my nose, and I scratched his head. Poor thing deserved a better life than what I gave him. Thankfully, I had a charitable ex-boyfriend who checked on him, or else I was sure he'd have gone feral.

I stood slowly and made it to the bathroom where I showered, changed clothes, and then collapsed on my bed. I knew I had things to do, people to find, and a world to save, but I was bone-weary, and being back on Earth made all those problems seem so far away. Almost as if they didn't exist. Plus, it was half past two AM, and I wouldn't be tracking down any weathermen at this hour.

Sleep wouldn't come. My mind kept replaying my conversation with Kull. In my half-conscious state, I couldn't think of anything else, and his words kept repeating over and over again. *He shall kill the one he loves, for love shall bring her end.*

At half past six, I crawled out of bed, feeling more worn

194

down and tired than when I'd lain down. I put on my tennis shoes and headed outside, hoping the sea air would help to clear my head. A few stray stars dotted the slate-gray sky. A chilly breeze gusted past, but I didn't mind it as it helped to clear the cobwebs from my head.

Waves crashed along the shore. Even here, fifteen feet up and away from the beach, sea spray flecked the sidewalk and splattered cold drops on my skin. Going from Faythander to Earth always took a bit of adjustment, and the cars passing by, coupled with the sounds of running motors, electric lights, and the absence of Faythander magic, made me feel as if I were missing something—a part of myself that I only found when in Fairy World.

When I'd finished my jog, I felt more like myself again, so I made my way back to my apartment and got to work. I found my file on Zack Zimmerman and studied it, looking for anything I may have missed, or any clue that would tell me whether or not he'd actually come into contact with the vachonette egg. Nothing new stood out. He was a typical guy from the Houston suburbs. Married with two kids. Didn't have a history of mental instability until recently when he'd started having panic attacks and a compulsion to buy very specific Fabergé eggs—of the black and gold variety.

Other than that, I couldn't find any useful information and knew my next step would be to set up another appointment with him, assuming he ever wanted to speak to me again. The last time I'd seen him, I'd gotten the impression he hated me. Call it a hunch.

I found my phone and dialed his cell, but he didn't answer and I was forced to leave a message. He'd listed his wife, a Mrs. Andrea Zimmerman, as his alternate contact, so I tried her next. She picked up on the second ring.

"Hello?" she answered.

"Hi, Mrs. Zimmerman. My name is Dr. Olive Kennedy. I worked with your husband not long ago, and I wondered if I might speak to him?"

"Yes, I remember you," she said, though I couldn't mistake her unfriendly tone. "Zack isn't here."

"Do you know when he'll be back?" I asked.

"No, sorry. You misunderstand. He's gone. He doesn't live here anymore."

"Oh. I see." *This complicates things.*

"I tried his cell, and he didn't answer. Is there another

number I can reach him at?"

"Sorry. If he has another number, I don't have it."

"I see. Thank you for your time."

"Of course."

She hung up without another word. I stared at my phone, wondering what had happened to Mr. Zimmerman. Had he split from his wife? It seemed the logical assumption. If that were the case, how would I ever find him?

Scanning his files again, I tried not to let my frustration win out. There had to be some way to get into contact with him, but as I looked from one page to the next, I couldn't find a single clue to help me. If I didn't find him, then I'd have no way to locate the vachonette egg, and my stepfather would be lost to me forever. I couldn't let that happen. Not only would the entire continent of Faythander suffer because of his absence, but my heart would be irreparably broken. He was the only being who'd ever been a parent to me, and if he died on my account, I would never forgive myself.

A hard lump formed in my throat as I searched desperately from one page to the next. I bravely tried to keep from crying, but deep inside, I knew the reality of my situation. The silverwitch wouldn't let my stepfather live a moment longer than necessary, and unless some miracle happened, I didn't know where else to turn.

The phone rang on my lap, startling me, and I was surprised to see Mrs. Zimmerman's number on the screen.

"Hello?" I answered.

"Dr. Kennedy, this is Andrea Zimmerman again. I called back because I thought you'd like to know something."

"Go ahead."

"Zack is still working at the station. You may be able to catch him there."

She gave me the address, and I found a scrap of paper and scribbled it down, thanking God for small miracles.

"He's there until noon working on the hurricane story, so you may be able to catch him today. Also, there's something else," she said.

"Yes, what is it?"

"I'm not sure how to say this, but... we're expecting another baby. He was so excited when I first told him. He—he'd always wanted a big family. I don't know why I'm telling you this, but if you can get through to him, will you tell him we love him? Will you... will you tell him I love him?"

"Yes, I'll tell him. I promise."

"Thank you so much. That means a lot to me."

She ended the phone call. I didn't want to waste another minute, so I grabbed my keys and mirror case and then rushed to my car.

Outside, gray soupy clouds blanketed the sky, casting a pall over the cracked asphalt parking lot. I found my car, a 1971 T-bird, black with yellow stripes down the sides. I'd almost thought the thing would have been stolen by now, but I had no such luck. The car was a creature of deceptive beauty—a classic on the outside, a disaster under the hood.

The door squealed as I opened it and climbed inside. I sat in the car but didn't crank the engine as feelings of nostalgia tried to overwhelm me. The car reminded me of my old life before I'd returned to Faythander. I'd been a different person then, before I'd met Kull, before I'd encountered Theht.

Yes, I'm changing you.

Pushing the voice out of my head as best as I could, I attempted to start the car. After half a dozen tries, some praying, and then some cursing, the engine cranked. I drove away from my apartment complex and onto Seawall Boulevard. Beyond the seawall, the Gulf was calm with only a few rippling waves moving the water, not enough to break its surface. The sea reflected the sky, a mirror of silver against gray. I'd only seen the water that calm a few times before, and it was usually followed by a hurricane.

Hadn't Mrs. Zimmerman mentioned something about a hurricane?

I would have tuned into the local weather station, but my radio was busted. I figured since I was headed to a news station anyway, I was bound to find out what was going on. After merging onto the freeway, I made good time, even after crossing the Houston city limits. The traffic was unusually light, and I found myself wondering where everyone had gone. Had the storm scared them off?

I exited the freeway and drove into the heart of Houston's downtown district. Skyscrapers overshadowed the narrow roads, keeping the streets hidden in their never-ending shadows. I finally made it to the news station and found a parking spot on the third level of the garage. By the time I grabbed my mirror case, rushed out of the car, and locked the door behind me, it was five minutes till noon.

"Please still be there," I whispered as I dashed for the stairwell and made it down the steps, then to the bottom floor, across a street, and finally into the building's lobby. The news station was on the fifth floor, so I searched for the elevators. I navigated across the marble floor in my scuffed Doc Marten boots, and then past the elegant indoor waterfall feature as it trickled down a modern-looking, glass-tiled backboard.

I pulled the knit scarf tighter around my neck, feeling inadequately dressed in jeans with holes worn through the knees and my *The Wand Chooses the Wizard* T-shirt. Someday, I would have to seriously consider upgrading my wardrobe. If Mr. Zimmerman didn't take me seriously before, he certainly wouldn't do it now. But now wasn't the time to worry over my clothing choices.

I found the elevators and hurried inside before the doors closed. A few professional-looking men and women, dressed in business suits and skirts, stood in the elevator with me as we rode up to the fifth floor.

When the door opened, I followed a few of the people out of the elevator and into the lobby of the news station. Beyond the main desk, a large white star and the red letters *KHTX* took up the back wall.

A young woman in her mid-twenties sat behind the desk, and she looked up as I approached.

"May I help you?" she asked.

"Yes. I'm looking for Mr. Zimmerman. Is he still here?"

"Let me check." She smiled, then picked up her phone and pressed a few buttons. After a pause, she spoke into the receiver. As she spoke, she scribbled something on a notepad and then hung up. "I'm afraid he's out in the field," she said. "He's covering the storm. I'm so sorry, but you just missed him."

"Oh." My heart sank. Was it too much to ask for something to go my way just once? "Is there any way I can get in touch with him?"

"Sorry, no. When our meteorologists are covering a dangerous weather situation, they're not allowed to take anything but emergency calls. It's for safety reasons. But he'll be back at work next Monday. That is—assuming we're all still here. Would you like to set up an appointment to meet with him?"

Next Monday? That was in three days. In three days, Fan'twar could be dead. "That won't be necessary," I said. "Please, isn't there any way I could get in touch with him today? It's really very urgent." I hoped she heard the desperation in my voice.

The lady sighed, looking annoyed, then glanced at her phone. "I guess I could make another call," she said, picking up the receiver. She glanced up at me before dialing. "I wouldn't get my hopes up if I were you. Zack's been really off lately. It's no wonder he got put on field crew, what with all the drama he brings to work with him every day. It'll be a miracle if he even shows up next Monday. I just want you to be prepared in case I can't track him down for you."

"I understand." But I didn't really. First, he'd left his pregnant wife. Now, he was in danger of losing his job? Zack Zimmerman was more mentally unstable than I'd thought. A feeling of guilt weighed on me. If I'd diagnosed him when he'd first visited me, none of this would be happening. But I'd had no way of diagnosing him then and certainly no way of helping him. I only hoped I wasn't too late to help him now.

The receptionist dialed another number and pressed the receiver to her ear. She spoke softly, but with my elven hearing, eavesdropping came naturally.

"You're sure?" she said. "But that's suicide. What's he trying to prove?" She paused. "What about severance pay and breach of contract? No? All right. I won't say anything yet. You too. Thank you." When she hung up, she glanced at me with worried eyes. "I've gotten word that his news van was parked at the Conoco in Jamaica Beach. I have no idea why he went there. He knows full well what happened to that place the last time a storm came through." She let out a nervous laugh. "I'm not sure if you want to go down there with the storm and all, but that's where he is."

"Storm?" I asked.

"The tropical depression is due to make landfall this evening. Didn't you know?"

"I've been out of town for a while."

"Oh, then you should be warned that there are damaging winds and waves predicted, plus a severe tornado threat. Why Zack decided to park his van down there is a mystery to me. But he is a meteorologist. They're not known for being cautious around storms, are they?"

"I guess not."

"I'm really sorry about all this," she said with a brief smile.

"No, it's okay. I'm sure I can find him at the beach."

She raised an eyebrow. "You're still going to the beach?"

"I don't really have a choice."

"I told you about the tornadoes, right? And the winds—up

to seventy miles per hour predicted. Not to mention what the waves and flooding will be like."

"Yes, you did."

"Ma'am," she said quietly. "I know this isn't really my place to say, but Zack's been really depressed lately, as in suicidal depression. He's been volatile at work to the point of violence. It's a dangerous situation, and I can't even imagine how much more stirred up he'll be down on that beach. I wish you would reconsider."

If Zack was suicidal, then I didn't have a moment to waste. "I understand, and that's the reason I have to go."

CHAPTER
Twenty-two

THE WIND LASHED OUT, MAKING THE STEERING WHEEL jerk as I drove down I-45 toward Galveston. A few large raindrops splattered my windshield, followed by a resonating rumble of thunder. As I crossed the causeway over the bay, only a few cars traveled along with me. For the second time today, the traffic hadn't been a problem, but I wasn't so sure that was a good thing.

After crossing onto the island, I took 61st Street toward the seawall and then drove west toward Jamaica Beach. The clouds churned in a roiling gray soup as lightning burst through the thunderheads. The waves, no longer the mirror of calmness, had erupted into frothy, churning walls that crashed with violence on the sandy shore.

My palms grew sweaty as I clenched the steering wheel. Magic tingled under my fingertips. Storms like these had a nasty habit of interfering with my magic. Mr. Zimmerman couldn't have picked a worse time to go AWOL.

The seawall ended, and I drove onto Highway 3005 toward Jamaica Beach. As I left the protection of the seawall, apprehension came over me. Zack must have known how incredibly dangerous it would be out here away from the seawall's protection. The storm of 1900 had claimed more than a thousand lives, and that was before the seawall had been built. Out here, past the seawall and civilization, we were subject to Mother Nature.

The wind picked up, making a shrill wail as it whipped my car back and forth. After fifteen minutes of white-knuckle driving with my heart thudding in my chest, I finally found the gas station. As I pulled into the lot, I spotted a white news van with a large red *KHTX* painted on the side and a small satellite dish on top, speeding away from the Conoco and down a road headed for the beach.

I pulled my car out of the gas station's parking lot and followed the van, trading asphalt for sand as I pulled onto the drive leading toward the beach. The sand shifted beneath my car's tires, and I prayed I didn't get stuck. I found the news van stopped near the shore, and I parked my car, shut off the engine, and then climbed outside.

The beach looked much more intimidating from this angle, with the waves towering over me. The wind almost knocked me down as I struggled to walk across the beach toward the van. Sand and salt, carried on the air currents, stung my eyes. I approached the news van, looking for Mr. Zimmerman or his cameraman, but found no one outside, so I went to the driver's door.

Mr. Zimmerman sat perfectly still in the seat as he stared at the approaching storm, not blinking an eye, making me wonder if he were alive. But when I knocked on the door, he jumped and then rolled down the window. His eyes widened as he looked at me.

"Dr. Kennedy?" he yelled over the wind. "What are you doing here?"

"I'm sorry to bother you, but I need to speak to you. It's sort of urgent."

His expression turned sour. "Now?"

"Yes. As I said, it's urgent."

"I can't talk right now. The storm's coming in, and I have to document it. You really should go. It's not safe."

"It's not safe for you, either. Can't you at least come back to the gas station with me so we can talk?"

"Talk about what? You said you couldn't do anything to help me."

"I know, but I've had a few developments come up that I think you'd like to hear."

He shook his head. "I won't leave!"

"Not even if I can help you?"

"Help me? You ruined me! I should sue you is what I should do. You said you'd never failed to cure a client, but you failed me. My life is a total, screwed-up disaster. Now, will you please leave?"

The waves came closer, crashing with a thunderous fury

as the sea level rose. Bits of foam flecked the air. Cold droplets splashed my skin. I tasted their salty brine on my tongue. It didn't take a genius to realize that the water would soon rise to where I stood. What in the world was the man thinking?

As far as I could tell, he'd brought no camera crew with him, which meant that he intended to be out here on the beach by himself as the waves rolled in. Drowning seemed like an awful way to go, but then again, he wasn't in his right mind.

Zack pressed the button to roll up the window, but I grabbed the glass and he released the button.

"You can't do this," I said. "You have to come back with me. Please. You can't leave your family."

"What do you know about my family?"

"I spoke to your wife earlier."

"My wife? Did she tell you that she kicked me out? Left my stuff on the driveway and changed the door locks? She wouldn't even let me visit the kids, even though I'd done nothing to hurt them. I'd never even raised my voice. Not once. She made me leave because I was a bad bookkeeper, because I squandered all our money and life savings on trinkets. Do you know how I felt the day I realized I lost my family? Nothing compares to that kind of pain. I don't care what they say—losing your family is the worst pain you'll ever experience. And even after that, after all that heartache, do you know what I did? I went online and purchased another one."

His voice cracked as tears formed in his eyes. His hands shook as he removed his glasses.

"Let me do this, Dr. Kennedy. Let me go so they can have their lives back. They'll get the life insurance, and my debts will be erased. I owe them that much, at least."

I tried to remain calm, but having my suspicions confirmed that he was indeed trying to commit suicide came as a shock. "Zack, listen to yourself," I said. "They don't need your money. They need you. Your wife and your kids and your unborn baby—they all need you."

"No they don't! I've ruined their lives. Can't you see that?"

Beyond the van, the sky roared with tornadic fury. I felt as if I stared into the gaping maw of hell itself. Gray clouds spiraled, making a huge funnel-shaped formation. The wind roared like a freight train.

"Goodness gracious," Zack muttered, "is that a tornado forming over the water?"

He grabbed his camera, unlatched the door, and jumped

out of the van. I followed as he ran toward the water. The waves had risen to the van's front tires. Zack splashed through the water as he stood on the beach, facing the storm head-on with the camera on his shoulder, waves crashing around his ankles.

"Mr. Zimmerman," I called over the raging wind. "What are you doing?"

"If I'm going to go," he shouted back, "then I'll do it like this. That tornado is headed straight this way. I couldn't ask for a more perfect moment. I'm sorry, Dr. Kennedy, but this is the opportunity I've been waiting for. You should leave now."

"I can't leave. I need your help. Please, just come away from the beach so we can talk."

He ignored me to stare into the face of the storm. With the waves crashing in my ears, coupled with the deafening roar of the wind and the sand blasting my skin, I felt as though the storm would tear me apart.

Fear trembled through my veins as I watched the waves tower over us, some the height of two-story buildings, and beyond them, the greenish-gray sky loomed. I could distinctly make out the shape of a funnel cloud, an enormous dark gray block against the lighter gray sky. The wind ripped past with a fury so strong it nearly knocked me over as I trudged toward Zack. Cold water splashed my ankles, then my calves and thighs as I struggled forward.

I refused to let him go this way. Zack was right—I'd never failed to cure a client, and I damn well wouldn't let it happen now.

A wave rose over us, so tall it blocked out the sky. As it crested, my mind went blank, absorbed by fear.

Water crashed around us, so cold it stole my breath. The current tugged me under. The salt-saturated liquid filled my lungs, burning my throat, and stinging my eyes. Brown, silt-laden darkness surrounded me. My ears popped as they filled with water. I kicked for the surface when the wave retreated, leaving me and Mr. Zimmerman alone on the beach. As I sat up, I choked on the water, and then took several deep breaths. Mr. Zimmerman sputtered and coughed as he lay on the sand.

Shivering, I crawled toward him and grabbed his arm, then tugged him upright. His eyes were wide and filled with fear. Perhaps the rogue wave had been his wake-up call.

"What are you doing?"

"We're getting to my car. This is insane."

"No, I won't go." But he didn't sound as determined as earlier, so I managed to get him in a standing position and tug him to my car. Thankfully, I'd parked far enough away that the water hadn't reached it yet.

I opened the passenger side door and shoved him in. The wind was so strong it nearly tore the door from its hinges, and it took several tries for me to slam it shut. After I walked around the car and attempted to open the driver's side door, I briefly glanced at the sky. Palm fronds and plastic bags whipped through the air. Beyond the debris, the tornado took up half the sky.

After yanking my door open, I slid onto the seat, then slammed the door shut behind me. With shaking hands, I cranked the car, but only the rumble under the seats told me the engine had ignited as the raging roar of the wind drowned out any other sounds.

As I backed the car off the beach, Zack kept his hands tucked in his lap as he rocked back and forth, his eyes unmoving from the sky. He looked on the verge of bolting out the door to face the storm once again, but Heaven help me, I refused to let him do it.

"Stay with me, Zack. We're going to take shelter in the gas station. You've got to pull through this, okay?"

He mumbled something, but I couldn't understand the words.

Hailstones pelted the car's windshield, small at first, but growing larger as we neared the gas station. I parked the car in front of the store, then killed the engine. The clatter of the ice pellets echoed through the car. Zack remained motionless in his seat. With the haunted look in his eyes, he seemed close to a nervous breakdown.

"We've got to get inside," I yelled.

He buried his head in his hands. "No," he moaned. "I can't."

"Yes, you can. Just follow me. We'll do this together."

He looked up, his face filled with rage. "Why are you even trying to help? I'm this way because of you. You deserve to die with me!"

His words stung, but I tried not to let it show. "Please try to understand, I wish I could have helped you sooner, but I didn't know how. Now, I think I may know how to help you. Just come inside the store with me. That's all I'm asking."

He sat for a moment longer, seemingly mulling over my

words, and then he grabbed the door handle and flung it open. I followed him outside. Hailstones pummeled my head and neck, making me sprint to the double glass doors and fling them open. Zack stayed behind me as we darted inside the gas station.

The door slammed behind us. Inside, two women huddled behind the counter. Zack and I headed for the hiding place as the hailstones pelted the glass windows, fracturing them. The sound of cracking glass mingled with the roar of the wind.

"Mind if we hide with you?" I shouted over the noise.

"Go ahead for now, but we'll be moving into the bathroom if it gets any worse," one of the women answered. "And pray we survive."

Zack and I ducked behind the counter, leaving me with a partial view of the world outside. Several palm trees surrounded the station and the road across the street, and the wind battered them, tearing off entire sections that got sucked into the storm. Streetlights illuminated the pitch-colored sky in pools of hazy orange. I wasn't sure I'd ever seen the sky so dark during daytime.

The sound of the wind changed in intensity, from a high-pitched wail to a low, deafening howl—the characteristic sound of a freight train.

"It's coming," Zack said beside me.

"In here," one of the women said as she unlocked a bathroom. We crammed inside as she shut the door behind us. We huddled near the sink, and although I was indoors, I wasn't sure the thin layer of boards and roof shingles would be enough to protect us from the mammoth tornado I'd seen over the ocean.

I squeezed my eyes shut as the sounds of crashing came from outside the door. My heart echoed the sound of the freight train, beating so forcefully I was surprised it didn't crack my chest. Something banged against the door, making me jump back. One of the women let out a muffled scream.

The sound of ripping came from overhead, and water dripped in streams from the ceiling and pooled onto the linoleum floor.

"Have we lost the roof?" one of the ladies asked.

Tiles ripped away from the ceiling, revealing patches of the outside sky, a sickening greenish-gray. Overhead, pieces of debris whipped past as the funneling winds sucked them away.

"Are we gonna die?" one of the women screamed, her voice panicked. I wanted to reassure her that everything would be okay, but the fear wouldn't let me speak, and I wasn't sure I would be telling the truth anyway. Maybe Zack would get his wish after all.

I kept my arms tucked over my head as the tornado passed over us, tearing off large sections of the roof. A massive clatter erupted around us as the wind ripped apart the tiny bathroom. The sink tore from the wall, spraying water over us. Chunks of cinder blocks crumbled onto the floor, raining bits of sharp stone down onto the floor.

Broken pieces of plywood combined with the stones. Something heavy struck my head. I fell back, screaming, realizing I was going to die, and then everything went black.

I awoke with the metallic taste of blood in my mouth. As I opened my eyes, I found Zack hunched over me. As I scanned the area surrounding us, I realized I was lying in what was left of the bathroom—half a wooden frame, a portion of the roof, and the toilet remained sticking up in a sea of boards and debris. I rubbed my head, feeling a tender bruise on my cheek and along my hairline.

"Where's everyone else?" I asked.

"They're fine. They both made it back to their cars, and we're waiting on an ambulance. You got it the worst, I'm afraid."

"Oh." My head felt as if it had turned to lead, and I had trouble focusing on Zack's face. But I didn't have time to wait for an ambulance. I'd been in Earth Kingdom for far too long already, and now that the tornado had passed, I was desperate for answers.

"Zack," I said, "please, will you let me help you now?"

"Help me?" he asked, confused. "What do you mean? I'm helping you. Come on, let me at least get you back to your car."

"My car? It's okay?"

I glanced over his shoulder to find the beast still parked where it was. Except for a few new dents, the car looked pristine.

"Fine," I grumbled and allowed him to help me stand. I hobbled on shaky feet back to my car, unlocked the door, and sat in the driver's seat. I had trouble focusing on anything. My thoughts felt like a jumbled mess. But one thing I did know—I needed Zack's help finding the vachonette egg. That one thought played through my head as I found my bag in the backseat, thankful my mirror was still intact inside. The feel of the plastic casing under my fingers gave me a sense of relief and helped me clear my head. My stomach felt sick and my head pounded. I'd most likely suffered a concussion, but none of that mattered right now.

As I opened my mirror, the familiar Faythander magic enveloped me.

"You're really doing this now?" Zack asked.

"Yes. I don't have a choice." I turned to him as he knelt on the ground outside my door. "There are some really bad things happening in Fairy World. My stepfather, the dragon king of Faythander, has been captured, and the only way to get him free is by trading him for a very rare dragon egg. It's called the vachonette, and it's black with gold bands—the only one of its kind."

His eyes widened. He pulled the pendant from beneath his shirt collar. A tiny black-and-gold egg hung suspended on the silver chain. "Like this?"

"Yes. Exactly like that."

"But I don't understand. Why do you need my help?"

"Because you've most likely seen it. And you're the only person who may know where it's located. That's why it's so important I do this spellcasting. If we can figure out where you saw that egg, then I may be able to get my stepfather back."

He shook his head. "Dr. Kennedy, you're in no condition to be working right now. Let the ambulance get here first. Let the medical team examine you. Then we can talk diagnosis."

"But I can't wait that long. Please, every second we waste brings him closer to death. You don't understand what sort of monster is holding him captive. She will do what she says—she will kill him."

He looked out over the landscape. Palm trees stuck up like matchsticks, stripped of their leaves. Ruined piles of lumber mingled with broken windows. In a few places, shelves were still standing, holding on to their stacks of canned corn and mixed fruit. Although the tornado had passed, we still had the storm to deal with, yet the rainy drizzle seemed like nothing compared to the tornado. Zack's breathing grew shallow as he wiped beads of sweat from his forehead.

"You know," he said, "it was a short time ago that I was begging you for help." He looked at me. "If I do this, will it cure me of my compulsions?"

"I can't say for certain, but there's a very good chance

you'll never struggle with your mental disease again."

"And... do you think I'll be able to have a normal life again?"

"I've seen it happen for many people. I don't think you'll be any different."

He nodded, finally seeming to make up his mind. "Very well," he said with a sigh. "Show me what's in the mirror."

CHAPTER
Twenty-three

SIRENS WAILED IN THE DISTANCE AS I SAT IN MY CAR with Zack kneeling beside me. The ruin the tornado had left behind littered the ground as far as we could see, but despite the destruction, I was focused on something else.

"What makes you think you'll be able to work the spell now?" Zack asked me.

"Because now I have a way to focus on what happened when you went there. Could you take off your necklace, please?"

He did as I said and pulled the chain off his head.

"May I hold it?" I asked.

He nodded, then placed it in my palm. "Careful," he said. "That's worth twenty-two grand."

"I'll keep that in mind. You remember how we did this last time?"

"I think so."

"Good. Just try to stay calm while the magic works. Remember, we'll only be seeing your memories. Nothing can hurt you."

"I understand."

Magic formed in my hands as I held the egg pendant. Blue and amber light glowed from my hands and into the stone, reflecting in the mirror. My hope was that the stone would serve the same purpose as the figurines and we'd have better results this time. But I wasn't certain of anything, so when the mirror's screen reacted to the magic and swirled with color instead of remaining empty like last time, I felt a tiny bit of hope.

"Now," I told Zack, "put your hand on the screen."

He hesitated, looking from me to the screen, as if uncertain whether or not he could trust me, but finally, he seemed to make his decision and placed a hand on the screen.

Warm magic poured from the glass, enveloping us both as we got sucked into the memory.

Zack and I stood in a small room made of metal and copper wires. A quiet, mechanical hum came from somewhere as the floor vibrated beneath our feet. The small cubicle seemed to be made for a purely functional purpose, although I noted elven aspects of the architecture—the way the metal panels were lined with ivy vines etched around their edges, the elegant curve of the room's only table.

The room wasn't what I'd been expecting. Usually a person's memories took us to a typical Faythander location, somewhere in nature, but this room was like nothing I'd ever seen before. I felt for magic in the room, and a spell came to my senses. The bluish color surrounded us, hard to detect, but it felt like Queen Euralysia's magic.

I spun around, searching for some explanation to our location, when Zack spoke up.

"I remember this." He took a step forward, running his hand over the smooth metal table. "It's difficult to recall, exactly. I remember the portal opening... I remember going through and finding a field full of these beautiful blue flowers. I'd never seen anything like them. Beyond the field, there was a strange building standing on top of a hill. After I went inside, I saw... elves inside. I know that sounds strange."

I cleared my throat and smoothed my hair away from my ears. "I've heard of stranger things. Keep going. You saw elves inside the building?"

"Yes. They were building something—it was made of metal, and it was tall." He tapped his fingers on the table. "I didn't know what it was. And then... the elves spoke to me. They said they'd brought me here because they thought I could help them. I was confused and wasn't sure what they wanted, so they threatened me. I remember being frightened. I thought they would hurt me—kill me, possibly—but then, something happened." He paused.

"What happened?"

"I cooperated." He stepped away from the table and searched the room, looking from the copper wires to a panel with symbols etched into its face. He traced his finger over the symbols. "The elves said they were interested in some research

I'd done. I was a weatherman back on Earth, but that wasn't how I'd originally started out. Before that, I was determined to be rocket scientist. In college, I'd even written a paper on an alternate form of rocket fuel using ions. I won an award for it.

"The elves wanted to know more about it." He spun around as realization lit his face. "That's it," he said. "They were running out of their own fuel and needed something else. That's why they'd taken me. I helped them engineer an alternate fuel, and then they put me on this ship and sent me to their base on the moon." He spun around, his eyes wide. "I remember," he said excitedly. "Dr. Kennedy, this is where I saw the egg."

The room faded, replaced by a building with a domed, glass roof that looked out onto a gray, rocky landscape. Amazingly, the blue orb of Earth rose above us.

"We're on the moon," I gasped.

"Yes!" Zack said. "This is where they took me."

I scanned the room and found neat rows of stacked treasures. Sitting apart from the rest, I found what I had been searching for. The vachonette egg sat on a silver pedestal. It was smaller than I'd imagined, about the size of a beach ball, and its golden bands swirled like clouds. Zack approached the egg.

"This is it," he said quietly. "This is where they put the egg."

Despite my elation at finding the egg, I felt my heart drop.

"So that's where the egg is? On the moon?"

I'd suspected it was somewhere hard to find, but this? I would never be able to get it back, and that must have been exactly why the elves had put it there. I rubbed my forehead, feeling a headache blossom. There had to be a way to take the egg back. There always was. I just had to think of a way.

A mist of magical fog surrounded us, the room faded, and we reappeared on the island.

Zack moved away from the mirror, then stood and started pacing, his feet crunching over the stray bits of sticks and palm leaves as rain pelted down around him. He didn't seem to notice.

"But there was something else." He grabbed his head. "What was it? Why can't I remember?" He spun around, his face scrunched as he concentrated. "Why can't I remember?"

"I suspect a spell is at work," I answered. "I felt something inside that ship, something odd that shouldn't have been there. It was a spell, one conjured by an extremely dangerous practitioner—the elven queen. If she was involved, that may explain why you were having such horrible mental delusions and side effects from the lost memories. The elves used your knowledge of rocket mechanics to help them fuel their spacecraft, and then they stole your memories from you. They wouldn't have wanted anyone to know where they'd transported the egg."

"Yes, yes, the egg. It had something to do with the egg."

"You remember something else about it?"

"It's a hazy memory, like trying to recall something you saw a long time ago. It feels like I'm grasping at smoke. There was more about that egg than I remember, and I think the elves were trying to hide the truth from me."

"If that's the case, then how will you be able to remember?"

"I thought you would know."

I glanced at my mirror. "We could try the spellcasting again. But this time, I want you to focus on the lost memories, the ones you didn't see just now. Maybe that will help. I will warn you, though, I've never done anything like this. I don't know how safe this is."

Zack breathed deeply. "Let's try it."

He knelt by the mirror once again. I held the egg on the chain, letting my magic flow into the stone. With the second spellcasting, a wave of dizziness washed over me and I felt my energy being drained from my body.

"Are you all right?" Zack asked.

"Just a little dizzy. Are you ready?"

"I'm ready, but are you sure about this? You look very pale. Maybe you should rest. We can pick this up tomorrow after the doctors have looked you over. You took a nasty blow to the head."

If only I could make him understand how dire the situation was. My stepfather would die if I didn't get that egg back. It didn't matter how I felt at the moment. I could rest later. But once Silvestra killed my stepfather, I would never be able to get him back. No amount of begging or pleading would save him once she'd killed him, and the frightening thing was—I knew Silvestra would do it. She was too proud and too precise not to follow through with her threats.

I pushed away my panic to stare at the mirror's surface, coming face to face with the desperation reflected in my own eyes. Glancing away from the screen, I focused on Zack.

"I can't rest now," I said. "Please understand when I say this is the most important thing you may ever do. If you help me retrieve that egg, you'll be saving more than just my step-father. You'll be saving an entire kingdom—an entire world."

He studied me a moment, then reached for the screen and placed his palm on the glass. I touched my own hand to the screen, keeping the egg between the mirror and my hand, letting the magic absorb all the energy from us, when the world faded around us, the light dimmed, and an uncontrollable shiver of fear raced down my spine.

We stood in a dark, cavernous room. Sounds of dripping water echoed through the stale air. The smell of damp earth filled the room, and the chill air prickled my skin. Usually, the memories didn't replay with such clarity, making me wonder if we'd entered a memory at all.

Zack stood beside me, his eyes wide as he took a step forward. We stood on a balcony overlooking the room below. Beneath us was a circular platform. Fanning away from the raised area, I counted seven ornately carved coffins.

Seven coffins. Like the seven Madralorde brothers.

A magical presence pushed against my own, forcing itself against my skull, a gradual pressure that slowly increased. I rubbed my temples as I tried to concentrate on the scene unfolding beneath us.

I counted four elves gathered in the room and recognized one of them as Queen Euralysia. She wore dull gray robes, and unlike the first time I'd met her, she looked aged and sickly. The color had drained from her cheeks, and her limp hair was more gray than golden.

An elven man with red hair and pale white skin also stood in the room. He had an unusually thin frame, even for an elf, and he moved slowly, as if it pained him to walk. I was certain I'd seen him before, but couldn't remember where.

An elven woman with long, midnight blue hair and velvet, navy-colored robes stood with the others, but my gaze snagged on one man in particular.

He stood taller than the rest, with dark, stringy hair and chalky-white skin. A shiver of fear ran through my body as I stared at the man. I'd never seen him before, yet the taint of his magic was unmistakable. It came to me, challenging my own, making me step away from him, although I knew I had nothing to fear as this was a memory.

"Do you remember this?" I asked Zack.

He shook his head. "No. I don't remember any of it."

"Then why did the spell bring us here?"

214

"You don't know?" he asked.

"No. It should have brought us someplace where you were, but I don't see you anywhere."

Fear settled in the pit of my stomach. I wasn't sure what sort of magic had brought us here, but it wasn't something I was familiar with. Below us, the elves gathered around a raised pedestal atop the center dais. The man robed in black placed something atop the surface. As he stepped back, I gasped.

The egg.

Its golden bands shimmered in the dim light, swirling against a backdrop of onyx. Its warmth radiated through the room, even up here, I felt its power and strength.

"That's it," Zack said. "That's the egg I saw. I remember that feeling because it's stayed with me all this time. Even after I returned to Earth, I knew that feeling, even though I didn't know where it came from, I know now. I've seen that egg, but I didn't see it here."

"Then why did the magic bring us here?" I asked.

The four elves circled the egg.

"When will it hatch?" the queen asked.

"Not long," the man in black answered. "Another week at most."

"Good, that gives us enough time to locate the staff."

The woman with the dark hair spoke up. "My hunters will infiltrate Danegeld and remove the staff within a fortnight. We shall have it in time."

"What of the sword?" the red-haired elf asked.

"We don't need it," Queen Euralysia answered.

"But how will we control Theht's powers without it?"

"I have my ways, Echorion. You've no need to question me."

"If I fear for the life of my wife, then I feel I should question you."

His wife? Yes, this must have been the queen's new husband. I'd heard she'd married but didn't know anything about him. I scrutinized the man. He seemed frail and sickly, and it made sense why she'd married him. She needed someone she could manipulate. If she'd married a man of power, she'd have a harder time controlling him.

Now that I thought about it, I remembered where I'd seen the man. He'd been a guard in the queen's palace when I'd gone there to seek the Wults' help finding my godson, although he'd changed since then and looked more frail. I was surprised I remembered him. But why did she marry a guard? Perhaps to bridge the gap between the more common folk and nobility?

But those were questions for later. Right now, I had bigger problems to handle than elven courtship.

"Are you sure the staff is in the Wult keep?" the queen asked the woman.

"Yes, I'm positive. My source will not fail me. I have faith he will help us retrieve the staff in time for the ceremony."

Source? Who was the woman referring to?

The magic grew stronger as it pressed against my skull, squeezing tighter and tighter until I was forced to shut my eyes. Gasping for air, I stumbled back.

"Dr. Kennedy," Zack said, "are you all right?"

Buzzing filled my ears. The magic wormed its way into my brain, searching, trying to identify me. Had the elves known I was coming? Where did the magic come from?

As if from a great distance, I heard Zack's screams. My eyes opened, and the face of the man with black robes filled my vision.

"You," he said, "should not be here."

I turned to where I'd last seen Zack to discover two elven guards on either side of him, dragging him away.

"Zack," I called as the man grabbed my arm, "take your hand off the screen!"

The air grew thick with magic as it surrounded me and sucked me into its portal. Relief washed over me as the pressure in my head disappeared.

Zack and I appeared back on the beach, both of us gasping for air. The mirror lay in my lap, and as the magical fog disappeared, I focused on the screen. A crack split the mirror in half.

CHAPTER
Twenty-four

I REACHED FOR MY BROKEN MIRROR AND BRUSHED MY FINgers over the glass. The magic faded, leaving me with two ordinary shards of broken glass. My heart fell. The mirror had been one of the only possessions I cared about. Now it was gone, and I wasn't sure how I could replace it.

"What was that?" Zack breathed beside me. "Those people—were they going to kill us?"

"If they'd gotten the chance, yes, I believe they would have. I've seen what the queen is capable of."

I shuddered as I recalled the day I'd witnessed the queen exterminate the entire race of goblins. The elven queen scared me more than anyone I'd ever known. I'd known some pretty dangerous people, but no one wielded the kind of power she possessed.

Overhead, the sky grew dim as evening approached, and I knew I was running out of time. I had to get back to Faythander, tell Kull and the others what I had seen in the mirror, and then somehow figure out where that place was located. But how could I get back now that my mirror was broken?

I rubbed my head, the dizziness making the world spin around me. The concussion, coupled with the loss in magic, made it hard to think straight.

As I brushed my fingers over the glass, I forced my brain to cooperate. Getting back to Faythander shouldn't be too hard. Really any sort of reflective surface would do, although I could never be sure if the glass were tainted or not. As it was, I had no choice.

Crafting a new mirror box would take time I didn't have

right now. But I could still use the mirror—I would just have to fuel it with my own magic.

"What are you doing?" Zack asked.

"I'm sorry, but I have to go back. Thank you for all your help."

His forehead wrinkled in confusion. "What do you mean? You can't leave without me. You have to take me with you."

"If I did that, you would lose all your memories again."

"But, no! I won't let you leave without me. You need to go to the hospital first, and I need to help you."

"I wish it were that simple."

"But I haven't even paid you." He reached for his wallet.

"Zack, don't worry about paying me. Where I'm going, your money is useless, and I'm not even sure I'll make it out alive, so there's no point in giving it to me."

"But why do you have to go?"

"Because that egg stands between the life and death of my stepfather. I have to get it back. No matter what the price, I can't let him die."

Zack only watched as I moved my hand over the glass. My magic flowed weakly to the surface, sluggish and slow, making me even dizzier as it rose to my fingertips. I directed the magic into the glass and focused on opening a portal.

In my mind, I conjured an image of the Wult keep. If the elves were intent on taking the staff from the keep, then I had no other choice but to go there and stop them. With my mind not cooperating, it was the best plan I could come up with.

Blue magical mist gathered around me and made my skin tingle. The portal opened with a loud howling wind, sucking me inside before I had a chance to catch my breath. Bursts of magical energy surrounded me as I flew from one reality to another. Air hissed in my ears as bright spots of light blinded me.

The violence of the portal caught me by surprise. If anything, I'd expected the portal to be weak, so what caused it to be so powerful?

An image of a woman formed in front of me. The form was too blurry to see the features, yet its glowing, ember-orange eyes focused on me, and I knew who it was—Theht.

The phantasm didn't speak. It only stared into my soul, giving me the feeling of familiarity, making me realize that this was the part of Theht that lived inside me.

"Go away," I screamed, although my words had no effect on the creature.

The wind quieted, the portal dissipated, and I crashed onto a stone floor. I felt as though I'd broken my spine, and making any sort of movement at all was beyond me. I only lay there, my breathing heavy as it echoed through the room.

I clutched my head with the image of Theht still fresh in my mind. The urge to vomit welled up inside of me as I contemplated the evil inhabiting my own body. There had to be a way to get rid of the creature inside me. But how?

Fan'twar would possibly know, and that made my quest to free him even more dire. There was no other being alive who possessed as much knowledge as my stepfather. I couldn't afford to lose him. The world couldn't afford to lose him.

I'd never asked him before because I'd been too afraid to admit that a piece of Theht existed within me. But I realized now that hiding from the problem wouldn't fix it. I had no choice but to ask for his help... after I freed him. And I would.

When I caught my breath, I sat up and stared around the small space, recognizing the room as one of the chambers in the Wult keep. Outside, I heard raised voices. I stood cautiously, feeling the characteristic dizziness as I tried to walk, but I managed to make it across the room and grab the doorframe for support.

I inched the door open and found I stood inside a broom closet that led into the dining hall where large wooden beams crisscrossed the cavernous ceiling. Inside, Kull and his mother stood arguing.

"I blame you," Halla said. "Our keep was not breached once during your father's reign. And now that you are king, this castle has become the gathering place for the entire continent. Elves and pixies alike frequent our halls, yet no one bothers to check if they are guests or enemies. Now look what has happened. The staff is gone with not a single guard able to tell us who took it. This would have never happened when your father was king."

"Please don't compare me to him. You know I am nothing like him."

"Yes. I am well aware of it—I am reminded daily."

I entered the room. Kull's eyes locked with mine, and relief spread over his face. He crossed the room in two strides and caught me in his arms.

"Thank the gods," he breathed in my ear. He pulled away to stare in my face. "You're okay?"

"Yes, I'm well enough." I tried to sound convincing, hoping he couldn't see the turmoil in my eyes. I swallowed the lump in my throat. Being with him again was like breathing air after drowning. I never felt complete when we were apart, yet after his revelation that he was destined to kill me, he held me a little closer and with more gentleness, as if he would break me.

"You always worry me when you go on those quests," he said.

"And you worry me more when I leave you behind."

He grinned. "Very well. I suppose we're even." He took my hand and led me to where his mother stood.

Halla gave me a guarded smile. "Olive, your arrival is a surprise, especially considering you've arrived in our broom closet."

"Yes, that's the trouble with portals. They're never very accurate, but at least I managed to make it inside the keep."

"Yes," she said with narrowed eyes. "What a convenient talent to have. Entering a place without needing to pass by guards or through doorways must be a handy ability."

I met her gaze. "It is, and luckily, I can only travel places I've been before, and I've never traveled anywhere forbidden to me."

"Tell me, do the other elves possess these same abilities?"

"No. I'm the only one who can travel from Earth Kingdom to Faythander and back and still retain my memories."

She crossed her arms. "I see."

Kull cleared his throat. "Much has happened since you left," Kull said. "Our castle has been breached, and the staff was stolen. No one seems to have seen who took it."

"I think I might know," I said.

"You do?"

I nodded. "I did a spellcasting in Earth Kingdom on Mr. Zimmerman. As it turns out, the elves forced him to help them work on a rocket that transported the vachonette egg to their moon base."

"The moon base is real?" he asked.

"Yes, but that's not all. They recently brought the egg back to Faythander. I'm not sure where it is, but during the casting, I overheard the elves. They had sent out a squadron to steal the staff. It must have been them who took it, and they were working with someone here, but I don't know who."

"Elves," Halla said with scorn, "I knew it. We've never been able to trust them."

"But the question is," Kull said, "who took the staff? And where are they taking it now?"

I shook my head. "During the spellcasting, I didn't recognize the building we were in. But there were seven coffins inside, and I believe it may have been the seven tombs of the Madralorde brothers. I'll have to do some research, but it's very likely that the elves have found Tremulac."

"Tremulac?" Halla questioned. "It doesn't exist. That island is a fairy tale."

"I thought so, too, until recently. But now I believe it is real because I'm fairly certain I saw it in the vision."

"If that's so," the queen said, "then where is it?"

"I have no idea."

She scowled. "Then I refuse to sanction any sort of expedition to find a lost island that doesn't even exist—"

"Mother," Kull said, "trust Olive on this. If the elves did indeed take the staff, then they would have brought it to that island—the same place where the egg is located. They would need both items to initiate their spell to recall Theht."

"Assuming that is all true, then how do you find the island? Although there have been many expeditions, no one has ever found it. You'll never find it."

"I disagree," I said.

"Why?"

"Because the elves took the staff, and all we need to do is track the elves." I glanced at Kull. "Luckily for us, we've got *him*."

He gave me a knowing smile, the one that made my heart flutter.

"She's right, Mother. I will track the elves and find the staff. That I promise."

"Don't be so hasty. We're not even sure it was the elves. No one saw a thing. I doubt you'll even find their trail."

"Where is your confidence, Mother? You know I can do this." He wrapped an arm around her shoulder.

"And kill yourself in the process, no doubt. What will the elves do to you once you find them?"

"We'll worry about that once we reach the isle."

She looked him in the eye, her face grim. "I know this is a quest that cannot be avoided, but I worry about you. I shall not get a moment's rest while you are gone. Battling beasts in the wilds is not the same as confronting the elves. There are some in the capitol who want nothing more than our extermination. They'll wipe us out the same way they did the goblins if we give them the chance."

"What are you saying? Do you believe I shouldn't stop the summoning?"

"No, but I am saying that tact is preferred to warfare. Don't give them an excuse to murder us all."

"I agree," Kull said, "which is why I have been in constant negotiations with them since Father passed."

Halla cupped her son's cheeks. "I see him in your eyes. You're all I have left of him. Please be safe on this quest."

"I will return safely to you. I promise."

She nodded, seeming satisfied. "Very well."

"We will take your leave, if you've no objections."

"No. You are free to go."

Kull walked toward me and took my hand. We turned toward the tall double doors, walked outside the dining hall, and then into an open hallway. Windows lined either side as we turned toward a set of doors.

"I'm in need of some fresh air. Will you join me outside?" Kull asked.

"Yes. I could use some fresh air, too."

Kull led me out the doors, into a courtyard, and over a bridge paved in cobblestones that led into the forest. The air smelled of rain, and water glistened as it dripped from leaves to puddles on the ground.

We followed a trail that led to the lake, to the same place where I'd seen Fan'twar not long ago. Sadness gripped me as I remembered how the sun had shimmered on his scales, or the way his eyes had glittered when he thought he'd said something mischievous. I missed him more than I thought possible. Kull squeezed my hand, bringing me out of my thoughts.

"What are you thinking about?" he asked.

I shrugged. "I'm thinking that I would like to have my stepfather back."

"I agree. I think everyone agrees. Faythander is not the same without him."

I nodded. "We'll get him back," I said, mostly to assure myself, although in truth, I feared I would never see him again.

The wind blew through the tree branches overhead, making the boughs sway and creak. Gray clouds blocked out the sun, causing the air to grow chill.

"Olive," Kull said quietly. "I'm afraid there's a traitor in our castle, and I'm afraid to admit who it might be."

I looked up at him.

"Maveryck," he said. "He conveniently led us into that desert and away from the keep, which happened to be during the time the staff was stolen. We were nearly killed by Jahr'ad, which was no accident. Maveryck is one of the only people who knew the staff's location. Also, he dresses and acts like elven royalty, and as of yet, nobody seems to know anything about him. Someone tipped off those elves to the staff's location. Given that he's a professional thief, it doesn't look good for him."

"I agree. I overheard the elves talking in the castle on Tremulac. Someone betrayed us."

"Do you believe it was Maveryck?"

"I can't say for sure, but I agree. It doesn't look good for him."

Kull worked his jaw back and forth as he stared over the lake. "Then we'll have to find him and ask a few questions. He won't like it."

"No, but it has to be done. What will you do if he is the traitor?"

Kull shook his head. "I'm not sure."

"Heidel won't like you interrogating him."

"No. But even she has to admit he can't be trusted. The only reason I've allowed him to stay with us is because your stepfather trusted him, but I'm afraid being in good graces with the sky king can only benefit him so much. His luck is about to run out."

He took my hand and tugged me back toward the trail, and I followed him toward the castle. When we reached the gates, the sun sank toward the horizon, casting slanting rays of orange light over the paving stones and castle walls. Crickets chirped in the distance, announcing the impending arrival of night.

We entered through the back gates and into a large foyer, where we crossed a room that housed Kull's stuffed beast collection. A giant burbonski—a creature resembling a polar bear with curved ram's horns—stood near the room's hearth. I also spotted a crocodile in one of the corners.

We crossed through the chamber and ascended a stone staircase.

"Where are we going?" I asked.

"To find the thief. We need to have a word."

"Where is he?"

Kull shook his head. "I thought my sister would know."

We took the hallways leading to Heidel's room, passing a few people along the way. Kull received a few formal greetings, and for the most part, the castle staff seemed pleased to see him. Although I knew his relationship with his people was strained, it seemed the servants, at least, didn't hate him.

We reached the end of the hallway where a red rug led toward the door at the hall's end. Kull knocked on the door several times with no response. As he turned the handle, the door was flung open from the inside, and a disheveled Heidel stood in the room. Her hair was down, which was odd as I'd never seen her without her hair in a braid or ponytail, and her cheeks were flushed and pink.

"Sister, is everything okay?"

"Yes, why wouldn't it be? And what are you doing here?"

"I came to see if you knew where I could find the thief?"

She cleared her throat as her face visibly paled. "I have no idea."

"Really?" he asked.

"Did you check the dining hall?"

Kull leaned against the doorframe to glance past his sister. She moved to block his line of sight. Kull exhaled.

"You might as well let me in so I can get this over with," he said quietly.

"Are you going to send him away?" she whispered back.

"Most likely."

She stood for a moment without speaking and then looked up at her brother with pain in her eyes. "Fine. Come in," she said, then moved aside.

We entered a large suite with separate sitting and sleeping areas. I found a bed and some heavy wooden dressers on one end of the room, and on the other side were a pair of sofas decorated in animal skins and antlers. Swords and battle-axes cluttered the walls, and I wasn't sure if I stood in a bedchamber or an armory. A large picture window took up the back wall of the room, and long, sweeping curtains partially hid the glass.

"You can come out," Heidel called.

Maveryck moved away from the curtains and stepped into view.

Kull puffed out his chest as he approached the man. "Maveryck, as you have likely heard, the staff has gone missing, and since you are a professional thief, and because you are affiliated with the elves, we are forced to acknowledge that you may be involved in taking it."

Maveryck narrowed his eyes. "I would never be involved in such a thing."

"Yes, I realized you would say that. But as I have found you in my sister's bedchamber, I can no longer pretend that you are our friend. I know the sky king trusted you, but I do not."

"Yet I was invited by your sister into her room. Does that mean nothing?"

Kull glanced at Heidel. "Is this true?"

She crossed her arms. "Yes," she answered quietly.

"But, why?"

"Must I give reasons for my actions?" she said. "This is my home as well as yours. I am entitled to invite visitors into my chambers, am I not?"

"Father would not have approved."

"Father is not here. And he didn't approve of Olive, either, yet you are not questioning her."

"Yes, because Olive is not a professional thief."

Heidel shrugged. "Have it your way. Accuse him of something he didn't do. But I can tell you, he is not your traitor."

"Even if he is not, he has earned my distrust. Maveryck, did you take the staff?"

"I did not take it, although I suspect that whoever has stolen the staff will have had a very good reason to do so. If you recall, I risked my own life to steal the staff from the witch's castle, and then risked further injury by battling a goblin wraith in the Earth Kingdom to return it to the sky king. But it was not me who took—"

"Wait a minute," Heidel said, "how could you know that we battled a *goblin* wraith in the Earth Kingdom?"

His face paled. "I don't know. That is to say, I didn't know until recently."

"Recently?" I asked. "What does that mean?"

"A lie?" Kull asked.

"No, not a lie. I can only tell you that some of my memories have begun to return."

"That's not possible," I said. "Memories don't return for anyone. Ever."

"This time they did."

Kull sighed.

"It may be because of my unusual brain chemistry," Maveryck said hastily. "I have the ability to recall certain events with unique clarity."

"What do you mean?" I asked.

"I can't tell you why, but trust me when I say that I am not like you. I'm not like anyone."

Heidel pressed her hands to her forehead. "Yes, I remember you told me this once before, didn't you?"

"In the Earth Kingdom, yes. You remember?"

"Olive did the spellcasting, Maveryck. Yes, I remember."

Maveryck swallowed as sweat beaded his brow. "You remember everything?" he asked quietly, as if he didn't want anyone else to hear.

"I remember enough."

Maveryck clutched at his chest, exhaling, and then pulled at a chain around his neck to reveal a crystal hanging from the bottom. "Then there is no use hiding this now," he said.

I eyed the shard. It reminded me of another I'd seen before—one worn by the now elven queen. "Is that an Illumina crystal?" I asked.

He nodded. "Yes. This belonged to my elven grandmother. This may be partially to blame for my memories returning. Long ago, it was spellcasted to be used as a memory charm. And although the magic has faded quite a bit, it has slowly been returning my memories to me. Since you are accusing me of not being honest with you, I thought I should start here. Whatever it is you wish to know, you have but to ask."

"What did you mean when you said you're not like us?" I asked.

"Because I'm cursed."

"How so?"

He paced the room, clenching and unclenching his hands in a nervous gesture. "If I tell you, you must all give me your word that you will not repeat what I say."

"You are in the company of Wults," Kull said. "You know we will keep our word. And you have them. That goes for all of us."

"Very well," Maveryck exhaled. "I should start from the beginning. My grandmother was elven but fell in love with a Wult man. Unfortunately, he didn't care for a courtship with an elven woman, and so she thought it best to bewitch him, which resulted in the birth of my mother. The child was an embarrassment and cast away from the elves for a time to be raised by Wults. Although eventually, she was again accepted by her mother, though that is a long story. Needless to say, I was born to a Wult father and half-elven mother. They were killed before I was old enough to remember, and then I was adopted by a rather noble elven family. Relatives, actually. They took good care of me, but it seemed my lot in life was to be surrounded by death. Both my elven parents died of the lung sickness when I was thirteen, leaving me in the care of my elder brother. He was not so kind. In fact, Navarre was insane."

"Insane?" I asked. "How so?"

"For one thing, he had a fascination for setting things on fire. Waking at night to find the furniture or tapestries ablaze became commonplace. Our servants made it a habit to sleep with buckets of water at their side."

"Yes," Kull said, "that doesn't sound normal."

"Navarre was also obsessed with prolonging his life. He traveled to the northlands to study goblin potions, leaving me alone for several months. When he didn't return, I assumed he was dead. But then, one evening, he returned. He was horribly disfigured, but he'd found what he was looking for. He returned with two potions, one of which he gave to me, and the other he kept for himself. He instructed me in its use, an elaborate ritual that involved drinking it under the new moon.

"We each took our turns drinking from the vials, but only one worked. Mine."

Silence filled the room.

"So how old are you?" I asked.

"Five hundred years, give or take. For an elf, my age wouldn't be so unusual."

"Yes, but for a human, it's unheard of," Kull said.

"Perhaps, but the potion did more than prolong my life. It also gave me perfect health, including making it impossible for my memories to fade. I do not consider this to be a gift. As I've had many loved ones die during my lifetime, this, to me, is a curse."

"Heidel, did you know this?" Kull asked.

"He told me in Earth Kingdom, but I'd forgotten until Olive did the spellcasting. Even after that, some of the memories are vague." She narrowed her eyes at Maveryck. "What does that crystal do?"

"It's an heirloom of my elven royal house, and at one time it was used as a memory charm."

"How did you get it? Did you steal it?" I asked.

"No. As I said, it was a gift from my elven grandmother, the former queen of the elves."

We stared at Maveryck without speaking. At least now I

knew why the man acted like elven royalty.

Maveryck tucked the crystal under his shirt. "Now you know my secrets," he said. "Will you still insist on accusing me of stealing the staff?"

"How could I possibly reconsider? You have only made yourself look guiltier," Kull said. "You've admitted to being kin to elven royalty, and as they are the ones who have taken the staff, and as you are also a professional thief, I can only conclude that you must have been involved in some way. I have no other choice but to ask that you leave our lands."

"And that is your final decision?"

"Yes, unless you can tell us who took the staff or where it is now, you must leave for the safety of our kingdom."

His face fell. "I cannot."

"Very well. As you have helped us in the past, I will do this as quietly as possible. I shall personally escort you out the gates and into the forest, and then you are to leave our lands and never return, at least, not until the staff has been recovered and I am satisfied that you are not the one who took it. Do you understand?"

"Brother," Heidel said, "this is unjust. You cannot force him—"

"Heidel," Maveryck interjected, "it's all right. I will leave."

"But it's unjust!"

"No, he has every right to protect his kingdom. I will go."

"Good. Follow me."

Heidel and I followed the two men out of the room and into the hallway. As we made our way to the main floor, I pondered Maveryck's words. To be honest, I wasn't sure he had taken the staff, but if he hadn't taken it, then who had?

Heaviness weighed on me at the prospect of losing the staff. The elves were even closer to being able to perform the ritual, and we were no closer to stopping them. Worse, if the elves were successful, what would happen to the piece of Theht existing within me?

As we exited the castle, Kull found a torch and carried it aloft through the courtyard and down a narrow trail leading into the forest.

The bobbing lights of nobbinflies and maywelters lit our path in bursts of purple and blue. Leaves crunched beneath our feet, accompanied by the sounds of chirping night insects. The brisk fall air made my skin bristle from the chill and turned my exhalations to white cloud puffs.

We reached a clearing where we found a wide path leading toward the rails. As we stopped in the clearing, moonlight shone overhead, casting its glow over the leaves and sticks strewn across the ground.

Kull spoke up. "The rails will take you wherever you need to be, preferably away from our lands."

Maveryck nodded and moved toward the road leading to the rails, but Heidel stepped in front of him.

"Brother, this is unjust. There is no proof he has done anything wrong. He has been falsely accused. Keeping secrets is not a crime."

"It is when it leads to the staff getting stolen by the elves."

"You are only sending him away because he shows interest in me."

"That's not true."

"It is true. At least you've fulfilled one of your life's missions as you are like Father in at least one respect. He wouldn't let you have Olive, and you will not let me be with whom I choose."

"That's uncalled for."

"Heidel," Maveryck said quietly, "I will go. There is no need to argue."

He took her hand, kissed it gently, and then turned away from us. The sound of his footfalls treading quietly over the leaf-strewn ground was the only noise to break up the silence. As he walked, a form appeared in his path. In the darkness, I could only make out that it was some sort of creature with fur and liquid silver eyes.

Maveryck knelt as the creature approached him. Kull had his sword out in an instant, but as we approached, the gray coat of Maveryck's wolf stood out under the moonlight.

"Grace," Maveryck said softly, "you've returned."

"Where has she been?" Heidel asked.

"I sent her on a journey, and it seems she has been successful."

"How do you know that?"

He ran his hand over her head. "Because she brings us news from Lauressa."

He removed a small scroll from a cylindrical pouch attached to her collar. He stood, then moved to stand under the light of Kull's torch. After reading the message, he looked at each of us.

"It seems the missing staff has been found."

CHAPTER
Twenty-five

"WHERE IS THE STAFF?" KULL DEMANDED AS HE, Heidel, Maveryck, and I stood in the forest and surrounded Maveryck's wolf, Grace. A fragile stillness clung to the frigid air, yet tension lay beneath Kull's words.

"The staff was stolen by the elves and taken to the capitol in Lauressa."

"How do you know that?"

Maveryck patted Grace's head. "I tasked Grace with keeping watch on the staff while we were in the desert. She saw the infiltrator aid the elves in taking the staff, and then she followed them back to the elven capitol where she met up with a contact I have there. He is someone I trust, and he was able to write this note and send it back to us. If we hurry, we may be able to meet up with him."

I eyed the wolf. "Did the message say who the infiltrator was?"

"It shouldn't come as a shock. It was Euric."

"Euric?" Kull said. "Are you sure?"

"Yes. Quite sure. Euric wants nothing more than to see you disgraced. He thought that by aiding the elves to remove the staff from your supposedly impenetrable keep, he would make you look like a fool."

Kull balled his fists. "I will deal with him."

"You may not have to," Maveryck said. "It seems Euric has been detained by the elves."

Beyond the forest, a carriage arrived, a brilliant bauble of golden light that looked like a marble from our perspective.

"Well," Maveryck said, "it seems I have found the staff for

you, which should put me back in your good graces and ensure that I am no longer banished from your lands. Am I correct?"

"Not so fast, thief," Kull said. "How can we trust that what you say is true? How do we know you didn't invent this story just to save your own skin from banishment?"

"I will prove it if I must. Journey with me to Lauressa, and we shall find the missing staff."

Kull glanced at Heidel. "Convenient, isn't it? Moments before his banishment and suddenly the staff is found."

Heidel shrugged. "Perhaps."

Maveryck turned to me. "Olive, you will join me, won't you? Magistrate Pozin is your father, is he not?"

"Yes, but what's that got to do with anything?"

"Because he is the contact I spoke of earlier. If anyone can help us find where the elves have taken it, it will be him."

I shook my head. "No, you're wrong. My father left Lauressa months ago so he could be with my mom. They were in Africa in Earth Kingdom the last time I checked. He couldn't be in Lauressa."

"I assure you, he is there. He returned several weeks ago. He spoke of a secret quest, though he didn't say more. He has been there ever since."

A breeze stirred the boughs overhead as I pondered Maveryck's words. Why would my father have returned to Lauressa? If he were traveling with my mom, the elven capitol was the last place they would have gone. The elves had a standing order to execute witches within their borders, and since my mom was a witch, she would be putting herself in unnecessary danger by entering the heart of elf country. What was so important that would make my parents travel back to the capitol?

"Are you sure?" I asked Maveryck. "You actually saw my father in the capitol?"

"Of course I'm sure. I realize he has been gone for some time, which is not characteristic of him, but he returned several weeks ago."

"Was there anyone who returned with him? A woman, maybe?"

"No one that I know of."

My heart sank. Where was Mom? "He was alone? Are you sure of that?"

"Quite sure."

My shoulders sagged. Had they split up again? Or had something happened to her? I'd been out of contact with them, but I'd assumed they had wanted it that way. The only way to know for sure if my mom was okay would be to travel to Lauressa and find out. It looked like I had more than one reason to go to the elf kingdom.

"We'll go the capitol and discover the location of the staff," Kull said. "And I expect complete honesty from you, Maveryck. We've had enough secrets."

Maveryck gave a curt nod. "Very well. We shall journey to meet with the head magistrate. But be prepared—Lauressa is not the place it once was. The queen has spies everywhere. You must all be wary and follow my lead. I know how to get inside the city, but we must do it quietly." He turned and led us toward the carriage. Grace followed at his heels. We traded forest for open field as we approached the carriage, leaving the glow of nobbinflies and the safety of the forest behind.

As the light from our waiting carriage spilled over the open field, a chill crept down my spine. We were traveling to Lauressa, to the heart of the queen's territory. I didn't want to contemplate what the queen would do to us if she found us, but we had to stop the summoning and find the egg. The consequences were too dire if we failed.

Maveryck spoke a few words to his wolf, and she turned and trotted back into the woods. He and Heidel entered the carriage, but Kull and I hesitated. With a quick glance behind us, I found the towers of the Wult keep stretching above the treetops and toward the moonlit sky. I had a nagging feeling that I would never see them again, that maybe the keep would never be my home, and that maybe the life I wanted—the one where Kull and I lived happily ever after—would never exist.

The story of Kull's prophecy surfaced. In my mind, I saw him stab me and kill me so Theht would die with me. The image scared me so badly that I had to force it away.

I felt Kull's hand on my shoulder. As I turned to look at him, I found the same fear I felt mirrored in his eyes.

"We'll get through this," he said.

I nodded. "Yes, I'm sure we will." But as I entered the carriage, the fear stayed with me.

Kull climbed inside behind me. After he sat next to me, the door slid shut with a mechanical hiss, then locked us inside.

The carriage sped forward. Inside, soft hues of blue and yellow lit the plush, ivory-colored cushions. The air smelled faintly of sweet flowers and perfume, and the cushions felt velvety-soft beneath my fingertips. The carriage interior was the epitome of calmness, yet it did nothing to soothe my unease. The closer we sped toward the capitol, the more my mind re-hashed my worries.

My thoughts turned to my stepfather. Guilt gnawed at me. If I'd played by the witch's rules and used the box to free Kull, I would have not only released Kull, but kept my stepfather from being captured as well. But as far I knew, the only way to open that box was with black magic.

I glanced at my hands resting in my lap. My fidgeting fingers were evidence of my unease. Opening and closing my hands, I wondered at the magic inside me. I'd only ever known of my Earth and Faythander magics, but was there more? The idea baffled me, but if I didn't possess black magic, why had the witch been so sure that I did? Was it because a piece of Theht now resided within me? Was Silvestra trying to get me to harness the power of the dark goddess? Or was there something else she'd wanted me to learn?

Kull took one of my hands in his, bringing me out of my thoughts, and I met his eyes. He didn't say anything, but I knew he worried about me. He was the one person who kept me going through all this. Without him, I was sure I would have succumbed to insanity by now.

Outside the carriage, we saw only darkness. It would be several hours before we reached Lauressa, and going all night without sleep wasn't the way I wanted to start the journey, so I laid my head on Kull's shoulder, and despite my worries, sleep took me.

I woke as morning approached, though it was still too dark to see much outside the carriage. Thick clouds stirred overhead, highlighted by occasional bursts of lightning. Fog snaked along the tracks, and as the carriage zipped through it, the mist swirled in eddies.

Maveryck cleared his throat. I turned and found him staring at me. His eyes turned silver in the glow from the carriage windows, and I perceived a faint hum of magic, making me think that perhaps there was more to him than what he'd already told us. Did the man ever sleep?

"You're awake early," he said.

"I've never slept well in these carriages. Plus, it's hard to rest with the balance of the world in danger."

"I agree, but perhaps no one knows that more than you."

I eyed him. He was right. I'd battled the forces of evil for so long and had saved the world so many times, I should have at least earned a medal by now. But I didn't need it. Knowing that my loved ones were safe was enough. I'd religiously kept in touch with my godson Jeremiah since the Dreamthief had nearly killed him. He was living in Kansas now, having the sort of childhood most kids dreamed of. He was happy, but most importantly, he was alive. Knowing that he was safe was better than any reward.

Jeremiah wasn't the only one I'd saved. I'd restored magic in Faythander, too; I'd saved the fairies' stone. The list kept growing. But even after all my accomplishments, I couldn't help but feel that all I had to do was slip up once, and the balance would crumble. There were forces out there far greater than me, and with Theht's powers festering inside me, I knew my time was short. If I didn't find some way to remove that part of the goddess's consciousness soon, the vision Kull had seen would come true.

I refused to let it happen.

"When we reach the city," Maveryck said, "I shall take you through an entrance no longer in use and linked through the city sewers. The elves have not guarded the entrance since the disappearance of the Gravidorum."

"You know of the Gravidorum?" I asked, shocked. The secret society wasn't common knowledge to elves or to anyone, for that matter. Maveryck shouldn't have known about them either. Yet he did.

"Yes, I know of the Gravidorum."

"How?"

He shifted. "Most elven nobles were inducted into the society in their youth, before they had a chance to make their own decisions, but that was the way things were half a millennia ago. However, I haven't been a part of that organization for nearly a hundred years. Now, with the extinction of the goblins, they've all disbanded. Well, that is, all but a few."

"A few? The Gravidorum still exists?"

"Yes. Their numbers are few, but those who remain are not to be taken lightly."

"I'm confused. With the goblin race eradicated, what purpose do they have left?"

Maveryck didn't answer immediately. "Once we arrive at the city, perhaps you shall see."

I stared at him, uncertain of his meaning. The Gravidorum had existed for hundreds of years for the express purpose of rewriting history. They'd kept the truth of the goblins' origins a secret, but after the queen had used a spell to destroy the entire goblin race, I'd assumed the Gravidorum would have no longer been needed. What purpose did they have in remaining?

The implications frightened me. I recalled seeing the elves gathered around the vachonette egg during the spellcasting. Could the elves I'd seen be the last remaining members of the Gravidorum?

"Maveryck," I said, "is it possible that the Gravidorum still exists for the purpose of harnessing Theht's power?"

"Yes, that is one aspect of their purpose. But you must ask yourself, what is their ultimate goal?"

"That's easy. To take control of Faythander."

"True, from the outside looking in, that may seem to be their purpose, but there are other powers at play in Faythander. Not every elf wishes for power. There are some who want something else altogether." His eyes darkened, from silver to black, sending a shiver down my spine.

"What else do they want?"

He shook his head. "Once we reach the capitol, you will see."

I hadn't been to the elven capitol since Euralysia had destroyed the goblins, but had it really changed so much? With the queen in power, perhaps it had.

The sun crested the horizon, driving away the fog, yet the storm-shrouded sky remained. Ahead, the glittering towers of Lauressa appeared. The castle sat in the city's central square, and its parapets rose above the rest of the buildings.

Kull and Heidel woke as the carriage slowed. When we reached the city's wall, the light-carriage stopped. The doors slid open, revealing towers bathed in red from the glare of the morning sun.

We exited the carriage in an area filled with people gathered along a road that stretched toward the capitol. Tents and small stone buildings crowded the road, and getting through the densely packed bodies took longer than I'd hoped. When we finally reached the gates, we didn't enter as everyone else. Instead, Maveryck led us away from the looming gates and walked down a worn-looking dirt path that took us around the gates to a grate in the stone.

The echo of voices came from behind us as Maveryck knelt and removed the fake grate, which wasn't secured to the wall, and then ushered us through. The opening was only wide enough to allow us to crawl inside. Soon my palms were coated in a layer of grit and my claustrophobia made it hard to breathe, but after shuffling through the tunnel and making it down a steep grade, we entered a broad, brick-lined passageway.

As I dusted off my leather pants, I scanned the tunnel. Fae lanterns glowed in sconces along the walls, casting our world in an eerie glow of blue. The light only illuminated small areas of the walls and floor around them, leaving the rest of the tunnel in darkness. My skin bristled at the chill in the damp air filling the corridor. Water dripped in slow, rhythmic beats somewhere up ahead.

"How did you know this was here?" Heidel asked Maveryck, her voice echoing around the chamber.

"There are perks to once belonging to a secret organization. Follow me." He waved us forward as he walked into the depths of the tunnel.

Kull fell into step beside me as Heidel and Maveryck walked ahead.

"Once again," Kull muttered, "we follow him blindly. I had hoped to be done with this, especially after last time."

"I know you don't like it, and neither do I, but I don't know of a better way inside the city. Plus, if he takes us to my father, we'll at least have one person to trust." I cleared my throat. "Sort of."

Kull kept his hand wrapped around his sword's pommel. Maveryck and Heidel made conversation up ahead, but they spoke too softly to hear. I supposed I could eavesdrop and allow my elven hearing to let me in on their conversation, but I resisted the urge.

The tunnel grew narrower and ended at a plain wooden door. Maveryck waited for us to catch up, then lifted the latch and led us through. We entered a small, circular room with a ladder leading to a grate in the ceiling. Maveryck ascended the ladder first and removed the grate, and then the rest of us followed.

We climbed out of the tunnel and up to a narrow alleyway. Wind whipped through the passageway, carrying the scent of herbs and flowers. In most cities, one might expect to find the scent of rotting garbage in a back alley like this one, but not here. In Lauressa, the elves expected everything to be honed to perfection.

Still, the alley had a barren feel created by its stark black stones and cramped buildings, an atmosphere made worse by the biting cold wind.

Maveryck pulled his cloak's cowl low over his face.

"I'll make sure we stay in the alleys and back passages," Maveryck said, "but I can't guarantee we won't be noticed. You'd all be wise to keep your hoods up and your heads down."

We pulled our cloak hoods over our heads and then followed the thief as he led us through the alley. A few elves passed us, but they kept their distances without giving us a second glance.

The city felt different from the last time I visited. For one thing, I didn't see any children on the streets, and the only sounds came from wagon wheels creaking and the shout of an occasional vendor. Colors were muted, lights seemed dimmer—there seemed to be a pall cast over the entire city.

The castle's main tower rose above the rest of the buildings, and as we approached it, I began to recognize the area near my father's cottage. We passed by an open park with spindle-straight trees and a pond with water that rippled in the wind, making waves lap against the pebble-strewn shore. The park benches, crafted to look like roots growing from the ground, sat empty. After the park, we entered the district surrounding the castle. Ornate stonework covered the buildings; cobblestones mixed with sparkling crystals paved the streets.

We took a road that led us behind the buildings. Soon, we entered another open park area where mossy grass grew like carpet and fairies built homes in the trees. Beneath the trees' sprawling green canopies, we found cottages built in the style of the elves' ancestors. Some were built around the trees and spanned several stories, while others sat away from the rest. It seemed an odd place for a woodland village, right here in the heart of the city, but elves had a thing about nature, so they reserved these homes for important people—people like my dad.

As we approached my father's cottage, I hesitated to walk to the door with the others. I'd never gotten along well with my dad. Although he had his reasons, he'd never visited me much when I was a kid, and even after his explanations and apologies, I half expected him to turn me away again. Rejection was a hard emotion to live with. Still, if I wanted to know what had happened to Mom, and if we wanted to know where the elves had taken the staff, then I had no choice but to face him.

CHAPTER
Twenty-six

MAVERYCK KNOCKED ON THE DOOR. AFTER A MO-
ment, the door opened, and my father stood on the
other side. His eyes snagged on me.

"Olive?"

"Hi, Father."

He looked from me to the rest of the group. "Maveryck,
you received my message?"

"Yes. We must speak with you, Magistrate Pozin. As you
know, it's of the utmost importance."

"Very well. Come inside quickly. You shouldn't be out in
the open like this."

My father ushered us inside. After we entered, he shut the
door behind us, locking us away from the howling wind and
outside world.

A fire crackled in the hearth, sending warmth throughout
the room, radiating ocher light over the parquet floors, the pillars carved with vines and bunches of grapes, and the mahog-
any furniture accented with mother-of-pearl and gold leaf. We
removed our cloaks and hung them on pegs near the door. Father's home hadn't changed much, except I did notice books
strewn on the couches and chairs, and several more tomes
piled on one of the round tables near the couch.

Father hastily picked up the books and shelved them.
"Did you have any trouble getting here?"

"No," Maveryck answered. "The city seems unusually quiet."

"Yes, it's been that way for some time now. Please, have a
seat. I shall prepare the tea."

We sat on the couches and waited on my father. Kull and Heidel sat with straight backs and shifted uncomfortably. The cushions had never been made for comfort, though my dad didn't seem to mind.

The scent of mint filled the room, and the hissing of the teakettle whistled from the kitchen. Soon, Father returned and placed a tray on a table near the couch. We took our cups and Father sat across from us, his face lined with worry.

I hadn't realized it earlier, but Dad looked older. He had several more gray hairs threaded through his long hair, and wrinkles lined his eyes and forehead. I knew the magic loss last year hadn't been easy on him, and it seemed life hadn't been kind to him, either. I wanted to ask if he knew where Mom was, but I held my tongue. If she were here, the last thing he would do was tell me with the possibility of being found out.

"The staff," Maveryck said as he placed his cup on the table. "Your message said you know its location."

"I do not know its location, exactly, but I am close to finding it." Father steepled his fingers as he peered at us. "I have been keeping a close eye on the nobles. My status gives me access to almost all places in the castle. Several days ago, I watched a Wult man being locked in the dungeon. I found it strange that the elves would imprison him, so after the guards left, I visited him.

"He told me his name was Euric and he had worked with the elves to remove the staff from Danegeld. He was angry with the king and thought that by taking the staff, it would make him look incompetent. The Wult man aided the elves in bringing the staff back to Lauressa, and then aided them further still by helping them hide it in a new location. However, he'd seen too much, and so instead of rewarding him as he had thought, the elves locked him up.

"After I met with him, I sent the message to you."

Kull spoke up. "Did Euric say where the staff is now?"

"He said only that the elves had taken it through a gateway located in the inner sanctum in the catacombs. I tried to go there, but it was heavily guarded. Not even I could enter."

"A gateway?" I asked. "Gateway to where?"

Father stood and removed one of the books from the shelf. "That is what I have been trying to determine. We know that the staff belonged to the Madralorde—assuming the stories are true—and we know the talismans were once housed on Tremulac Isle. But no one has ever been able to discover the location of the rumored isle."

Father laid the book on the table and opened it to a map of the city of Lauressa. "There may be a reason for that," he said. "If you look at the map, you can see that our city is built with a series of underground tunnels beneath it." He pointed to the map, which showed an elaborate web of tunnels below the city's foundation.

"Yes," Heidel said. "Didn't we travel through one of those tunnels in order to get inside?"

"We did," Maveryck answered, "but I thought those tunnels were built by the Gravidorum."

"That is what I believed as well, except after doing some research, I learned that those tunnels date back thousands of years, well before the Gravidorum came to this city."

"Then who built them?" I asked.

"It's possible those tunnels were built by the Madralorde. They may have created a gateway from Tremulac to Lauressa, but in order to open the gateway, one would have to be in the castle at Tremulac."

"How do you know that?" I asked.

Father leafed through the book to a page near the back. On the paper, a map of the elven continent, Laurentia, had been inked in detail onto the parchment. In the center of the page, where the city of Lauressa should have been drawn, sat empty space.

"What happened to the city?" Kull asked.

"It's hidden," my father answered. "Several hundred years ago, the elven nobles tasked several of their best wizards with the project of hiding the city. Their experiments were successful, and they managed to cloak the city for several days. Outside the city walls, the countryside seemed to continue on forever. And above, it seemed as though only fields were beneath."

"That's interesting," I said. "Do you think the same thing happened to Tremulac?"

"I'm not sure. It took a great amount of power to fuel the spell that hid Lauressa, so if the same thing were to happen at Tremulac, and for it to last for so long a time, seems improbable."

"But not impossible," Kull said.

"Even if the island was hidden by magic, how would we find it?" I asked.

"What if we were to follow the elves through this gateway you spoke of?" Heidel asked.

"No, I'm afraid that is not a possibility. The elven queen is expecting you to come after the staff, and she has prepared a trap for the four of you. If any one of you were to pass through her gateway, the queen would immediately be alerted to your presence and take you prisoner. She needs a blood sacrifice to initiate the spell, and it would be within her reasoning to use any one of you. I believe we would be safer finding an alternate path to Tremulac."

"Is it even possible to find?" Kull asked. "Some have been searching for centuries and have never found it. It doesn't seem likely that we will."

"Except that we have an advantage," Father said.

"What advantage?" Heidel asked.

"For an entire castle to be hidden by a spell, it would put off a great deal of magical energy. In theory, we should be able to find the castle by searching for the spell."

"If that's so," I said, "then why hasn't anyone found it before us?"

"Because they never knew what sort of spell to search for. The queen and her royals discovered it recently, and if they could find it, then we should be able to do the same."

"But where do we start?" I asked. "It could take ages to roam through the countryside looking for a spell."

"We won't have to."

"Why?"

"Because I've already narrowed down the search area." Father flipped to a section of the book that mapped the wild lands. He pointed to several large lakes at the center of the page. "I believe Tremulac exists on one of these lakes."

"The wild lands?" Maveryck said. "Have you been there yourself?"

"No, of course not."

"Then how do you know it's there?" Heidel asked.

"Because I have been closely following the royalty. I was able to scry upon Veladon, the queen's vizier, one evening as he left the castle. He entered the wild lands, and I could see no more after he entered, but when he returned, a gateway was opened up in the catacombs beneath the city—a gateway that led to Tremulac."

"So you believe Veladon found Tremulac in the wild lands and created a portal back to Lauressa?"

"Precisely."

Kull worked his jaw back and forth. "I still think it would

be easier to enter through the catacombs under the city. The wild lands aren't far if we take the rails, but we'll only get as far as the border. Once we arrive, we'd be lucky to survive crossing that waste."

"At any other time, I would agree," my father said. "But it's too risky. The sky king will perish, the queen will harness Theht's powers, and there is more at stake than even you can fathom. I must insist that you make this journey. The wild lands are dangerous, yes, but they are safer than the alternative."

"What do you mean?" I asked, confused. "What else is at stake? What could possibly be worse than my stepfather's death? Or the queen ruling with Theht's powers?"

After I asked it, I realized what a dumb question it was. By now, I should have known to never ask how things could get worse.

My father took in a deep breath, then he stood. "If you will promise not to speak of what I reveal to you, I shall show you all."

"Show us what?" Kull asked.

Father shook his head. "Follow me if you wish to see. But be warned, this must stay between us."

We stood and followed my father down a short hallway, but we passed the doors and stopped instead at a blank wall. He lifted his hand and whispered a word of magic, making his fingers glow blue. The power of his spell made my skin tingle with an electrical intensity. I took a step back just to be away from that amount of power.

The glow from his hands spread outward toward the wall, revealing a door hidden by magic. As the spell gave way, the door came into full view. Without speaking another word, Father lifted the latch and led us inside a large room.

As I stepped inside, I gasped.

My mother sat on one of the many beds inside the chamber. She held a baby in her arms. Other women were in the room also, and I found several cribs lining the walls. Sounds of babies cooing and softly whimpering came from the cribs. When my mom looked up, her eyes met mine. Surprise lit her face.

"Olive?" she gasped.

She handed the baby to one of the women and came to me. Without hesitation, she wrapped her arms around me, catching me by surprise. I had to remind myself that this was Kasandra Kennedy without the spells. The old Kasandra would have never hugged me so publicly, but the new mom, the real mom, did it without a second thought.

"You have no idea how happy I am to see you," she said. As she pulled away, tears shone in her eyes, and she hastily brushed them away.

Unlike Dad, she looked younger than when I'd seen her last. Her auburn hair was longer and fell to her shoulders, and her eyes seemed brighter. She wore elven clothing—a leather tunic with a white peasant's shirt and a long, sweeping skirt. I'd only ever seen her in name brand Earth clothing. Oddly, the new look suited her.

"What are you doing here?" Mom asked.

"They came to find out about the staff," Father answered.

"The staff? Well, they've found a bit more than that, haven't they?"

Mom took the baby she had been holding in her arms once again and cradled him to her chest. I stared in confusion at the infant when Father spoke up.

"Olive, this is what I meant to show you. This is why you haven't heard from your mother and I for so long. We've discovered a secret that could bring down the queen if she knew about it."

I glanced around the room. "Let me guess; it's got something to do with these children?"

Mom took a step closer. "Yes. It's got everything to do with them."

"Do you notice anything odd about these children?" Father asked.

I scanned the baby Mom had in her arms. He seemed young, perhaps only a month old, and had the characteristic pointed elven ears. His two tiny hands were fisted near his face. As he slept, he kept his heart-shaped lips parted and made soft sighing sounds. An odd emotion came over me, something akin to a feeling of longing. I'd never exactly contemplated becoming a mother, but I supposed many women dealt with the emotion from time to time. It occurred to me then that someday, I wanted children.

At that thought, another emotion followed. Fear. If parenthood ever did happen, how would I raise a child with the crazy scary life I lived?

I pushed my thoughts aside in order to think logically. Obviously, there was something special about this baby. But what? He looked like an ordinary elven baby. I couldn't find anything unusual. I had supposed that he must have been infected with some sort of virus or been born carrying deadly pathogens, but as I stretched my magical senses to encompass the baby, nothing stood out. I even used my elven hearing to listen to his heartbeat, but that sounded normal as well.

"He seems perfectly fine to me. I can't find anything wrong with him."

"Are you sure?" Mom asked. "Here. Hold him, and you might think differently."

She placed the baby in my arms. The emotion I'd felt only moments ago came back even more strongly. Kull stood behind me and watched as I held the baby, and I couldn't help but realize how natural it felt, to have him close while I held the baby.

But that wasn't the reason Mom had let me hold him. My goodness, what on earth was wrong with my head? How could I even contemplate motherhood when I could barely take care of my cat?

I took the baby's tiny fingers in mine, but all I could think was that he seemed perfect. Not a single flaw at all.

"There's nothing wrong with him."

"Look at his magic," Mom said.

I did as she said, extending my magical senses to detect the baby's magical color. Since the baby was elven, I expected to see the usual blue. As the magic appeared, I stared, shocked, as his powers turned gray.

"Gray magic," I gasped.

"Yes," Mom said.

"But how is that possible? Goblins use—used—gray magic. This child is elven."

Father stepped closer. "We've learned that nature has a way of balancing itself out. Wiping out the goblins should have put an end to all gray magic, yet since their extermination, babies to elven parents have been born with gray magic."

I tried to wrap my mind around the situation. "I didn't think that was possible."

"Neither did anyone else. That is, until now. For magic to stay balanced in Faythander, some believe it must be made up of five different parts. It could not survive with only four. Gray magic has found a way to return."

"It's amazing. Do you think these children will have the ability to control liquid elements like the goblins?"

"Yes, some of the older babies have already begun to exhibit characteristics that lead us to believe so."

My heart clenched with fear as I contemplated what the queen would do once she found out. "How many are there?"

"Seventeen that we've discovered in the city so far."

"Are they all hiding here?"

A pained look crossed Father's face. "No. Only a few are here. Some parents opted to leave the city altogether. Everyone knows how dangerous it is to be found with a child who possesses the same sort of magic the queen had thought to eradicate."

Mom spoke up. "But these arrangements are only temporary. This room has been spellcasted with powerful magic in order to hide them, but we can't keep these babies hidden forever."

"No, they'll need somewhere else once they start to grow, and we can't house them all," Father said.

"Then what will you do?" I asked.

Father shook his head. "We don't know."

"The queen will find out eventually," Mom said, "and when she does, I don't want to contemplate the consequences."

Silence fell over the room, broken by the occasional cry of a baby. Kull spoke up from behind me.

"There is one thing we can do," he said. "We must stop the queen from taking Theht's power, for once she has it, hiding from her will become impossible. Nowhere will be safe, not even in a room protected by powerful spells."

"He's right," Maveryck said. "We must not waste another moment. We must journey to the wild lands in order to find the lost castle. If we don't, if she gains more power than she has now, spells will not stop her. Theht's power is greater than any of us understand. She will not stop with the extinction of the goblins, but will eradicate all creatures who oppose her."

Chills prickled my neck as Theht's presence stirred at his words.

He's right, it said.

"I agree," Heidel said. "Wild lands or not, ghosts or specters or pools filled with blood, we cannot let that stop us."

"Pools of blood?" I asked.

"Yes, that is what my people say exists there."

"I'd not heard that one."

"It's a rumor, Sister," Kull said.

"A rumor founded on facts, I'm afraid," Maveryck said.

We all turned toward Maveryck.

"How would you know that?" I asked. "Have you been there?"

"A very long time ago. Yes, I've been there."

"How would you know what's inside the wild lands?" Heidel asked. "No one goes there and survives."

"That is not completely true. I did it, and others have done it as well."

"The bloodthorn traveled the wild lands," Kull said, "but he had his immortality protecting him. We won't have such a luxury."

My mom spoke up. "I don't see how you are to survive such a quest. Pozin, isn't there another way?"

"Yes, and it's through the queen's catacombs, where she has warded the entrance with her most powerful spells, where she has posted half of her guards, and where she is waiting for them to enter. You may not have seen many guards roaming the city, and there is a reason. She has moved half her regiment to the catacombs."

"Still, it sounds less dangerous than the wild lands," Mom said.

"No," Maveryck said. "I can get you through the wild lands. I cannot make the same promise for the queen's catacombs. Plus, if we do enter through the wild lands, we shall have the element of surprise on our side."

"Either way sounds pretty bleak to me," I admitted, "but it has to be done."

I glanced at the baby still cradled in Mom's arms. Emotion welled within me, and a knot formed in my throat. For a child to be killed because of the color of its magic appalled me, yet I knew Euralysia. I knew her motivations. I'd witnessed her execute the entire goblin race.

It would not happen again. God help me, I would not let it happen again.

CHAPTER
Twenty-seven

WE WAITED UNTIL THE COVER OF NIGHT TO LEAVE the city. Fog shrouded the desolate streets. I felt as if I walked on an alien planet. It seemed fear lurked in every corner, that it drove the people to stay indoors and forced the once vibrant, musical city into oppression. I didn't envy the people who lived here.

Maveryck led the way as Kull, Heidel, and I followed. We took the same passage to leave the city as we had to get in, but I didn't think it mattered. There were no guards or people any-where, making me wonder if we'd stumbled upon a graveyard rather than the elven capitol.

After crossing through the streets, Maveryck led us into the tunnels, and then out beyond the city wall. Dewy grass squished under my leather boots as I followed the others to-ward the light-rails. The single thread of light cut through the darkness like a beacon, and I breathed a sigh of relief as we finally climbed inside the carriage and away from the city.

"Lauressa is a different place," I said as the carriage sped forward, its mechanical whir a soft purr in my ears and its mag-ic making my senses tingle.

"It hasn't been the same since the queen took control," Maveryck answered.

"Faythander won't be the same either if she manages to get control of it," Kull said.

I stared through the window and watched as the carriage sped away from the city. Lights shone from the top of the cas-tle, making my thoughts turn to Mom and Dad, who'd stayed behind. Worry nagged at me. I didn't like leaving them behind in that city, where they could be discovered at a moment's notice, but what other choice did I have? The only thing to be done was to stop the queen, and that thought gave me the strength to keep going forward.

Kull grabbed my hand and kissed my knuckles.

"What was that for?" I asked.

"You looked worried."

"Shouldn't I be?"

"No."

"No? Our world is on the brink of destruction, and I shouldn't be worried?"

"Right this moment, there's nothing you can do about it. So I say no, don't be worried."

I eyed him. He never seemed to worry about anything— well, except maybe one thing—but for the most part, he held it together. It was a talent I envied.

"Tell me, Maveryck," Kull said, "what can we expect to find in the wild lands?"

Heidel had rested her head on Maveryck's shoulder, but she sat up as he shifted.

Maveryck's eyes darkened. "My memories of that place are not ones I care to recall." He heaved a heavy sigh.

He'd said he had the ability to recall events with perfect clarity. I was reminded that it would most likely bring him pain to speak of such a memory, but it couldn't be avoided. We had to know what was in the wild lands.

"My journey into the wild lands happened when I was much younger, just a boy really, while my elven parents were still alive," he started. "My elder brother Navarre wanted to take me on an expedition. What I didn't know was that he was leading me into a trap. Looking back, I am sure he was jealous of me. I was the youngest, adopted, and doted on by our parents. He was the eldest and expected to be the leader, and he hated it. Needless to say, he didn't like me, and so he led me into the wild lands. Whether he wished to kill me or merely scare me, I cannot say for sure. But he left me there alone.

"Unlike what most people think, the wild lands aren't merely a desolate waste. In fact, they're the opposite. They're a place of enormous magical energy, so potent that plants and creatures grow mutated. After time, the magic began to wreak havoc on the area's ecosystems, decimating some, causing others to warp into different species altogether.

"But the most dangerous aspect of the wild lands is neither

the plants nor the animals—it is the magic that gets into your head. It makes you see things, makes you lose your senses, and eventually, makes you lose your mind.

"I was only able to survive because my family returned for me. Navarre had let it slip what he'd done, and so my parents came and found me. If not for them, I don't think I would have made it through."

"Is there any way around it?" Heidel asked. "Some way to get past the magic?"

"Yes, I believe so. Since then, I have made it a point to never be in such a situation ever again. Although I have not returned, I have done a fair amount of research and learned that there are trails protected from the magic in that waste, and if one were to find one of the trails and stay on it, it would be possible to navigate through the wild lands and avoid the most potent magic. However, I'll have to know where we're going. Magistrate Pozin spoke of a lake, but how are we to know which one?"

I rummaged in my pack and found the journal. Recalling something I'd seen inside, I placed the leather-bound tome on my lap and opened it carefully. The paper creaked as I flipped to a map near the middle of the diary.

The picture had been drawn by hand, although its detail and clarity were remarkable. The map had no name, but around the outer edge of the landmass were the words OUTER RIM. And inside were the words ACASER FORMATION. Other points of interest had been given names as well, but I focused on the lines crisscrossing the map.

"Look at this," I said to Maveryck and passed the book to him. "Do you think this could be a map of the wild lands?"

He studied the map several minutes before speaking, turning the pages, then back to the map, then turning it one way or another. "Yes," he finally said. "I think this most likely could be a map of the wild lands. But it has changed since this map was drawn."

"Do you think we can rely on it to get us through?" Kull asked.

"There is only one way to know for sure," he answered, then handed the journal back to me.

I studied the picture, wishing we had more than only this to help us get through the waste.

A large lake had been drawn near the map's center. Several other bodies of water had been drawn as well, but the lake caught my eye, perhaps because the image of a skull, similar to the one I'd seen in Silvestra's castle, took up the lake's center.

"What do you make of this?" I asked.

"Could it be Tremulac Lake?" Heidel asked.

"It seems the most likely place. However," Maveryck said, "not all is as it seems in that place."

"Then why would Dracon draw this symbol?" I asked. "Come to think of it, this symbol looks similar to the skull symbol I saw in Silvestra's castle. It means black magic. Do you think black magic is at work in the wild lands?"

"No, not that I'm aware of," Maveryck answered. "It's possible that the skull means something else—death perhaps, or a warning."

"A warning about what?" Heidel asked. "Is there something in that lake we should know about?"

"Hold on," I said, staring at the map. A small, five-pointed star was drawn in one of the skull's eye sockets. "There may be something here. What do you make of this?"

Maveryck took the book once again and studied the picture. He shook his head. "I don't know. Perhaps it has no meaning at all."

"I doubt it." I took the book back from him as I contemplated the star's meaning. The longer I looked at it, the more I thought the star was oddly shaped, with the ends ending not in points, but in curves, like an asterisk.

My breath caught in my throat. "Theht," I whispered. "This is the symbol for Theht." I looked up. "I think I've found our lost castle."

"Are you sure?"

"I'm fairly certain that we'll find something here, whether it's the castle or not, I think this should be the place we travel to."

"But if it's the symbol for Theht," Maveryck said, "shouldn't we avoid it?"

"Logically speaking, yes. Why Dracon decided to mark this lake with Theht's symbol must have been for a good reason. But if we want to stop the summoning, then this is where we'll have to go."

Running headlong into dangerous, possibly life-ending situations was becoming a habit of mine. One day, I'd have to consider breaking it.

"Then it's settled," Kull said. "We'll have to make it to that lake and hopefully find our missing castle. Maveryck, how long will it take to travel through that wasteland?"

"The lake sits at the center of the area, and if we are able to locate one of the trails, then we should be able to make it there in less than a day, assuming we are not attacked and killed by some sort of mutated beast."

"I'll handle the beasts," Kull said smugly. "Monsters don't worry me, it's what's at the center of the lake that's troubling."

"You won't slay the beasts without help," Heidel said. "Not without Bloodbane, anyway."

"Which is why you are coming with me," Kull said. He sighed as he glanced at the sword he'd placed on the floor of the carriage. "Bloodbane would come in handy right about now."

"But Bloodbane is not here," Heidel said, "which is why you must let me help you."

Kull raised an eyebrow. "One would think you are glad my sword is gone."

"Glad? No. I am merely making the best of an unfortunate situation."

"Or taking advantage of it."

"Those are your words, Brother."

Kull and Heidel, at it again. Would they ever get tired of their back-and-forth bickering?

"What will you do with Euric?" Heidel asked.

Kull shrugged. "Nothing. He's been imprisoned by the elves. I don't see that there is anything I can do."

"You can demand the elves release him so he may serve his penance in the Wult dungeons."

"No need. As long as he is detained, he can do no further damage to me."

"Yet," Maveryck said, "the damage may have already been done."

"Why do you say that?" I asked.

"I heard Euric's speeches he made at the Wult inn near Dragon Spine Mountain. He was intent on rallying the people against the king. Some of His Majesty's subjects may see Euric as a sort of martyr."

"I disagree," Kull said. "Once they learn that Euric stole the staff from the keep, they won't see him as anything more than a traitor."

"Forgive me, Your Majesty, but I believe you fail to understand the power of a cult mentality. There were some who claimed Euric to be Odin reborn. And he did nothing to stop

251

that belief. They followed him blindly."

"What are you saying?" Kull asked. "If that's the case, what would you have me do? Execute anyone who professes to follow the man?"

"No, of course not. His following was too small and insignificant to make a difference. But you must keep an eye on his followers."

"This started because you lost Bloodbane," Heidel said. "It was your symbol of power. Now that it is gone, they have lost their faith in you."

"Unfortunately, I see no way to remedy the situation. Short of traveling to the outer isles and forging another sword, I am not sure what to do to restore our people's trust."

Silence filled the carriage once again. I rested my hand atop Kull's. He seemed like he needed something to lift his spirits. I couldn't help but feel guilty that I was the one responsible for destroying Bloodbane. The heirloom sword had been the symbol of his power, and it seemed I had become the symbol of his failure.

He stared out the window, though there was nothing to see but blackness broken up now and again by the lights of an occasional town or village, or a random flock of maywelters or nobbinflies.

Soft yellow lanterns illuminated Kull's profile. Although tiny wrinkles lined the edges of his eyes and scars marred his deep bronze skin, I couldn't help but find him irresistibly attractive. If not for him, I would still be dead inside. He'd saved me more than once, physically and emotionally, and I hadn't been the only person he'd helped. I knew he cared for his people and worried about them, so to see him being rejected by his own kind made my heart feel heavy. Perhaps stopping the elves from summoning Theht would prove his worth once and for all.

Spending another night on a carriage wasn't a habit I wanted to keep up, but since I knew I would need my strength, I gave up rehashing my worries and slept with my cheek resting on Kull's shoulder, listening to the sound of his breathing and realizing I should probably take his advice and stop worrying.

Easier said than done.

⟆⟑⟆

I awoke with the whir of the carriage resounding in my ears. When I opened my eyes, I found the sky outside had lightened to a dull, gunmetal gray. Acid churned in my stomach as my thoughts returned to my daily to-do list.

Travel through the wild lands without getting killed.
Find an evil castle.
Steal a lost egg.
Stop a maniac queen from taking over the world.
Do it without dying.

At least I couldn't complain of being bored.

I lay with my head on Kull's shoulder a moment longer, feeling the strength of his deltoid against my face. I gently traced my fingers along his arms, letting the warmth of his skin thaw my chill. But with his nearness, I was reminded of the prophecy.

Would he really be the person who killed me?

That thought made me shudder. Somehow, I had to figure out a way to keep Theht from controlling me. I had to rescue Fan'twar—I wasn't sure if he could remove Theht's presence from my mind, but he could at least point me in the right direction.

As the sky lightened outside, I began to make out the shapes of mountains against the gray horizon. But before we reached the peaks, the carriage slowed. The others woke as we pulled to a stop.

"Have we arrived?" Heidel asked.

The doors slid open, revealing a desert of sand dunes pocked with rocks, reminding me of the surface of Mars.

"Yes," I said, "we've arrived."

CHAPTER
Twenty-eight

THE CARRIAGE SPED AWAY AS WE APPROACHED THE wild lands. Despite Maveryck's description of the place, I couldn't see life anywhere. No monsters or mutated plants, no pools of blood, only an endless, desolate landscape as far as we could see.

A dry, hot wind rushed past, stirring the sand into clouds. "This isn't so bad," I said.

"That's because this is only the outskirts," Maveryck answered. "We've yet to cross the border."

I tightened my grip on my pack's strap. Father had given us enough supplies to support a small army, and my pack's weight was proof. But would food and weapons do us any good in the place we were going?

As the sun rose over the desolate valley and the empty expanse seemed to stretch forever, I began to doubt Maveryck's word. This seemed no different from an ordinary desert, and I saw no signs of creatures mutated by magic. As I prepared to question him once again, we passed through a magical barrier.

A blast of hot air radiated around me as we crossed through the magical shield. Kull and Heidel didn't seem to notice, but Maveryck winced as we crossed it. The air shimmered in shades of white and blue, and as if we had flipped a switch, the world transformed.

The sun shone with an orange haze as it filtered through layers of billowing, sulfur-smelling clouds. We stood in a jungle of tangled vines with carnivorous-looking flowers in shades of orange and purple. Humidity saturated the air as sounds of insects chirping came from the forest. Magic pulsed with a fever pitch from the smallest shrub to the clouds overhead. The feeling was so overwhelming, I had to stop and catch my breath.

"What?" Heidel spun around. "Where are we?"

"We crossed through the barrier," Maveryck said.

Kull unsheathed his sword. "You could have warned us."

"I had no way of knowing where it was."

My arms and legs tingled with magic, making me feel as if ants crawled under my skin. "I didn't sense it either until we crossed through."

The sound of a creature howling echoed in the distance. Something disturbed the leaves overhead, making me jump back. Water pooled from the canopy, splashing us with large droplets. I wiped the liquid off my face, tasting its brine on my tongue.

"Well," Maveryck said, wiping the moisture from his tunic, his eyebrows raised as if the water had offended him somehow, "welcome to the wild lands."

"Where do we go from here?" Heidel asked.

"I'm not the best person to ask. It's all changed quite a bit since I was here." Maveryck looked at me. "Olive, do you have the map?"

"Yes." I pulled my pack off my shoulder and dug through it until I found the journal. I flipped through the book until I came to the sketch of the map, although I wasn't sure how useful I would be at reading it, so I handed the book to Kull. "You're better at navigating than me."

Kull studied the map as the rest of us looked on. "We'll need to find one of these trails as soon as possible. I believe we entered here, in the south. If we travel due north, we should run into this trail here, and that in turn should lead us to the center of the lands where we'll hopefully find the lake."

"Sounds good to me," I said as I replaced the journal in my pack. When Fan'twar had given me the diary, I had never planned to use it to navigate through an unholy land full of magically mutated plants and monsters, but then again, my life never seemed to go the way I planned.

Hoots and whistles came from the canopy as we trudged forward. We all used our swords and knives to cut away the vines and plants blocking our path. The sun rose higher, making the heat even more oppressive. Sweat beaded on my neck and forehead as I chopped through a thick vine that sprayed white fluid as it burst open, then shriveled back.

Near me, Kull severed a vine that lashed out, cutting his

hands with sharp barbs.

"You okay?" I asked.

"Fine." He wiped his hand on his tunic. "This cursed forest better be worth getting through."

"It will be if we get that egg back," I said.

Rumbling came from overhead. At first I assumed it to be thunder, but as it grew louder, I glanced up to find a horde of bat-like creatures flocking over the canopy, blocking out the sun. I'd never seen so many creatures in one place.

Thousands of wings created a rushing sound, brushing the hot air, creating a maelstrom of wind. After they passed, only silence remained.

"That was odd," Heidel said. "Do you think they were flying toward something?"

"Away from something, most likely," Maveryck said.

"Let's keep going," Kull said. "Whatever disturbed them is something I'd rather avoid."

Pressing forward, we hacked through the brush until blisters formed on my fingers. We entered a small, circular clearing. Neatly trimmed grass grew around a single flowering plant blooming in the center of the glen. The air seemed cooler here than in the rest of the forest. Bunches of flowers in pastel purples and blues sprouted from its delicate branches, moving gently in the breeze. The bush reminded me of the hydrangea flowers blooming around my grandmother's house. A low, crumbling brick wall had been built around the plant, and in places, it looked as if words or symbols had been etched into the stone.

I wiped away a bead of sweat as I stared at the flower. "That's odd," I said. "Who would have built that wall? Maveryck, has this place ever been inhabited?"

"No, it would have been impossible for anyone to inhabit the wild lands. The magic here would take over any man-made structures a person built. I imagine the castle—if it exists—is protected by powerful spells in order to survive the magical onslaught. Anything else would have been destroyed ages ago."

"Then how did that get there?"

He shook his head. I reached out, feeling for enchantments in the glen or surrounding the wall, but the magic from the forest was too strong and overpowered any spells I might have felt.

"Is it safe to approach?" Kull asked.

"I can't say for sure. The magic here is too strong for me to detect spells."

"Maybe Dracon built it," Heidel said. "Is it pictured in the journal?"

"Good idea," I said and pulled my pack off my shoulder. After I found the journal, I flipped through the pages until I found the map. The others gathered around me as we scanned the drawing.

"What about that?" Kull said, pointing to a small circle near the southern border. The label read *HEARTSTONE*.

"Well, that plant doesn't look like any sort of stone I've ever seen, but it is drawn circular, just like that wall."

We moved toward the flower, keeping an eye out for enchantments or traps, but found none. Sunlight, unhindered by brush or tree limbs, shone down onto the ground, highlighting the flowers and making them sparkle.

Kull knelt, lightly touching one. "These aren't flowers at all. They're jewels."

I knelt by the flower and inspected the petals. Cradled inside each bloom, I found a jewel. Pink, purple, and cobalt stones glittered in the sunlight, refracting around the small grove.

"I guess we know why it's called the heartstone," Kull said.

I reached out and gently touched the leaves, feeling a steady hum of power coming from the plant. As I touched it, the stream of magic joined my own, a presence that reminded me of the Everblossom tree that had once grown beneath the pixie lands. Its magic seemed to speak to me, but whatever it wanted to say was snuffed out by the influx of magic surrounding us.

"I've never seen anything like it," Kull said. "It's beautiful."

"Yes. It's odd, but it reminds me of the flowers that bloomed around my grandmother's house. And it also reminds me of the time I heard the wind chimes when I went near the Everblossom tree. Do you think it could have been put here for a reason?"

"What sort of reason?"

"I don't know. Maybe to help us or something? Do I sound crazy?"

"We're in Faythander. Anything's possible."

"True."

I touched one of the jewels, the cold stone smooth under my fingertips. Magic pulsed from the jewel, and I had an urge to take it from the flower but decided against it. I wasn't sure what it would do to me. What if it had been cursed? Or what if the magic was unstable?

I stood and stepped away, looking from the plant to the wall instead. "Maveryck, can you read this?" I asked.

"Not very well. Some of the symbols are familiar, but it's old elvish. *Flourish for eternity.*" He ran his fingers over the symbols, his face puzzled. "I can't make out the rest."

"It's an odd place," Heidel said, glancing around, "but we'd be wise not to linger here. We'd be easily ambushed in a place such as this. It's too dangerous for us to stay any longer."

I glanced at the plant as we left the clearing, wondering how the wall had gotten there and wanting to know why the plant felt so familiar. Was it connected to the Everblossom somehow? I wanted to stay longer and learn more about the flower, but for the time being, I would have to wait to get any answers.

We entered the dense jungle once again. The suffocating air returned, making me feel as if I'd been smothered in plastic wrap. When the sun reached its zenith, we still hadn't found the path, making me wonder if we were traveling in the wrong direction.

Something fell from the canopy and landed in front of us. I stumbled back as a large, scaled creature stood before us. Black, prismatic scales covered its body, and it had a snake-like tail studded in barbs that whipped back and forth. Its lithe body reminded me of a panther. The creature had a snake's head, with long, slitted pupils focused on us. A forked tongue licked the air as it took a step forward. The beast stood as tall as two men. Its mouth gaped open, revealing fangs dripping with saliva.

"I'm just guessing here," I said, "but I don't think it's friendly."

"I believe that is a well-educated guess," Kull answered.

We scrambled as the thing leapt forward, lashing out with hawk-like talons. It nearly missed gouging Heidel's midsection. She cursed and drove forward with her dagger in a powerful attack, ripping a hole in the beast's leg.

The creature let out a scream that sounded almost human-like. Maveryck lashed out with a short dagger, but the beast knocked him backward.

"Maveryck," Heidel shouted, "you're useless in a fight. Let us handle it."

Maveryck stood, brushing off his tunic. "I fight just as well as you!"

"No you don't!"

"I do too!"

"Then shut up and prove it!"

The monster snapped at us, so close I felt its fetid breath from where I stood.

"Split up," Kull yelled. "Don't stay in one place."

I clenched my knife hilt tight as I scrambled into the forest. With the thick jungle obscuring my vision, I only saw flashes of scales and claws as the monster pursued us. Kull's screams came from somewhere as I readied a spell, only to find that my magic refused to come to the surface.

I focused on calming my mind and tried again, but when I called the magic a second time, it still wouldn't come to the surface—as if the potent power surrounding us kept it from responding.

"This isn't good," I muttered as I tried a third time with no success.

The monster broke through the jungle where I hid, its eyes livid and yellow, magic pulsing hot and strong from its body. I fisted my hands and faced the beast, a flimsy dagger my only protection. A quick search for Kull and Heidel revealed them both struggling to get to their feet behind the beast. Maveryck was nowhere in sight.

Backing away, I stayed focused on the monster as it dove for me, its massive talons outstretched, intent on tearing me in half, when a burst of silver light blasted from the jungle and hit the beast square in the chest. The monster's body exploded in a fireball of white-hot heat. As the flames died away, nothing remained of the beast but wisps of glowing embers carried on the jungle breeze.

Maveryck stepped forward holding a basita weapon as Kull and Heidel both limped toward us, focused on Maveryck's gun.

Maveryck stood tall as he clicked the gears back into the safe position. "Does that prove I can fight?" he asked smugly.

Heidel only stared with her mouth agape. Finally, she found words. "Fine. That proves it."

CHAPTER
Twenty-nine

AFTERNOON APPROACHED WHEN WE FINALLY SPOTTED the path matching the drawing on Dracon's map. Despite the massive growth of foliage, the path looked untouched, as if a lightning strike had burned through the forest. Mirror-smooth, black stones paved the trail, and magic emanated from the path, so strong it made my hands grow clammy and my stomach sicken. I closed my mind against the magic to keep it from affecting me, but doing so only masked the symptoms.

"Didn't you say we were supposed to be protected from the magic on these paths?" I asked Maveryck.

"Yes," he answered. "I feel the magic, too—it's unusually strong. Perhaps there is a spell keeping the paths protected from the forest's magic."

"Yes, maybe so."

The forest grew quiet as we walked down the road. The constant sounds of insects chirping disappeared altogether, and only the echo of our footsteps—clinking as if we walked on glass—rang through the open expanse above us.

"I thought you said nothing manmade could exist here," Heidel said. "How do you explain this road?"

"It's a spell," I answered. "It feels stronger than the forest's magic. It must be keeping the road intact and the forest's magic at bay."

"How is that possible?" Kull asked.

"I don't know. For a spell like this to exist, there has to be something fueling it."

"Then the question is, what's fueling it?"

"I have no clue. But there's definitely something weird happening here. My best guess is that we'll find out at the end of this path. At least, I hope so."

"And I hope it's not something that will kill us," Heidel said.

"Good point," Kull said.

Clouds thickened overhead, a mass of gray that overpowered the blue. At least it made the heat less intense. We found a few large stones alongside the path and stopped for a small meal of bread, honey, and some dried meat, though I wasn't focused on the food. The pathway's magic was getting harder to block out the deeper we traveled. It called to me with an almost overpowering voice, tempting me to test the magic. Theht's voice chimed in, awakening more the closer we got.

The time for my awakening draws nigh.

"Is something the matter, Olive?" Heidel asked.

I looked up and found the others had already packed up and were ready to go. I hastily stuffed my half-eaten hunk of bread into my bag and stood. "No, I was daydreaming, I guess. We can go."

Kull eyed me. "You're sure?"

"Yes. Positive. Lead the way," I said with as much enthusiasm I could muster.

Kull gazed at me a moment longer, not seeming to buy my relaxed attitude. "Maveryck, Heidel, go ahead; we'll follow. I'd like to have a word with Olive."

Maveryck and Heidel walked away, leaving me to keep pace with Kull.

"Olive, what's going on?" Kull asked quietly.

I shook my head.

"You can tell me."

"I'd rather not."

"Why?"

"Because it's... just... it's hard to talk about."

"Does this have something to do with Theht?"

"Yes," I said grudgingly. "The magic here is stronger than anything I've felt before. I don't understand how it behaves or what's fueling it. And it's... calling to Theht. In my head. I know that sounds ridiculous, but you asked. So there it is."

Kull frowned as he pondered my words. "Calling to the goddess how?"

I wrapped my arms around my stomach, feeling the contents agitated and roiling. Every step we took made it harder to control the beast inside. A clammy sweat broke out over my skin.

"I'm not sure how to describe it," I said. "I just feel like I've kept the goddess locked away, and now, the lock is crumbling apart." Our footsteps echoed over the glassy stones with an eerie, musical quality. "This isn't right. Maybe I should go back."

"By yourself?"

"I know. Dumb idea. But I'm not sure how much longer I can control my magic."

"Do you think we should turn around?"

"Turn around? No. We have to stop the summoning. I'll deal with it."

"You're sure?"

"Yes, I'm sure. We don't really have another choice, do we?"

"But we can turn back if we have to. I can go with you."

"And let Maveryck and Heidel go alone?"

Kull knit his brows. "Well, I suppose it wouldn't be the best solution."

Inhaling a deep breath, I did my best to keep Theht's powers locked inside, but with the outside magic growing stronger, I wasn't sure how much longer I would succeed.

"We can do this," I said. "We always have."

"Yes. But not without casualties."

I knew he was speaking of his father. He was right—confronting the elven queen would come with consequences. I tried to tell myself it was for the greater good, that I was doing something noble and heroic, but deep inside, I was afraid, and not just for myself, but for all of us. Who else would die because we chose to face evil? Heidel? Maveryck? Kull? My stepfather?

As dusk approached, the trail sloped downward and we entered an ancient crater. The jungle suddenly disappeared, replaced instead by a barren land of stones and sand. In the center of the depression, far in the distance, we found a lake, and at its center sat the glittering towers of an ancient fortress.

"Tremulac," Maveryck said in a hushed tone. "We've found it."

"You're sure that's it?" Heidel asked.

"What else what it be?"

"I don't know. A mirage, maybe?"

"It's not a mirage," I said, feeling the magic of the fortress in waves so potent I wasn't sure I could withstand it. "That's definitely real. What could be causing so much magic to be focused around one place?"

"We may not know until we go inside," Kull said. "Olive, you look even paler than before. Can you manage?"

I took several deep breaths, trying to let the extra oxygen clear my head. "Yes, I'll manage."

"You don't always have to be brave, you know," Kull said.

"I know."

He wrapped his arm around me, and with his strength, I found the power to overcome the darkness. Theht shrank back at his presence, making me wonder if perhaps Theht's presence knew he would be the one to destroy it. And to destroy me.

We continued forward. Another invisible ward blocked our path, but we moved through it with ease. Perhaps it was too old to function, or perhaps it was meant to keep someone else out altogether. Or perhaps it was meant to keep someone inside. Whatever the case, we hiked down the sloped path toward the shimmering shore of the dark lake.

From this angle, the water was glassy and black, and it didn't ripple in the wind as normal water would. The wind stirred the sand, making dust clouds billow through the air. No one spoke. It seemed that if we did, we would break the spell of silence, or awaken the ghosts that haunted this land.

I gripped Kull's hand in mine, his presence the only thing keeping Tremulac's magic from overwhelming me. The castle's slender spires seemed to pierce the sky as the sun set behind them, reflecting off their sharp angles. The slim, black towers reminded me of Egyptian architecture.

Could the castle really be the legendary fortress of Tremulac? It seemed so impossible, yet there it stood. I'd heard the stories as a kid, as I lay on Fan'twar's dais, listening to the deep sound of his voice as he told me of the seven brothers creating weapons meant to unite the world.

This was the feeling I would have gotten if I'd discovered King Arthur's round table—giddy and scared at the same time—yet this place was tainted with evil. Unlike the legendary Earth king's Camelot, Tremulac was not a place of peace, but of power, of ultimate control.

It seemed the elves had always had a thing for subjugation.

We drew nearer and found a narrow bridge spanning from the shore to the castle gates. I saw no guards and felt no wards on the bridge. Still, I wouldn't cross until I'd made sure it was safe.

Maveryck and Heidel made it to the foot of the bridge and waited for Kull and me to catch up. I still hadn't let go of Kull's hand, and I wasn't sure I would until we'd left this place.

"Is it safe?" Heidel asked.

I studied the arched, narrow beam that extended from shore to gate. It was made of the same glassy material paving the road. Beneath the bridge, the black water remained still, with only small ripples breaking the surface and lapping the sand-covered shore. The air near the castle tasted strongly of salt.

"I don't feel any spells," I said, "but I would still be careful crossing. I don't trust that lake."

"I agree," Kull said. "It hardly looks inviting. Maveryck, what do you say? Is it safe to cross?"

Maveryck didn't answer. He only stared out over the water, his eyes seeming distant, as if he were looking at something else, something too far away to be seen. Finally, he seemed to focus on us. "Sorry, this place... I feel like I've seen it before... but it doesn't make any sense. If I'd been here, I would remember with perfect clarity."

"Maybe you saw it when you were a boy?" Heidel suggested.

"No. If I had, I would remember."

"Then what would cause you to forget something?" I asked.

"Nothing."

"Perhaps you dreamed of it," Kull suggested.

Maveryck clenched his jaw. "Yes, maybe that's it."

"Should we cross now?"

"Yes," Kull answered. "I should like to get this over with."

Heidel stepped carefully onto the glassy surface, and I followed her. Kull walked behind me, and Maveryck came last. As we traversed the narrow bridge and made it to the center, the view of the castle and the surrounding landscape came into sharper view. The quiet air was interrupted by a gentle hum, but I couldn't decide where the noise came from. Magic, perhaps?

Past the castle, the lake spread out beyond the horizon, so large it seemed to reach the edge of the world. The castle spires glistened in the last rays of sunlight as the water's reflection shimmered on their surface. The building was much taller than structures the elves had built in modern times, and as we drew nearer, I realized it was much larger than I had first thought. The sight was awe-inspiring on a grand scale, from a time long past, when chaos ruled the world.

We finally made it across the bridge and to the island where the castle stood. White sand covered the beach, punctuated by small, water-worn pebbles. A chill lingered in the air on this side of the bridge, making goose bumps prickle my skin. Up ahead, we found a large gateway bored into the castle wall, and we headed toward the entrance, our feet shifting in the sand.

I clenched Kull's hand so tightly I was surprised he didn't complain. The fear was almost overwhelming. Usually, I did a pretty good job at controlling my fear, but being in this place, where the magic overpowered mine, where I felt powerless against the goddess within me, made me want to turn around and run as far away as I could. Focusing on my stepfather's life was the only thing that kept me taking one step after another. I had to do this for Fan'twar. I had to bring him back.

We traded a path of sand for a cobbled courtyard. Crumbling pillars surrounded us. A few statues of elven gods and goddesses remained intact, standing like sentinels as tall as three men, looking down on us with detached gazes.

My heart beat wildly in my chest, its persistent thumping echoing loudly in my ears.

"What will we find when we get in there?" Heidel asked.

"I'm not sure, but we're looking for a chamber where the elves are keeping the egg," I said. "In my vision, the elves were inside a large chamber, and the egg was on a raised platform in the middle of the room. It looked like the room was underground or deep inside the castle because I didn't see any windows."

"Wherever the room is, we should be careful inside," Kull said. "We have no idea where the queen is. She may be in Lauressa, or she may have entered the gateway under the catacombs and arrived here already."

"If she's inside the chamber, what then?" Heidel asked. "Do we fight her?"

"If we must, but I'm hopeful we'll be able to sneak inside and steal the egg before she notices."

"How do you plan to do that?" Heidel asked.

Kull nodded toward Maveryck. "I thought we'd let the professional thief handle it."

I glanced back at Maveryck, who didn't seem to be paying attention to our conversation. His pensive eyes were locked straight ahead.

"What do you say, Maveryck?" Heidel asked. "Can you handle stealing the egg?"

Finally, he seemed to focus. "The egg?"

"Yes, can you steal it quietly?"

He nodded. "Stealing the egg won't be a problem."

"You see?" Kull said. "We shall be in and out and home in time for our evening meal."

"I don't share your confidence," Heidel said. "These quests never go as we plan."

"I have to agree," I said.

"Why not? Just because we've had rotten luck on every single mission in the past doesn't mean it will happen this time. I, for one, intend to have a positive attitude. We shall walk inside, reclaim the egg, and be on our way."

"Keep dreaming," I muttered.

Behind us, Maveryck mumbled something, and when I turned to look at him, I found him running his fingers along the walls. His fingertips lightly brushed the stones, and his other hand was clenched in a fist. I felt magic in his fisted hand, and his fingers glowed with a faint bluish light, casting shadows beneath his eyes and highlighting his elven cheekbones.

"Are you all right, Maveryck?" I asked.

He looked up, seeming to come out of a trance. "I'm not sure. I believe the castle's magic may be affecting me."

"That makes two of us," I said.

"It's hard to withstand the power. I feel like the magic is trying to speak to me, but I don't know how to answer. I apologize if I am not myself."

I squeezed Kull's hand. He was the only thing standing between me and this place's power.

The path ahead widened into a large chamber supported by pillars. Overhead, it looked as if there had once been a large glass dome, but now, only a metal frame remained. Glass littered the floor, but beneath it, a mosaic of tiles reflected the moonlight. A large marble statue of an elven goddess stood watch at the center of the room, though cracks fractured its surface in several places.

"This must have been a beautiful place," I said. Although I spoke quietly, my voice echoed.

"Yes," Maveryck said, scuffing at the glass with his boot. "It must have been amazing."

"Keep to the corners of the room," Kull said, "and stay alert."

We followed Kull as we paced the edge of the room. As we did, I began to see a pattern in the tiles. The mosaic made a picture of waves and a castle, but I couldn't make out much more.

"Do you recognize that goddess?" I asked Maveryck.

"It may be Philigrene, the ancient goddess of the sea, but that's only a guess."

I kept my eyes on the statue as we crossed the room. Elves hadn't worshipped the old gods in several centuries, preferring science to religious studies, but part of me lamented their abandonment of the old ways. Somehow, the ancient elves had managed to balance religion and science, a trait not found in the modern society.

After crossing through the domed chamber, we entered an area with a spiraling staircase. It reached below ground level and down into a dark chamber.

"We'll need light," Kull said.

"I'll handle that," I replied. "At least, I think so."

I wasn't sure if my magic would cooperate in this place. It hadn't worked in the jungle, but I hoped I would be able to manage such a simple spell.

Balling my hand into a fist, I whispered a word of magic, and a sphere of bluish-white light formed around my hand. I felt the magic leave my body in a painful jolt and had to focus to keep it under control. If that was how all my spells would react, I wasn't sure how well I could depend on my magic. But the others hadn't noticed my discomfort, so we started down the staircase without another word.

The world transformed as we descended into the bowels of the castle. The smell of mold and damp earth filled the air, and images of skulls replaced the gods and goddesses. It seemed that the castle's creators had had two faces—the one they displayed above, and the one that lurked beneath.

As we climbed down the stairs, the air grew chillier. The blue light glowing from my hand made everything look silvery and eerie, and I wondered how long it had been since light had touched this part of the castle. If this place was as old as some thought, it might have been thousands of years since any light had touched the carved-stone walls or the broad, glassy staircase.

I felt as though we had entered another world. Our footsteps rang out against the glass-like stone. A chill crept up through the stone steps, and as we descended from one level to the next, the intensity of the magic increased as well.

Glancing at the tall staircase spiraling overhead, I noticed the light from the world above had disappeared completely. We were alone in the darkness, the cold as our only companion, on a mission that could easily end in our own deaths, yet we kept going.

After what felt like an eternity of climbing, we stepped off the staircase and entered a broad foyer with smooth stone walls. Directly in front of us was a set of large doors made of the same onyx-type stones paving the pathway leading to the castle. A large, orb shape was carved in the middle, continuing through both doors, with lines fanning outward, away from the circle pattern. A sunburst—the symbol of elven royalty.

"The room I saw in the vision must be inside these doors," I said, feeling the ice-cold tendrils of magic coming from the doors' surface.

Maveryck stepped to the doors and pressed his ear against them. I also used my elven senses to detect any sounds beyond the doorway but noted only silence inside.

"I don't hear anything," Maveryck said.

"If we enter, how do we know the elves won't be alerted to our presence?" Kull asked.

"We don't know for sure," I said. "But, the elves would have entered through the gateway in the catacombs, not through here, and they would also be expecting us to enter the same way. They didn't anticipate we would cross through the wild lands and enter through this passage. If we're going to get inside that room, this would be the best way to do it."

Heidel inspected the doors, pulling away bits of cobwebs that clung to the surface. "It looks like these doors haven't been used in some time."

"I'm still not sure," Kull said. "The elves would be foolish not to have these doors guarded."

Maveryck pressed his hand to the door, his fingers splayed, letting his magic weave into the fabric of the stone. He closed his eyes, humming gently, a sound imbued with magic. After a moment, he pulled away. His gray eyes glittered with magic, and I wasn't sure I liked the feeling of power coming from him.

"It is safe," he said. "The room is empty."

"You're sure?" Heidel said.

"Quite sure."

Kull crossed his arms. "I don't know. Perhaps we should find another way inside."

"We may not have time," I said. "The elves will start the ritual soon. It could take hours to find another way inside, if another way even exists."

"I agree with Olive," Heidel said. "We have to take our chances."

Kull sighed. "Very well. But we do this quietly. In and out and home for our evening meal, understood?"

"Not happening," I mumbled.

"Yes, we understand perfectly," Heidel answered.

Kull nodded to Maveryck, who slowly pushed the doors open. The heavy stone doors slid across the floor, creating half-moon patterns in the dust on the floor.

We stepped onto a narrow balcony overlooking the depths of Tremulac castle. Far below, we saw the vachonette egg, a tiny speck sitting on a raised platform. Lit only by firelight, the egg sat in a seemingly empty void.

"Finally," Kull said in a whisper. "We've found it."

CHAPTER *Thirty*

My heart raced as I stared at the egg so far below. Kull, Heidel, and Maveryck looked on as the egg shone with a golden luster, reflecting the firelight cast from wide biers surrounding the room. I scanned the huge chamber—seven raised coffins around the vachonette's platform, the expanse of empty floor, the pillars spanning to the cavern's ceiling, and the balconies surrounding the walls—but the place was empty.

"It looks like we're alone for now," Heidel whispered, the immense room making her voice echo.

"Yeah, let's hope it stays that way," Kull said.

Maveryck scanned the room, his eyes intent. "I'm going to go down there," he said. "I'll have to do it alone. If there are traps, I can find them, but it's harder if I have to find them for four people."

"So we just have to wait here while you take the egg?" Heidel asked.

"Yes."

She crossed her arms. "I don't like it."

"Like it or not," Kull said, "he's right. One person has a better chance of avoiding traps than four."

"But we don't even know if there are any traps," Heidel said. "What if he is attacked? What then? We get to sit here and watch him die?"

Maveryck smirked. "I won't die."

Heidel sniffed. "I still don't like it."

"If it makes you feel better, you can keep watch from here. If anything tries to attack, shoot it." He reached into his pack

270

and handed her the basita.

She glared as she took it. "I'd rather go with you."

Maveryck smiled but said nothing and backed away. Then he turned and walked toward the staircase, his footfalls quiet, though not silent. Anyone paying attention would hear him.

Heidel adjusted the weapon and clicked the gears into place. We watched as Maveryck paced down the stairs, his dark blue robes blending in with the background. He moved with practiced stealth. From this distance, I could no longer hear the sound of his footsteps. When he reached a landing midway between the top of the dome and the bottom, he stopped and outstretched his hand. A faint bluish glow emanated from his fingers as he treaded from one edge of the landing to the other.

"What's he doing?" Heidel asked.

"Checking for enchantments, most likely," I said.

When he seemed satisfied, he leapt over the staircase banister and climbed the rest of the way down.

"Do you think he found a spell?" Heidel asked.

"He must have found something," Kull said.

Heidel sighed. "I don't like this. I'm following him." She moved toward the staircase when Kull caught her arm.

"Wait," he said. "Give him a chance."

"I don't want to."

Maveryck reached the bottom of the staircase and walked out onto the floor. Heidel stayed put as he crossed the expanse of tiles, his footsteps silent, his blue robes swirling behind him. The onyx floor swam with patterns of cobalt blue, an odd enchantment that was stained by Maveryck's shadow as he passed over it.

When he reached the raised platform, he sidestepped the coffins and headed straight for the egg.

My heart pounded as I watched him near the pedestal where the egg rested. As he approached the egg, he held his glowing hand out and approached the dais. It took him longer to reach the egg than I would have liked, but I knew he was only being cautious.

When he finally stopped by the raised column supporting the egg, he circled it several times and then snatched the egg up and placed it inside his bag. I wanted to breathe a sigh of relief, but I knew he still had to get back up to us.

He walked quickly off the platform and toward the open floor. Heidel's shoulders relaxed a tiny bit, though she kept the weapon focused below.

Maveryck slowed, then stopped, as his gaze snagged on one of the coffins. He peered up at us, although from this height, I couldn't make out his expression.

"Something's wrong," Heidel said. "What does he see?"

Maveryck stayed by the coffin, unmoving.

"Can you see what's inside that coffin?" Heidel asked me.

Elven eyesight wasn't nearly as effective as hearing, but still, it gave me a slight advantage. I scanned the coffin but saw nothing out of the ordinary. "I can't see anything," I said. "Maybe he found a spell or something that's trapped him."

"Kull, we've got to get down there," Heidel said.

"Wait. If he needs help, he'll let us know."

Heidel growled but remained where she was. Maveryck glanced up, his eyes locked with ours, and he motioned us down to him.

"Very well," Kull finally conceded. "We'll go down. But stay alert. Olive, lead the way and keep a lookout for enchantments."

I nodded and walked toward the staircase with Kull and Heidel following behind. Keeping my hand open with my fingers outstretched, I let the magic flow into my palm as I searched for foreign spells. Down below, I sensed the spell on the landing where Maveryck had leapt over the edge and climbed down.

"We'll have to avoid the stairs here," I said as we reached the landing. Kull, Heidel, and I each took turns climbing to the floor. When I reached the bottom, I turned and stared out over the enchanted floor.

Everything looked so much larger from this perspective, making me remember that I stood in Tremulac castle, a place of enormous power and ancient magic.

Although my skin tingled with the magic, I was able to keep the overwhelming feelings of its sheer power at bay, but I wasn't sure how long I could keep it up. I focused instead on Maveryck, who stood hunched near one of the coffins.

As we approached, I saw the terror in his eyes.

He backed away as we neared him.

"Maveryck, what's the matter?" I asked.

He looked from me to the other coffins surrounding him. "Help me get these lids off," he said.

"Get the lids off?" Heidel asked. "We can't! We've got to get out of here."

Kull unsheathed his sword as we approached the first coffin—the one that had frightened Maveryck. As we neared it, I saw that the lid was missing, leaving its contents open. What had Maveryck seen that had scared him so badly?

In a place this old, I didn't expect anything to exist except a mummified corpse. Instead, I found an elven man with long, ornate robes lying in the tomb. His body and clothing were untouched by decay. Except for his skin, which was gray, he looked as if he slept. The man had to have been one of the Madralorde brothers, but what had kept his body so preserved? Was it a spell? I stretched my hand over the tomb, searching for the spell, when a wave of power hit me, making me stumble back. I slammed my mind closed against the magic just in time. Kull steadied me as I pushed the magic away, taking deep breaths and finally closing it off completely.

A loud crash came from one of the other tombs. I rounded and found Maveryck standing in a cloud of dust, the coffin's lid at his feet. He gasped and drew back as he looked inside the tomb.

"It can't be," he mumbled. "It's not possible."

Heidel went to his side and took his hand, but he shrugged her off and rushed to another tomb. Maveryck strained against the lid until it slid off and crashed to the ground. I glanced around the room, wondering if he had already alerted the elves to our presence with the noise.

"We've got to stop him and get out of here," Kull said.

"I agree, but what's gotten him so stirred up?"

"I don't know."

We stepped onto the raised dais and approached Maveryck. Heidel stood near him with her hands balled into fists, her silver arm guards gleaming in the firelight.

"Do you know what's wrong with him?" I asked.

"He's gone mad," she answered as another crash echoed through the room.

Kull hefted his sword as he approached the thief. Heidel and I followed behind Kull. I glanced into another open tomb, finding a corpse similar to the first, this one with crimson robes.

"Come away from there," Kull said to Maveryck. "We've got to get out of here with the egg. We don't have time for this."

"No! I won't leave. Look what's inside."

"It's a body. What else did you expect?"

"Look again. Look inside this one!"

We approached the tomb he stood beside and glanced

into its depths. Inside, the tomb was empty.

My heart pounded as realization struck me. Was it possible?

Maveryck rubbed his temples as he paced the length of the coffin. "The potion didn't restore me, it altered me. It changed my memories, and now I know who I am. Who I really am."

"Who are you?" Kull asked.

From behind us, a familiar, musical, yet bone-chilling voice answered, "He is Dracon. The last of the Madralorde brothers."

We rounded to find Queen Euralysia emerging from a portal, along with several other elves wearing long robes and dark cowls. Was it true? Could Maveryck really be the last Madralorde brother?

The portal closed as the elves surrounded us. Kull cursed under his breath and gripped his sword.

Queen Euralysia approached us, her footsteps ringing out against the stone. She wore an unadorned black gown, and the color was gone from her cheeks, leaving her skin chalky and white. She wore her hair pulled back in a severe, straight ponytail. It seemed the only color on her body was the red rimming her eyes.

But it wasn't her appearance that made me shudder. The magic she held felt tainted and impure, the way magic became when exposed to death.

Ice ran through my veins as I backed away from the queen, but I knew it would do no good. With Theht's presence attempting to take control of my own magic, I wasn't sure I trusted my powers.

The elves removed their basita weapons as they surrounded us.

"What do you want from us?" Kull demanded.

The queen gave us a wan smile. "Want from you? We are friends, remember? Return the egg, and I will ask nothing more."

"And if we refuse?"

I glanced at the gleaming basita weapons surrounding us. Was there any way for us to fight them? With my unstable magic, Kull's sword, Heidel's knife, and Maveryck's weapon, it seemed we had a pretty slim chance. Still, we could try.

Maveryck walked forward. His fear had disappeared. Instead, he walked with an air of confidence.

"No," he said. "We will not give it to you. You have no right to be in this place."

The queen's smile disappeared. "I have every right to be here."

"No, you do not. This is a sacred chamber, and you are not welcome here."

"You cannot make me leave."

"Actually, I can." He outstretched his hand, and a flash of brilliant silver light blinded us. I fell back as the magic hit me in the chest. The queen and her men also stumbled backward. Magic buzzed around us, filling the room with its energy.

But Maveryck had never been a powerful practitioner, and even if he were the last Madralorde brother and wielded more power than we realized, it must have been hundreds of years since he'd used it last.

Queen Euralysia reached out, and dark energy swirled around her fist. It grew into a large void and then snuffed out all of Maveryck's power.

"Don't toy with me," she snapped. "I've enough power to bring down this castle if I wanted. Guards, shoot them all and bring me the egg."

Bolts of lightning erupted from their weapons. I ducked and hid behind a coffin as the energy bursts filled the room. Kull and Heidel also managed to dodge the weapon fire and hide beside me, but Maveryck fell back with a scream, landing on his back, clutching a hand to his chest.

"Maveryck," Heidel screamed, lunging for him, but Kull caught her arm and drew her back to us.

"Stop," she yelled, "I have to go to him!"

The elves closed in on Maveryck and grabbed his arms, dragging him toward the altar where the egg had been. In horror, I watched as they searched his clothing, and then his bag, until they found the egg.

My heart thudded as the elves placed the vachonette egg back on the pedestal.

"We've got to get him back," Heidel whispered.

I knew we only had a matter of seconds before the elves were no longer distracted by the egg and came for us, so I conjured a masking spell to hide us from view. It was a temporary solution, but as the magic left my body and enveloped us, I felt safer.

With the ease of using my magic, and Theht still not able to take control of me, my confidence was boosted. If my magic were cooperating, maybe we would have a fighting chance against the elves after all.

"Find the others," the queen said, "and prepare the weapons for the sacrifice. We'll use him." She nudged Maveryck with her boot.

"Use him for what?" Heidel asked. "For the sacrifice?"

"I'm afraid so," I answered. "They'll need some sort of dark energy to fuel the spell. Maveryck's death would be a good solution." Having been nearly sacrificed once or twice, I felt I was becoming an expert on the subject.

"We won't let it happen," Kull said. "We'll get him free."

"How do you plan to stop them?" I asked.

"I don't know yet," Kull answered.

Flames crackled around us as the elves stoked the large biers surrounding the coffins. A few elves emerged carrying weapons, one that I recognized—the staff of Zaladin. I counted six ancient-looking weapons that they placed around the egg.

"They still don't have the sword," I said. "This is not going to turn out well."

They must have been planning to harness her power with only six weapons. If they failed, they would unleash Theht on the world, and if they succeeded, the elves would control the goddess. Either way looked bleak.

"Do you think Maveryck is really one of the Madralorde brothers?" Heidel asked.

"It's possible," I said. "It explains why he was acting so strangely as we traveled here. He must have been remembering this place."

"But why didn't he remember sooner? He said he had perfect memory."

"He might have believed he had perfect memory. I suspect someone must have tampered with his long-term memory and created an alternate past for him, one that was similar to his real past, but different enough to make him forget his true identity."

"But who would have tampered with his memories?" Kull asked.

I shook my head. "He said his brother gave him the potion, but he was remembering a false memory. It could have been anyone."

We watched as the elves moved Maveryck's limp body atop a long slab of stone. The heat from the fires enveloped the room, creating a dense fog of smoke that drifted up to the ceiling.

Beside me, Kull glanced up, and I followed his gaze.

"What would happen if we brought the castle down on us?"

"Are you serious?" Heidel asked.

"Olive, do you think you could manage it?"

Above us, I could only make out the faint X-shaped outline of the arching stones illuminated in the firelight. "Maybe. I couldn't bring down the whole place, mind you, but I might be able to manage a wind spell and dislodge a few of the larger stones."

"Good enough," Kull said. "You stay here and wait for my signal. Heidel, come with me. We're going to rescue your thief."

"And then what?" I asked. "How do we escape? Leaving the way we came is out of the question. It would take too long, and by the time we made it to the top level, the elves would have caught up."

"Could we use the portal the elves made?"

"Yes, we could use it, but there's an entire squadron of armed elves on the other side. They'd capture us before we got a chance to escape."

"Couldn't you create a portal, Olive?" Heidel asked.

"Possibly, but creating portals requires much stronger magic than masking spells or wind spells. I don't fully trust my magic. Plus, my mirror is broken. It won't be an easy portal to create, if I even manage to create one at all."

"But it may be our only way out," Kull said.

Once again, everyone had way more faith in me than they should have. "I'll do what I can." *And hopefully not release Theht in the process.*

Kull eyed me. "Your mirror is broken?"

"Yes. Massive tornado. Long story."

He stared at me a moment longer but didn't press the issue. Maveryck's moans came from where he lay, which was a good thing—it meant he was still alive.

The queen and her elves surrounded Maveryck and locked hands as they began chanting. Déjà vu returned as I was reminded of a scene similar to this, one I'd witnessed in the presence of the Everblossom tree, when I'd seen a vision of myself as an infant prepared to be sacrificed.

Time had come full circle. In a place like this where magic was so strong, it wouldn't take much to bring Theht back into the world, and with the amount of power they already had, they wouldn't need the sacrifice of an innocent like the others had needed when I was an infant.

Gathering my magic within me, I turned to Kull and Heidel. "Whenever you're ready, I'll release the spell."

He nodded, gripping his sword tight. "Heidel, follow me."

They crept to the next coffin. Several elves wandered the room as they searched for us, but with the aid of the shadows and my masking spell, spotting us wasn't easy to do.

When Kull and Heidel reached the tomb closest to Maveryck, Kull turned to me and nodded. Inhaling deeply, I stared overhead and focused as best as I could.

"*Cirrus*," I whispered, letting the wind spell flow from my fingertips, up through the air, brushing the fires and making them flicker and dance, until the wind dashed against the domed roof.

Rumbling filled the chamber as the stones tore loose of their mortar.

The chanting stopped.

Debris rained down around us, followed by a massive stone that gained speed as it sailed to the floor and landed with a deafening crash.

Chaos ensued as more and more stones dislodged from the ceiling. Clouds of dust choked the air, making it hard to breathe. I moved away from my hiding spot as a boulder-size rock smashed the tomb in front of me.

"Get back," one of the elven guards yelled as another giant stone fell inches from where he and his companions stood.

It seemed that I'd unleashed more destruction than I'd hoped for as one stone after another crumbled from the ceiling. My heart raced as I realized we had to get out before we were buried.

Kull and Heidel appeared in the dust cloud. They each supported Maveryck, who stood upright between them but seemed too weak to walk on his own.

The queen yelled over the chaos, "Bring him back! Don't stop the summoning!"

I felt the queen's power fill the room—a tight feeling in my chest that made me wonder if I was having a heart attack—as the blue swirls dusted the air and shored up the ceiling. Only a few pebbles continued to fall. As the queen's magic dissipated, I felt my own spells diminish. The flimsy masking spell I'd used began to disappear. It wouldn't be long before the elves spotted us.

"Run to the staircase," I said to the others. "Hide under the stairs."

I prayed it gave me enough time to remove my ruined box and create a portal. As we ran, I pulled the bag off my back and grabbed my mirror case. My blood pumped with added adrenaline as we made it to the staircase and hid beneath it. Sitting deep in the shadows beside the others, cold radiating from the stones surrounding us, I lifted the mirror case's lid.

The cracked mirror stared back at us, reflecting the fear in our eyes as I pressed my fingertips to the fractured glass. My fear of being captured wouldn't let me think properly as I unleashed the magic, and it exploded through my chest and into my arms and joints. As it collided with the mirror, the spell refracted off the broken glass and blasted outward, causing a storm of electrical intensity to radiate around us.

Sweat beaded on my clammy hands as I reached out again, feeling as if I couldn't breathe, as though the spell had sucked away all my magic and left me an empty shell, but I knew we had only one way out. I had to create a portal.

I tried to ignore the queen shouting to her guards. They'd most likely spotted the magical spell I'd just used, which meant they would've spotted us, too.

"You can do this," Kull whispered, reassuring me.

I nodded, tears blurring my eyes as I pressed my fingers to the broken shards, praying I could open the portal. Trying again, I listened to the pounding footsteps of the elven guards as they drew closer to us.

I can do this. I can open the portal...

But as I attempted to call the magic once again, my weakness was unable to keep Theht at bay, and the piece of her that had invaded my mind broke free from its prison.

I cried out as it took me, pain shooting from my head into my hands and down through my feet. Gasping, I felt my body growing numb.

I can't let this happen!

Another voice intruded on my thoughts. *Yes, you can. It is time for me to come forth.*

No! Please, no!

The world seemed to fade around me as the goddess took control. From the edges of my consciousness, I watched the elves close in on us. I watched as they shot my friends, stunning them motionless on the ground. I watched as they smashed what remained of my mirror, a waterfall of crystal shards that broke into thousands of pieces. A piece of my soul went with it.

The sound of shattering glass was the last thing I remembered.

CHAPTER
Thirty-one

LIGHT PIERCED MY EYES AS I GASPED AWAKE. A MASSIVE headache pounded through my skull. I wanted to cry out but only managed a hoarse moan.

As my consciousness returned, I realized I was tied up near the altar where Maveryck had been. The light came from a portal that was open above the altar, though I saw no signs of anyone until I was able to focus better.

Bodies lay scattered around the room.

Most of them were covered in blood. The room was barely recognizable from how I had seen it earlier. The destruction was epic—only piles of rubble remained where the coffins had been. In fact, the only objects still intact were the six weapons of the Madralorde brothers, which were placed around the raised altar and glowed with an intensity that blinded me.

Acid churned though my stomach as I tried to make sense of the situation. I sat up straight and focused on my breathing, feeling the headache diminish as I did so. The sound of footsteps came from somewhere, but piles of rubble blocked my view. I grasped at the ropes tying me and found them loose, so I pried them off.

As I stood, dizziness disoriented me for a moment, but I steadied myself and managed to make it to the altar. My stomach sickened as I found a pool of dark, drying blood staining its surface.

Behind the altar, I found the remains of the vachonette egg. Tears stung my eyes as I knelt by the shell. Hopelessness tried to overwhelm me. With the egg destroyed, I had no way to get my stepfather back. I wanted to sit on the floor and cry—

nothing ever worked how I planned, and now I'd failed at saving the one person who had cared for me my entire life.

I carefully picked up a piece of the fragile shell, finding it surprisingly heavy. Such a waste! That my stepfather should be destroyed over such a small item didn't seem fair, but nothing ever seemed fair.

Magic no longer coursed through the eggshell, making its destruction weigh even heavier on my heart. But I couldn't give up yet. Was there still a chance I could save Kull and the others? I placed the shell back on the ground where I'd found it. Standing, I stumbled away from the altar and searched for my friends, or for anyone alive. I had to stay focused on them. If I thought of anything else, I knew I would lose it.

The violence was worse than I'd thought from my vantage point on the ground. The elves had been massacred. Limbs lay strewn about, discarded like garbage. Tattered clothing and blood were all that remained of others. Frantically, I searched for Kull, Heidel, and Maveryck, but I couldn't find them.

"They're not here," a voice said.

What appeared to be queen Euralysia emerged from behind the rubble, although her form was blurry, her skin tinged in orange, and her eyes glassy.

The instant I saw her, I knew everything I had feared most had happened. She had used the vachonette egg and the Madralorde weapons to call Theht back. The queen and the goddess were now one. She grimaced as she clutched her hands to her stomach, making me realize that whatever power the queen was using to control the goddess must not have been working well.

"I have become Theht," the queen said, approaching me. "The same that has happened before has come to pass once again."

"Where are my friends?"

"I will tell you soon, but first, you must know something else, something I have been trying to communicate to you for a very long time—a mystery you have been grappling with—the truth of the nature of our universe." She outstretched her hand. "Let me show you."

Mystery? What was she talking about? Part of me was curious to find out, but my fear won out and I drew back. "No."

"I beg you to reconsider. There is more you must know. The queen and I are one, but this is not the first time I have inhabited another's body. I was male, long ago, when the first books were written. I had taken another form, and since then, I took another form still—that of a woman. Now, I have taken the queen."

Her body shimmered as waves of magic, so intense I felt queasy, coursed through her skin.

Theht fisted her hands until the waves of magic stopped pulsing. "But the queen cannot contain me, and I cannot last in this form for long. A piece of myself exists within you still. You must give it to me."

So, that's what she really wanted. She wasn't whole yet—she still needed the piece of the goddess that existed inside me.

"What if I don't?" I asked.

"Then I will take it from you," she said, "but that is not my first choice."

I connected the dots. She needed what was inside me to be whole, and she needed me to give it willingly.

"Show me where my friends are first," I said, "and then I might consider it."

She smiled, a look that made me shudder. "Yes, I was hoping you would ask."

My heart fell. That was her plan. She was using my friends as leverage to get me to give up the piece of the goddess I held. But maybe that was good news. It meant they were still alive.

"Take my hand, and I will show you everything. There is so much you don't yet understand. Let me show you. You will understand why I have taken the queen. I am not your enemy, Olive. I never have been." For a moment, she sounded like the princess.

My heart pounded as I stared at her hand. "First, show me where my friends are."

She hesitated, not answering, then met my gaze, her glassed-over eyes making my heart race. "After I show you the vision, I will take you to your friends."

It wasn't what I wanted, but it was good enough. "Is that a promise?"

She only nodded.

I knew I couldn't fully trust her. I knew the moment I took her hand she would have power over me. But I had no other way to find my friends.

When the time came, I would do everything within my power to stop her. That thought stayed with me as I took her hand, making swirls of colorful magic ignite between us. My stomach lurched as the floor fell away beneath my feet. We rose above the floor, looking down. From the altar going outward, a burn pattern marred the floor, mingled with specks of blood. What remained of the egg glittered in bands of gold and black, its destruction threatening to overwhelm me again, forcing me to focus on my current task and not on the tremendous loss I would be forced to soon accept.

The room faded as we rose higher and higher, over the castle, above the jungles and wild lands, over Laurentia, and finally, over the clouds. We only stopped when we were floating above the planet.

Whether I was still in my body or not, I wasn't sure, but since I was able to breathe where there was no atmosphere, and since my pain was gone, I realized we must have been caught up in a memory.

The goddess floated beside me. Sparks of lightning danced through her eyes and coursed through her arms like blood through her veins.

"Why have you taken me here?" I asked.

"Because it's important for you to know where you come from. To do that, I must show you the beginning." She glanced behind us. "Look."

I followed her line of sight and saw a dark object moving toward the planet. As it neared us, I realized it was an asteroid. Fear took hold of me for a moment when I realized the asteroid was on a collision course for our world.

"This is the past," the queen explained, "the first time I gave life to our worlds."

As the asteroid entered the atmosphere, it flared in an orange glow, then plummeted for Earth's surface, igniting the world in a blinding fire. Although the spell protected us and I knew this was only an image from the past, I still felt as if the heat singed my skin, a phantom pain that spanned eons of time. The explosion wrapped the planet, filling the world with a fire that engulfed an entire continent, then expanded to Earth's oceans. As the world exploded, I watched it split into two realities—Earth and Faythander.

I wasn't sure why Theht wanted to show me this. Perhaps as a display of her power, or maybe to show what she planned to do to the world again? Either way, watching the birth of Faythander was an experience I wasn't prepared for. I'd read about it my entire life, but seeing it now, so close I could feel the breath of life as it filled both worlds, was enough to make tears spring into my eyes.

Two worlds as one. Two different realities. One with magic, the other without, both filled with life.

Magic blossomed on Faythander, glowing in radiant beams that wrapped the world. *My home*, I thought as I watched the magic unfold.

Theht's voice intruded on my thoughts. *The time has come*, she said. *You, Deathbringer, shall know the truth of your existence.*

The truth? "I don't understand," I said.

"You will. Watch."

A shadow emerged from behind the two planets. At first, I wondered if one world had eclipsed the other, blocking light from the sun to create the illusion of a third planet. But as I watched, my heart began to pound and I realized that I was seeing not a shadow, but another world all together.

"Dalgotha," Theht said. "The world I inhabit."

My mind tried to grasp her words, but it was too much. Could it be true?

"There is a third world, separate from Earth and Faythander, though born at the same time. A castoff. A world born in the shadows. A world of fire and death, where the atmosphere is damaged and cannot protect its inhabitants from the cosmic rays of the sun, where life exits only by taking energy from others."

We moved away from Earth and Faythander to hover over Dalgotha. Although it was a planet, I felt the pain of the world—of its damaged atmosphere, of the plants barely able to survive, of the species living a truly horrific existence—and I felt people living there as well. Past the pain, I felt the fear and terror of the world's lifeblood being siphoned away. It was an odd feeling that was hard to describe, though it felt as if anything living on the planet would have been forced to take energy from others—a place where death and murder would have run rampant. Is that what Theht meant about taking the energy from others?

"This is my world," she said. "This is the place I have survived in for eons. It is my home. And it is my prison."

"Is that why you want to come to Faythander?"

"Yes. My world is dying. It will support life for only a short time more. It is time for me to move to another home, but to fully do so, I must have the energy. I can only inhabit this body for a short time. To fully enter into your world, another event is needed."

"Event? An event on an epic scale, you mean. Our world has to be destroyed, and you want me to do it."

"It will be reborn, not destroyed. In order for me to fully cross, I will need enormous amounts of energy. It was attempted once by the brothers you call the Madralorde, but the energy was not focused enough, and so it settled in the place where the castle now stands, fueling its spell for eons.

"But the time has come again. You must use your energy to set another asteroid in motion in this plane, and you will be the one to bring it to the world. It will be a glorious day, Deathbringer."

"But it will kill everything on Faythander!"

"It will eliminate most of the life, but not all. Just as before, some will survive, and then it shall grow and flourish."

I shook my head. "I refuse to be a part of this. I will do everything in my power to resist you."

"You have no choice. The prophecy has been spoken."

"Then I will stop it. I will do whatever I can to stop it."

"You will fail. You cannot change the future. Do not deny your destiny."

As she said it, I felt her words echo within me, stirring the piece of herself that existed in my mind. I was shocked to feel it take hold of me, grappling my power away. Resisting, I held tight to my magic, but in this state, without being in full control of my body, she easily overcame me and ripped my power away.

Our bodies traveled away from the three planets, past the moon and Mars, to the edge of the asteroid belt. We stopped near one of the bigger asteroids, so large it must have been three miles across. Bits of ice sparkled on its surface—beautiful, but exponentially deadly.

As I stared at the asteroid, pain rippled through me, shredding my energy apart, bleeding me from the inside out. The force was so violent I screamed but couldn't hear my own voice. Power exploded from every cell in my body, ripping and tearing until the magic collided with the asteroid, spinning it off trajectory onto a collision course with Earth.

"It has started," her voice said. "In a few months' time, the asteroid will arrive at our planet, and you shall be the one to guide it to our world."

Her words seemed to come from far away as the energy surrounding us faded.

"Know this," her voice whispered. "My purposes cannot

be thwarted. Those you call your companions cannot help you. Your dragon protector will die soon, killed because of your own inadequacy to save him.

"Indeed, the man you love will be the one to kill you. He does not love you, for you have never been loved. And you never will be. You shall die alone, as this is the lot of all our kind."

Her words pierced me deeper than I thought possible, hitting at some inherent pain that I'd always carried, a feeling that I had never been loved, that I never would be worthy of anyone's love. It was something I'd never admitted to anyone, and it was a scar that ran deeper than all the rest.

Those thoughts stayed with me as I reappeared not in Tremulac castle, but in the catacombs under the elven keep.

The headache returned to my body as I lay on the cold paving stones. As I lay there, I realized the queen was gone. Kull, Heidel, and Maveryck were in the cell with me. Kull and Heidel were both bruised and bleeding, but at least they were conscious. Maveryck, however, lay on the ground, his skin ashen, his chest unmoving.

"Olive," Kull said as he came to my side.

I couldn't make sense of anything. Being taken into a memory from the past, shown the destruction of Earth and the birth of not two planets, but three, and then having every ounce of energy drained from my body in order to set an asteroid on a collision course with Earth, was enough to make me collapse.

I grabbed Kull's hand as he came near, feeling the warmth of his presence melt the chills that had burrowed inside my heart. Tears burned my eyes as I realized what Theht had forced me to do. The worst part was knowing I had been powerless to stop her. She held so much power over me, and now, with the asteroid coming toward our planet, it was only a matter of time before she took over my body once again and struck our world.

"Kull," I whispered, shivering.

"Olive, what's the matter? What did she do to you?"

I couldn't find the words to answer. It was too much. The wall I'd built to hide my emotions threatened to break, and keeping my pain inside only hurt worse. But it's what I had always done, so instead of crying and releasing my pain, as a normal person would have, I kept my heartache buried inside, creating a canker that grew larger with Theht's words so fresh in my mind.

With my energy spent, not even able to lift my head, I lay on the stone floor, realizing I had doomed Faythander forever. I clutched Kull's hand as it if were my lifeline.

And perhaps it was.

CHAPTER
Thirty-two

TIME BLURRED. I KNEW WE HAD LEFT THE ELVEN CAS-
tle and headed south. I knew Maveryck was dead. Someone told me they had found a way to save my stepfather,
but I couldn't understand how. The only coherent memory
I had was of sitting in a light carriage, looking out over the
nighttime landscape and focusing on the stars, those glassy
orbs that haunted my vision, knowing that somewhere out
there a piece of a star was headed for us—for me.

After that, nothing made sense until we arrived at Silvestra's castle. The witch—her pitch skin sparkling under the light
of the moon, her silver dress moving like a fairy's wings filled
with magic, with a spell on her lips—touched her finger to my
head.

I exhaled.

My mind returned to the present. I was shivering and
cold, though I had a blanket wrapped around me. We sat in
her ballroom, and the ceiling overhead looked like the bands
of the Milky Way—appropriate and mocking at the same time.
Though the room's light was dim, I knew there were others
there with us.

Kull held both my hands in his. A few of the witch's wraiths
milled about, but none of them made eye contact with us. I
pulled away from Kull's hands, and he released me.

"Olive, can you hear me?"

I nodded.

"Thank the gods," he breathed.

He caught me in a tight hug, yet somehow he managed
to be gentle. When he pulled away, I found his glacier eyes
sparkling a familiar blue. I thought I might be human again, if

just for now.

"What's going on?" I asked. "Why are we here?"

Kull moved back so I could see Silvestra. She stood over me, tall and imposing, her odd, colorless eyes seeming to look straight through me.

Of all the places we could have gone, this was the last place I would have chosen, but then I remembered something someone had said—something about my stepfather.

"Fan'twar?" I asked.

"We saved him," Kull said, squeezing my fingers.

Hope filled my heart, but something had to be wrong. The egg had been ruined. How could we have possibly gotten him back?

"I never wanted the egg," Silvestra said.

"She wanted what was inside," Kull answered.

Silvestra moved aside, and I saw a sight that took me a moment to register. My stepfather lay sleeping beneath the enchanted ceiling, and curled near his tail, so small it could have been my cat, lay a tiny, black-and-gold-banded dragon.

"It hatched," I whispered.

"Yes," Silvestra answered. "The queen stole my egg many years ago, and she took it to a place where I could not find it, though I never stopped searching."

"During the sacrifice," Kull said, "the queen forced the egg to hatch, and she used the baby dragon's first breath to initiate the spell."

That explained the burn marks I had seen.

"But I don't understand. She didn't kill the dragon?"

"She had no need to," Kull answered. "The queen only needed the power from its first fire. She had no use for it after that, so she returned the dragon to us."

"But why didn't she kill us? How did we escape her?"

"We didn't all escape with our lives," Kull said, his voice somber.

"Maveryck?" I asked, my heart sinking.

Kull nodded.

"How is Heidel taking it?" I asked.

He frowned. "Not well. She refuses to accept that he's dead, although we both watched the elves murder him. I know his death must be especially painful for her, but she acts as though nothing happened."

"That's not good. If she can't accept that he's dead, then she'll never be able to move forward and heal. Is there anything I can do to help her?"

"No, not now. She won't see reason. When we went back for his body, we couldn't find it. It was most likely removed by the elves, but she is certain Maveryck must have arisen and walked away."

"But even if that were true, if by some miracle life could be restored to the dead, then wouldn't he have come back for her? It doesn't make any sense."

"I agree. I fear Heidel has endured too much trauma during her life. To be subjugated by Geth, raped and beaten, and then to lose not only him, but Maveryck as well, is too much for her. She cannot allow another traumatic event to enter her life or it will break her."

"Sadly, I have to agree. There's nothing anyone can do to help her until she accepts the truth. Perhaps given a few weeks, she'll be ready to move forward."

Poor Heidel. She seemed destined to lose the people she loved. It appeared her luck was worse than mine, and that was saying something. My heart hurt for her.

"What about my stepfather?" I asked. "Is he okay?"

"He's fine now, although if we had arrived any later, that wouldn't be the case."

I glanced up at Silvestra. I would never be able to forgive her for almost killing him, yet I knew that someday, I would. I would forgive her because Fan'twar wanted it. I had to remind myself that while she appeared human, she had a dragon's heart, and dragons lived by their own code. It was well within her rights to kill the sky king, and while I wanted to be angry with her, I'd been raised by dragons and knew that lashing out would only cause more pain—an emotion I never wanted to deal with again.

"Can I speak to him?" I asked her.

She nodded and moved aside. As she turned to leave, her wraiths followed. Kull helped me stand up. Walking the path to Fan'twar on my shaky feet took longer than I liked, yet I couldn't have been happier that he was alive.

We'd lost Maveryck but saved the sky king. One life for another. One taken, another saved.

Fan'twar cracked open his golden eyes as I neared him. I sat on the floor beside him, spent after crossing the room and too dizzy to stay on two feet. Kull knelt beside me, and we both glanced at the hatchling sleeping by Fan'twar's tail.

The baby dragon had a short snout and glossy scales that

sparkled with gold and black bands. I wondered at what she had already endured in her short life—to be hatched by the elves, her first fire used in a spell that would ultimately result in the planet's destruction.

"You came for me, young one," a deep, familiar voice said.

"Of course I did," I answered, running my hand over the smooth scales covering his neck. His skin was uncharacteristically cold to the touch, even to my frigid fingers. I realized he still needed time to heal.

"You did well," he answered.

I glanced at Kull. "Maybe. We still lost Maveryck, and the elves called Theht back. I'm not sure I count it as a win."

"But Theht does not have the power to destroy our world. Without the sword, the elves will not have the power to control the goddess, and she will be forced to abandon our world, for she does not have the power to stay here."

My stomach knotted. "Not yet. There's something I have to tell you." I glanced at Kull. "I have to tell you both."

"Go ahead," Kull said.

I exhaled deeply, wondering if I would be able to admit what I knew. "I'm afraid it's only a matter of time before Theht has the power she needs. She used my magic to put an asteroid on a collision course with our world. It's only a matter of time before it gets here. As soon as the asteroid collides with our planet, she will use its energy to cross from her world to ours. And... she's going to use me again, to destroy our world."

My hands were shaking and I didn't know how to make them stop, so I pressed them into my lap, but it didn't help.

"I can't do it," I said, my emotions trying to break free. "You can't let me do this." I looked from Fan'twar to Kull. "You'll have to stop me. It's the only way to save us."

"It's too early to talk that way," Kull said. "There's still time to stop it from happening."

"But how? Even Fan'twar said I can't stop prophecy."

"You cannot stop it, no," my stepfather said. "But perhaps there is a way to better understand it."

"What do you mean?"

"You must find the one who spoke the prophecy in the first place. Lucretian—the first high druid of Faythander."

"Is he still alive?"

"Possibly. He disappeared almost half a millennia ago, and no one has seen him since. But, he was last spotted on Dragon Spine Mountain, near this very palace. If anyone knows where he is, the witch is the one to ask."

"And if I find him, do you think he can undo the prophecy and stop it before it happens?"

"Stop it? No. But he can explain it to you and perhaps help you find a way to fulfill it without the consequences you anticipate. And that is not all. Lucretian was the last known person to possess the sword of Dracon. It is the weapon that will destroy Theht—that I know. You must find Lucretian, and you must recover the sword. As you see, all is not lost, for if even the tiniest glimmer of hope can be found, then goodness still exists. You will succeed, young one. That I know."

I uncrossed my arms. With his words, I finally felt as if fear didn't control me. Peering overhead, the bands of radiant stars reminded me of something else I'd seen, the truth of our universe.

"There's something else," I whispered, "something Theht showed me."

"What?" Kull asked.

Studying the stars overhead, my memories turned to an image of the world splitting apart. "I saw the birth of our world," I said, "but Faythander wasn't the only planet formed that day."

"What are you saying?" Kull asked.

"There are three worlds, not two. I think we finally know where the Regaymor come from, and where Geth took me when he imprisoned Mochazon, and where the bloodthorn tried to take me. The third world."

I almost said the name of the world out loud, but I stopped. The fairies had told me its name was a spell, and I would only say it if I had to.

"All this time," Fan'twar said, "I believed it to be a place in Faythander. I never thought to look to the stars." He chuckled. "Well, even an old dragon can learn a new thing or two."

"So you didn't know?" I asked.

He shook his head. "I doubt anyone in the history of our planet knew this. Even Geth, I suspect, did not understand the truth of the alternate reality he had had discovered. You are the first to learn of this. You are special in more ways than you know." He turned to me, his golden eyes intense. "You may think to be hard on yourself and believe you have failed. You have not. My life has been restored because of you. Theht has not destroyed our world yet because of your persistence. If ever a person could stop the goddess, it is you. It was no accident that Lucretian prophesied of you all those years ago, because if there were ever a person to beat a prophecy, it's you."

A lump formed in my throat as his words sank in. "I'm glad you have faith in me," I said. "That means a lot."

He nodded, then closed his eyes.

"Do you need to rest?" I asked.

"Only for a little while, child. Only for a while."

As he breathed shallow, ragged breaths, I stood and backed away quietly. My own body hardly felt recovered, but at least I felt I could walk without fainting. With nowhere else to go, Kull and I crossed to the staircase leading to the balcony overlooking the ballroom.

My mind was a mess. I still carried a piece of Theht inside me, but I knew that as long as it stayed there, Theht couldn't control our world, at least for now. The events that had happened in the last few days were hard to grasp, and even with Silvestra's spell working inside me to restore my mind, I felt as if I would lose it again if I thought too long about the future.

We made it to the top tier, where we stood looking out through the opened glass windows with the smell of greenery in the air and the smooth marble railing beneath our fingertips. Above us spanned the universe, and before us, the world of Faythander, with thundering waterfalls, trees that stood like spires reaching for heaven, and life that filled every corner—a place so beautiful it resonated not just with my physical senses, but with my soul as well.

"Olive," Kull said quietly. "I've been meaning to talk to you for quite some time. Well, since you arrived back in Faythander really, or perhaps before that... after we defeated the bloodthorn, to be honest—"

"Kull," I stopped him.

"Yes?"

"You're rambling."

"Oh, yes, I am. You're right." He leaned with his elbows on the balcony railing, looking out over Faythander. Of all the beauty in Faythander, I didn't think I could find anything more perfect than him. The way his eyes reflected the moon, the curve of his strong jawline, the wisps of his blond hair caught in the breeze. He was more than I deserved or expected, and I feared I would wake up and lose him, only to realize I didn't have to.

"What I meant to say," he said, "was that I was going to talk to you sooner. I wanted to ask you something."

My breath caught in my throat. I didn't want to let on what I suspected he would ask, and I also didn't want to get my hopes us. Although he'd pledged his love to me, he hadn't made it official. We weren't engaged, and most people still thought of us as acquaintances and nothing else. Still, it was hard not to get my hopes up.

"It's about Grandamere," he said.

"Oh." I exhaled, trying not to let the disappointment show on my face. "Is she all right?"

"She is well enough, but with her failing health, she has decided to move back into the castle."

"I see. That's probably a wise decision. It's better that she live somewhere with people around to help her." I eyed him. "Is that really what you wanted to talk to me about?"

He smiled, but I found nervousness in his eyes. "Well, this is bit harder to do than I expected."

He took my hand and then knelt in front of me. My body broke out in a clammy sweat, and I didn't know why, but I felt warm tears in my eyes.

"I want you to marry me, Olive. I know our lives aren't typical. I know we've no business trying to start a family with a world in danger of being destroyed, but goddesses be damned, because if we can't live and make a future for ourselves, then there's no point in carrying on."

His gaze was so intense I couldn't look away.

"Will you marry me, Olive?"

Had he really just said the words? I hadn't been in my right mind for quite some time. Could I be hallucinating? But his hands felt so real and warm as he held my fingers, and I couldn't mistake that overwhelming sense of joy. No hallucination could mimic that.

"Yes. I will. Of course I will." I brushed the tears off my cheeks as he kissed my knuckles, then stood and took my face between his hands. He kissed me slowly and gently, and I knew then that I'd made the best decision in my life. After he pulled away, he took my fingers in his and carefully slid a ring on my finger.

The cool metal warmed as it touched my skin. I stared, confused as I looked at the ring. Jewels sparkled in a faint, bluish glow from the silver band. Oddly, the bunches of tiny gems reminded me of the hydrangea flowers I remembered seeing in my grandmother's garden.

I lightly touched the gemstones and felt magic within.

"Are these...?"

"They're from the flower we found in the wild lands. I saw how much you liked the jewels, and I thought they suited you. I'd been trying for so long to find a ring, but neither elven nor Wult nor even Earth Kingdom jewelry suited you. But this flower, it seemed when you saw it, it knew you. I know how strange that must sound."

"No—actually, I had the same thought."

He kissed the top of my head. "You like it, then?"

As I studied the ring, I felt its magic combine with my own. I knew then that this ring was different; it was meant for me. Kull knew it as well. It represented who I was now, who I had become, and my potential to become someone better. I didn't know what the future held, if I really would destroy the world because of Theht, if I would be able to find Lucretian and discover a way around the prophecy, or even if we would have a world to live in. But with my stepfather's life saved and a real future with Kull to look forward to, I realized I had an actual chance at happiness, and that was good enough for now.

"As for Grandamere's cottage," Kull said, "she's given it to me. She said since I was the only one who ever visited her, she thought I should have it. With a bit of work, it would make an adequate first home for a newlywed couple, don't you think?"

"Yes," I answered with a smile. "But I think it would be more than just adequate. I think it would be perfect."

"It might not be perfect. We'll live next to the keep, you know. We'll have to deal with my mother dropping by at a moment's notice, and then there's Heidel, who will demand we accompany her on any quest she can come up with and leave any time she chooses—and that's not to mention her temper we'll have to put up with."

I laughed. "Fine. Maybe it won't be perfect."

He gave me his lopsided grin, the one he reserved only for me. We looked out over the trees and I found the stars glittering—not the light cast from the enchanted ceiling, but real light. It didn't seem probable that a star's light, burning billions upon billions of miles away, could ever reach us, or that it could even been seen, yet it was there, so real I could almost feel its heat burning against my cheeks, shining just as brightly as the jewels on my ring.

I gently ran my fingers over the ring's sparkling jewels, feeling a calming flux of magic, knowing that in the end, everything would be made right.

"We'll have a future," Kull said. "I don't know how, but some way, we'll survive this. And we'll do it together."

Acknowledgements

MY HEARTFELT THANKS GOES OUT TO EVERYONE WHO helped bring this book to life. First, I want to thank the ladies of Clean Teen Publishing: Rebecca Gober, Courtney Knight, Melanie Newton, and Marya Heiman. They took a chance on my books and helped the Fairy World MD series become a reality.

Next, I want to give a huge thanks to my awesome team of beta readers: Ann Jones, Julie Woods, and Tasha Priddy. I don't envy their job of reading my early drafts, but someone has to do it!

I would like to thank Chelsea Brimer for being my devoted editor through four Fairy World MD books. (So far!)

My PA, Courtney Whittamore, who is a true blessing in my life and I thank God every day for placing her in my path when I needed her the most.

To Misty McDavitt, who possibly has the hardest job of everyone. She watches my kids while I steal a few hours to write. As I am the mother of said kids, I know that is no easy task.

To my group of fans who are growing in number—thank you all! Your encouraging words help keep me going through the tough times.

To my mom and dad, who read my books and still like them.

To my husband, David, who helps me come up with these crazy stories. I want it noted that you got Fan'twar as a human and several dragon fights. You're welcome.

And to my kids, I have loved each one of you since the day

I met you—and possibly before that—and I always will love you.

Last, to my Heavenly Father, who saw fit to give me the talent to write—and many more blessings that I couldn't possibly list here.

About the Author

Tamara Grantham is the award-winning author of more than half a dozen books and novellas, including the Olive Kennedy: Fairy World MD series and the Shine novellas. Dreamthief, the first book of her Fairy World MD series, won first place for fantasy in INDIEFAB'S Book of the Year Awards, a RONE award for best New Adult Romance of 2016, and is a #1 bestseller on Amazon in both the Mythology and Fairy Tales categories with over 100 reviews.

Tamara holds a Bachelor's degree in English. She has been a featured speaker at the Rose State Writing Conference and has been a panelist at Comic Con Wizard World speaking on the topic of female leads. For her first published project, she collaborated with New York-Times bestselling author, William Bernhardt, in writing the Shine series.

Born and raised in Texas, Tamara now lives with her husband and five children in Wichita, Kansas. She rarely has any free time, but when the stars align and she gets a moment to relax, she enjoys reading fantasy novels, taking nature walks, which fuel her inspiration for creating fantastical worlds, and watching every Star Wars or Star Trek movie ever made. You can find her online at www.TamaraGranthamBooks.com.

CPSIA information can be obtained
at www.ICGtesting.com
Printed in the USA
LVOW11s0844070217
523450LV00002B/16/P